HER LOVER'S FACE

PATRICIA ELLIOTT

ISBN 978-1-7380272-3-1

Published in 2024 by Patricia Elliott

First published by Black Velvet Seductions Publishing in 2018

I dedicate this book to Heather Teston.

My story wouldn't be sitting in the hands of my readers without you. You gave me the courage to release it to the world. I'll never forget your support, nor will I ever forget reading your amazing stories on Wattpad. Keep writing! You have the heart of a storyteller.

I also dedicate this book to my family, my friends on Wattpad and Facebook, and my old high school muse who inspired this story idea.

Okay, I might as well dedicate this book to the whole world at this rate, ha ha. For all those who have struggled, are struggling, or will struggle, I encourage you to never lose hope. No matter what you're facing, you are not alone!

This one's for you...

PROLOGUE

Freedom.

The word played in Laryssa Mitchell's head like sweet music on the radio. She stared down at his coffin as the pallbearers lowered it into the waiting grave. It landed on the ground with a dull thud. She cringed, unable to take her eyes off the wooden casket. Expecting at any moment for her husband to shove back the lid and pull her into the grave with him.

Relax, Laryssa! He's dead.

She searched her heart for any feelings whatsoever for the man she'd been married to for seven years, but none surfaced. He'd put her through hell. That's why, when the coroner went to give her his personal belongings, the first words out of her mouth were, 'bury them with him'. The man's jaw dropped, and he'd simply stared at her.

She yanked off her wedding ring and dropped it onto the casket. Whispers could be heard behind her, but she didn't care. From her pocket, she pulled the divorce papers, which were drawn up earlier that month, and dropped them into the grave. She never did find the courage to tell him she wanted a divorce, not while the bruises on her back were still healing.

The positive pregnancy test she'd taken a few weeks ago only enforced her need to stay. There was no way she'd have made it on her own. She'd hoped a miracle would come her way, and he'd change when she told him the news. She learned the hard way he had no intention of changing. If he could speak, he'd probably say it should have been her in the grave instead of him. Fate intervened and brought her freedom, despite her hesitancy to step out into the world.

The only feelings inside her were guilt for being partly responsible for his death, and sadness for her child, who would grow up without a father. She turned away and walked through the crowd of people who, one by one, offered their condolences.

No one knew what he had put her through. He'd been a master deceiver, always putting on a lovey-dovey act when his friends were around. But the monster inside him lurked beneath the surface, waiting for the moment when they were alone. His words were warm. His eyes cold. She shivered when a snowflake slipped beneath the collar of her jacket.

His business partners made sure she gave him a funeral service. She agreed for fear of what might happen had she done otherwise. If it was up to her, she would have just had a graveside service and be done with it. Her heart remained cool and distant, as though she was viewing a stranger. He was no longer the man she'd fallen in love with in college. Now that was the man she could truly mourn for. The one she'd miss.

Her first tear slid down her cheek as she reached the last person in line who offered their condolences. He looked vaguely familiar, but her brain wasn't working well enough to remember him. A large bandage covered his left cheek. His friendly voice made him appear sympathetic, but his eyes, which concentrated on her so intently, looked as though they held a secret she'd rather not know. She shuddered with unease.

After saying a quick thank you, she excused herself. She felt his eyes watching her as she hurried away. The hair on her arms stood on end, and she wondered if she really was free after all.

He watched as Laryssa made her way to the car. "It's not over. Not by a long shot," he murmured. He noticed a woman beside him staring and pulled the brim of his hat down low. "Sad, sad day." He shook his head for her benefit.

Now there was nothing to stop him from taking what he wanted. For seven years he'd been patient. Seven bloody years. He ached with anticipation of having her all to himself. An ache that was all too familiar from watching her night after night. No more seeking relief by his own hand, not when she would soon be able to do it for him.

His gaze slid down her body. She wore a full-length black dress, but that didn't ease his excitement. He knew her body too well. His hands tingled at the thought of peeling the dress off of her, and he grew hard thinking of her naked. The veil she wore covered her face, but he knew the brown curly hair and matching eyes that hid beneath it. There was nothing about her he didn't know. What song she sang in the shower. What color her favorite underwear was. He'd left no stone unturned. He would bide his time. Let her mourn for her loss.

He chuckled.

Loss? What a laugh. How many times had he seen her crying in her bedroom at night? How many times had she pretended to be asleep, hoping that Aidan wouldn't beat her when he got home? Only Laryssa, his sweet Laryssa, could be upset over such a man.

He made the sign of a cross and walked back to his car. He put the key in the ignition and sat back in his seat, letting his gaze linger over her a final time. She sat slumped at her steering wheel.

"Make no mistake, Laryssa. I'm coming to take what's mine."

CHAPTER ONE

"Huh, what?"

Laryssa Mitchell bolted upright in bed, nearly smacking her head on the overhead lamp. The phone rang again, startling her. "Get a grip, Laryssa. You brought the phone in last night." She reached out and grabbed the phone off the nightstand. "Hello?"

"Laryssa, where are you?" a voice shrilled in her ear.

"What? Oh, Melissa?" Laryssa asked. She shook her head to clear away the cobwebs, her legs dangling over the side of the bed.

"Of course, it's me. Have you looked at the time?" Melissa's voice lowered to a whisper, "The meeting is in forty minutes."

"You've got to be kidding me." She turned the clock on the nightstand. Nine-thirty glared back at her in large orange numbers. "Peachy. I'll be right there."

Placing the phone on the bed, she stood up quickly and experienced a sudden bout of nausea, which had her rushing to the bathroom. Not again. Would this ever end? Every morning, she found herself with her head in the toilet. The only bad thing this time was she couldn't jump in the shower to refresh herself. Slowly standing back up, she went to the sink and splashed cold water on her face.

Exhaustion was evident by the dark bags under her eyes which was, she guessed, how she ended up sleeping through the alarm.

Laryssa rushed through her bathroom routine, and then she hurried back into the bedroom. She grabbed the red three-piece suit which hung in her closet and stared at it before putting it on. It was the first maternity suit she'd treated herself to. She'd bought it the day the doctor told her she was having twins. The revelation of that had dazzled her senses. She had finally accepted she would be a single working mother with one baby. The thought of having two frightened her, especially as she could barely afford to feed herself. And even though weeks had passed since the doctor gave her the news, she still felt overwhelmed at times.

Quickly grabbing a bagel, Laryssa rushed out the door. It wasn't the most nutritious of meals, but she couldn't afford to be late and lose her job. She had to work full-time to make ends meet. The days following Aidan's death had been agonizing. The lawyers informed her that she'd been left with nothing. He never had a cent to his name. Since the death had been his fault, the insurance company didn't have to pay her anything either. All his debt and bills had fallen squarely on her shoulders. She could barely pay the mortgage with her semi-decent administrative assistant wages, let alone all the other bills that plagued her.

She'd thought about selling the house, but there was no time to get it ready for viewing while working full-time. As it was, the doctors told her she needed to rest as much as possible. If she could afford it, she'd pay someone to help her, but whatever money she received disappeared as quickly as it arrived. It was times like this she longed for her parents. Unshed tears burned in her eyes. *Get over it, Laryssa.*

She slid into the driver's seat, started the car, and executed a perfect U-turn to get going in the right direction. She was glad she took the advice of her friend, Melissa, and applied for a job a month ago. The job helped her re-gain not only her independence, but her life as well. A life that didn't include him. Well, almost. His face still haunted her, not only in her dreams, but during her waking moments as well.

With only five minutes to spare, she pulled into the parking lot of Richards' Enterprises. Wasting no time, she hurried inside and skidded to a halt.

It couldn't be possible, could it?

No. No way.

A man, who looked frighteningly familiar, stood in the elevator across the lobby. She rushed to the elevator before the doors closed and squeezed inside, keeping her eyes trained on the floor, her heart pounding like a runaway freight train. Willing herself, she looked up at the man who stood beside her. Her stomach twisted and cramped as though someone had punched her. The ground opened, and she lost her balance, bumping into him. She reached for the hand rest on the side of the elevator as it ascended.

"If you're afraid of elevators, you should take the stairs," the man said in a low voice. "Not everyone appreciates being bumped into, even if it is by a pretty lady."

The voice, oh God, even the voice was the same. The elevator came to a halt, and she stumbled out of the car. The man strolled past her and started to walk down the narrow corridor created by two long rows of green partitioned cubicles.

Okay, she was going insane. First, she saw him at a club that she and Melissa had gone to a week earlier and now here. How could she be imagining him everywhere? She wasn't that crazy.

The doctor had told her that occasionally people suffer hallucinations after losing a loved one because they were in denial. She'd seen him in the coffin while it was lowered into the ground. Damn it, she was at his funeral. Who knew better than her that the father of her babies was dead? She had asked the doctor why it was happening now and not back then. He kept saying everyone was different, or that there was a part of her that needed closure.

Surely, it wasn't just her mind playing tricks on her. It couldn't be. He neared the end of the corridor and stopped to speak with one of her colleagues. How could she bump into a hallucination? She needed another look and started down the corridor after him, only to be stopped by her Supervisor, Dan.

"You're late," he said coolly, tapping on his watch.

"I'm so sorry. I went to bed early but was so tired I slept through my alarm." Tears sprung up in her eyes. Darn hormones, she thought to herself.

He looked down at her belly and understanding dawned in his eyes. "Do you need more time off? If we're working you too hard, I can always get someone to fill in an extra day or two a week."

"I'm fine. Really. Maybe I'm not getting enough iron or something. Did you find the papers I left on your desk last night?" She asked, attempting to change the subject.

"Yes, thank you. However, I do need you to find the company's complete personnel file. Mr. Richards' grandson has taken over for Brendan and decided to work out of this office for now. He wants to make a few personnel rotations. He's brought in some of his own people."

She looked around. The place didn't look like it needed changing, but then she hadn't been back for overly long. "He doesn't plan to fire anyone, does he?" she asked, biting on her bottom lip.

Dan chuckled. "Don't worry. I wouldn't let anything happen to my favorite assistant."

"I really am grateful for my old job back, especially after all these years." She rested her hand on his forearm.

"Don't mention it." Dan glanced down at his watch. "But better hurry up with those files, though. The meeting is about to start."

Laryssa approached the filing cabinets that lined the wall south of the elevator. Melissa must have heard her approach and looked up from her desk, eyeing her intently.

"Everything okay?" her friend asked. "You look pale." Trust Melissa to notice. She had too good of an eye sometimes.

"I'll tell you about it later. If I don't find the personnel file and fast, Dan will have my hide." Laryssa pulled open the drawer marked with a 'P' and raced through the files. "Ahaa, here it is. Catch you later."

With unsteady feet and a heart that wouldn't slow down, she made her way to the conference room. She stood at the door, her hand resting on the doorknob, when she heard his voice again. The familiar sound sent a snake-like shiver down her spine.

Gathering the courage, she opened the door. Her mind was not prepared for what she saw in front of her. There, at the head of the table, stood her worst nightmare. Her newly found freedom ceased to exist at that moment.

"Don't just stand there gawking at me, take a seat," he ordered. His cool voice cut through her like a newly sharpened sword.

The file fell from her hand, and her feet involuntarily moved towards him. Dan was on his feet in a split second and by her side. "Laryssa?" He touched her shoulder gently.

Silence spread throughout the room. The only sound was her labored breathing, which verged on hyperventilation.

"Miss, take a seat, please," the man said again.

She shook her head as she approached him. This wasn't possible. How could he be standing here? The doctors couldn't be right. She couldn't possibly be hallucinating again.

Confusion and frustration clouded his face. "Miss, is there a problem?"

Laryssa stopped an arm length away from him and reached up with a shaky hand to touch his face. "Aidan." She jerked back and bumped into the chair behind her. Distress overwhelmed her entire being.

"No," she gasped. "This isn't possible." She stumbled backwards away from him. "Go away, you're not real." The walls of the room closed in around her, and she struggled to breathe. Her vision blurred and everything faded. The last thing she saw was his ghost rushing forward.

Alexander Richards sensed what was about to happen and caught her, lowering her to the ground. "What on earth is she doing working in her condition?" he barked.

"Her condition is called pregnancy. Something perfectly normal."

He looked up and saw the young woman he had seen her with earlier rush into the room. She must have heard the commotion from down the hall. She dropped to her knees next to her friend.

"Laryssa, sweetie, talk to me. It's Melissa." She tapped her friend on the cheek. The only response was a groan. "Gosh, is everyone an idiot today? Call an ambulance."

He quirked an eyebrow at her, and she quirked her eyebrow back. He would have grinned if he didn't have an unconscious woman in his conference room. Obviously, Melissa wasn't afraid to voice her opinion.

"Forget the ambulance. I'll take her," he said.

Melissa's eyes widened as she stared at him. He couldn't say why he blurted that out. After all, he appeared to be the one causing her distress. It would stand to reason someone else should take her, but she intrigued him. Why did she freak out when she saw him? That was the answer he was hoping to find out when she woke up. This was not quite the way he expected to spend his first day at the company, although it was definitely more interesting than anything else he had planned.

Dan picked up Laryssa and walked towards the door. Alex left the meeting in the capable hands of his second in command and led them to his car. As he rushed through the city streets, the reality of what he was about to do hit him hard. He had actually agreed to walk into a hospital without thinking twice, except for now. The one place he always sought to avoid. Laryssa moaned and moved slightly on the seat beside him but didn't open her eyes.

Alex pulled up to the front of the Hospital's emergency doors. He hurried around to the other side of the car and lifted her into his arms. Shocked, he looked down at her. He hadn't expected such a feather weight, not with her rounded belly. While he studied her, a weird emotion ran through him that he couldn't identify. She snuggled closer to him and sighed softly. The sound wrapped itself around his heart. He couldn't help but feel oddly connected to her, and the need to protect her washed over him. Why? He didn't know.

Alex rushed into the emergency room. The nurse at the admission desk looked up from the patient she was currently dealing with and signaled another nurse who rushed out front with a gurney. He laid her down gently.

"What seems to be the problem," the nurse asked.

"She's pregnant. She fainted." Alex's eyes darted around the room as discomfort settled deep inside him. If it wasn't for his interest in her reaction to him, he'd leave and never come back. He was usually known for being able to keep calm in high stress situations, but that ability high-tailed it out the door when it came to being inside a hospital.

"Are you her husband?" the nurse asked him.

It was a truly reasonable question, but words failed him as he looked down at the woman on the bed, his past threatening to overcome him. Memories that he thought he had buried fought to resurface with a vengeance.

"What's her name?" the nurse spoke again.

"Laryssa."

He looked around the waiting room, thankful that it was relatively empty in case he had to wait. The last thing he wanted was to be surrounded by people. Within ten minutes, the nurse whisked them into the back. She wheeled Laryssa into an empty room.

Not long afterwards, a doctor walked in. "What happened?"

"I'm not sure, we were in a meeting at work, and then she started hyperventilating. Next thing I knew, she fainted."

"Why don't you go have a seat while I examine her? There is a chair just outside." The doctor nodded towards the door. Alex studied Laryssa for a moment, hesitant to leave her.

"Don't worry. I'll take good care of her." The doctor put the stethoscope in his ears and turned towards the bed.

Alex walked reluctantly out of the private room and plunked himself in the chair next to the door.

"Laryssa, can you hear me?"

In a small corner of her mind, Laryssa could hear the voice and struggled to open her eyes.

"Good girl. I'm Doctor Martin. Do you know where you are?"

With blurred vision, she could make out the white walls and heard the beeping of machines around her. "The hospital?" She squeezed her eyes closed and rubbed them. When she opened them, she could finally see again.

"Do you know how you got here?"

"Not really. What happened?" She tried to push herself up, but the doctor gently pressed against her shoulders and made her lay down again. "You fainted at work. Have you eaten today?"

"I ate a bagel." She noticed the look of disapproval on his face and quickly continued, "I know, I know. I was a little behind this morning. I was going to grab an early lunch after the meeting finished." Suddenly, all the details came flooding back and a shiver rippled through her. Thankfully, the doctor was too busy fiddling with the blood pressure machine to notice.

After a few moments, the doctor said, "Your blood pressure is a little high. Has your doctor mentioned anything about it before?"

She nodded. "It was a little high at my last appointment, but he said it wasn't too bad. He mentioned that since I was having twins, it might be higher than normal, and that I should relax as much as possible." Laryssa blushed sheepishly. She hadn't really been following the doctor's orders. Work left her with little choice.

"I think it is in your best interest to apply for maternity leave as soon as possible."

"I haven't worked long enough to qualify." She cursed under her breath. If only Aidan would have let her continue working, but, no, he had to make her quit. Tears filled her eyes for the second time that day. What was she going to do now?

"Here, let me bring your husband in."

"I'm afraid my husband is—"

"He's waiting just outside," he interrupted. "I'll go get him."

She tried to speak again, but the doctor disappeared out the door. Aidan, outside? No, that wasn't possible! The man she saw couldn't have been Aidan, could he? But the doctor was saying he was here. Oh God. Her stomach churned, and foul-tasting acid rose in her throat. She covered her mouth with her hand and made a beeline for the garbage can in the corner.

After she finished retching, she sat back down on the bed and wrapped the blanket around herself like a cocoon. She had to remain calm for her babies' sake. The hard part was getting her heart to listen. There had to be a reasonable explanation for all this. But logic and reason fled from her thoughts when the doctor re-entered the room, followed by...*him.*

"No. No. No." She grasped the railing of the bed as a wave of dizziness washed over her. Tears pricked at her eyes. "This isn't happening. This isn't possible."

The doctor looked from Laryssa back to Aidan, and then motioned for Aidan to follow him outside. She craned her ear to hear what they were saying.

"I think we might keep her overnight just to be on the safe side," the doctor said. "She seems to be upset over something, and I want to monitor her blood pressure to make sure it doesn't get too high."

Aidan looked back into the room and stared directly at her. The usual evil glint in his eyes had been replaced by what looked like sincere concern for her. If the doctor could see him, he wasn't a hallucination or a ghost.

"Give her a private room. I have to return to the office, but I'm going to send her friend down to keep her company." Wandering back inside the room, he gave her a gentle squeeze on the hand. "I have to go, but I'll send Melissa down to keep you company. She's worried sick."

Laryssa was unable to respond and could only stare at him as he turned to walk away. She had to be dreaming. The Aidan she knew would never have bothered saying good-bye or touch her as tenderly as this man had done. Not unless there were more people around to witness his husbandly acts.

Her wish for the perfect husband must have caused her to create this fantasy. No other explanation made sense. Any minute now, she'd wake up, and he would be dead. Buried deep in his grave on the other end of town, and she'd be safely inside her house.

She squeezed her eyes closed and willed herself awake. When she opened them, she was still in the hospital room, and Aidan, who now stood at the door, was staring at her with pure curiosity.

The nurse unlocked the wheels of the bed and started to push her out of the room. Once they were out in the hallway, he gave her hand another quick squeeze and said, "I'll come back soon and see how things are going."

He started to walk down the hall. She twisted on the bed and watched him disappear out the doors. The nurse took her up to the maternity wing and placed her in a private room. Her composure broke the minute the nurse left, closing the door behind her. She buried her face in her hands and cried.

The tears were still falling when Melissa arrived at the hospital.

"Oh, sweetie." Her friend sat on the edge of the bed and wrapped her arms around Laryssa. "It's okay, girl. Everything is going to be okay."

"I'm going crazy. I'm seeing him everywhere." She pulled another tissue out of the near empty box and blew her nose.

Melissa gave her a squeeze. "You'll be fine, you'll see. Just give it time. The mind can be a funny thing."

Definitely funny all right, and it would lead her straight to the funny farm. Maybe she had imagined it all. Yes, that was it. If she saw him again, he probably wouldn't even look like her dead husband.

Alex leaned back in his black office chair, unable to focus on his work. He couldn't help but think of the young woman he had taken to the hospital. Why were so many people mistaking him as a man named Aidan? She was the third person to do that in the past two weeks. Granted, no one else reacted quite so strongly. The others who questioned him just shrugged their shoulders and went on their way when he denied the claim. With her, he never even had the chance to get that far. Instead, she fainted in his arms. That was not exactly the type of reaction he was used to from the opposite sex.

He was used to women flirting with him and enjoyed it as much as the next man when he was in the right mood. But this, this was entirely new, and it intrigued him. She was riddled with mystery, and he would do whatever it took to unravel it. He never backed away from a good challenge and decided to learn more about her by reading her personnel file.

He glanced over it and learned she was a widow and twenty-seven years old. That meant she was single. Not that he cared about that particular fact. He continued reading and discovered she worked for the company a few years back but then resigned. What prompted her to come back? He didn't like that this created more questions than answers, so he closed the file.

Sitting forward, he tried to focus on the work in front of him. Since taking over this branch of the company for his grandfather when Brendan left, his workload had increased, and he couldn't afford to be distracted. Within minutes, though, he tossed his pen against the beige colored wall in frustration, and it landed in the brown ceramic planter of his green fern.

He was already a little behind with his detour to the hospital, and that irked him. He liked being on top of things, but he couldn't get her image out of his mind. The way she sat there on the hospital bed scared of him, cringing whenever he touched her. Most women he could forget while he worked, but something had pierced his soul during the trip to the hospital and seemed to link him directly to her.

He hoped that the next time he saw her the connection would go away, and he could get back to work. He couldn't say he relished the idea of her overreacting to him again, but something told him that it was his fault she was there, and it was his job to reassure her that he wasn't this Aidan fellow. Hopefully, he could put her mind at ease.

He stood up and quickly grabbed his jacket before rushing out the door to his car. A serious case of '*should he, shouldn't he*' played in his head. The 'should he' won, and he found himself pulling into the parking lot of the hospital. All he was going to do was go inside, introduce himself, and leave. Since they worked together, it was the least he could do. He couldn't have her reacting that way all the time.

If she couldn't figure out how to work with him, he'd have to let her go. This visit would determine their next step. The trip wasn't personal and had nothing to do with the fact he couldn't stop thinking about her. He just wanted to make sure she was well enough to do her job and see what he could find out about this Aidan fellow. That was what he kept telling himself as he parked his car. It was the only rational explanation for why he would willingly enter a hospital again.

Laryssa sat on the edge of her bed, picking away at the supper the hospital provided. Melissa had already left to go home and cook supper for her husband. She promised to show up bright and early the next morning since it was her day off.

The hospital food wasn't as bad as everyone always claimed it to be, but her stomach still refused to let her enjoy anything. Morning sickness was only supposed to last until the second trimester and then go away. She'd started the second, and it still hadn't shown any signs of disappearing. It was always worse when her stress levels were elevated. Pushing the tray away, she swung her legs up on the bed and rested against the mattress, which had been raised to a sitting position. She pulled up her gown and rested her hand on her stomach.

"It's still hard to believe I've got two of you in there." She ran her hand in little circles over her belly, laughing with delight when one would push out to meet her hand. "Bet it's getting a little squished, eh?" It was nice to have a serene moment like this after a stressful day. She loved sitting and watching her stomach before falling asleep. Something she would definitely miss once they were born. Gosh, it was hard to believe she was already twenty-one weeks.

She couldn't imagine what it would be like when they finally made their appearance. Excitement and fear mingled together as she thought about it. She couldn't wait to hold them, yet she couldn't help but feel afraid at the possibility of being alone when the time came. Melissa promised to be with her, but it wasn't the same. They deserved a daddy. Aidan's face appeared in front of her, and a ton of bricks fell on her heart.

If he had put in the effort, he could have been a good man. He showed her that when they first met. It was for that reason alone she tried to make it work, knowing what it could be like. Now, it would seem she was doomed to be haunted by his memory and his face the rest of her life. A memory so fresh that Laryssa swore she could hear his voice.

When the familiar voice got louder, her eyes widened in fear. "No, it can't be," she gasped. She stared at the door as if a ghost was about to walk through it, and within seconds, one did. The spitting image of her husband walked into the room.

"Go away! You're not real! You're not real!" Laryssa cried out, taking shelter under the covers.

Alex chuckled at the spectacle of a grown woman hiding under the sheets, the way a child would hide from a ghost. Her reaction only intrigued him more. "Miss," he inquired softly.

"Go away. You're not real. You can't be real. You're dead." She kept a death grip on the sheets as he tried to pry them down.

"Last time I checked, I was real," Alex commented. Finally, he managed to pull the sheets off her head. She swung her arms at him. He grabbed her forearms and held them away from him.

"You're dead. I saw them bury you." She wrenched her arms away from him and proceeded to keep swinging. He wrapped his fingers around her wrists and gently lowered her hands down beside her.

"Ms. Mitchell, I'm not sure who you saw buried, but it wasn't me. I'm not this Aidan guy."

Laryssa eyed him warily. "Who are you?"

She tried to pull away, but he didn't relinquish his hold on her. He was going to make her see the truth if it was the last thing he did. Her latest reactions re-enforced his need to share who he was.

"My name is Alexander Richards. I assure you we've never met before." He was sure of that. There was no way he'd forget someone as beautiful as her. "I'm sorry if I frightened you." He wanted to say more, but a nurse walked into the room.

"Is everything okay in here? We really can't have her getting upset right now." The nurse looked at the clock on the wall. "I'm afraid that, while we do allow family to stay, we really need her to get some rest, so unless you're willing to let her sleep, you'll have to come back tomorrow."

Alex didn't really want to leave. He wanted to pry more information out of her, but he knew the nurse was right when he looked back at Laryssa. She was tired personified. The dark bags under her eyes were more evident than before. Maybe time alone and a good night's sleep would allow what he said to sink into her mind. Hopefully, the next time he came to the hospital she would be more willing to speak with him. He grabbed his jacket and strolled out of the room.

As he drove home, the situation kept popping into his mind. Unease settled into the deepest part of him as he recalled the terror in her eyes when he walked in the room. Did he really look so much like this other man that she'd react so strongly? Maybe she was so distraught over her loss that everyone she saw looked like him.

He had heard of cases where a person couldn't accept the loss of a loved one and wanted them to be alive so badly that they were able to convince their minds that they were still alive. Would that have happened both times she'd met him? Or could there be something more to this than either of them realized? That was what he was determined to find out.

The next morning, true to her word, Melissa popped in bright and early. "Hey girl, how's it going today?"

"Lousy!" Laryssa sighed, cuddling deep beneath the covers. "What's wrong with me?"

"Do you want to talk about it?" her friend asked.

"I don't even know what to say." She leaned forward and whispered, "Hi, my name is psycho. I see dead people."

Despite the absurdity of the situation, they looked at each other and burst out laughing. After a few minutes, they calmed down, and Laryssa leaned back against the bed. "Gosh, that felt good."

"Glad I could help," Melissa said, grinning.

"I'm scared, Mel. If I keep having these hallucinations, they might take my babies away."

"Are you so sure they are hallucinations?"

Laryssa got up out of bed and walked toward the window, resting her hands on the windowsill. She leaned her forehead against the glass and looked at the cars in the parking lot below.

"I'm not sure of anything anymore," she said honestly.

"Did Aidan have any family? Maybe Alex is a relative. That might explain the resemblance."

"If only it were just a resemblance. He looks exactly like him. Almost as if, nah, it's impossible."

"What, what's impossible?" Melissa joined her by the window, and they watched a family climb into their car.

"What's impossible?" his deep voice spoke from behind them.

Laryssa jumped and grabbed Melissa's arm. It was him. He said he would come back. Now here he was. Her feet remained rooted on the floor, and she couldn't make herself turn around. All she wanted was for him to go away. She didn't want to see him.

"Hello, Alex," Melissa said. "Laryssa, can you lighten your grip on my arm? It's going numb."

"Oh, sorry." She released her friend but reached out for her again when she started to move way. "Don't go."

"You'll be fine, don't worry. I'll check in on you again later." Mel gave her a kiss on the cheek and then walked towards the door. "Alex, be gentle," she chided.

Laryssa's heart skipped a beat when the door clicked behind her, indicating that Melissa was gone, and she was alone with him. Shoes squeaked on the polished hospital floor behind her. She stiffened at the sound. He was coming closer, and there was nothing she could do but wait for the blows.

Breathe, Laryssa. In through your nose. Out through your mouth. When his hands came to rest on her shoulders, she jumped.

"It's all right. Don't be afraid," he said softly. The pressure on her shoulders increased a little as he tried to turn her around. At first, she resisted but knowing it was inevitable, she slowly turned.

She stared at the floor, unable to find the strength to lift her head. He placed his hand under her chin and, with great care, lifted her face to look at him.

The tenderness of his touch undid her and helped her realize the truth. "You're not Aidan, are you?" she asked in a quiet voice. He led her to the bed and coaxed her to sit down next to him.

"Afraid not, Miss, although I have a feeling you don't want me to be, do you?"

Numbly, she shook her head. "This is some cruel joke."

"My apologies for startling you yesterday," Alex let his hand rest on top of hers. She stared at his hand for a moment then pulled hers away. She lifted her head to study his features. Her hand reached up to touch his face for a second time. He let her fingers rest lightly on his unshaven face, tracing a small scar under his left earlobe.

"I need to lie down."

Alex helped her swing her legs up on the bed and lowered the head of it for her. Her eyes watered, and she closed them tightly. Tears slipped down her cheeks.

He brought his hand to her face and brushed the tears away.

"Please, don't," Alex spoke with a gentleness Aidan never used. "I hate when women cry, especially because of me."

Laryssa opened her eyes and looked at him. "Why do you keep coming back here?" she asked suspiciously.

"What can I say? I'm a sucker for women who fall all over me." He shrugged his shoulders.

"I didn't fall all over you," Laryssa said defensively.

"You didn't exactly stay standing either," he said, winking at her.

"Touché."

A few moments later, the doctor joined them. "Well, Ms. Mitchell, all the tests came back okay. Babies are healthy. You're free to go. However, you'll need to start visiting the obstetrician once a week from now on and be sure to remember to take your prenatal vitamins. I also want you to rest as much as possible. No more working. We can't risk the babies coming prematurely. I'm releasing you into your husband's care."

"My husband," she squeaked.

"Sure, Doctor. I'll make sure she's taken care of." Alex shook the doctor's hand.

"Just let the nurse at the front know when you're ready to go."

"Will do. Thanks, Doc."

She watched the exchange. Husband? An uneasy feeling washed over her. If Alex wasn't Aidan, why would he allow someone to believe they were married? "Why didn't you tell him you aren't my husband?"

"If he knew you were going back to your house alone, do you think he'd have let you go?"

"How do you know I'm alone?" Laryssa asked, folding her arms across her chest.

"Oh sure, you got a million men waiting in the wings. I don't think so." He pointed to her belly.

"There are many men out there who find pregnant woman attractive," she countered, holding her chin high.

"Oh, I know. I used to be one of those guys," he said in a despondent tone. "While you get dressed, I'll bring the car around. I'll phone my housekeeper, Joanne, and let her know we're having company."

"I don't know what gave you that idea, but I'm not staying with you." She widened her stance, ready to fight him.

"Yes, you are. You heard the doctor. You need to rest."

"Look, you're welcome to drive me, but I am going home and nowhere else. You aren't my husband. I'm never having a husband again." Her words spewed out of her mouth with more vehemence than she meant to display.

Alex placed his palm against his forehead and let out a breath. "Aren't you the least bit curious as to why I may look like Aidan? God knows, I am. I'm offering you a place to rest while we figure it out."

Curiosity didn't even come close to what she felt right now. She was an emotional mess, with anxiety and fear rolled into a ball, bouncing back and forth inside her stomach. "Thank you, but I—" she tried again.

"Good, then it's settled. Get yourself dressed. You're staying with me," he said. "I'll go pull the car around. See that you're ready by time I get back."

Even though she had no intention of staying with him, she did as she was told. She just wanted to get out of the door first and would deal with him when the time came. Once she was dressed, she walked over to the closet and grabbed her jacket, turning towards the door when she heard a noise. Alex must have told a nurse they were ready to go because she came in with a wheelchair.

"I'm fine. I don't need a wheelchair," Laryssa argued. She refused to feel like an invalid who couldn't do things on her own. After Aidan died, she took great pride in stepping up to the plate and being master of her own life. She wasn't going to let someone else take that control away from her.

If Alex thought she would just give in to him, he had another thing coming. Feeling pampered for once would be nice, but not at the expense of losing her self-respect. No man was going to boss her around a second time and get away with it. If she didn't fight for respect, she'd never get respect. She had no plans on being any man's doormat again.

Laryssa stood there and fought with the nurse about the wheelchair when Aidan's look-a-like stroll in. If she was honest with herself, she did want to find out the story behind the face. A face that looked pretty determined in the moment.

"Sit." Alex pointed to the wheelchair.

"Mr. Richards, I will not be told what to do. I lived with that long enough." Temper flared like a ball of fire inside her.

"I tried to explain that it is hospital policy. She won't listen," the nurse grumbled.

"Ms. Mitchell, sit! Or I will carry you to the car myself," he dared. A sparkle of humor danced in his eyes.

"You wouldn't," Laryssa gasped.

"Wouldn't I?"

When he took a step towards her, her mouth opened, and she let out a squeak. The corners of his mouth curled into a grin.

CHAPTER TWO

Alex watched as Laryssa's eyes tracked his every move. Her breathing quickened with each step he took. The best thing to do would be to walk out that door and never come back, but he was in it too deep. He challenged her already and couldn't back down now. Besides, for some reason he didn't want to walk away. She lifted her head, and their eyes locked. Her brown eyes darkened with interest, only a narrow ring of her true color remained.

He closed the space in a matter of seconds and scooped her up in his arms. She pushed against his chest and tried to pull her legs free, wiggling her bum in the process.

"Put me down," she pleaded, pushing even harder against him. "I'll sit in the chair."

He tightened his hold. "Watch it, or I might drop you," he warned. "Besides, you had your chance. Now sit back and enjoy the ride. You might find you enjoy it more."

"Fat chance," she mumbled. He barely suppressed the grin that was fighting its way to the surface. The first time he picked her up, she was unconscious. This time, she was very much awake and every time she wiggled, his hand brushed the corner of her breast. The contact created a fire under his skin that shot straight to his loins. He re-adjusted his hold and turned towards the door of the hospital room.

"You can't be serious about carrying me the whole way." She studied his face, her mouth open.

"There's one thing you should know about me. I mean what I say." With that, he started walking down the hallway.

He felt the moment of her surrender. Her hands came up around his neck and linked together. She let her head rest against his shoulder. His heart started to pound, and he wondered if she'd notice. If she did, she gave no indication. Instead, she snuggled even closer and sighed. Her breast pushed up against his chest, and a fizz of energy shot through his body, stopping in a place where he thought all interest left long ago. His body jolted at the intensity of his desire. She tilted her head and look up at him.

"Am I getting to be too much for you, tough guy?" She unlinked her hands from around his neck to squeeze his biceps.

He was definitely getting himself in over his head, but it was too late to change his mind now. He could see his car outside the hospital doors. When he reached it, he opened the door and gently lowered her on to the seat. He grabbed the seatbelt and fastened her in.

"What do you think I'm going to do, Mr. Richards, run away?" she asked him when he climbed in the other side.

"The thought had crossed my mind." He turned the engine on and pulled out of the parking spot.

"In case you hadn't noticed, I'm not exactly capable of running at the moment." She rested both hands on her protruding belly.

He shrugged and said, "Better to be safe than sorry." With how stubborn she was, he could imagine her trying to get out of the car the minute he pulled up to a red light.

They lapsed into silence as he drove through the city until he turned onto the highway. "Uh, you are taking me home, right?" Laryssa sat further up in her seat.

"Why?" He placed his foot a little harder on the accelerator to keep up with the flow of traffic.

"It's my home. Do I really have to give you a reason?" She folded her arms across her chest while her foot tapped on the floor.

The pout on her face sent another shot of desire through him. Since when did he get turned on by a pouting woman? There must be something wrong with him. *Of course, there is something wrong with you, you fool. You're getting turned on by a pouting woman who's pregnant with another man's baby.*

He fought an internal war for a few minutes and, by the time he glanced back at her, she was sound asleep. That was unexpected. He thought for certain she was going to argue about going with him to his place. Reaching over, he pulled her jacket closed to keep her warm.

If she was going to stay with him, she would need clothes. The only logical thing would be to take her home so she could pack. The car hit a slight bump on the road, and she stirred. Her head came to rest on his shoulder for the rest of the drive. When she exhaled, her warm breath tickled his bare arm, making his body ache for her. The sensation wasn't welcome. He didn't need or want a romantic entanglement in his life. He learned from the last time, and, if he wasn't careful, this would get out of hand. He was, after all, only human.

He drove into her driveway and turned the engine off. Alex contemplated picking her up and carrying her into the house, but he didn't want to rehash the way his body deceived him back at the hospital. Thankfully, a moment later, she stirred. He watched her cheeks blush when she realized that she had practically slept on him the entire trip home.

"I'm so sorry. You should have woken me up," she said, scooting closer to the door before opening it. "Thanks for driving me home and for bailing me out of there."

She climbed out and waddled to the door of her house. He caught up to her as she put the key in the lock.

"You don't need to come in. I'll be fine." She opened the door, stepped inside, and proceeded to close the door.

He placed his foot in the way. "Yes, I do! In case you don't remember, the doctor left you in my care," Alex said. She tried to move his foot, but he kept it firmly planted.

"Mr. Richards, I don't need a babysitter. I can take care of myself, and I'd rather you weren't here." She took her hands off the door to try to push him away.

He used that opportunity to push it open and stroll inside. "I hate to remind you again, but the doctor put you in my care."

"No. He put me in the care of my husband. Which, in case you haven't noticed, isn't you." She grabbed his arm and tried to pull him towards the door.

He refused to budge, planting his feet on the floor. She may have been stubborn, but she would soon realize he was just as stubborn. He wanted answers to the mysteries that surrounded her, and he was going to get them.

"Where are your blankets?" he asked. She stopped the tug-a-war with his arm and stared up at him.

"Huh?"

"Your blankets? You know, what you cover yourself up with when you go to sleep." He motioned the pulling up of covers. "I'll need some if I sleep on your couch tonight."

"No, you won't, because you are not staying here." She shook her head. "My, uh, my place is too small."

He glanced around the living room. It was smaller than his own bedroom, and he didn't think the rest of the house would be much bigger. Although, he had to admit she made good use of the space, making it look livable with the strategic placing of her furniture. Spider plants hung from the ceiling in the corners of the room, and there were flowers on the coffee table in a pink vase. The beige sofa was placed under the window, and the entertainment centre on the opposite wall. The size of the house would put him in close contact with her on a daily basis.

The thought had a certain appeal to it, yet warning bells were going off in his head. Being surrounded by all things feminine, including her, in such a small space, wouldn't be good for him. He had made a pact never to get closely involved with another woman.

"Okay, if I can't stay here, then pack some clothes. You're staying with me," he said.

"Mr. Richards, I can't stay with you, and you can't stay here. I won't have some strange man sleeping in my house," she said with a firm voice.

"Hmm, I'm Alex Richards. I'm thirty-four years old. I was born..." He laughed and ducked out of the way when a multi-colored couch pillow flew in his direction.

"Argh, you're impossible." She threw her hands up in the air and stormed out of the room.

Yes, this was definitely going to be interesting. Alex looked around the room again and noticed it wasn't like normal family rooms There were no pictures that lined the walls or shelves. Nothing to indicate why she reacted the way she did at the office or the hospital.

He heard the sound of water flowing and figured she must be running herself a bath. That meant he had more time to explore his new surroundings. There had to be something in the house that would help him figure her out. Something to stop the restlessness that had etched itself deep into his soul from the moment he'd met her. Rubbing his hands together, he glanced at the bathroom door, hoping she'd be in there a while. It was time to find some answers.

Laryssa turned on the radio, switched it to the country station, and lowered herself into the bath. "Heaven," she sighed. Bubble baths were her favorite way to relax and, after what she had been through today, she deserved it. She leaned her head back against the bath pillow and closed her eyes.

She tried to forget that there was a man downstairs who, if she didn't know better, could pass as her husband. A man who had forced himself into her house. If she had any sense, she'd be on the phone to the cops.

"Ha."

They'd probably send the men-in-white to come and get her instead. "That's right, guys. Mommy is insane." She ran her hand over her belly where a little foot protruded; or at least she thought it was a foot. She'd read how some people could tell what part of the baby was sticking out, but she still couldn't figure it out. Hopefully that didn't mean she lacked maternal instinct. "I'm definitely going to have an interesting story to tell you both when you're older."

She hoped that if she stayed in the tub long enough, he would let himself out, but that thought was thwarted when there was a knock on the bathroom door. Laryssa didn't want to answer. She wanted time alone; time to think. The whole situation held an unrealistic quality to it, like a dream she couldn't wake up from. Maybe if she tapped her heels together three times, she'd wake up.

Another knock resounded. "Laryssa, are you okay?" he called.

Why wouldn't he go away? She slid down further in the bath and let the water run over her ears.

"If you don't answer now, I'm going to come in!" he threatened. She heard a moment of silence, followed by another pound on the door. "Damn it, Laryssa. Answer me!"

Couldn't he take a hint that she didn't want to talk to him.

"Laryssa?" Alex said, panic lacing his tone.

She heard the door handle shake. *He wouldn't dare*. She shot up in the bath, reaching for a towel.

The door burst open. She watched in horror as the towel she was reaching for fell to the floor. "What do you think you're doing," she screeched, covering herself with her arms.

The gentlemanly thing to do would be to pick up the towel, hand it to her and leave the bathroom, but Alex couldn't make his feet move. Her hair, straightened by the weight of the water, rested like a curtain over her full breasts. His eyes drifted downward to where her hand covered the mound between her thighs.

He swallowed hard when his insides heated and his friend, yet again, decided to perk up at the sight of her. He'd read about sirens, but never in all his life did he ever think he'd meet one. She stood there staring at him, not saying a word, but her song sang out to him.

Alex tugged at the waist of his tightened jeans. He felt like a teenager again.

"I—you..." He slammed his hand on the door handle in frustration when he heard the huskiness in his own voice. Letting out a growl, he grabbed her by the arm and hauled her out of the tub.

She gasped as her hand pulled away from her chest, revealing her ample breasts and darkened centers, nipples puckered. She crossed her legs and attempted to cover herself with her free hand, not very successfully.

Were they aroused because of him, or because she was cold? He fought the urge to pull her close to find out. The smell of strawberries tickled his senses. His gaze traveled down her body and back up, making it harder for him to let go. Her cheeks were flushed by the time his gaze locked with hers. Involuntarily, his hand reached out and stroked her cheek. Her eyes widened, and she jerked back.

Fear! She was afraid of him. The thought was like a mental cold shower. He dropped her arm and took a step back. What else would she be for goodness' sake? He just burst into her bathroom and stood there gawking like a schoolboy.

He shoved his hands in his pockets to prevent himself from reaching out to her again. "Why didn't you answer?" he snapped.

"I didn't feel I had to. It's my house." She turned away and reached for another towel, wrapping it around her body.

From behind, she didn't look pregnant. His eyes lowered to her ass, and he fought the urge to test and see how firm it was. He was still looking when she turned back around.

"Take a picture, Mr. Richards. It lasts longer." She held her head high and walked by him to her bedroom, without so much as a second glance.

He followed her and leaned against the door frame. "I'm not a pervert, Ms. Mitchell," he said, crossing his arms.

"Could have fooled me." She walked to her closet and pulled out a blue, short sleeved maternity dress.

The fact she thought of him as a pervert irked him. Sure, he stood there staring at her in the bathroom, but what else was he to do. She shocked him. He only did what any red-blooded male would have done.

"If you had answered me, I wouldn't have barged in. I was worried about you," he reasoned.

"And that is your reason for drooling over me? Look, I don't need anyone worrying about me." Laryssa placed her dress on the bed and turned back to him.

"Can I have some privacy, please?" She gestured toward the dress.

The towel slid down slightly, showing her cleavage, and his body quickened. Angered at his own response, he turned and left the room, slamming the door behind him. He raked his hand through his hair. From the very beginning, he knew she was going to be trouble. The sooner he got her to his house to be watched over by Joanne instead of him, the better. There he'd be able to do some digging of his own and learn about his look-a-like, without running into her every minute. He discovered nothing during his search of her living room.

As soon as the door closed, Laryssa rushed across the room and locked it. She let out a deep breath and leaned back against the door. She'd never had such an intense sexual moment before in her life. Her pulse still raced, beating against the skin on her neck. Her arm tingled where his hand had held it securely. The strength in his hand had excited her as it flexed gently on her arm, but it also frightened her. She knew just how dangerous it could be.

"Relax, Laryssa. He's not Aidan," she murmured. "Aidan's dead. He can't hurt you anymore." She pushed herself away from the door and walked toward the floral pattern covered bed, letting the towel slip to the floor. How could this man make her feel so alive? He had barely touched her. Apparently, her libido hadn't dropped off the end of the earth like she had thought.

When Aidan looked at her, she felt nothing in the end, except fear. When he touched her, she struggled not to tremble, knowing he would get angry if she did. Alex was identical to him, yet her body reacted in a way totally foreign to her. While her mind was registering Aidan, her body knew instinctively that it was another soul. The feeling left her perplexed.

When he reached out to touch her in the bathroom, she didn't jerk back in fear; but at the intensity of the feelings that coursed through her body when his finger brushed her cheek. It rocked her all the way down to her toes. She'd never felt so sexually alive before.

After a while, Laryssa finally gained the courage to go downstairs. Alex was sprawled out on the couch, sound asleep. The beige leather couch looked awfully small with him lying there. He took up the whole length of it. One of his arms had slid off the cushion and dangled over the side. The other was propped under his head. His feet were crossed and hanging off the other end.

She grabbed a flannel sheet out of the linen closet and went back to cover him up. She took a seat in the chair off to the side and stared at him. How was this possible? Aidan had no family. He had told her that he was alone, too.

This man on the couch proved otherwise, didn't it? If she went by her heart, it alone knew. Even her eyes proved it as she studied him. Aidan favored brush cuts, but Alexander's dark brown hair was longer. A few stray hairs had fallen across his forehead, curling above his left eyebrow. His nose was smooth and straight, while Aidan's had a bump from being broken in a bar fight. She already knew his eyes had passion. She saw that in the bathroom. Aidan's eyes had held no feeling unless he was angry, then they shot out daggers.

With just this bit of time together, she knew he wasn't Aidan. Not just because of slight differences in their appearance but because of how he acted. Alex had a maturity that Aidan seemed to lack and was more sophisticated. He carried himself with a certain confidence. Somehow, he even looked more handsome. *Oh, don't go there, girl. You've sworn off love.* She couldn't trust her judgment of men and didn't want to find herself in the same situation as before. But, yet, here she was, watching a man sleep on her couch. A man so identical to her husband, it was mind-boggling.

Were they long-lost brothers or simply a case of look-a-likes? After all, didn't everyone in the world have a double? As much as she didn't want them to be, they were connected. If he was Aidan's brother, then the children she carried were related to him. She couldn't just make him leave. She wished to God she could because, with just a look and a certain tone of voice, the painful memories she buried deep inside bubbled to the surface.

How could she find the strength to keep him in her life? His face was part of the life she'd been trying to leave behind. What if he turned out like Aidan? Laryssa shuddered.

Her stomach growled at her. She hadn't eaten anything since lunchtime and, judging by the pale light shining in the window, it was evening already. Laryssa whipped up a few meat and cheese sandwiches to ease the hunger pains that never seemed to stop. After eating hers, she placed one on the table in front of Alex and went up to her room.

She flopped down on her bed and put a pillow behind her so she could lean up against the wall. He appeared determined to be a fixture in her house unless she agreed to go with him. Having him here gave her mixed feelings. Would it be easier just to go with him to his home? At least there she wouldn't be filled with the memories of what took place inside these walls. Maybe her mind wouldn't be so confused. Here, all she had were rooms and things that reminded her of Aidan. And seeing Alex sitting there on the couch didn't help either. She couldn't separate the two of them so easily yet, not here anyway.

Laryssa stared at the door, half expecting him to come charging into the room, demanding her to take her clothes off. Aidan was an inconsiderate, demanding sex fiend. She might as well have been a blow-up doll for all the affection he showed. If he didn't make her give him a blow job, he would just stick it in with a wham-bam, thank you ma'am.

She did her best to purge the house of Aidan, including purging herself of his last name, Peters. The neighbor's son had helped her move the furniture around. They moved the double bed from the guest room into the master bedroom and tossed the king-sized bed. She refused to spend one more night in it after his death. Real-estate agents approached her about selling the house, but where would she go? Not to mention, she really wasn't in the condition to pack and move right now anyway.

Besides, why should she let any man chase her out of her own home, including Alex? She was in control of her own life now and was not about to let any man take that away, not without a fight.

CHAPTER THREE

Alex rolled over and was jarred awake when his bed dropped out from under him. He flung his arms out and his elbow connected with a hard surface, causing him to wince. Before he knew it, he landed face-first on the floor. He opened his eyes and found himself staring at a sea of blue. He ran his fingers across the carpet. Since when did he have blue carpet in his bedroom?

He propped himself up on his elbows and gave the back of his neck a rub. From his line of view all he could see was the sofa, coffee-table, recliner, and a thin ray of sunshine which shone over the sofa.

Birds chirped, greeting the morning sun. Softly and tenderly another sound reached out, wrapping itself around his heart. Craning his ear, he listened carefully. The familiar tune of a country favorite carried through the house. He knew it was her, and all the recent events tumbled into his mind. The need to get her into his territory hit him stronger than ever.

He took a deep breath. The strong, rich scent of coffee filled his nostrils. Lured by the smell, Alex pulled at the pink linen blanket wrapped around his feet and stood up. After doing a few simple stretches to work the kink out of his back, he followed the sound of her voice.

He found Laryssa in the kitchen, stretching to reach something on the top shelf. She wore nothing more than a light pink, silk nightgown with spaghetti straps. The further she stretched, the more skin she revealed, leaving little to the imagination.

Without turning around, she gestured to the coffee pot. "There's fresh coffee if you want some." She grabbed a chair from the table and placed it below the cupboard.

How had she known he was there?

When she went to climb on the chair, he grabbed it and took it back to the table. The last thing he needed was for her to get up on the chair in that poor, incredibly sexy excuse for a nightgown. She'd already given him a good view, and he didn't need another one. Not when his body decided to painfully remind him of his lack of sexual intimacy over the years. He reached up, grabbed the bowl she wanted, and placed it on the counter.

"Thanks." She leaned down to pull a pan out of the cupboard.

He swallowed hard as he watched her nightgown slide dangerously high, giving him a glimpse of a mound of white flesh. She wasn't wearing any underwear, he thought with a start.

"Are you a tease, Ms. Mitchell?" he asked, leaning back against the counter to enjoy the view. She jerked upright and stared at him questioningly. "You're not wearing any underwear."

Her face went a deep red, and she couldn't meet his eyes. "I didn't think you'd be up yet. I came down to get some underwear out of the wash, but it was still wet."

He grinned at her choice of words and watched as a bright crimson color filled her cheeks.

"They were wet from being washed," she said, rolling her eyes, "so I came here to make something to eat while I waited. Can't you men ever think of anything but sex?" She tried to push by him, and he blocked her with his arm.

She turned to walk the other way, but he enclosed her against the counter, arm on either side, his hands resting on the counter. "Well, with this little flimsy gown being the only thing between me and your body," he said, capturing the silk of her nightgown between his fingers, "what man could resist?" She shivered and her eyes darkened with lust. A heady sense of power coursed through him.

"A man who wishes to have children in the future," Laryssa said with conviction.

Children? Memories assailed him and took him back to a time he didn't want to remember. He let his hands drop, and she shoved by him. Without turning to watch her leave, he tugged at the collar of his shirt as panic bubbled inside him, robbing him of his breath. Children. There would be no children. None of his own. Not again. Pain spiraled through him, piercing his heart like a knife. A pain so raw, not even a decade diminished it.

He wasn't going to break-down. He took three deep breaths and forced the thoughts from his mind. Of course, they were never really gone. They hovered like demons in the dark recesses of his mind, threatening to attack at any moment. That was why he never stopped working. Never went to bed until overwhelming fatigue gave him no other choice. And the reason he never allowed himself to have a close relationship with a woman. He looked around the small, intimate kitchen. Here, he was in danger of what he tried so hard to avoid. The need to get her back to his home re-surfaced with a vengeance. He'd get her there one way or another. He just didn't know how yet.

Laryssa leaned down and pulled the clothes from the dryer, placing them in the laundry basket to take upstairs. When she turned around, there he stood, filling the expanse of the doorway. Her only way out. His feet were a shoulder width apart. His lips were pressed together, and his arms folded so tightly across his chest that they pulled at the seams of his shirt. His eyes were dark and remote. She recognized those eyes and that stance. Aidan did the same thing when he was determined to have his own way.

"Whatever you have to say, forget it!" She steeled herself against the look. The one which, in the past, frightened her into immediate submission. No man was ever going to have that satisfaction again, especially not one who looked identical to the man who nearly destroyed her. She moved closer to him to leave the laundry room, but he was an immovable mountain. "Move, please."

"After you agree to come back with me." He placed his hands against the door frame.

"Alex, if you don't move, I'm going to be late for work." She pushed against his chest with her free hand, but he refused to budge.

"You aren't working anymore."

Her heart skipped a beat, and a tingling sensation crawled up her spine. Her legs turned to jelly. She squeezed her eyes shut and reached out to the dryer to steady herself. *Breathe, Laryssa. Breathe!* Behind her closed eyelids, she could see Aidan's silhouette. He had stood in the exact same spot as Alex and uttered those exact words.

She had cowered in fear and did his bidding, but that was then.

She steeled herself against her new enemy. "And how do you suppose I pay my bills, oh bright one?"

"Just pack your clothes. I'll pick you up after work later."

"Mr. Richards, I'm not staying with you. How many times do I have to say that?" She rubbed her temples. "Now, if you'll excuse me, I have to finish getting ready for work."

"You're not working,"

She poked him in the chest. "Who the hell are you to tell me what I can and can't do?"

"Your boss."

Laryssa immediately dropped her hand and stared down at the floor. The scene in the office replayed in her head. Alex was at the head of the conference table when she walked in. His last name was Richards, and the company was Richards' Enterprises. That alone should have clued her in.

Lifting her head, she asked, "Are you telling me that if I don't move in with you, you'll fire me?"

"Don't call it firing. Call it a lay-off till after the babies are born. You need to relax. The doctor even said so."

"If there is one thing I know as a P.A, it is the rules that govern the workplace. I've re-written them enough for that precious employee handbook. You can't fire me just because I won't move in with you. That's sexual harassment."

His eyes narrowed. "I know perfectly well what harassment is, Ms

Mitchell. I also know you are unfit to carry on your duty without personal risk, not only to your health, but theirs as well." He pointed toward her stomach, "I wouldn't be a good employer if I allowed you to keep working."

"So, instead, you fire me? How does that make you a good employer?"

"I'd love to sit here and argue with you, but I have to head to work. If you show up, I'll haul your butt back here so fast you won't know what hit you." He leaned in closer and spoke with a low voice, "You might want to be dressed by time I get back. If I see that strap fall off your shoulder one more time, I won't be held responsible for my actions." He slipped his thumb under the spaghetti strap that slid off her shoulder and stroked her skin. Goose bumps covered her arms. He slid the strap back up where it belonged, and then disappeared down the hallway.

When Laryssa heard the door close, she rushed to the phone in the living room and picked it up to call human resources. After a moment, she placed the phone back on the receiver and flopped on the couch. What good would it do? Like it or not, this man was in her life. He appeared to be as curious about her as she was about him. The least he could be, though, was sociable and not downright infuriating.

Alex looked around his office and then back at the stack of papers in front of him. It was late afternoon, and he was no closer to reaching the bottom of the stack than when he started. If he managed to fill any out, which was a task in and of itself because of her, more were brought in to replace them. He had to get his mind off her cute little rear-end and big brown eyes. He wasn't sure which he stared at more. The more he thought of her and the feel of her soft ivory skin against his thumb, the less work he got done. He banged his fist down on the desk.

"You're usually cranking out the paperwork, what's up?" He looked up and saw his friend, Ron, in the doorway. "Come, sit." Alex motioned to the black leather chair in front of his desk. "Have you ever been mistaken for someone else?"

"Once. I think almost everyone has been. Why?"

"Laryssa called me Aidan."

"Who is Aidan?" His friend leaned forward.

"Unless I'm going out on a limb here, I'm going to say it's her dead husband."

"She thinks you're her dead husband?" Ron asked with a perplexed look on his face.

Alex nodded his head. "Well, initially. But, after a day of staying with her, I don't think she believes that anymore."

That earned him another puzzled look. "You've been staying with her? You can't stand the sight of a woman for more than a couple of hours."

"I know, but there is something suspicious going on here, and I'm not letting her out of my sight till I know what it is." He weaved the pen in and out of his fingers.

"Maybe she's conning you, thinking she can get a hold of your money?"

"That thought had crossed my mind, but I don't think even the best actress can faint like that or control her own blood pressure." He rested his elbow on the desk and cradled his chin with the palm of his hand.

"What are you going to do?"

"I've asked her to move in with me."

"You what?" Ron's mouth dropped open. "You definitely need a drink. Come on. Let's lock up, and I'll take you out for a beer."

"Thanks for the offer, but I better get back to her house before she decides to skip town."

"All right, your loss. See you tomorrow." Ron shook his head and left the room.

Alex stopped at a Chinese restaurant before he went back over to

Laryssa's place. He pulled into her driveway and sat paralyzed in his seat when he saw her figure swaying back and forth, her back facing the window. When he opened the car door, he could hear music flowing through the open living room window. He continued to stare, catching glimpses of her. Watching her like this, uninhibited, left an odd feeling in his chest he couldn't identify. She had changed out of her nightgown into what looked like a sundress, with equally enticing straps. God help him.

He walked up to the house and knocked on the front door. No answer. Obviously, Laryssa couldn't hear him over the music. He turned the handle and walked in.

She jumped and spun around, hand over her heart. “Have you ever heard of knocking?”

“I did. You didn't hear me,” he grumbled and shoved the food at her.

“What's this?”

“What does it look like?” He didn't like how good she looked in her blue sundress, which fit her perfectly. He could see every curve of her luscious body.

“If all you're going to do is snap at me, then you can walk right back out the way you came.” She turned and carried the food into the kitchen.

He watched her walk away. He heard how pregnant women waddled, but she walked with confidence, aware of whom and what she was. Helpless, he followed her.

“Mr. Richards, if you're so desperate to help me, you can grab those cups.” She pointed high into the cupboard.

“Please call me Alex. You make me feel like my father.” He grabbed the cups and placed them on the table.

“If it's all the same to you, I prefer Mr. Richards. You can have your pick of drinks from the fridge. I'm afraid I don't keep beer stocked, though.”

He grabbed a soda and sat at the table. A piece of paper caught his attention. He picked it up and examined it. “What the hell is this?”

"That? Oh, it's my resignation." She continued to dig around in the Chinese food bag as she spoke.

"I can see that," he seethed. "What's the meaning of it?" He crumpled the paper and held it tightly in his fist.

Turning towards the cupboard, she pulled down two plates. "Under the circumstances, I think it would be best if I moved on."

Tired of being ignored, at least attention wise, he grabbed her arm, sat down, and pulled her onto his lap. Now, there was no way she could do anything but talk with him. She had fought him so hard that morning regarding the job. Why on earth would she decide to resign now?

"What the!" she cried, squirming to get loose.

He held her firmly. "We're going to talk, you and I."

"But our food is getting cold."

"Screw the food! I want to know why you are resigning."

"What's it to you? You're the one who couldn't wait for me to leave this morning." She pulled at the arms which held her.

"If it makes you feel any better, Dan isn't too happy that I won't let you come to work. He says you're invaluable to the team." He wound a strand of her hair around his finger. All he had to do was tug and her lips would be on his. The thought had crossed his mind many times since he'd left her standing in the doorway of the laundry room in her pink flimsy nightgown.

Now she sat in his lap with a sundress on. Curiosity plagued him; he ran a finger along her hip and across her lower back and felt the faint outline of an undergarment. He heard her draw in a breath. Did she wear a thong or panties? The thought nearly did him in. He knew he had to change his line of thought before she wondered what the hard object was that pressed against her.

He took a deep breath and asked, "Does this mean you've chosen to move in with me?"

"Please stop pushing. I already told you that I won't move in with you." She gave him another push. "Let me go."

"After we've talked," he said. "This morning you fought me like a tiger when I asked you to take time off."

"Ordered is more like it," she huffed.

"Whatever, so why resign now?"

Laryssa stared at the floor, chewing on her nails. How do you explain to someone that they look exactly like a person you lost? That ordering her not to work left a sour taste in her mouth. It was too much like her past, and she needed to pull away from it, to let it go. She was a new woman now and wouldn't allow herself to be controlled by anyone, let alone a man who looked like Aidan.

She'd spent the whole day thinking and decided hell would have to freeze over before she let another man make a decision for her. That was what prompted the resignation letter. If he was going to fire her, at least it gave her some control over the situation. Where she'd go from here, she didn't know. At least Dan would give her a good reference and would probably give Alex heck for losing her, which sounds like he did a little already.

As she sat there contemplating how to answer, his finger stroked her cheek. The touch was so gentle, a sigh escaped before she could stop it.

"I only meant until the babies were born, you know. You could come back to work after," he said.

"What do you suppose I do in the meantime?" When he opened his mouth to speak, she continued, "and don't say move in with you because that isn't going to happen."

"Why not? My place is big. It has a pool, and my housekeeper is more than happy to help you out."

"Gosh, why are you so persistent? What's in it for you?"

"Are you always this suspicious of men, Ms. Mitchell?" He studied her expression. "Is it so difficult to believe that someone wants to help you out?"

"If you want to help me out, you can start by letting me go and stop touching me." His hand paused where it had been caressing her upper arm.

"But you are so tempting." He pulled at the strap of her dress and let it snap back in place.

Suddenly, she wished she would have put on the pant suit she owned, instead of the dress. She had decided against the suit, thinking she would have been too hot. But right now, with her skin exposed and his fingers dancing lightly on her shoulder, her body was ten times hotter than the suit would have made her.

"Mr. Richards, let me go," she pleaded.

"Say yes then." He moved her hair aside and brushed his lips against her neck, sending a tidal wave of pleasure through her body.

Rational, think rational thoughts, Laryssa. Her body was betraying her. She did not want to have feelings for another man, especially a man who looked as deathly handsome as Alex and whose face could sweep her into the past in a split second.

Would his house have the answers she was looking for? *Good rational thought there.* She rolled her eyes. It would be like stepping into the lion's den with one great big lion, except this lion had deep, ocean-colored eyes and a smile that could knock you off your feet. He was a puzzle, extremely charming one minute and downright rude the next. Laryssa didn't need another charmer or a lion. All she wanted was to live her life on her own terms and not have to answer to anyone else. It was charm that got her in the first mess.

"Let me go," she said in a cool voice. "I mean it."

"I'm not letting you go until we finish talking." He tightened his arms around her waist.

"I'm done talking." She grabbed one hand and tried to pry it off. He grabbed her arms and trapped them beneath his own. "I'm not joking. Let me go. Now."

He had the nerve to grin at her. "If I don't let you go, what will you do?" he teased.

"This." With all the strength she could muster, she kicked his shin with the back of her heel. He let out a curse and released her. She stood up and put the table between them.

"God, you could have at least warned me." He rubbed his shin.

"I'm sure you aren't so dense that you don't understand what 'let me go' means. But, in case that wasn't clear enough, maybe this will be. I will not be manhandled into making a decision." With that, she turned and high tailed it out of the room. Alex was right behind her and caught up with her at the stairs. He grabbed her arm and pulled her close to him.

"After nearly ripping open my shin, I think I deserve this. I was a good boy in there." He placed one hand behind her head, and he leaned down till his lips were a fraction away from hers.

She should pull away, but his citrus and musk scent swirled around her and made it impossible for her to do anything except wait with anticipation. His lips gently skimmed over hers, and she felt oddly disappointed. But before she could complete that thought, she was being devoured, and her mouth wonderfully assaulted. His tongue slid skillfully over her lips, encouraging her to open to him and, when she did, he swept inside. She melted against him, and her heart rate sped up. She could do little else but cling to him.

The life in her womb protested against the pressure as he attempted to pull her closer to him. It was enough to break the moment, and they pulled apart. He couldn't take his eyes off her lips, likely swollen from the kiss.

She swallowed hard and cleared her throat before glaring up at him. "Kiss me like that again, and your other shin will be black and blue."

"If our next kiss is anything like that one, it'll be worth it." He gave her a wink and then walked away.

"Of all the men in the world, I had to meet this one. Insufferable, infuriating," she mumbled as she walked up the stairs. What were the odds, after years of not feeling anything for Aidan, she'd be so quickly turned on by his double? Something was wrong with that picture. Fate was delivering her a low blow. For Pete's sake, her husband died just a few months ago, and here she was, exchanging kisses with the first man inside her house since then. How much more pathetic could she get?

If he insisted on staying with her, then she would just have to avoid him as much as possible. Playing the perfect hostess was not on the top of her to do list. Let him live in his deluded world that she would come back with him. Hopefully, he would eventually tire of the idea and leave her be. She could only hope. Still, she couldn't help but wonder what his secret agenda was. No man tried this hard without an ulterior motive. Did he think she knew something, and that she'd break eventually? Good luck, Alex. She knew even less than he did.

CHAPTER FOUR

Alex pulled up to her house and put the car in park after going for a drive. He wasn't going to wait any longer. He had given her two weeks to come to a decision on her own, but it didn't appear it was going to happen that way. Every time he had tried to talk to her, she would come up with some excuse as to why they couldn't. Like tonight, for example, she complained about being tired and waddled off to bed. Tomorrow they would talk again, and this time they'd discuss everything. His house. Aidan. All of it.

He had tried to snoop around her house but found nothing, not even a photo album. Not that he had much chance to look since she was always there. Did Aidan look like him, or was she just stringing him along because he was rich?

Since she lost her husband, she might be looking for someone to help her out financially. She was probably in debt up to her eyeballs and was trying to rope in some poor sucker with her sob story. It wouldn't have been the first time a woman chased after him for his money, but her story topped all the others. However, if she was in such dire straits, why did she so adamantly refuse his help?

Was she telling the truth? Did Aidan really look like him? He found the whole thing a little hard to believe. He hoped that all he had was a doppelgänger. Someone who only kind of looked like him. A situation that was merely coincidental. It was either that, or his family had lied to him all his life. Neither sounded very plausible. He could dismiss her claims and leave her be, like she wanted him to, but he was never one for turning down a good mystery. Granted, this one could change his life, and that was the one thing that made him wonder whether it was all worth it.

Alex hung up his coat in the closet and collapsed on Laryssa's couch. His back ached at the idea of sleeping on it again. He wanted to be in his own house, in his own bed. He stripped off most of his clothes and climbed under the covers she had left for him.

Could she be carrying his nephews or nieces? He hadn't really asked her to present evidence or even a picture, but he was hesitant to do so because he might lose her. They were walking around on eggshells, never broaching the topic. But when the shocked look of recognition entered her eyes, he couldn't help but wonder if his double really did exist. She also gave him another look. One that caused desire to rocket through him.

He knew she'd be upstairs in bed, wearing a more modest nightgown. A grin spread across his face as he remembered the flimsy night attire she wore the first night he was there. When she came downstairs after the second night, he was disappointed to find that her latest nightgown went past her knees. Boy, he was pathetic. One of the curses of humanity; attraction! It was something he could do without. The kiss they shared had been more potent than anything he could ever remember. Had his heart gone into overdrive when he'd kissed Valerie?

Valerie.

He couldn't control the unpleasant tremor that rocked his body at the mere thought of his ex-wife. Why couldn't he get past the pain she'd caused him? There'd been a time when he went from woman to woman, trying to erase her memory and her betrayal, but it never worked.

Eventually, he swore off women completely. Swore off anyone who could hurt him, except for those who he was close to before.

Those he trusted implicitly, like his family, but could it be possible that even they abused his trust? His grandparents, Mitch and Ruth, had raised him from birth. He looked back on his childhood and recalled all the questions he'd ask them about his parents. He never did receive a thorough answer, only enough to appease a child. Did that mean they were keeping something from him? Why would they hide something this important if it were true? No! He wouldn't even entertain the thought. It was preposterous. Rolling onto his side, he forced all thought from his head, closed his eyes, and fell asleep.

Only moments later, his eyes shot open as a scream pierced the air. He hopped up and whacked his shin on the coffee table. *Mental note: move coffee table*. With his shin aching, he took the stairs two at a time. His heart skipped a beat as another cry rang out in the darkness. When he reached her door, he could hear muffled sobs.

Slowly, Alex opened the door and poked his head in. He saw her body rocking back and forth on the bed. Unable to let her continue to live through the terror of her nightmare, he approached her.

The dream held Laryssa captive. She couldn't break free.

"You aren't working anymore," Aidan barked, backing her into the corner of the laundry room. He grabbed a fistful of her hair and brought her face close to his. "I've heard about the way you look at him. If I see you with him again, I'll make sure you regret it the rest of your life."

She pleaded with him and insisted nothing was going on, but he wouldn't listen. He tightened his grip on her hair and dragged her upstairs to the bedroom. "You're mine! Do you hear me?" he growled. "Mine!"

She tried to protect herself, but he was too strong. He tossed her on the bed and ripped off her clothes. Clutching her breast, he said, "No one else is allowed to touch you. No one!" Aidan took her nipple between his teeth and pulled. She cried out in pain.

"Laryssa," a voice called. "Speak to me, for God's sake. Say something."

She heard the voice, but Aidan's lips weren't moving. In fact, Aidan was no longer groping her. He appeared to be hovering in the air above her. She reached out and her hand passed right through him.

"Laryssa, come on." Unseen hands shook her shoulders. "Wake up, you're dreaming."

"Go away!" She swung her arms at the invisible foe, praying for him to go away. Her hands came in contact with a hard, warm body. Afraid to open her eyes, she pulled away and took shelter on the far side of the bed. A dream? Was she still dreaming? The bed moved slightly as the other person shifted. She felt his eyes staring at her.

The sheets were cool and damp. Sweat caked her hair against her forehead. With a struggle, she opened her eyes and broke free from her nightmare. Her gaze came to rest on a dark form sitting on the edge of the bed, not three feet away from her. A scream ripped from her mouth, and she dove under the covers.

Her heart pounded beneath her rib cage. Aidan. How could he be here? It was not possible. No way! Aidan was dead, and only God could raise himself from the dead. Slowly, her mind played over the events of the last few weeks. She lowered the sheets and stared at the man who sat next to her.

Reaching out, she touched his cheek. This was Alex, not Aidan. Aidan couldn't hurt her anymore, and Alex, who she didn't know a lot about yet, sat there with concern etched into his brow. She took a moment to study him, afraid to speak, not wanting to break down. Since he'd come to stay with her, he'd shown more sympathy and kindness than Aidan showed in his lifetime. A sigh of relief broke the tense air.

The streetlight shone in through the window giving her a clear view of him. At first glance, she thought it was Aidan. The odds were just too outrageous. But the gentle look in his eyes told her another story. Just who was this man? She let her gaze travel down his body. Boxer shorts. This man had nothing on but boxer shorts, blue ones, at that, with tiny yellow ducks. She coughed to cover up a giggle that bubbled inside her.

He cleared his throat, causing her to bring her gaze back to his face. "You okay?" he asked.

"I...uh." She couldn't help it, her gaze traveled down his well-toned body again. No doubt, if she pinched any part of him, no fat would exist. She watched his hair roughened chest take in a deep breath as her eyes drifted lower. By the look of things, he worked out constantly, unlike his counterpart. Aidan was a lazy butt. He would plop himself down in front of the television with an open beer, hand resting in the front of his pants. At the time, she had laughed. It reminded her of Al from Married with Children. But Alex, his body conjured up images of Hercules. Every time he took a breath, the muscles in his stomach flexed. Pleasure spiraled through her body.

"You were screaming. Are you okay?" He reached for her.

She shrunk backwards and smacked her head on the overhead lamp. "I just had a nightmare, that's all," she croaked, rubbing her head. Her gaze drifted down to the only article of clothing he wore, which didn't prevent her imagination from visualizing what was beneath it. Anxiety and lust intertwined in her belly. Thanks to her vivid imagination.

"That's all? You were screaming bloody murder. Do you want to talk about it?" He shifted under her scrutiny and stood up. "Be right back."

Laryssa leaned back against the headboard and watched the door. Moments later, he returned, fully clothed and with a glass of water in hand. He rejoined her on the bed. Disappointment filled her. She liked his semi-nude state. He handed her the water, and their fingers brushed as she took it from him. The intimate feel of the moment brought tears to her eyes. Her hand shook, and water sloshed over the edge.

He took the glass, placed it on the nightstand, and put his arm around her, pulling her close. It had been a long time since she was held so tenderly. She couldn't help but bury her face against him and let the tears flow. She had longed to be held like this by Aidan, but he refused any tender moments. He said they were a sign of weakness.

After a few minutes passed, she lifted her head, trying desperately to regain her composure. He grabbed a tissue off the nightstand and handed it to her. His eyes watched her carefully. "Do you feel better?"

"Yes, much better." She noticed a wet spot on his shirt from her tears and attempted to wipe it away. Her hand was stopped by his, sandwiched between his heart and hand. Suddenly shy, due to the closeness of the gesture, she attempted to pull her hand away. His fingers curled around hers and held it there, his other arm still wrapped around her shoulders.

With her fingers linked with his, he brought them to her chin and raised her face to meet his. He released her hand and brushed the remainder of her tears away. She trembled under his soft touch. Something was happening here, and she was powerless to stop it.

His eyes traveled over her face, following the movement of her tongue as she moistened her lips. He angled his body towards her. Desire evident in his eyes. She knew he was going to kiss her again. The anger that coursed through her the last time he tried never surfaced.

She watched as his head lowered, and his lips paused an inch away from hers. Her body tingled with anticipation. She could feel his breath on her lips and found herself closing the distance between them, unprepared, yet again, for what his touch could do to her. The moment their lips joined together she was lost. A silky moan rose from her throat when he swept inside her mouth, mating with her tongue a second time.

His lips dropped to the hollow of her neck. She rolled her head back against the headboard, one hand resting on his shoulder. His breath on her neck made heat pool between her thighs. She lost all coherent thought as he continued his assault on her body. All she could think of was how long it had been since she had been touched this way. His hands curved around her hips and ran up her sides till they laid to rest below her breasts. Alex paused, and she sat stone still. She was unable to tell how long they sat in the trance-like state.

How could she feel this way? Was she falling back on her old feelings for Aidan? She couldn't remember the last time she had her world of reality rocked by the touch of a man. Was it wrong to feel this way? Could her body tell the difference between them?

His arousal pressed against her side. "Lara, sweet Lara. I so desperately want you," he moaned huskily. His hand traced the outline of her breast before caressing the fullness of it. She put her hand on his chest to push him away, but the sensations held her hand motionless. They boggled her mind. Push him away. Let him stay.

What did she want? Before she could decide, his mouth crushed against hers again.

When she attempted to protest, he took advantage of her parted lips and thrust his tongue inside, teasing hers like a merry-go-round. Her complaint was swallowed by a moan she couldn't prevent, followed by a guttural sound from within Alex, which made his chest rumble beneath the palm of her hand.

His hand caressed her stomach before it slid lower, stopped by her nightgown. "I want to see you. To touch you." His voice was thick with desire. He stood up and pulled her up next to him.

Her nightgown brushed uncomfortably against the hardened peaks of her breasts. His hands bunched up the nightgown and lifted it over her head. She attempted to cover herself. With her protruding belly, she had trouble feeling sexy.

"Don't." He grabbed her hands and pulled them away from her body, taking a step back to look at her.

She knew her body was not in perfect shape, stretch marks attacked her breasts and hips, making her want to cover up. The only bonus was that her breasts, which were always petite, had grown considerably. That wasn't the only thing that had grown, though. Her hips wouldn't even let her fit into her old jeans anymore, and she had the sneaky suspicion she'd never fit in them again. She stopped being able to wear them when she was eight weeks pregnant. She was twenty-three weeks now and feeling every pound of it. Well, at least he hasn't caught you in your granny panties yet, she thought to herself. Her cheeks heated under his careful scrutiny, and she tugged at her hands.

"You are beautiful," he said.

She stared at him in stunned silence. Beautiful? She'd never felt beautiful before and definitely didn't have the confidence to flaunt herself, but here she stood, stark naked, in front of a man she barely knew. His eyes feasted on her swollen body, making her feel every inch the woman she was. He hadn't touched her much, but the intensity of his gaze had her shuffling her feet. She bit her lip with fervor. How long was he going to stand there and stare at her?

He sat her on the edge of the bed and knelt on his knees, face level with her breasts. She never liked her breasts being touched, so why was she eagerly awaiting his administrations? Anticipation fluttered through her at the thought of his mouth on them.

She watched his lips part as he blew a gentle breeze against her sensitive peaks, and her nipples pulled painfully tight. She placed her hands on his cheeks and drew him closer, eager to let him taste her. His mouth closed over one nipple, while his thumb and forefinger teased the other.

Laryssa moaned. Never in her life has a man been able to touch her this way, both physically and emotionally. There was something she was supposed to remember, but with his mouth suckling her breast, thinking was impossible. Round and round, his tongue played. Her back arched at the pleasure of his moist full lips as they nipped and tugged gently on her breast. No part of her body was asleep. Every inch hummed with awareness.

He pulled his head back and looked up at her, licking his lips. "Tasted as sweet as I thought you would." He said, his voice low and eyes dark with lust.

A shudder rippled through her. She shifted so that she was lying down on the bed. He came to rest beside her, propped up on his elbow, other hand resting on her thigh. Her body was ready for him, and he knew it too. She could see the knowledge playing in his eyes. With great tenderness, his hand came to rest on the place that cried out for him, as it had never cried for another soul. His fingers parted her and found her sensitized bud.

She almost cried out when his hand pulled away. She looked up at him, and noticed he was watching her belly intently, eyes wide. Another movement pushed against her stretched flesh.

Babies. High risk. No sex. The thoughts pummeled her mind. Now she remembered what she was supposed to remember. With twins, she was considered high risk for pre-term labor. Doctors warned her to avoid sexual intercourse due to earlier complications. How could she have forgotten? She got up, picked up her nightgown and started to slip it over her head. Hands appeared out of nowhere and seized the gown before she could put it on.

She whirled around and found herself face to face with Alex. He pulled the gown away from her and held it behind his back. His other hand slipped around her waist and pulled her close. His arousal pressed firmly against her belly.

“We have unfinished business,” he reminded her. All too aware of what he meant, she lifted her hands to his chest to ward him away. She watched the nightgown float to the ground as his hand gently gripped the nape of her neck. The gentle caress of his fingers had her wishing she could get closer to him. And as much as she wanted to, she couldn't, not only for her babies' sake, but for her own as well. This was not a complication she wanted in her life. She didn't even want him in her house. Yet, here she was, naked in her bedroom with him.

An unpleasant shiver went up her spine as she recalled the last time she stood in this room with a man who looked like him. Alex misread her reaction and lowered his lips to hers. She turned her head at the last second and placed her hands on his chest.

“Alex, please stop.” She pushed against his chest more forcefully this time.

He pulled back slightly and looked down at her with concern. “What's wrong? Am I hurting you?” he asked, his hands resting on her upper arms.

She took the opportunity to step back and pull out of his reach. “I can't do this.”

When he took a step toward her, she held her hands up, ready to push him away again if she must. Her body was still vibrating from his touch. If he touched her again, she wasn't sure she would have the strength to deny him and not end up giving in to her desires. How could she want him of all people?

Again, he took a step toward her. Laryssa backed up and sucked in her breath when she realized she had nowhere to go. The cool bedroom wall pressed up against her back. The predatory gleam in his eyes had her heart thumping against her chest.

He let his forearm rest against the wall just above her head and leaned down to whisper in her ear, "We're at the point of no return here."

"Girls don't have a point of no return, Alex." This was getting to be a habit, him boxing her into a corner. One habit she intended to break, here and now. She had no intention of becoming his next meal to satisfy his sexual craving, "Take a cold shower."

"Why would I want to do that when your body responds to me so perfectly?"

"Of all the nerve." She lifted her hand and thought about hitting him. In that split second while making the decision, Alex took hold of her wrist, trapping it above her head. "Let me go."

Alex studied her face and then abruptly dropped her hand but didn't back away. The muscles in his jaw flexed and his nostrils flared. "What type of game are you playing?"

"I'm not playing games. I just don't want to complicate my life with just sex." Before she could barely finish the sentence, his lips pressed firmly against hers. The kiss revealed a passion that had not yet been unleashed. His hand curved around her neck, his thumb caressing her jaw. Her legs turned to mush, and she rested her hands on his shoulders to keep from falling.

He pulled back and looked down at her. "Did that feel like it was going to be just plain sex to you? I could feel your heart pound beneath my hand. I can see the desire in your eyes, even your body responds to me." As if to prove his point, he let his hand brush her femininity. Her body jerked involuntarily against his hand. The personal touch reminded her that the only barrier between them were his clothes.

"You really should buy more crimson-colored clothes. The color is very becoming." He caressed her cheek with his thumb.

"My clothes and my body are of no concern to you. I'm not on the market for a fling. Good night, Mr. Richards." She emphasized his formal name, hoping to create distance between them in some way. She ducked under his arm and took refuge in the bathroom till he left.

They had crossed a line tonight. Her defenses slipped, and she'd let herself feel, and, man, did his touch ever feel good. She couldn't lay all the blame on him. She was partly responsible, too. Thankfully, she managed to come to her senses before they did something stupid. She had a funny feeling the future held a lot more than she bargained for.

~

"Oh, baby. Do it just like that." The man from the graveyard wiped the drool off his chin with the back of his hand. After the golden boy left, Laryssa had wandered out of the bathroom and flopped on her bed, pleasuring herself with a dildo. How he wished he was there in person to help her.

He'd been patient since Aidan's death, but it was now wearing thin. If he didn't find some way to get rid of the latest man in her life, he'd never have her. But what could he do? There was no way he'd be lucky enough to have Laryssa throw the man out of her house, not without some incentive. She was such a softy when it came to people.

"*Kill him*," a voice whispered in his ear.

"*Kidnap her*," another one suggested.

He covered his ears with his hands. "Shut up!"

The last thing he needed right now were the voices to start up again. They always wanted him to do bad things. He didn't want to hurt her. He just wanted to make her see that they belonged together. She'd love him if she gave him a chance. He knew she would.

He had no delusions of grandeur about himself. He knew he was ugly. His head was bald, and a jagged scar ran from his left ear all the way to his mouth. But he still deserved someone who loved him, and the person whose love he wanted was right there on his computer monitor. He'd stop at nothing to get her.

He didn't want to kidnap her, but that didn't mean he couldn't threaten the golden boy. If she felt his life was threatened, she might kick him out. The idea was worth a try. He'd have to be careful though. No fingerprints or names. Nothing that could connect him to the note.

He leaned in and watched her on the monitor. She was nearly ready to orgasm, and his jeans could no longer contain him. Lowering his hand, he freed himself and joined her in ecstasy. The day would soon come, and they'd do it together. And that was a promise he intended to keep.

CHAPTER FIVE

"Women!"

Alex tossed the unread inspector's report onto his desk. His mind kept straying to a gorgeous brunette whose actions kept him awake all night, and every night since he'd met her. If it hadn't been for the efficient work of his vice president, Ron, his grandfather probably would have been biting his ear off at his lack of concentration. He knew he was not pulling his weight lately, but, thankfully, Ron had been more than willing to pick up the slack.

The downside was that Ron always wanted to butt in and share his two cents on Alex's personal life. *If a woman disrupts your day, it would be best to be rid of her.* That was Ron's advice and, after last night, Alex wished it was as easy as his friend made it sound.

He leaned over his desk and grabbed the cup of coffee his secretary had dropped off earlier and took a sip. It had not been easy walking out of Laryssa's bedroom after their midnight encounter. He tried a cold shower, hoping to cool his libido, but it didn't work. The jog in the cool night air didn't work either. He was thoroughly disgusted with himself at nearly begging her to take him. He had never done that before, and there was no way he wanted to start now. She brought out the Neanderthal in him.

If anything, this just decided what his next move would be. The thought of clubbing that stubborn woman over the head and taking her back to his cave had a certain appeal. He grinned at the idea.

What started out as an innocent mystery to find out why she reacted the way she did, now turned into game of dodge the flame. The flames she threw in his direction were unmistakable. She did not want him there and made sure he knew it daily. They hadn't talked much about the reason as to why he was there, but he knew for certain she was as clueless to this situation as he was.

Laryssa was unlike anyone he'd ever met before. He enjoyed rattling her chain to see the spark fly that, when unprovoked, sat like a wilted flower within her. To see the passion stored inside her come to life by a simple touch was incredible. A yearning stirred inside him, and he smiled. He wanted to be the man who made that passion soar and show her what it was like to touch the moon. *Forget it, Alex. You tried that once already and it blew up in your face.* He let a hand run down his roughened face. Another thing he had forgotten to do in his haste to leave her house that morning. Shave.

He needed to remember his mission, to find out about this supposed doppelgänger. When he went back to her place after work, they'd have it out. Then and there. Before the day drew to a close, he'd get his answers. His restraint wouldn't last much longer under her roof.

Last night, he'd barely been able to contain himself. She looked so desirable and delectable. Her wavy brown hair had fallen like a veil over her shoulders. His pants grew tighter as an image of her perky breasts snuck into his mind. Even the way she wrapped her arms protectively around her belly played havoc with his system. It made him want to gather her in his arms and promise that everything would be okay, but that was not his promise to make.

Alex spun in his chair and stared out the office window. As a boy he made that promise, as a man he knew better. He would never forget the nasty twists of fate life could throw at you. It only took a second and your life could be drastically altered.

When he took Laryssa in his arms, she allowed him to forget that temporarily. There was a thread connecting them; it didn't take a genius to figure that out. It felt nice to forget the past for a while and explore the connection between them. But now that thread seemed more like a noose closing around his neck. He grabbed his tie and loosened it. The pressure in his throat eased slightly. He picked up the phone and dialed his house number.

"Hello?"

"Joanne, prepare the room please. We *will* be having a guest tonight." Not waiting for a response, he hung up the phone, grabbed his jacket, and headed back to Laryssa's house.

He found her sitting at the kitchen table with a piece of paper in her trembling hands. Her face devoid of all color. A cup of what appeared to be coffee lay on its side on the table, its remnants dripping onto the floor. A nearly empty pot of water sat steaming on the stove. Potatoes on the counter, in various stages of readiness, had begun browning.

Laryssa appeared oblivious. She was sitting on the edge of the seat. Her back straight and mouth quivering. Her eyes glued to the paper in her hands. Her knuckles white.

"You need to go," she said in a barely audible voice, not once taking her eyes off the letter. He turned off the stove and then snatched the paper out of her left hand. It read:

'Get him out of your house, or I'll kill you both while you sleep. And I do know when you're sleeping. No police, or I'll know.'

Short and to the point. He let a few choice words fly as his eyes scanned the letter again. It had been typed on a computer and had no signature. He glanced back at Laryssa, who now had her fists clumped in her lap. "Do you know who wrote this?"

She shook her head.

"No idea at all?" he pressed further.

"I..." Laryssa stared at the paper in his hand.

Aidan had done business with a number of unsavory men, and they all creeped her out. She tried to recall all the men they had entertained over the years. Could one of them have left the letter? How many of them were capable of murder? Did Aidan, had he? The thought that she may have shared a bed with a murderer made her lose any resolve she had left. Uncontrollable spasms jerked her whole body, and tears streamed down her cheeks.

Through blurry eyes, she watched Alex pull out his cellphone and begin dialing. That snapped her back to attention. "Who are you calling?"

"The police," he said.

Panic coursed through her veins. She struggled to stand up, using the chair as leverage while supporting her back. She grabbed his cell-phone and flipped it closed.

"You can't do that. The letter. The note."

"I know what it said." He snatched back his cellphone and attempted to dial again.

She placed a hand on his arm. "Please, don't."

He looked down at her as if she'd lost her mind. Maybe she had, but there was no way she was risking all their lives after the warning in the letter. They had no idea what they were up against.

"You need to go." She attempted to pull him out of the kitchen.

"And leave you here to fend for yourself? No way." He stayed firmly rooted in his spot. "If I go, you go."

"For the love of God, Alex. This is no time to be chivalrous. Someone is mad that you're here with me." She paced back and forth across the linoleum, biting her nails. "They never bothered me before. If you leave, I'm sure I'll be fine."

He slammed his fist on the dinner table. "Damn it, Laryssa. You don't know that for sure."

She jerked backwards, away from him, away from the fist which hit the table beside her. "Surely I'd be safer than I am with you." Her legs threatened to give out at any moment. She walked around the table and collapsed on the chair farthest from him. That temper. That fist. A familiar terror shot through her.

She let her hand roam over the life in her womb. What would she have done if she had lost her babies that fateful day? Her hands shook. She placed them between her legs to stop them, but her legs started to shake instead. Tears welled up in her eyes. Losing Aidan had been a shock, but she survived and came back stronger than ever. She wouldn't do anything to put them in jeopardy again. If she lost them, she'd never be able to live with herself.

By the time she broke herself out of the past, she saw Alex standing close by. His eyes fixated on her with curiosity. She tried to wave him away but shivered when her gaze came to rest on his clenched fist. He unclenched his fist and dropped to his knees in front of her. He took her face between his hands with great care, so gentle that a tear escaped down her cheek.

"Dear God, Laryssa. I'm so sorry. I didn't mean to scare you. I'd never hurt you."

Promises. So many promises. She longed to believe him. He was the master of broken promises. She gave her head a quick shake. No. Aidan broke them, not Alex. Other than the odd bout of anger and his demand that she moves in with him, Alex hadn't given her any reason to fear him. At least, not on the physical level anyway. The emotional level was a whole other matter.

Last night, she barely controlled herself. The feel of his hands on her body almost undid her resolve. His amazing green eyes, with specks of blue, had made every inch of her tingle as they traveled from her head to her toes.

"Don't make promises you can't keep, Alex." She took his hands and removed them from her face. Their hands came to rest on her lap together.

"I don't make promises I can't keep. The only thing I'm promising right now is a safe haven for you, away from whoever wrote that note. I have twenty-four-hour security. You'll be safe there."

Even with the best security system she knew there were flaws, not to mention that going to live with him wasn't what the note wanted her to do. It also went against everything she stood for, and the promises she made after Aidan died to never get involved again.

Granted, Alex wasn't asking her to be his girlfriend. He was just offering her a safe place to stay until this blew over. And she couldn't deny that being able to relax would be nice. The doctor told her she needed to rest, and since Alex moved in here with her, rest had been slim to none. Not only was there sexual tension, she also half expected him to come charging into her room in the middle of the night. The same way Aidan used to when he had had a rough day at work, expecting her to please him.

She shook her head. Alex didn't deserve these thoughts. She knew it, although it was strange that this note showed up after she repeatedly turned down his offer to move in. Since Aidan's death, she had never experienced a single problem or even a harassing phone call. He wasn't involved in the writing of it, was he?

There was no easy answer to that question. He could say yes to scare her into submission, or he could say no to get her to trust him. They both worked in his favor, not hers. There was really no point in asking, but she couldn't help herself.

"Did you send it?"

He stared at her like she'd lost her marbles. "You can't seriously believe that I'd stoop that low? I need some air." Grabbing his jacket, he stormed down the hall and out the front door.

She pushed herself up off the chair and followed him outside. "What am I supposed to think? You uproot my life by storming into it, making it barely recognizable. You push me to move in with you, despite my constant rejection of the idea, and now this note shows up."

He turned away from her and gripped the porch railing. "Don't you think if I was going to do something I'd have done it by now, instead of breaking my back each night on that couch of yours?"

"That wasn't my choice, you know. You were the one who bombarded your way into my house and insisted on staying on my couch."

"Only because you refused to come with me."

"Do we always have to go around in this circle?" she huffed. "Why do you feel that this is your responsibility?"

"I..." His eyes took on a distant look as he stared across the road. "I don't have an answer to that right now. Something connected me to you. I don't know." He turned and looked at her with confusion. "You feel it, don't you?"

Her pulse sped up, and she glanced down at his hands, which were turned up in question. Warmth flooded her cheeks. Their actions of last night replayed in her head. The way she felt when wrapped in his arms.

Men should come with a warning label. He was a lethal weapon. She realized her question about the note had been way off base. Alex was not a man who'd write a letter to get his way. Not the man who held her at night, whispering sweet words into her ear after a nightmare.

As grateful as she was for the revelation that she hadn't allowed a psycho into her house, she didn't want there to be a connection either. All she wanted was her life to go back to normal. The life she had before the ghost of her abusive husband came back to haunt her. A ghost so frighteningly familiar, yet so different.

He moved closer to her, took her gently by the shoulders, and then cupped her face in the palms of his hands. "I promise you, I didn't write it," he said. "Scout's honor."

"I know," she sighed, leaning into the palm of his hand.

He caressed her cheek and lifted her face to look at him. "I'm relieved that you believe me, but you never did answer my question."

She didn't want to talk about her feelings with him. Of course, there was a connection between them. If looks were anything to go by, he could pass as the twin brother of her dead husband, and that alone gave her a connection she didn't need or want. As a woman, her body betrayed her, making her feel things for him she couldn't control. Even now as his hand moved behind her head, her skin tingled, and her breath quickened.

"Just like I thought." He lowered his face to hers.

"I didn't say anything," she whispered against his lips.

"You didn't have to." His lips crushed against hers, and all the heat of the previous night rushed back to the surface. Pictures of her being naked and in his arms, flooded her mind. How could she want to have sex with this man? It didn't make sense. Her body screamed for him as his tongue swept across her lips, seeking the warm moisture within.

Before she had a chance to open to him, he pulled back ever so slightly and murmured, "Shall we pick up where we left off?"

He held her tightly against him as her knees buckled. She leaned her forehead against his chest and struggled to breathe. His kiss never failed to take her breath away. Once she was steady enough, she stepped away from him.

"Let's not and say we did." The last thing she needed was for them to start this up again. It was hard enough to stop last night.

"How about yes and say we didn't?" He walked over and leaned down to whisper in her ear, "Haven't you thought about last night, and what it could have been like? You and me. I know I have."

She froze, afraid to move. His words made her want to forget everything. She wanted to throw caution to the wind and fling herself into his arms. Only the babies prevented her from doing so. Thank God for them, at least they helped her keep her common sense.

"Alex, the doctors told me I can't."

When the doctors told her she couldn't engage in sexual intercourse, it hadn't bothered her until this moment. She had gone into false labor when she was thirteen weeks pregnant after spending the evening celebrating that she was having twins. Being only twenty-three weeks now, she had a long time to wait before she'd get permission to have sex again. The twins acted almost like chaperons.

"Party poopers," he mumbled good-naturedly. He wrapped his arms around her again and nibbled on her earlobe. "Do you think if you ate an apple a day, it would keep the doctors away so we can?"

She laughed and swatted him on the shoulder. "I don't think it works that way."

He continued his pursuit of her ear, and his hands slid down to the hem of her shirt, skimming underneath to touch her bare skin. He moved closer to her. His arousal pressed against her belly, sparking a desire that spread like wildfire through her.

Her hand lowered to touch him, but a car horn pulled her out of her daze. They were standing on the porch for the whole world to see. This was not exactly how she wanted to be thought of by all her neighbors, as the one who couldn't keep her hands to herself in public.

Neighbors. People. The letter. She leaped away from him and scanned the surrounding houses. A curtain moved in a window next door. The house on the other side appeared dark, with no car in front. Neighborhood kids played in a yard across the street.

A black Cadillac slowed as it neared her house, and her pulse spiked. Tinted windows prevented her from seeing who was in the car. An agonizing second later, the Cadillac picked up speed and stopped in front of a house halfway down the block. The afternoon sun glared off the bumper. Must have been someone looking for a certain address. She hoped and prayed anyway. The thought that she may be living in a neighborhood where a madman resided made her shudder.

She jumped when hands came to rest on her shoulder. "Cold?" he asked. She went to shrug her shoulders and shivered instead. He turned her in his arms. A lopsided grin on his face. "I can think of a way to warm you up."

She rolled her eyes. *Men! Can't they think about anything else?* Not that she should talk. Her body desperately wanted to be touched by him. She wanted to feel his hands on her bare skin. *Oh, shut up, Laryssa.*

"Get your mind out of the gutter, Richards." She dislodged herself from his arms and moved back into the house, away from prying eyes. Halfway into the living room, she turned to call him inside, only to find him right behind her.

"Gosh, don't do that!" She leaned on the arm of the couch. One hand pressed against her chest.

He feigned innocence. "I was just following you." The grin plastered further across his handsome face, and his eyes sparkled with humor.

"Yeah, right." Her insides did a strange flip flop with each moment that passed. She ran the tip of her tongue over her lips, wishing he would bring those kissable lips her way.

"Now whose mind is in the gutter?" he said, flicking her nose.

"I know who I'd like to toss in the gutter." She rubbed her nose and took a step away from him. He threw his head back and laughed. Mortified, she clasped a hand over her mouth. Had she really said that out loud?

"I'd love to see you try." His voice took on a deep sexy drawl.

"Man, you're a pain in the butt."

And, from the look on his face, he relished being a thorn in her side. However, if he didn't take a hike now, he wouldn't be around long enough to be a thorn in anyone else's side.

He needed to go torture someone else. With looks like his, there were probably plenty of women who'd love to be tortured by him. She, however, wasn't one of them. One man already put her heart through the cheese grater, making sure no part of it was left intact. She wasn't going to give that power to another.

Needing to put space between them, she went down the hallway and into the kitchen. She stopped dead in her tracks when she noticed the note on the floor beside the table. Fear, anger and frustration worked their way through her again. A knot the size of a bowling ball lodged in her chest, her breath shallow. She wanted to tear the paper into tiny pieces, toss it in the garbage and set it on fire. Pretend it didn't exist. But she couldn't get the courage to reach down and grab it, knowing it had been touched by a crazy man. She heard Alex approach but couldn't remove her eyes from the paper.

Alex watched her stare at the paper like it was a rattler poised to strike. He leaned down, picked it up and stuffed it in his shirt pocket. Her fear-filled eyes drifted to his pocket. It annoyed him that someone would set out to threaten an innocent woman like her.

Equally annoying was his need to protect her. Something he felt the moment they met. For years, he had no trouble avoiding women. Not that he had been celibate by any means. He just had no desire to get romantically involved. Any decision they made tonight would purely be for her protection.

Taking her hand, he led her back to the living room and sat with her on the couch. "I'm not going to let anyone hurt you." He placed an arm around her shaking shoulders. "You'll be okay, I promise."

After a few moments of silence, he knew what had to come next. It was high time he asked a few questions about the elusive Aidan. “Laryssa, was Aidan involved in any shady dealings?”

“As much as I hate to say it, I don't know.” She shook her head. “He never spoke about his work. There were times when he was away for days, and then he'd come back in a foul mood.”

“Any enemies you know about that might try to take advantage of you now that he's gone?”

Her head shook again. “You might say he was a force to be reckoned with. The leader of the pack if you will.” She rubbed her hands up and down her arms. “Is it cold in here?”

“What kind of work did Aidan do?” He watched as a blank look took over her eyes. How could one live with someone and not know much about them? What a joke. Hadn't he done the same with Valerie?

“Please, can we talk about something else? You—he—this just feels weird.” She got up from the couch and crossed to the window.

“Okay, let's talk about getting you moved into my house.” He really didn't want anything to happen to her. Fate brought them together, and he'd be damned if he let anyone take her away from him now, especially before she shared what she knew about Aidan. He watched her body stiffen, but she held her position, staring out of the window.

“Alex, I've already told you I will not move in with you.”

“You're not safe here, damn it.”

She whipped around to face him. “Stop talking to me that way!”

Alex got up and walked over to her. “Be reasonable, then.”

They stood head-to-head now. Well, head to chest given their height difference. He wanted to gather her up in his arms and kiss some sense into her pretty little head.

“I'm being perfectly reasonable. I was raised better than to live with a man I'm not married to.”

“Won't live with a man you're not married to, but will have sex with him, eh?” He watched her eyes fill with fire. How he loved that spunk.

"We did not have sex."

"Only because I didn't force the issue," he said, tucking his thumbs in the belt loops of his jeans. He leaned back against the wall beside the window and watched her. The topic always returned sex no matter how hard he tried to avoid it.

"If you had, I would have screamed." She lifted her head defiantly and placed her hands on her hips.

"Wanna bet?" He hooked one arm around her waist and drew her to him. Before she could scream, he covered his mouth with hers. Her body stayed rigid for all of two seconds before she melted in his arms. He moved her away from him and let her go. "See."

He watched her eyes open. A dazed look stared back at him. Moments later, he watched as pure fury replaced the innocent dazed look.

She took one step closer to him. "Don't you ever do that again!" Her heel landed heavily on his right foot before she hurried out of the room. He flopped on the couch and flexed his sore foot, making sure his toes weren't broken.

Satisfied with his assessment, he flew up the stairs, anger building inside him. He met back up with her at her bedroom door.

"Kindly leave my room." She attempted to shut the door, but he forced his way in.

"I don't take *kindly* to my foot being stepped on," he ground out between his teeth.

"Oh, boo hoo." She crossed her arms over her chest and looked at him with raised eyebrows. "Mr. Manly Man can't handle a woman stepping on his foot?"

He grabbed her arm. "Don't goad me."

She was getting under his skin like no other woman before her. If it had been any other woman saying those words, he'd be out that door without so much as a second look. But something was going on here, and nothing she could say or do would drive him away.

"I've been trying to be a gentleman, but I'm getting to the end of my tether."

"Don't threaten me. I'll do whatever I darn well please." She attempted to pull her arm away, with no success.

"Well, right now, you'll do what I say and pack your bags." He marched to her closet and pulled out a suitcase. He placed it in her arms, but she shoved the suitcase back in the closet.

"How many times do I have to tell you? I'm not leaving." Her cheeks glowed red with annoyance. "I don't live with men I'm not married to." She turned and headed toward the bathroom.

He grabbed her arm within two steps. "What do you call me staying here?"

"A frustration," she all but yelled at him, as she tried to pry his fingers off her arm.

The thought suddenly dawned on him. If she married him, then her last name would change, and whoever was after her wouldn't be able to find her. Maybe then she would come and stay at his house. Of course, it wasn't permanent. He didn't do permanent anymore, and it didn't appear Laryssa had any plans on permanency herself. It was the perfect arrangement, not to mention it would get his friends and family off his back about dating again. After Valerie, there was no way he'd get sucked into a relationship. She'd trampled on his heart and fed it to the birds.

"Okay," he said.

"Okay?" Her forehead creased with confusion as she looked up at him, temporarily forgetting about his hand on her arm.

"Let's get married."

CHAPTER SIX

Laryssa stumbled and grabbed onto the side of the couch for support. "You've got to be kidding me." She gave her ear a quick pat to make sure she hadn't lost her hearing. "Did I...did you—I didn't just hear what I thought I heard, did I?"

"Depends on what you thought you heard me say," Alex said, winking at her.

"How can you stand there and joke around? This is serious." She wrapped her arms around herself and paced the living room.

Alex walked over and pulled her onto the couch, sitting down next to her. "Sit! You're going to wear a hole in your carpet."

Marriage. He couldn't seriously be contemplating it, could he? They had only known each other a few weeks. She couldn't marry him. No way. No how.

"You can't love me," she blurted out as she slid to the other end of the couch. The day was going from bad to worse. What was she going to find out next? That she was on candid camera? Things like this don't happen in real life. Someone out there was having a laugh at her expense. A death threat and a marriage proposal all in one day. That had to be a record of some sort, she thought with a short, hard laugh. Not to mention the marriage proposal being from her own personal poltergeist.

"I'm going crazy. I have to be going crazy." She covered her face with her hands and silently wished for him to go away.

"No worse than I am, I assure you," he said with a chuckle of his own. "I never thought I'd hear myself utter those words again."

"Why, on God's green earth, did you? You don't love me." Déjà vu! Didn't she have a marriage without love once already? Taking a deep breath, she laid her head back and closed her eyes.

"I don't recall saying that. I just said we should get married."

Opening her eyes, she turned to face him. "Been there. Done that. Got the goods to prove it." She pointed to her belly. "And will never, ever, do it again." *Especially not with you, of all people.*

He would be a constant reminder of the man who should have been the love of her life. How could she not have seen exactly who Aidan was before? The dating had been awesome, but once he slipped the ring on her finger, the polite, sweet guy she knew disappeared. Why could she not see all the quirks beforehand?

Her only excuse was she'd been blinded by love, but it definitely hadn't been love near the end. All she had was a hope and a plea that somehow, someway, she could change him back and, once again, have the man she thought she fell in love with. She had hoped the baby would have been able to accomplish that.

She let a hand roam over her belly. "It just wasn't meant to be," she whispered. A single tear slid down her cheek.

No matter how hard she tried, that one winter day would never be forgotten. The knock at the door. The two cops who stood on the other side, hats pressed against their chests. She had looked from one to the other as pity filled their features. A dark cloud descended over her. In a split second, she knew why they had come.

She squeezed her eyes at the memory. One she tried so hard to forget. Most days she could push it away, but she could never forget. The guilt bubbled inside her, making her stomach churn. She was the reason Aidan got behind the wheel. Abuse or no abuse, she was the cause of his death.

Having Alex around would be a further reminder of her selfish dreams and the life she no longer wanted to remember. If the two men were related, and he found out she had a hand in Aidan's death, would he show the same fury? The hair on her arms stood on end as spider-like sensations crawled up her spine. They would have to talk about Aidan eventually, but she couldn't bear to share her past right now. Not until she knew Alex a little better. She hadn't even shared the story with her best friend, Melissa. Some things weren't meant to be discussed, not even between friends.

Alex cleared his throat. "So?"

She put her hand on the arm of the couch and tried to stand up too quickly. Her stomach churned even more. "Excuse me."

She covered her mouth with her hand and took refuge in the bathroom just in time. Leaning over the toilet, she lost the remains of her lunch. After a few moments, her throat stung beyond belief. Tears streamed down her face as another bout of gut-clenching heaves overtook her.

She jumped when she felt fingers on the side of her neck. He swept her hair back away from her face.

"I didn't know I was that hideous," he said wryly.

She wanted to protest but was rocked by a fit of dry heaves. In the intimacy of the bathroom, he stood there holding her hair and tenderly stroking her back with his free hand until her body calmed. By the time she was ready to stand up, her back was on fire from the strokes of his hand, and her eyes were full of fresh tears that had nothing to do with getting sick. He helped her upright, and they stood in an awkward silence for a moment.

"I must say I've never had that response to a proposal before," he commented. "You're hell on a man's ego."

Sheesh, how many times had this man proposed in his life? "It didn't really have anything to do with you. Well, it did, but not really." She clamped her jaw closed before she said anything else, and heat rose in her cheeks. A burp escaped and her stomach rolled again at the foul taste. "Uh, do you mind?"

"You sure you'll be okay?" he asked. The tenderness in his voice wrapped itself around her heart like a soft flannel blanket. She reined in her emotions, fortifying the wall around her heart. She couldn't let his sweet words make a home there. Pain always followed, no matter how kind they appeared to be.

She looked up at him with what she hoped was a sincere smile and said, "I'll be fine, really. You can go now." Her voice cracked slightly, and, for a second, she wasn't sure if he was going to buy it.

He took a few steps out of the bathroom and stopped, looking back at her with genuine concern in his eyes. She wanted to fall into his arms and cry her eyes out, but she couldn't afford the luxury.

"Don't worry. I'm not going to collapse on the bathroom floor. I just want to freshen up," she persisted. *Go away before I puke on your shoes.* She needed to brush her teeth before she gagged again. He gave her one final glance and then walked down the hallway. She closed the door and grabbed the toothpaste.

Later, she found him in the kitchen reading the collections notice she'd received in the mail earlier.

"In a wee bit of trouble, are you?" He placed the letter on the table and leaned back in his chair to look up at her.

She walked over and grabbed the paper, shoving it in the junk drawer. "I don't recall asking you to read my mail." She walked to the sink, flung a cupboard door open and slammed a cup on the counter, chipping a piece of china off the bottom.

"Kind of hard not to when it's sitting in plain view. This actually reinforces my earlier idea." He waved a hand towards the table. Laryssa raised her hand to silence him, but he continued, "Look, you're obviously in trouble in more ways than one."

"That doesn't mean I want to get married. In case you haven't realized it yet, my first marriage didn't go so well. I've got no desire to put myself through that again." She shuddered at the thought.

"Neither do I. I've gone through hell and back more times than I can count." His words were forced, and his eyes took on a haunted look. Pain emanated from every single pore of his body, and her heart ached for him. She wanted to throw her arms around him and soak up all the pain, but to prevent herself from doing so, she walked around the small brown oval table and took a seat at the opposite end.

"I'm here to talk if you need to," she said in a soft voice.

And just like that, the blinds came down, shutting her out. He looked at her with a blank stare. "There is nothing to talk about."

"Fine, whatever." She grimaced when a sharp pain attacked her side. It hurt even worse when she breathed. The doctor told her she'd experience stretching pains, but they grossly under-exaggerated how much it would hurt. If stretching pains hurt this bad, how on earth would she handle labor? She closed her eyes and massaged her side till the pain subsided.

When she looked back at Alex, he was staring at her with his head cocked to one side. "You okay?" he asked.

Her eyes dropped to the ominous note that threatened to fall out of his pocket and to the drawer holding the collections notice. "As good as can be expected after..." She let her voice trail off.

"I meant what I said, you know." He reached out and placed her hand between his. His gentle touch sent a wave of heat up her arm. The feelings were new, and it sent fear flying through her like a hurricane. Love always had a victim, and she had no plans on being a victim any time soon. If she agreed to his proposal, she knew she would fall for his charms and lose herself in those adorable sea-colored eyes.

"Why? It doesn't sound like you want to get married any more than I do. I mean marriage should be when two people love each other, and we don't."

"I'm proposing a marriage of convenience."

She opened her mouth to oppose, but he put two fingers on her lips.

"You need my help," he said. As if to prove it, he removed his other hand from hers and pulled the note out of his pocket. "If we get married, then your name changes and whoever wrote this won't be able to find you anymore. You'll live with me in my place and be able to relax the rest of your pregnancy." He took a breath. "I'm also willing to clear your debt for you."

"What's in it for you?"

"My family would finally leave me alone. They think I need to get help. This way, they'll think I've moved on and won't bother me anymore." His voice cracked as he spoke.

What did he go through that hurt him so badly? She wanted to smack whoever put that pain in his eyes. He turned his head away.

When he turned back, the pain was gone, and a smile was in its place. "You'd be doing me a huge favor."

"Let me get this straight. You want my help in deceiving your family?" she asked. That would certainly go down well now, wouldn't it? Her unsettled stomach didn't seem to favor the idea either as it gurgled away.

"Not really deceiving, we'll be married after all. I promise that it's a no strings attached marriage. I just ask that we stay married a year. At least, until after the babies are born. Then, if you want to leave, you can."

That alone should have been reason enough to say no to him, but she found herself drawn to the idea, although, one question kept popping into her head. "But what about," she stammered, "you know."

"If you don't want me to touch you, I won't. Although, you have to admit if we did, it would be damn good."

She sat up straight as he rounded the table and stopped next to her chair. He knelt in front of her and took her face between the palms of his hands. She placed her hands on his forearms. Butterflies fluttered inside her stomach, or it could have been the babies moving. In that moment, she couldn't tell.

He dropped a kiss on her nose. "Please say yes."

"If we don't do anything, will you—I mean, won't you..."She let her question trail off.

"If you mean, will I be faithful, the answer is yes. I don't go for casual flings." He pulled her up and wrapped his arms around her.

"But last night we..." She stopped, her face heating at the intensity of his gaze.

"Last night would have been anything but casual. You felt it, and so did I. We're definitely compatible. But, as I said, if you don't want to, then we won't. However, if you do come to me, I promise it will be better than anything you could ever imagine."

She shook her head to break the spell she found herself under every time she got lost in his eyes. "What if I don't?"

He studied her intently for a moment, and within seconds, she found his lips on hers. A fire sizzled in her belly before spreading to each limb, making her lean closer to him. The butterflies in her stomach got stronger, and she felt a distinct boot against her skin, which had them breaking apart.

"They definitely pack a wallop, don't they," he said with a chuckle. "Do we have a deal?"

She backed away from him and rubbed her belly. "Okay. But I want to lay down some ground rules."

"Anything your heart desires." He took a seat in the chair, leaned back and rested his hands behind his head, as if all was right in his world...while hers was so messed up it wasn't funny.

"I want my own room," she started to say, and he opened his mouth to protest, but she continued, "I also want you to stop touching me. I can't think when you touch me."

His lips curled up in a grin. "Here are some of my own ground rules. I'm okay with your rules, in private, of course, but we'll act like husband and wife in public. My family has to believe this is a real marriage. Also, if you don't wish me to touch you, I'll need you to wear a robe when you're in your nightgown. After all, I'm only human."

She swallowed hard at the gleam of desire in his eyes as they roamed over her body. He didn't have to tell her twice.

"Why don't you go and get yourself ready," he said.

"We're not married yet, so I'm fine staying where I am for now, thank you." Didn't they already have this conversation? They were going in circles, and it was getting downright irritating. She didn't agree to move in with him just yet.

"We have to get you a ring."

"I don't need a ring. You're just going to have to sell it after anyway."

"No one is going to believe we are getting married if I don't get you a ring. We're going to head to the jewelers."

She relented and went to get ready. Twenty minutes later, Laryssa climbed into the car next to Alex. He backed out onto the street, and soon they were on Highway One.

"Where are we going?" she asked.

"There is a cute jewelry place I know in Vancouver," he said.

"Why don't we just go to one here?"

He waved off her protests. "Don't worry. It won't take us long to get there."

She sat back in the seat and stared out the window. Surrey had many jewelry stores. There was no reason for them to go all the way to Vancouver. Why the sudden urge to go there? She knew he had a plan, but what, she didn't know. And she could bet twenty dollars he wouldn't share it with her. Not long later, he pulled the car to a stop in front of a very prestigious jewelry store. Diamonds and rubies glittered in the window displays.

Her jaw dropped. "We can't go in there. This places charges more than I make in a year."

He ignored her and proceeded to get out. Seconds later, her door opened, and he was helping her out of the car.

"Alex, please. Let's go somewhere else. I'll feel bad if you get me something here," she pleaded.

He continued to direct her inside the doors with one hand on her arm and the other on the small of her back. The jeweler showed them numerous rings.

"I don't want anything this big." She shook her head. They both looked at her like she was crazy.

Alex took her hand and turned it over, sliding a ring into place. "Fits perfectly."

She held her hand up and watched as the sun glittered on the platinum diamond ring, displaying numerous rainbows on the ceiling. "It's gorgeous, Alex. But I can't accept it. I mean it's not like we're—"

"Excuse us a moment." He took hold of her arm and pulled her to the door, away from the prying ears of the clerk. "Remember what I said. In public, we're supposed to be in love. You won't tell anyone otherwise. Got it," he growled in a voice so quiet she could hardly hear him.

She rolled her eyes and gave him a salute. "Yes, sir. Your wish is my command."

He placed his keys in her hand. "Here, take the keys and go wait in the car." His voice was that of a parent telling their child to go to their room.

She placed her hands on her hips. "Don't treat me like a child."

"Quit acting like one, damn it." He kissed her hard before taking her outside and back to the car. She watched as he went back inside without her.

"How on earth am I going to stand living with him?" she mumbled. No wonder he didn't stay married the first time. He was the most stubborn, pig-headed jerk of a man she'd ever met.

He re-joined her about twenty minutes later, and they pulled back onto the road again. She watched the signs as they drove by them. To her surprise, the sign that would take them back to her place came and went.

"Uh, you missed our turn."

CHAPTER SEVEN

The stalker slammed his fist on the mahogany desk. The force shook the monitors stacked high along the wall. Laryssa had been gone for over an hour, off gallivanting with that pretty boy. Didn't she learn her lesson from the note he sent her?

And what was with that guy carrying a suitcase out to his car? He'd switched to the hidden bedroom camera and watched the man pack a few articles of clothing while she'd been in the shower. Now, an hour later, they still had not returned. He switched from camera to camera, each displaying a different room in the house, hoping to catch a glimpse of her.

He stopped momentarily when camera eight popped up on screen. Installing a camera in the bathroom without Aidan's knowledge had been a little tricky, but he pulled it off without a hitch. The man wanted him to install cameras everywhere, but even Aidan wanted a little bit of privacy when he took a crap.

This camera view gave him more pleasure than the other seven put together. He loved watching her naked in the shower and had wanted to lick the drops of water that clung to her breasts. He loved watching her rub soap all over herself. How her hand would close over the sexy flesh between her legs, lathering it with soap. It made him want to come just thinking about it. He wanted to run his tongue over every inch of her body and have her screaming for more.

He threw the remote against the wall and the back popped off. The batteries rolled under the desk.

"*She'll be back*," a little voice said to him.

"*She's gone, gone, gone*." Another voice pierced his thoughts.

"*You should have done something when you had the chance*," a third voice taunted him.

Leaning forward in his chair, he gripped his head tightly. "Go away," he cried. They were always there—the voices, never giving him a moments peace. Laryssa was his only peace. She could make the voices stop. She'd come back to him. He could feel it.

Laryssa's stomach clenched, and her hand tightened on the handle of the door. "We need to turn around."

When Alex didn't answer, her grip tightened even more. This must be what he'd been planning. The reason he wanted to come all the way to Vancouver.

"If you don't tell me what's going on, I'm going to roll down my window and scream."

He still remained silent. She pushed the button to roll down the window, and it started its descent. The window stopped its descent when Alex hit the master control.

"Relax," he said with a chuckle. "We're just taking a detour to my place."

"Detour, my butt." She slumped in her seat with a resigned sigh. She was stuck in a moving car with no way out. *Peachy*.

"I'd love to take a detour to your beautiful behind, but I'm afraid that has to wait till we're in private." He gave her leg a squeeze.

She pushed his hand away. "That's not what I meant, and you know it." He threaded his fingers through hers and held it firmly on his lap.

"Let me go." She wiggled her hand, trying to get it loose.

"You might as well get used to it. We'll be doing this a lot in public."

She didn't think she would ever get use to the way his thumb created tiny circles on her wrist, making her blood sing. "I doubt the rest of the drivers are going to be too concerned if you keep your hands to yourself."

She yanked her hand away from him and folded her arms across her chest, scooting closer to the door. Maybe she could call for a taxi when they got to his place. He couldn't keep her there. That would be kidnapping. Could that have been his intention from the start? He seemed genuine, though, but what did she know about the criminal mind anyway?

"I think you should just take me home."

"Look, we're getting married soon. You might as well stay at my place to prepare for the wedding. We'll be holding the reception there."

She hated how he tried to make all the decisions. "There is no way I can stay with you."

"Why not?"

She grasped for the nearest straw. "I...uh...have no clothes."

Keeping his eyes on the road, she watched him reach around behind her and pointed at a suitcase. "Problem solved," he said.

It was the same one she tossed back into the closet during their earlier exchange. She frowned. When did he have a chance to pack a suitcase? Must have been when she disappeared into the shower before they left.

She ground her teeth together. "How dare you go through my things!"

"Would you rather walk around my house naked?" he challenged. "I wouldn't mind, of course. But I had to think of Joanne."

"Pig," she said under her breath.

He covered his mouth with the back of his hand to stifle what sounded like laughter. She could see the sparkle of humor in his eyes. A repartee of similar taste occurred off and on for the rest of their trip. She had never been so glad to see a driveway in all her life.

"Wow!"

But that was no driveway. It looked like the freaking freeway. He stopped the car at a gate and punched in his code. The large iron gate swung open, and he drove the car through. The gate had to be at least ten feet tall. Each bar looked about the size of a small tree trunk.

Trees littered the side of the road until they reached the center of his estate. Her eyes widened, and her jaw dropped as she stared in awe at the sight before her. In the centre of a meadow, behind a mermaid water fountain, stood the most gigantic, gorgeous house she'd ever seen. No. Not a house. A castle! It was like had they stepped back in time to the medieval days with knights and lances.

The car came to a halt, and Laryssa stumbled out, unable to take her eyes off the house. "This is yours?"

"Yes. Well, my grandfather's actually. It's a family heirloom of sorts." The gray limestone building stood at least three stories high. The windows were made of beautiful stained glass, each with its own design. Gargoyles sat perched on the roof, as if guarding the house in every direction. She'd visited Craigdarroch Castle in Victoria years ago, but it paled in comparison to this place.

"What, no moat?" she asked.

He laughed. "My great grandmother was afraid of water, so they just built a wall around the place. I've had to rebuild most of it now, though. The storms have slowly weathered parts of the wall. "

"I'm not surprised. We took some real beatings over the last few years. Stanley Park was a mess the last time I went there to walk around."

Even the mermaid water fountain that stood beside them hadn't escaped unscathed. There was a faint outline of a crack on the mermaid's neck, and a chip missing out of her cheek where a heavy object must have hit her. The mermaid sat on a rock, with water spurting out of her out-stretched hands. Her face had a welcoming look as if she was beckoning a sailor to come to her. Goldfish swam in the water which gathered in a circle around the rock below.

"Shall we head inside?" He held out his hand.

Laryssa took it without qualm, too mesmerized by the house to care about being deceived, at least temporarily. The thought still sat there in the corner of her mind. She'd talk to him later.

They walked into a huge foyer. It was larger than her house and reached up to the top floor. Staircases on either side of the room led to upper walkways which wrapped around the room like balconies in a concert hall. Several hallways and doors branched off the main floor, leading to who knows where. Pottery artwork sat on pedestals around the outer edges of the room, illuminated by lamps which were mounted on the wall above them.

In the distance, she heard the clickity-clack of shoes on the cherry hardwood floor. She turned toward the noise and watched as an older woman entered the room from one of the many corridors. She was wearing a simple light purple blouse and black slacks. There was a slight limp in her gait and, as she got closer, Laryssa noticed one eyelid drooped lower than the other. Her brown hair, with strands of gray, was pulled back into a loose bun, pins nearly ready to fall out. This must be the house-keeper Alex had told her about, but she wondered what her story was. The woman didn't look like she could maneuver well enough to keep a house of this size clean.

"Joanne, this is Laryssa Mitchell. Laryssa, this is my housekeeper, Joanne," Alex said.

The older woman walked forward, and Laryssa found herself in an awkward embrace. Joanne pulled back away from her after a few moments. A faded scar ran from her right ear to her eye. The older woman's greenish blue eyes were warm and friendly. Those eyes looked faintly familiar, though, but she couldn't place them. There was something about her that drew Laryssa in immediately, and she couldn't help but like her. Maybe it was the way her whole face lit up with her smile, like the Fourth of July. She knew the woman's emotions were genuine.

"I'm so glad you finally agreed to come, it gives me someone to pamper. Alex doesn't let me pamper him." She slapped him on the arm. "Come, my dear, let me show you to your room."

"I'll leave you two ladies to get acquainted. If you need me, I'll be in the study." He turned and walked down another corridor in the opposite direction from where Joanne had appeared.

"All work and no play makes for a dull boy," Joanne whispered in her ear. Laryssa burst out laughing, despite the contradiction. Alex was anything but dull. He was stubborn, manipulative, and a huge annoyance. She followed Joanne as they walked toward an elevator.

"So how far along are you now, dear?"

"Twenty-three weeks. Although, I feel like it's forty." She ran her hand over her protruding belly.

"Are they fairly active?" Joanne asked as they entered the elevator, and she pushed the second-floor button.

"Today they certainly are. It feels like they're fencing."

They arrived on the second floor and traveled down another corridor.

"You don't, by any chance, have a map of this place, do you?" Laryssa asked.

"I'd give you a tour, but I think Alex would kill me. He says you are to be resting. Have there been problems?" Joanne's eyes filled with concern.

"A couple. But hopefully, the worst has passed."

"Well, I'm here to take care of you. We'll be sure you get plenty of rest and relaxation." Joanne stopped in front of a door on their left and opened it. "This is your room."

Laryssa couldn't stop the strange feeling that rushed through her as she entered the room. "This isn't your room, is it?"

"Nope. I'm just down the hall."

Something didn't feel right.

"I'm not booting anyone else out of their room, am I?" Laryssa asked. The room was completely covered in pink. Pink wallpaper, pink lush carpet, and even the queen-sized bed, which was along the wall and opposite the door, had a pink comforter lined with lace. This room seemed completely out of character for Alex. Out of character for a man who had sworn off women.

"No, not anymore." A deep underlying sadness wrapped around every word the older woman spoke. Laryssa thought it a strange answer, but she had no right to pry. She did have to admit the bed looked very inviting. After arguing with Alex all day, her energy level had dipped tremendously. She forced her attention back to Joanne who was opening another door.

"You have your own bathroom in here and a huge bathtub if you like baths. There should be a full assortment of toothpaste, shampoo, etcetera." She checked the drawers. "Yes, all here. So, tell me, when are the babies due?"

"August twenty-seventh, but I doubt I'll last that long. I really don't think my belly can stretch any further."

"You'd be amazed at exactly how far your skin can stretch," Joanne chuckled. "Well, with my help, we'll hopefully keep them in the oven for as long as we can." She patted Laryssa's stomach, and the babies leaped at her touch.

The babies wouldn't move for most people who touched her stomach, but now for both Alex and Joanne they did somersaults. It was as if they instinctively knew them.

"I had better go. Alex informed me you both haven't eaten yet. I'll go warm up some supper."

She wondered what else Alex informed her about. Did she know anything about their situation? She would definitely need to have a word with him.

Alex rummaged through his desk, looking for the phone book. He wanted to make a few extra calls to beef up security. If there was one thing he learned, it paid to play it safe. Despite having Laryssa here, the note bothered him.

He pulled out the bottom drawer and froze. Her smiling face stared up at him. Momentarily stunned, all he could do was stare at his little angel. His heart pounded and tears blurred his vision. He couldn't remember the last time he willingly looked at her picture. Anytime he tried, pain radiated throughout his body. This was her personal sanctuary. He'd placed the photo on top of her old baby blanket years ago.

He reached down and grabbed the portrait, placing it on his lap. His fingers traced the outline of her face. Sharp pains stabbed him in his chest. Why did he think looking at it this time would be any different? Images of that day had been forever burned into his brain. She was so small, so tiny. His heart twisted in agony.

Agony turned into anger. Anger at the one who stripped her away from him. He'd never truly hated anyone until then. She was the reason he vowed never to let anyone get close enough to hurt him. Now, here he was letting another woman into his home, and not just into his home but into the most special room in the house. He wanted to refuse to let her use it, but Joanne was right. There was no other room prepared that was so close to Joanne's room. If something were to go wrong, Joanne would need to get there fast.

His gaze dropped again to the photo. This was the only way he would ever get to hold her again. It didn't seem fair. Why do the good ones often get punished? She never did anything wrong. If angels existed, she would be the most beautiful one now. Her laughter could turn even his worst frown upside down. If he was upset, all he had to do was look at her and his heart would burst with joy.

Footsteps pierced his conscience, and he placed the picture reverently back in the drawer as Laryssa blew into his office, eyes blazing.

"You all settled in?" He cleared his throat. His words had come out huskier than planned.

"Sorta. The room is lovely, thank you."

"I feel a 'but' coming." He leaned forward at his desk.

"You knew I didn't want to stay with you. I don't like not being given a choice," she growled at him, placing her hands on her hips.

"As if you would come if I had given you a choice." He rolled his eyes.

"Let me teach you one thing about me." She walked towards him, placed her hands on the edge of the desk, and leaned forward. "I don't like being made to do something I don't want to do." She looked him dead on as she spoke.

He lifted a hand and cupped her chin. "And if there is something I want, I'll do anything to get it." He knew she registered his meaning as her eyes flickered with interest, although she disguised it rather quickly.

"Let me assure you, that is the last thing on my mind. The other reason I came down is to make sure I'm not booting anyone out of their room. Joanne says I'm not, but thought I better double check."

"The room doesn't belong to anyone now, except you."

"Are you sure? I mean I kind of find it strange that you have such a pink room with just you and Joanne here."

His chest constricted. He didn't want to be having this discussion, not so soon after studying her picture. The pain was still too raw and immediate. "Do you think I haven't had other women stay here?" That wasn't the truth, but right now, he didn't care.

Her face went a bright crimson, and she backed away from the desk. "All I wanted to know was whether I was kicking someone out of their room. Not a history of your love life."

He stood up and walked around to where she was standing and gripped her shoulders. What looked like fear registered on her face, and she shied back slightly.

"It is none of your God damn business why I have that room. You should be grateful you get to use it. Do not speak of it again, do you understand?"

She gave a slight nod. He watched her eyes fill with tears and felt her tremble beneath his grip.

"Excuse me." She pulled free and fled the room, slamming the door behind her.

He banged his fist down on the desk. Inwardly, he felt nauseous that he'd frightened her, but she had gotten too close to what he held most sacred. Something he never wanted to speak of again.

The door opened again, and in limped Joanne, waving her finger at him. "What did you do to that poor girl, Alexander Michael Richards?"

He cringed at the use of his full name. Joanne may not be his mother, but she certainly acted like one. "It's not my fault. She's too nosy for her own good," he grumbled.

"I will not have you upsetting her in her state, Alexander." She pointed out the door. "You go right up there and apologize."

He rocked back on his heels and crossed his arms. "Remind me why I keep you on?"

"Cause you'd fall apart without me. Now shoo. Dinner is ready. Go apologize, then bring her to the kitchen."

He grumbled under his breath.

"Don't grumble at me, mister." She pushed him out the door and headed toward the kitchen, leaving him staring upstairs.

For some reason he felt strangely outnumbered. And here he thought he'd have the upper hand. It seemed Laryssa had already made a strong ally. He stomped up the stairs, the sound of each step vibrating throughout the foyer.

CHAPTER EIGHT

"Insufferable man. Who does he think he is?" Laryssa shoved open the balcony door and stepped out into the cool air. She rubbed her shoulders that still burned from Alex's grip. When would she learn it didn't pay to be curious? Maybe she should re-think the whole marriage thing. The fury she saw on his face brought back frightful memories. Before the fury, there was something else in his eyes when she first walked in. It had looked like pain, but he had masked it so quickly.

Something bad must have happened to whoever used this room. It didn't take a genius to figure that out. But he didn't have to take it out on her. She had only asked an innocent question. Thankfully, she had Joanne. Joanne wouldn't let anything happen to her. Again, she wondered about the two of them. They appeared to have a close relationship, more than the typical employer and employee. She supposed if they'd known each other for a while it could evolve into a close friendship, but didn't the rich usually place servants in a different class than them? At least, that was what books and movies portrayed.

She leaned on the railing and looked out over the fields, the wind blowing her hair back from her face. This probably wasn't a good idea. Her hair would be full of knots by the time she got back inside, but the wind felt so cool against her skin and eased the tension in her shoulders. The breeze carried the aroma of salt water. Had they really traveled that far from her place? They were too busy bantering for her to notice how long it took to get here.

A shuffle on the carpet behind her had her mind pause all thought as she whipped around. "Oh. It's you." She turned back toward the open field and gripped the railing. "What do you want?"

"Joanne made me come."

She would have laughed at the whiny tone of his voice if she had felt anything like laughing.

"I mean, I'm sorry for barking at you."

The soft undertone in his voice made his apology sound believable, but she'd experienced it all before. "You're sorry? I find that hard to believe. You probably wouldn't even be up here if Joanne didn't make you."

He stood beside her and rested his forearms on the railing. "You're right, but I should apologize. I was out of line."

"Were you? It's your life, and I'm not part of it. It's not my business." She shivered at the sudden chill that swept through her.

"You're cold. Let's go inside and talk." He grabbed her arm to lead her inside.

"I would appreciate it if you didn't touch me." She pulled her arm away and walked into the room.

When he didn't follow her inside, she turned and looked back at him. He stood there, still as a statute, staring into the room. His face ashen and eyes were wide. She walked over to him and waved her hand in front of his face. He didn't even blink, and trepidation filled her.

"Alex?" She placed her hand on his shoulder.

He jerked back away from her touch and bumped into the railing, nearly toppling over it. She grabbed his wrist and pulled him inside the room, closing the double doors safely behind them. His pulse raced beneath her hand. Her heart rate increased to match.

“What's wrong? What is it?” They sat down on the edge of the bed and for a few minutes he never spoke.

“I—this is not something I'm comfortable talking about,” he said in a voice so broken that tears filled her eyes.

She lifted a trembling hand and brushed her fingers across his cheek. “I know it’s not what I’m here for, but if you need someone to talk to, I'm here to listen,” she said, half hoping he'd take her up on the offer. The other half wished he'd just leave the room. She didn't want to care about what caused his pain, but the slump in his shoulders and shaky voice hit her square in the heart.

After a few moments of silence, she went to stand up, only to have him pull her back down. “Don't go, please. I promise I won't pull anything,” he pleaded. “Just let me hold you.”

The pain in his eyes made her insides ache. As much as she didn’t want to be touched, she knew it just wasn't in her to walk away. A lone tear drifted down his cheek, and she found herself reaching for him. She'd never seen a man lose composure before. Whatever happened still held a vice grip on him. Tears fell down her cheeks as she held him.

Her tears dropped on the back of his hand which rested on her leg. He pulled back to look at her. His face wet with tears of his own. She lifted her hand again and brushed his tears away. “I'm here for you, Alex,” she said in a soft voice.

He took hold of her hands and kissed the back of each before standing up. “I'm afraid this is something no one can help me with.”

With that, he turned and left the room. She sat there staring at the empty doorway. It looked as though ghosts haunted them both, and hers just walked out the door.

Moments later, he poked his head back in rather sheepishly. “I'm supposed to take you down to dinner.” He held out his arm. “Shall we?”

Throughout dinner, her back ached, and she could barely keep her eyes open. She answered any questions directed her way. Mostly she watched the interaction between Joanne and Alex with fascination. There was such affection in their gazes when they looked at each other, and she wished, just for once, someone would look at her that way.

"Tell us about your family?" Joanne asked.

Laryssa let her fork rest on the side of her plate, as she looked up at the two curious faces looking in her direction. "My family?"

"Your parents. Do you have siblings?" Joanne took a sip of her tea.

Her hands went clammy, and thoughts pushed to the surface she had long since tried to forget. "My parents died in a boating accident when I was four."

Joanne's eyes widened, and her fork dropped on to her plate with a loud clang. "Oh, how awful."

Awful didn't even begin to cover it. She still remembered the fear of being alone. Her babysitter sitting on the couch crying, holding her so tight she could barely breathe.

'When is my mommy coming home?' she had asked. The babysitter just placed her on the ground and started crying again.

The memory wasn't nearly as vivid as it used to be, but she could still remember sitting curled at the foot of the couch before a police officer picked her up and took her away.

She shook her head, trying to push the memory away and looked at Joanne and Alex. "Yes, it was awful, but I made it through." She tried to beam a bright smile their way, but a lump gathered in her throat.

Alex looked at her with grief evident in his own eyes, and Joanne, who initiated the conversation, had guilt in hers.

"It's okay, guys, really. It was a long time ago." She turned to Joanne. "Dinner was wonderful, thank you."

"Do you want more?"

"No, I'm good, thanks. I think I'll just head up to bed. It has been a long day." She pushed her chair back and stood. Alex did the same.

"Do you need help finding your way back?" Alex asked.

She remembered Alex's earlier reaction to her room and shook her head. "No, I think I can manage."

After one wrong turn, she managed to make it to the elevator and take it up to the second floor. She washed up in the bathroom and then sat on the edge of the bed. How on earth had she make it through dinner without bawling her eyes out? The easy camaraderie between Joanne and Alex made her feel so alone, made her remember what she once had with her parents and never found again. Sure, she had foster families, but they always had so many kids and didn't have time to focus on her.

She'd left for college the minute she could and never looked back. No doubt the feeling of being alone made her fall hard for Aidan when he lavished her with attention. Even the feeling of possessiveness he showed had its own allure. Now, as she looked back, she recognized it for what it was. He never cared about her. She was just a fixture, an object of possession. Shame filled her at all the friends she'd lost over the years because she let him take over her life.

She thought of Melissa who, even after six years of not contacting her, welcomed her back with open arms. She picked up her purse and rifled through it to try and find Melissa's number. She pulled out a folded piece of paper and started to unfold it. The larger the paper became the faster her heart pounded. The top of a brown head started to show. By the time she opened the final fold, her hands shook uncontrollably, threatening to rip the paper in the process. Unable to look at it, she let the photo of Aidan slip out of her hands.

Love. It should have been love. She lifted her head toward the heavens. "God, am I really so unlovable?" As if in protest, the life in her womb pushed out. She played tag for a few brief moments with them. Here were two lives that would depend on her and expect her to love them. How could she give them what they needed when she never experienced it herself?

Cradling her belly, she moved to the middle of the bed and let herself fall back against the pillow. She rolled onto her side and turned off the ballerina table lamp. Her future was uncertain, but for the moment she could pretend all was well. Pretend that she belonged. Alex made something come alive inside her. She longed to let her inhibitions go and ride the tidal wave he brought with him, but the crash against the shore could cripple her. She needed to be strong, to fight him and his endless witty charm.

Aidan wasn't without his charm. That was how she fell for him to begin with. Now look at her. Were the feelings she had for Alex just a repercussion of what she used to feel for Aidan? It couldn't be something new, could it? Had she ever felt butterflies in her stomach when Aidan kissed her? She moved to the edge of the bed and stared down at the paper that landed face up beside the bed. Tears flooded her eyes as she stared in the eyes of the one she used to love.

The last night they spent together flashed before her eyes. She recalled the twin taillights of his car as it drove down the driveway, disappearing into the snowy night, never to return.

She squeezed her eyes tight. “I refuse to remember,” she whispered to the shadows.

The cool air from the open window rustled the curtains and blew the picture under the bed. Too lazy to get up, she decided to leave it for the night.

“Joanne!” Laryssa groaned as she covered her face with a pillow.

Every day this past week, her sleep had been disrupted by Joanne. She'd come into the room and throw back the dark curtains, flooding the room with light.

“I thought you were supposed to pamper me, not give me sleep deprivation.”

“Sorry dear, but it is breakfast time, and we have a busy day.” Joanne placed the tray in front of her and wiped her hands on her apron. “You have a doctor's appointment this morning, and we have a meeting with the wedding coordinator this afternoon.”

“But my doctor's appointment isn't until next week.” She glanced at Joanne who limped around the room, picking up her discarded clothing.

“For security reasons, Alex switched you to another doctor. In case, well, you know,” Joanne replied with a wave of her hand.

She shifted to sit higher in bed. “Man, it's harder to get up these days.” All she wanted to do was lie back down and go back to sleep.

"I wish I could say it gets better."

"You mean it doesn't?"

"Don't sound so shocked, dear. Even ancient me had kids at one time," she spoke with an underlying sadness in her voice. "Now, eat up. I'll go run you a bath."

She wanted to ask what happened, what caused her to look so shattered, but the housekeeper had already disappeared into the bathroom. By the time Joanne came back into the room, Laryssa's plate was empty.

"That was delicious, thank you." Strawberries, Raisin Bran cereal and orange juice really hit the spot. "I feel bad having you wait on me, though, especially when I can do it myself."

"Don't feel bad. Enjoy it." Joanne gave her a pat on the shoulder. "You'll be busy soon enough with those little darlings."

She let her hand rest on Joanne's. "Thanks."

"Are you up to coming into the garden today? You can keep me company there while I work."

"There's a garden?" She never saw one when they drove up. The garden back at her house had been her pride and joy. It was the only thing that took her mind off her troubles and got her through the day. The only time it had been a problem was when she didn't clean her hands good enough. Aidan wouldn't want her to touch anything that belonged to him if her nails were dirty.

"Yes. It's hidden behind the house. The door in the kitchen is fairly close to it." Joanne picked the breakfast tray up off the bed and started towards the door. "I'll be in the kitchen. Meet me there when you're ready."

"Hey, is Alex still here?" Laryssa asked.

"No, he left early for work."

Good, no chance that he'd burst into the bathroom again. She couldn't forget the first time it happened. The look in his eyes as he stared at her made her nervous. She didn't relish the idea of it happening again, not now anyway, when she was three weeks further along. Usually, she took a book with her in the bath, but since Alex saw her in the bath, the last thing she wanted to do was read. Get in and get out was more her style these days.

Walking into the bathroom, she stared at the water in the tub and found herself wishing they could replay the scene. She replayed the scene in her head often, and, in her fantasies, she wasn't pregnant. Why on earth was she teasing herself? *Because you're pregnant and not getting any!* She'd never spent so much time thinking about sex before, and now that she'd met Alex she couldn't stop. How could she want him? He looked exactly like her husband, and she'd stopped wanting Aidan a long time ago. She closed her eyes and plugged her nose, submersing herself underwater, coming up for air only when her lungs burned.

Not long later, she met Joanne downstairs, and they walked out to the garden. She collapsed on a swing which hung in the gazebo and watched as Joanne dug in the dirt, removing weeds from around the tulips. Walls of bushes surrounded the heart of the garden. A huge apple tree rested off to the side of the gazebo with a branch resting slightly on the roof. Little rivers of water ran throughout the garden, covered occasionally by a small bridge. Flowers in shades of red, yellow, and orange grew throughout, reminding Laryssa of a beautiful sunset.

She rested her head on the swing and pushed on the ground with her shoe. Amidst the sound of running water, she could hear the chirping of birds. A robin perhaps. "This is such a beautiful place. It reminds me of the secret garden."

"That was the movie that gave me the inspiration for the garden so many years ago when we moved here," Joanne said with a smile.

"Cool." She glanced around the garden. "Have you known Alex long?"

Joanne froze for a second and then plucked a weed out of the ground, her sunhat low over her face. "I guess you could say I've been there from day one." It sounded like her words were carefully calculated.

She tilted her head to the side and watched Joanne cut a flower, placing it in the basket beside her. “Then you would know if he had a brother?”

Joanne's fingers slipped and the gardening shears cut into her hand. Blood started to drip down her wrist.

“My word, I'm clumsy.” She pulled a hankie out of her pocket and wrapped up her hand. “I better go in and clean up. You are more than welcome to stay out here. I could bring you out a drink when I'm done.”

“After all you've done for me, the least I can do is help you.” Intrigued by the older lady's response to her question, she pushed herself up and followed Joanne into the house.

“Do you have any bandages down here?” Laryssa asked.

“Yes, in the drawer on the right side of the sink.”

She found what she was looking for and took a seat next to the older woman at the kitchen table. Removing the hankie, she studied the cut. “It doesn't look deep, thankfully.”

“I'm not usually so clumsy,” Joanne groaned when the antiseptic wipe touched her skin.

She watched Joanne beneath lowered eyelids and saw the weariness in her eyes. Something had concerned her enough to make her slip.

“It was my fault, I apologize.” Laryssa pulled out a bandage and placed it over the cut. “I should not have pried.”

“No harm done.” Joanne chuckled and looked down at her bandaged hand. “At least, not really.”

“It's just...I'm going to be part of this family soon, and I really don't know anything about his family or his past. Alex is not exactly forthcoming.”

The housekeeper glanced at her watch. “I'm sorry, my dear, but I have to start lunch. Why don't you go into the sitting room and relax? I'll call you when it's done.” Her eyes seemed to be pleading with her to go, yet, at the same time the older woman's mouth opened and closed as if she wanted to say something more.

“Okay.” She got up, went into the sitting room, and took a seat at the bay window.

The tree branches on a willow tree swayed in the late morning breeze and hid the garden from her view. It would seem that, just like the movie Secret Garden, everyone here had their own secrets and burdens to bear. Joanne wanted to tell her something, she could feel it.

CHAPTER NINE

Alex sat at his desk, looking over some paperwork for his latest landscaping project, when a knock disturbed him. He looked up and saw Melissa standing in the doorway.

"The file you asked for, sir." She walked to his desk and placed it in front of him. "Oh, and Craig Henderson phoned while you were out." She lingered at his desk for a moment before turning away.

"Is there something on your mind, Ms. Johnson?" She had been looking at him strangely for the last few days now, sneaking peeks at him when she thought he wasn't looking.

Melissa walked to the door and closed it, no doubt so no one could hear what she had to say. She was the most outspoken employee on his team, never afraid to say what was on her mind. She had a good head on her shoulders and excelled in her job, despite her mouth. He had to admit he was grateful that he had to put up with her only when his personal assistant phoned in sick.

"Mind if I speak freely?"

"Have you ever done anything else?" he regarded her wryly with half a smile.

"I know I've put my foot in my mouth a few times, but when it comes to my friend, I'll do anything to keep her happy." She paced a few steps in his office and stopped to stare out the window.

"Ah, this is about Laryssa."

"Yes. She phoned me a week ago. I'm concerned for her."

"I can assure you she's fine, and you're welcome to visit her whenever you wish." Alex picked up the pen he'd placed on the desk and started to sign the next paper on his pile, expecting to hear the door open and close. When it didn't, he looked up and saw her staring at him with morbid curiosity.

"Why are you marrying her?"

He leaned back in his chair and threaded the pen through his fingers. "Why do most people get married?" The last thing he wanted to do was get into a discussion about this with her best friend. One wrong word and she'd high tail it to Laryssa, and then he'd have a fight on his hands. Not that he'd mind fighting with Laryssa. Their battles always led to the most interesting outcome.

"You can't honestly tell me you've known her long enough to be in love with her, so don't give me that load of bull." Melissa crossed her arms and tapped her foot on the floor.

"Okay, I won't. Now is there anything else I can do for you?" He waved his hands at the stack of paperwork on his desk. "I do have more pressing matters to attend to."

Melissa spun on her heels and stormed to the door of his office. He could hear her muttering under her breath and his ears caught one or two of the words.

"...Cursed...handsome."

He raised an eyebrow as she spared him one last glance before opening the door. Her eyes were narrow, and a frown marred her model like features.

"Don't marry her if you don't love her." She left, slamming the door behind her.

Love, of course he didn't love her. Why would he do something so foolish as to fall in love again? If he hadn't learned the first time, someone might as well shoot him. There was no way in hell he wanted to go through it again. Loving Valerie destroyed him, and he had the distinct feeling loving Laryssa would kill him.

She hadn't been living with him long, but she'd already put her stamp on the place. Every time he walked in the door after work, he'd hear her laughing with Joanne, while the aroma of supper tickled his nose. He'd find them sitting together at the dinner table, chatting.

He didn't want her to fit into his life so easily, and it irked him. Being attached to his housekeeper would make it harder for them when they ended things. Joanne, too, had grown fond of her in such a short time. He wanted to say, don't get close to her, but then he'd have to explain the marriage was a fake. If he did that, the news would get back to his parents, and he'd be right back at square one again.

The door hinges squeaked as it opened again. This time Ron poked his head in. “It's quitting time. I thought you may want to go for beer.”

“Sure, why not,” he shrugged.

After Melissa's visit, he definitely needed one. Thankfully, Laryssa never spilled the beans to her friend, or he had a feeling Melissa would have ripped him to shreds. He debated phoning Joanne or Laryssa to let them know he was going out, but he was only planning to have one beer, so he shouldn’t be late. If plans changed, he’d call them.

They drove to a nearby club and walked inside. Alex hesitated at the door. Loud music made the floor vibrate beneath his feet. Men were gathered in groups around the stage just to get a glimpse of the woman sliding down the pole, hoping to get close enough to shove bills down her thong. The waitresses, unfortunately, were the ones who had to put up with the turned-on men as the dancers stayed just out of reach.

“Come on, chicken.” Ron grabbed his shirt collar and hauled him to a table next to the stage. “It's been ages since I've visited this place.”

“If your wife knew, she'd skin you alive.”

Ron laughed. “You're probably right, but I won't tell her if you don't.” His eyes followed the dancer on the stage. “I wonder if Elaine still works here.”

"What can I get you handsome fellows?" a cheery voice behind them asked. The waitress wore a white halter top and skimpy black shorts that barely covered her behind. Who needed the dancers when these girls were working the floor?

"Just two Genuine Drafts, sweetie-pie," Ron said.

Alex watched as his friend's gaze followed the waitress around the counter and laughed. "Stop drooling."

"Give it time. They'll have you drooling, too."

He highly doubted it. The small interest he had in woman for sexual purposes disappeared when Laryssa walked into his life. God only knew why. It wasn't as if he was getting anything from her, other than a few cold showers. When she was around, his body had a mind of its own.

The waitress slid their beers across the counter. "Here you go, boys."

"Mr. Ice Man, why are you glaring at the dancers?" Ron's voice broke him out of his stupor. "I thought this would help bring you out of your funk."

"I'm not in a funk." Alex took a large swig of his freshly opened drink. "I've just got better things to do with my time than watch naked women."

Ron gave him a bemused look. "Okay, where's my friend, and what have you done with him?"

"This is more your scene, Ron, not mine." He hooked a thumb toward the stage. "These women don't do anything for me."

His friend's eyes lit up like fireworks. "It's her, isn't it? You've gone and done it."

Alex took a final chug of the beer and spun the can on the table. "Gone and done what?" He picked up the empty beverage container to spin it again.

"You've fallen for her."

"No way in hell." He tightened his grip, and the aluminum crunched beneath his fingers. "And the last thing I need is you talking about her. I heard enough about it from Melissa today." He grabbed his jacket and stood.

Ron lifted his hands in the air. "Okay, okay. Sorry."

Instant guilt rushed through Alex, and he sat back down. Ron had been nothing but a good friend. One who stood by him after the accident. "I don't mean to be a killjoy. Why don't you have another beer? I'll buy."

"Gladly. You owe me." Ron slapped his back.

The waitress brought another beer for Ron. "You want anything else, honey?" she nodded towards Alex.

"No thanks." He put on his jacket. "I had better go. They'll be worrying if I don't get back soon." He stood up and glanced towards the stage. The new dancer seemed to have him in her sights and gravitated towards him. "I'll see you tomorrow, Ron."

As he went to walk away, something landed on his head. The smell of perfume snuck its way up his nostrils and down into his windpipe. His lungs squeezed closed, and he doubled over in a coughing fit. It was like something an old granny would wear when her sense of smell started to go. He grabbed a bra off his head and tossed it back onto the stage.

"Great, just great," he mumbled.

Ron smacked his hand down on the table and roared with laughter. Of course, his friend would find the humor in this. Maybe in another life he would, too. But with Joanne and Laryssa, he didn't relish trying to explain how he reeked of another woman's perfume. "Good night, Ron."

He walked away, hacking up a storm, as the woman's perfume filled his lungs a second time. What did she do, bathe in the stuff? Every time he took a breath, it wrapped itself around his nose and knocked the air right out of him. Now he understood what it felt like to be asthmatic.

He climbed into his car and rolled the windows down, hoping the fresh breeze would get rid of the stench. Why couldn't she have worn something subtler like Laryssa's perfume? She always wore one that smelled like flowers and put on just enough to tickle his senses.

Even as he pulled up to the gate leading to his property, he still reeked of the dancer's perfume. Joanne and Laryssa were sure to notice the smell. The only hope he had was to sneak inside the house and jump in the shower before he ran into them. Chances were good. His place was large enough that you could go a week without running into someone.

"What the hell am I worried about? I didn't do anything wrong."

He opened the gate and drove down the driveway. Maybe he shouldn't have gone, but how did he know what would happen? He did try to leave as soon as he was able to. What happened to him could have happened to anybody.

His mind suddenly went blank, and all his reasoning power went out the window. The two women were sitting on the front porch, and they did not look happy.

"Shoot me now!" he grumbled, letting a few choice expletives fly off his tongue.

They turned and watched his car pull up. Joanne pointed to her watch and gave him a firm look. He looked down at the time and realized he had been gone longer than he thought. So much for the 'leaving right away' theory. He took a deep breath, put his car in park and climbed out. Time to face the judge, jury, and executioner. Joanne never let him get away with anything. She always kept him out of trouble, or at least tried to. As a boy, and now as a man, she clucked like a mother hen around him. Warmth spread through him. He couldn't imagine his life without her. She was the one thing he could always count on.

His gaze drifted to Laryssa who sat next to her, and Ron's words played in his head, *'You've fallen for her.'* Why did everyone believe he'd fallen for her? Granted he'd gotten use to having her around, even enjoyed it, but in love with her? Forget it.

Duh, it's because you're marrying her, remember?

He'd have to be more careful in public. He was, after all, supposed to be a man in love. He walked up the steps and approached them.

With a frown on her face, Joanne pushed herself up out of the seat. "Supper is sitting on the stove. I'll go warm it up for you." She hurried by him and went inside.

Laryssa followed Joanne inside, but not before he noticed the hurt evident in her eyes. She walked inside stiffly with her hand on her back and disappeared up the elevator.

The dark ball of dread that sat in the pit of his stomach grew larger. In the safety of his room, he pulled off the clothes that stunk of perfume and jumped in the shower. Satisfied that the shower had removed the worst of the stench, he put on new clothes and headed to the kitchen.

Joanne turned to him as soon as he walked into the kitchen and waved her ladle at him. "You're supposed to phone if you're going to be late. We had supper waiting for you."

Since Laryssa moved in, they'd been eating together every night. He raised his hands in surrender. "I'm sorry. Ron asked me to go out for a drink."

Joanne pressed her lips together, tilted her head and regarded him with raised eyebrows. "He was wearing perfume?" She swatted him on the arm gently with the ladle. "Honestly, Alexander. I thought I taught you better."

"I didn't do anything, honest." He sighed when she made her, 'I don't believe you,' grunt.

"It's not me you need to convince, my dear boy. You have your future wife living with you, but you come home smelling of another woman. She's in a delicate state right now, and this is the last thing she needs to worry about." She waved the ladle at him one final time before turning back to the stove.

She placed his food in front of him and left the room without another word. *It's a conspiracy to make me feel guilty, I swear, and doggone it, it's working!* He pushed his plate away and, yet again, found himself heading upstairs to Laryssa's room.

Why did it have to hurt so much? Laryssa knew it would happen eventually. How long could a healthy man go without finding some willing woman? She wanted to believe he wouldn't; that he would keep his end of the bargain.

You turned him down. What did you think would happen?

"Get a grip, Laryssa." She paced, trying to ignore the dull pain that radiated in her back. What right did she have to be upset? It was not like they were in a real relationship, with any real commitment. This was what she'd been trying to avoid, giving another man the power to hurt her. Try as she might, she couldn't dismiss him. In the month she'd known him, he'd squeezed into a corner of her heart. She'd even started to consider him a friend.

She heard a light knock on the door. "Yes?"

Immediately, she wished she hadn't answered. He pushed open the door and leaned against the door frame. He wore a white t-shirt with black, tight-fitting jeans that hugged his narrow hips. His hair damp and wild from the shower he had taken to remove the other woman's scent. He did smell of soap and shampoo, but the stale scent of her still lingered. Tears pricked her eyes again. That had been happening a lot lately. He stood there, staring at her with uncertainty in his eyes. Discomfort wrapped around her like a glove.

"I wanted to explain." He moved towards her.

She shook her head and held up her hand. "Look, forget it. You don't need to explain."

He took her by the shoulders and made her sit down next to him on the bed. "Yes, I do. It's not what you think."

"And what am I thinking, Alex?" She moved away to put a bit of distance between them. She couldn't focus with him sitting so close.

"That I've been with a woman. That's not true, technically."

Laryssa lifted her head to the ceiling. Her ears wrapped around the word technically. "What do you call *technically*? You went to supper with her but didn't sleep with her?" She pushed herself off the bed with a groan and walked toward the balcony door. The spring rain fell heavily against the glass. "I'm tired, Alex. Just go."

Instead of hearing the door close, a hand came to rest on her shoulder. "Lara, please."

"Look, I've said there's no use explaining. We're not married. We're not even a couple, for Pete's sake. Can't you leave well enough alone?" Tears gathered in her eyes, making her feel even more foolish. The last thing she wanted to do was make him feel sorry for her.

His fingers flexed on her shoulders before he slowly turned her to face him. "I came up here to explain why I smelled like a woman's perfume."

"If this is for Joanne's sake, save it! I know she's the only reason you came up here." She shrugged him off her shoulders and moved a few steps back. Suddenly a light dawned on her. "Or maybe the woman turned you down, and you wanted to come up here to see what you could get from me."

"Damn it, Laryssa. That's not it at all. Why do you have to be so difficult?" He rested an arm against the balcony door and leaned his forehead against it, before whipping around to face her. "The only woman I want around here is you, and it is driving me insane." His voice was low and husky.

The intensity of his gaze had her stumbling backwards. Her heel hit the bed, and her bum plopped down on the edge of it. "You have a strange way of showing it, coming home wearing another woman's perfume."

"Do you really want me to show you?" He took a step toward her. "It wouldn't be a problem."

She supported her belly with one hand and crawled across the bed. Her heart palpitated in her chest. One strand of hair flopped against his forehead, which gave him a boyish look as he grinned at her. His eyes remained serious though and seared her with a look that was anything but boyish.

He started to walk around the bed, but she placed her hands out in front of her. "No, stay there."

"What? Don't trust me?" He cocked his head and shoved his hands in the back pockets of his jeans.

Trust him? Ha! Not as far as she could throw him. Not when all their talks ended up with a sexual innuendo. Her body reminded her daily of what she was missing. She'd woken up drenched from an erotic dream, featuring none other than him. Dreams so explicit she didn't dare share them with Melissa.

After a few minutes, she finally found her voice. "Need I remind you, that you were the one who came back wearing another woman's perfume? I wouldn't bother asking about trust."

"That's it!" He stormed around the bed faster than she could move. He grabbed her hands and forced her to sit down beside him. For a moment, he said nothing, only stared at her as if lost in thought. "You look so gorgeous." He traced her lips with his thumb.

She couldn't prevent her lip from quivering and hated herself for not being able to control the way her body reacted to his touch. "Our deal was no touching, Alex." She pushed his hand away.

"Will you just shut up and listen to me." Frustration was now evident in his voice. He knelt beside the bed, bringing himself eye level with her. "After work my buddy, Ron, asked if I wanted to go for a drink."

"You drove after drinking? What are you-" Before she could finish, he pressed his lips hard against hers. He pulled back, and she lifted her hand as if to slap him. "Don't do that," she said between her teeth.

He grabbed her hand and held it in her lap. "It's the only way to shut you up. Now will you be quiet, please?"

Realizing she had no choice, she bit her lip and nodded her head. The sooner she let him speak, the sooner he would leave.

"Anyway, Ron took me to a club near work, not mentioning, of course, that it was a strip club, or I never would have gone. We bought some drinks, and then I went to leave..." He paused. His cheeks and the tips of his ears changed to a bright crimson color before he continued. "As I was leaving, the dancer tossed her smelly bra on my head."

CHAPTER TEN

She stared at him and pictured what he'd look like with a bra on his head. The image made a bubble rise in her chest and soon a giggle escaped out of her mouth.

Before long, she was laughing so hard tears flowed and her sides hurt.

"It's not that funny," he mumbled, turning brighter red by the minute.

"I'm sorry." She tried to make a straight face, but the look on his had her break into fits of laughter again. "I wish...I could...have been...there with my camera," she said between giggles. Hiccups attacked her from laughing so hard.

"Does this mean you believe me?" he asked with hope in his voice.

She gave him a once over, and then with a poker face she asked, "You aren't wearing—hiccup—woman's lingerie now, are you?" The look of horror on his face had her burst into hysterics again.

"Don't you be getting any ideas!" he warned her.

She glanced over at her dresser and then back to him again as she tried to picture him with one of her brassieres on his head. "Wait here." She squeezed by him, walked to her dresser and pulled out one of her bras.

"If you think about putting that on my head, I'll really give you something to laugh about," he forewarned her as she started to walk towards him.

"I just want to get a better visual of what happened." She gave him her most innocent smile and continued her quest toward him. Teasing him probably wasn't a good idea, but she couldn't help herself. The situation was too comical to let it pass.

Before she could place the bra on his head, he grabbed it, and with speed she could only dream of, he wrapped it around her hands like handcuffs and pulled her down carefully onto the bed. She let out a shriek and tried to pull away, but he pinned her against the bed.

"Now I'll give you something to laugh about." He held her hands with one hand and began to tickle her with the other.

She howled in laughter. "Mercy, mercy."

After a few moments, he stopped his assault. In fact, his hands went stone still and were resting on her sides. She looked up at him while he studied her intently. It was at that moment she realized their predicament, and there was a change in the atmosphere.

The heat in the room tripled and her heart skipped a beat. His eyes, which were filled with humor, now were filled with desire. His hands started to stroke her sides, sending mini shocks through her body. She tried to stand, but no matter which way she moved she ended up touching some part of him. He was half on top of her.

"Alex, I..." she whimpered.

His hands brushed her breasts, but it was only a fleeting touch that left her aching. She wanted. No. She needed him to touch her. Alex shifted his weight, but never let her go. Her face was flushed, and he could feel her rapid heartbeat beneath the palm of his hand.

He rested his head on her shoulder and whispered with a deep husky voice, "Why do you have to be so sexy?"

"Same goes...for you," she said between breaths, her breathing still heavy from laughing so hard.

His jeans grew tight, and his heart hammered against his chest. “Damn it, Laryssa, don't say that to me,” he groaned. “I want you.”

The minute he said it, he knew he'd made a mistake and should have kept his trap shut. She tensed and rolled onto her side to get up. He let her go.

“I meant what I said about no touching, Alex,” she said in a firm voice. “I know I instigated this, I apologize.”

The words were a contradiction to the look in her eyes. Her eyes said ‘touch me, mold me with your hands’. He ached to do just that. He wanted to lie with her on the bed and remove each article of clothing, one by one, and run the tips of his fingers over her breasts, down her sides before feeling the heat between her thighs.

He rolled onto his back and rubbed his hand down his face. For once, he wished he could think rationally while in the same room with her. She made him think with the wrong head and there didn't seem to be any way to control it.

He looked up at her as she stood a few feet away from him. It would be so easy just to grab her and pull her down beside him, but she'd probably knee him in the crotch if he tried. Her knee was just the right height to do it, too. He pushed himself off the bed and put a little more distance between them. The tension fizzled in the air between them, like electricity traveling through the power lines. The hair on his arms stood on end.

Afraid that he would get shocked if he touched her, he turned and walked to the door. “Be ready bright and early tomorrow. We've got a wedding to plan.”

He stormed into the kitchen, grabbed a cup out of the cupboard and banged it closed. Having her in his house was not making it any easier. He thought they could live in peaceful harmony, especially with the size of his place, but knowing she might be naked just down the hall from him had his body crying out with sexual fantasies.

He hoped by placing her in his daughter's old room it would dampen any sexual interest in her, but it didn't work. He walked over to the coffee maker and slammed the cup onto the counter.

“Don't you dare break those, young man.” Joanne walked up to him, pulled the cup out of his hand and proceeded to pour him a coffee.

"Don't start." He crumpled into a chair at the table and laid his head down on his arm. "Not tonight, Joanne."

"Mind your manners," she said in a calm, stern voice. She let her hand rest on his. "Do you want to talk about it?"

He lifted his head and looked at her. "I don't even know, really," he confessed, before letting his head fall back on his arm again. Everything was getting to him these days. He didn't even know if it was one thing or a whole bunch of things combined.

"Did Laryssa get upset over what happened?"

"Nothing happened. Ron and I went for a beer and the striper tossed her bra on my head."

When she didn't speak for a moment, he looked up at her. Her mouth was pressed in a firm line, but her eyes danced with laughter as if she couldn't decide whether to get mad or laugh. The mother in her prevailed, and she whacked his shoulder. "That is no place for an engaged man to be."

"Man, for an old lady you sure pack a wallop," he said with a grin, while rubbing his shoulder.

"Oh, shush up. Did she believe you?"

With a creased brow, he scratched his head. "Yes, I think so. She couldn't stop laughing."

He watched Joanne fight to remain serious but couldn't stop a chuckle from breaking through. He glared at her.

"Sorry. So, if she's not mad, what's wrong? Is it Valerie?" she asked softly.

He sat up straight, his back stiff. "I thought I told you never to mention her name."

She nodded her head, her eyes filling with compassion. *Damn it.* He didn't want her sympathy. He wanted to forget his ex-wife's name; forget she ever existed. Valerie took the most important person in his life away forever and it was not something he'd ever forget. The pains in his chest grew, threatening to swallow him whole.

Joanne placed her hand on his, and he gripped it tightly as he struggled to take deep breaths.

"As hard as this is, you have to let it go, Alex."

"How can I?" he gritted through his teeth.

"It's not easy, but you have to find a way to make peace before you can find the true treasure, which, just so happens, to be sitting right under your nose."

"What do you know about it?" he spat at her.

"More than you think, sweetie. More than you think." She gave his shoulder a quick squeeze and then got up to put the cups in the sink.

When she turned back around, he saw a deep level of pain in her eyes. "I guess we've all got our sorrows to bear, don't we? I'm sorry, Joanne."

"It's not you, dear. I've carried my own share of regrets from the past, but it's the past, and we can't change it. We can only find a way to move forward."

He didn't want to move forward. Moving forward meant letting her go. How could he do that? How could he betray her memory? His stomach turned over at the thought.

"Alex, if you don't, the past will find a way of repeating itself. Maybe not to the same degree but it will."

She spoke the truth, he knew it, but no one would make him forget his little girl. Not Joanne. And certainly not Laryssa. If she left because of that, then he didn't need her. Didn't need whatever was building up between them. He had lived ten years on his own and could do it another ten if that card came up.

Joanne leaned down to his kiss the top of his head. "Don't let it eat you up inside. You deserve to live, Alex."

"Damn it, Joanne. So did she!" Pain coursed through him, and he smacked his hand on the table. The sound echoed through the kitchen. "Doesn't anyone understand?"

He squeezed his eyes closed and sucked in a sharp breath. *How could they?* They hadn't lost a daughter. He had. No amount of therapy would give her back to him. He pushed himself up from the table and walked away.

Joanne watched him leave the kitchen with his head low. His feet shuffled across the floor as though he had no strength left to lift them. She placed a hand over her heart and swallowed hard. "Oh, my sweet dear boy, no one understands more than I do."

Someday she'd have the strength to tell him, but not today, not with all his pain still locked up inside. If she told him now, she might lose him completely.

Alex tore his shirt off and tossed it on the floor. Slipping off his shoes, he kicked them into the corner. What did Joanne know about it? She didn't live in his shoes. She didn't know what it was like to watch your dreams fade away into a sea of nothingness.

He stripped off the rest of his clothes, except for his boxers. He let his hand run over the cotton, his finger tracing a faded yellow duck. He would treasure the gift forever, despite the worn fabric, and the threads hanging out of the seams.

His vibrant daughter had bounced into his room on Father's Day, carrying a present covered with blue and white wrapping paper. 'Daddy, Daddy, I got you a present. Mommy let me pick it out all by myself.' She had hopped up on the bed and smothered him with hugs and kisses. He remembered holding her high in the air, as he pretended to eat her belly while she giggled and squealed with delight.

His chest constricted, and his throat clogged at the memory. He remembered the excitement in her voice and the proud expression on her face at being old enough to pick her own present that year. The last present he'd ever receive from her.

How could he have been away so much? He should have been able to see his relationship with Valerie going down the drain. Should have been able to stop it before...

With sudden fury, his fist connected with the wall. Sharp, needle like pains raced through his hand and up his arm. He gave his hand a quick shake and stared at the red, swollen knuckles. Blood dripped down his middle finger. He sucked on his knuckle and gave his head a rueful shake. Chalk up another point on his stupidity meter.

Burdened with grief, he flopped on the bed and buried his face in his hands. For years he had managed to keep his emotions in check, but since Laryssa arrived, they'd hit him head on with the force of a tornado. Too much free time on his hands to dwell on his thoughts. No, that wasn't right. He tried to work, tried to keep busy. She kept slipping into his mind, making him think. She made him face the pain he wanted to forget. Made him remember what it was like to feel. Whenever she walked in the room, his heart rate sped up, and his hands itched to touch her. The vortex that swirled around her sucked him in, knocking all common sense right out of him.

At least one of them still had their senses. She didn't seem to have any trouble walking away, although he could feel the passion burning beneath the surface. His groin stirred to life. "Not now, you stupid thing," he mumbled.

The door squeaked behind him. He looked over his shoulder, and there she stood. Cursing, he tossed the comforter over him. *Perfect timing.* He glared at her.

She shifted uncomfortably. "I heard a bang and wanted to make sure everything was okay."

"Yes. Go back to bed," he snapped. He didn't want her to come closer, didn't want her to see his obvious discomfort that the comforter only half hid, not when his emotions were this raw. He adjusted the comforter and winced as part of the comforter brushed his sore hand.

She walked towards him and gasped. He watched her gaze go from his hand to the indent in the wall. He could see the gears turning as she came to her conclusion. She quirked her eyebrows up at him, and he shrugged.

Shaking her head, she headed into the bathroom. He hardened even more as his eyes followed the gentle sway of her hips. He didn't want to be aroused, not by her, and especially not while he lay virtually naked on his bed. He sat up, still keeping himself covered with the comforter.

"I told you to go back to bed!" he shouted at doorway.

Shortly, she re-appeared, carrying a first aid kit. "You need someone with two hands to help." She struggled to lower herself to her knees on the floor in front of him. After opening the first aid kit, she reached for his hand with an antiseptic wipe, getting dangerously close to his hidden bulge.

He shoved her hand away with his good hand. "Don't you listen? I said—"

"I heard what you said. Now, quit being a baby, and let me help." She rolled her eyes and reached for him again.

He wrapped his good hand around her wrist. "Unless you want to give me what I really need, I suggest you leave the room." With his sore hand, he tore back the comforter and watched her eyes register his reaction to her. He hadn't planned on being so blunt, but damn it, she wouldn't listen.

She drew in a sharp breath, and her eyes widened in surprise. "Surely you can control your raging sex hormones for two minutes while we fix this up." She peeled his fingers off her wrist and went to reach for the first aid supplies again.

His fist slammed down on the bedside table, and he watched her jump in surprise. "Get out of here, will you!"

She struggled to stand up and lost her balance, landing on her hands to cushion the short fall. He noticed she had tears in her eyes when she finally managed to stand up. Holding her head high, she turned and walked out of the room. He felt like punching another wall but opted not to this time. His hand still hurt like hell.

He fumbled with the first aid kit and cleaned the wound on his hand, mumbling words that would make Joanne rinse his mouth out with soap. How could he be so attracted to Laryssa, yet despise her all at the same time? On one hand, he wanted to hold on to her and never let go. On the other, he wanted to kick her behind to kingdom come. Go back in time and never meet her in the elevator. At least, he'd still be at peace or close to it anyway.

A cool draught blew in from the open balcony door and swirled around his sweat laden body. He welcomed the chill of the night air. The breeze cooled the fire that raged out of control inside him. Overwhelming exhaustion knocked him back on the bed. If he felt like this after every meeting with Laryssa, he'd be dead before his next birthday. Either he'd die from wanting her so badly, or she'd kill him for overstepping his bounds.

Laryssa waddled down the hallway as fast as she could and didn't stop until she stood safely behind her bedroom door. She hunched over and gasped for air, which seemed to be in short supply. Alex and Aidan were so alike. The look in his eyes and the bang of his fist on the table scared her senseless.

Alex had shown her compassion and sympathy this past month, but his anger always simmered beneath the surface. Did he have a time bomb inside him waiting to explode, just like Aidan? After tonight, she didn't want to wait around and find out. His fist could be coming towards her next time. She'd been a punching bag enough in her life and would never put herself in that position again.

Come morning, she'd take the first taxi home.

CHAPTER ELEVEN

Laryssa pulled her suitcase out of the closet and started to pack her clothes when there was a knock at the door. “Come in.”

Joanne limped into the room, favoring her right leg more than usual, and eyed the clothes on the bed. “You aren't leaving, are you?” she asked with a frown as she settled on the side of the bed.

“Joanne, you know I love you. But Alex...well...he...” She couldn't quite find the words she wanted to say for fear of hurting the older woman's feelings.

“Is stubborn, rude, and in need of a good kicking?” Joanne gave an all-knowing smile and grabbed Laryssa's hand, pulling her down beside her. “Oh, my sweet child, there is a lot you still don't know.”

“Then why doesn't he tell me?”

“To tell means he has to remember. There is a war going on inside him. Has been ever since...” Joanne let her voice trail off.

“Ever since?”

“I'm sorry, my dear. It's not my place to tell. But I will tell you that he has never recovered.”

Never recovered? He certainly looked perfectly healthy to her, other than the anger he carried. “After seeing him lose it last night, I'm not about to stick around and wait for him to take it out on me.”

Joanne's eyes widened. "You think he'd hurt you?"

She looked down at her hands and ran her thumb over her bare ring finger. "It wouldn't be the first time."

"You poor child, no wonder last night frightened you." Joanne put her arm around Laryssa's shoulders. "I know he displays anger, but I promise you that he would never hurt you. If he was going to hurt anyone, he'd have hurt me ages ago." She chuckled. "I've been in his face enough. He just needs someone to love him, no matter what. Help him see it's worth opening his heart again."

"Is that why you've stayed here so long? He couldn't be easy to work for."

"There isn't any other place I'd rather be. He really is a caring, loving man. You must have at least seen that, or you wouldn't have agreed to marry him," Joanne said with a certainty. "In the last ten years, he's never been this serious over anyone. He must have seen something in you to ask you to marry him."

She couldn't disagree with her about the caring part. Alex held her during her nightmare, stroked her back when she'd been sick, and agreed to marry her to protect her. Last night, however, reminded her of a time she'd rather forget.

Joanne stood up and walked to the door. "Come with me. I want to show you something."

She led them outside, across a small open field, and then into an old wooden red barn. They hid behind a stack of hay, which stood about ten feet tall. The barn had a fresh smell to it as though it hadn't been used in years.

"Watch." The older woman pointed towards another door.

Within moments, Alex appeared, carrying a small bowl. He walked over to the corner where there was a large trough, placed the bowl on the ground, and whistled. Laryssa heard the rustling of hay, followed by a noise that sounded like a cat meowing. A brown and black tabby cat approached him and rubbed up against Alex's leg.

Laryssa heard him murmuring to the cat in a quiet voice. She was unable to make out his words, but the cat rubbed up against him again and appeared to be enjoying the conversation.

"He found the cat injured outside the fence about two months ago and has been taking care of her since then. She, also, has a litter of kittens hidden in there somewhere," Joanne whispered. "They are just little darlings. She only lets Alex get close though."

Her heart warmed as she watched Alex interact with the cat. He took in stray animals, too, did he? Intriguing. Alex stood, brushed the hay off his pants, and looked their way as if he sensed them. She pressed up against the stack of hay and prayed he wouldn't come their way. Her prayer was answered when he turned and left the barn.

He proved to be an enigma to Laryssa. Could it be he would never hurt her? No man so gentle with animals could be capable of anything as horrendous as what Aidan put her through. Yet the hole in his wall showed her what his fist could do. She started to understand why his family wanted him to get help. Of course, she shouldn't talk because she has issues of her own. Maybe sticking around a bit longer wouldn't hurt.

Don't forget about the note. She shivered. How could she have forgotten about it? Living in the safety of this place had given her a sense of security. Well, for the most part, when Alex didn't go into one of his rages. Now she knew something happened in the past that made him this way, and no one has been able to help him so far. Could she be the one to break through the barrier he built around his heart? No, she wouldn't get involved. The last time she thought she could help someone, it turned out she needed help instead.

"Shall we go inside?" A woman's voice pierced her thoughts.

She turned and found Joanne staring at her. "Oh, sorry, I forgot you were there."

"Hey, you're not old enough to go absentminded yet." Joanne winked at her with her good eye. "Here, give an old woman a hand. My leg isn't what it used to be."

She put her arm around Joanne and helped her toward the house. "What happened?"

Joanne stayed quiet for a moment then said, "I was in a car accident many years ago. It's usually not too bad, but if the weather is about to change it flares up."

"I'm sorry. Was anyone else in the car with you?"

When the older woman didn't speak, Laryssa looked at her. Her shoulders hunched over, and a tear was sparkling in the corner of her eye. "I'm sorry, I shouldn't have asked."

"No, it's all right, my dear. Scott, my husband, was driving the car when the accident happened. He didn't make it."

"I'm so sorry." Life was not fair. Tears fought to come to the surface.

Joanne gave her a sad smile and a gentle squeeze on the arm. "Aw, you are a sweetheart, but don't cry, or you'll make me start."

As they walked back to the house, Laryssa realized that staying here would be safer than going back home. At least she had Joanne. Someone who could understand the pain she went through. Alex, well, he was a whole other ball game. And in terms of the note, she didn't even want to try and guess what author wanted.

The stalker's fists clenched so hard that his dirty, uneven nails dug into his skin. "Where the bloody hell is she?" He'd been watching her place day and night for the last month, but no sign of her. The witch had outmaneuvered him again. She had probably put that lame-ass guy under her spell, too. When he first saw that man in her house, he thought he was going psycho. The man looked like Aidan. But that was wrong, so wrong. Right?

'You aren't gonna get her now. He's back!'

He watched the man interact with his woman. Aidan would never have comforted her or have been so gentle. He had clapped with glee upon the realization she was still a free woman. When he watched Laryssa touch the man back, he wanted to march over there and kill the intruder. No one was supposed to touch her but him.

'Do it!'

'The gun. You know where the gun is. You could end it now.'

But he didn't. He had ignored the voices, and now she was gone. If he could find out the man's name, he'd find her again. She was probably staying with him like the whore she was. Maybe, if he called Matt, his detective friend, he would be able to track her down. After all, he did go out of his way to help Matt retrieve lost case files on a company computer that had crashed. The man owed him a favor.

He grabbed the cordless and sat down in the computer chair, placing his feet up on the desk. He dialed the number while his chair teetered on its back legs.

“Thank you for calling D&A Enterprises, Julie speaking. How may I direct your call?”

Go shove your cheeriness up your ass, lady.

“Get me Matt.”

'You should do it for her,' a voice whispered in his head.

A few moments later, the detective answered the phone. “Matt speaking. Can I help you?”

He let a sinister grin spread across his face. “You can indeedy.”

“Oh, it's you,” Matt mumbled.

“Hey, you can at least show some enthusiasm for the man who saved your job.”

His friend let out a sigh. “Whatever. What do you want? I'm in the middle of reviewing a case.”

“I want you to find someone for me.”

“No! Last time I did that I nearly lost my job,” Matt's voice lowered to a whisper.

He heard a distinct click of a door closing in the background. “Just hear me out. A friend of mine died a few months back, and his wife has disappeared. Her stuff is still here. I think something may have happened.”

His friend snorted. “When have you ever been concerned about anyone but yourself?”

'You going to let him treat you like that?'

“Shut up.” He growled and pushed a little too hard on the desk with his feet. His chair toppled backwards, his arms and legs flailed in the air. He landed on the floor with a thud. “Shit!”

"I'm hanging up now. I've got work to do," Matt said with exasperation.

"Wait, wait." He gripped the phone tight. Matt had to help him, or he'd never find her. "I didn't mean you."

"All right, tell me what's up."

He told Matt of Laryssa and the mystery guy but kept all the seedy details to himself. His penis hardened at the mention of her name. He lowered his zipper and freed himself from the confines of his black jeans.

"I'll see what I can do, but I can't promise anything." With that, Matt ended the call.

The phone almost slipped out of his sweaty palm at the anticipation of all that was to come. He placed the phone back on the base. With his excitement growing, he let his hand roam over his erection. She'd pay for leaving him, and he would enjoy every moment of it.

Laryssa shuddered. An underlying dread rushed through her system.

"Are you okay?" Joanne asked.

"I..." She paused, as she surveyed the living room where they had retired after lunch. "I can't really explain. I just had a very bad feeling all of a sudden."

"You aren't still worried about Alex, are you?"

"No. Well, maybe a little. But this was different." She shook her head. "Like someone was walking over my grave."

Laryssa slid a hand behind her back while she sat on the couch to help relieve an ache that resided in her lower back. The aches were more commonplace than she cared to admit. The children rolled in her womb, adding to the pain as they kicked her ribs. But relief filled her each time they moved.

"I'm sure it's nothing, my dear." Joanne gave her a quick pat on the knee and then placed her hand on the arm of the sofa, pulling herself up. "I had better go see what I can sort for supper."

Laryssa laid her head back against the sofa and closed her eyes.

Suddenly, she had the oddest feeling that someone was watching her. She opened her eyes, and her hand flew to her throat. Her heart pattered beneath the palm of her hand. "Gosh, do you have to keep doing that?"

"I like seeing you look relaxed. Sue me." Alex flopped on to the couch next to her.

She looked down and saw the mess of a wrap on his injured hand, the result of a one-person job. "I could have helped you with that, you know."

"Last night wasn't exactly the best night for me. Can I treat you to dinner to make up for it?"

"I'm afraid I'm in no condition to go anywhere. My back is hurting dreadfully tonight."

"How about dinner on the veranda with me?" he asked.

She guessed they were finally getting somewhere. He was actually asking instead of ordering her. That had to be a step in the right direction. "You forgot to say something."

"Pretty please." He looked at her with wide puppy dog eyes and made whimpering sounds before letting a grin spread across his face.

She couldn't suppress a giggle. "How can I refuse the puppy dog eyes?"

"You can't refuse 'em, eh? I'll have to remember that." His grin took on a more wicked style, and his arm slid around her shoulders.

"Alex, I only agreed to dinner, nothing more." She shrugged off his arm, but not before a shiver revealed her inner emotional turmoil when his fingers brushed the bare skin of her neck.

Her body wanted his touch in a more specific place. No amount denial seemed to make it change its mind. It irritated her to no end. How could she want his touch when he looked so much like...her mind trailed off. One side of her wanted him, but the other side of her couldn't escape from his actions of the previous night.

"You scared me last night," she said.

"I'm sorry. You came in at the worst time, but I shouldn't have lost my temper with you. I was not myself, and I feel horrible." His arm came around her shoulders again, and he squeezed gently.

She leaned her head back and closed her eyes. His hand stayed on her shoulder, playing with a lock of her hair. She just couldn't deny herself one simple little touch. His fingertips dipped to her shoulder and worked their magic on a knot that had permanently attached to the muscles at the base of her neck.

"Here, why don't you sit on the floor, and I'll give you a massage?" he offered.

Laryssa looked down to the floor and then back up at him. "Are you nuts? If I sit on the floor, I'd be like a turtle trying to get back up. Trust me. It's not a pretty sight. I only do it if I have to."

"I'd help you up."

"Thanks for the offer, but I'm comfortable here."

As much as she liked this side of Alex, it unnerved her. When he showered her with compassion and sensitivity, she didn't have any strength to fight him. It showed her what type of a man he could be when he let go of the pain. The type of man any woman would be lucky to have. The man in the barn and the man sitting beside her right now were the real Alex. She could feel it. He could crack jokes, laugh, and love like everyone else. Who else would give her space in their house when she needed protection?

She looked up at Alex who seemed to be watching her attentively. When their eyes met, a spark ignited inside her. She drew in a sharp breath. Here sat a man who could very well steal her heart, and that scared the crap out of her.

Due to her earlier revelations, Laryssa couldn't seem to initiate conversation that evening on the veranda. If she opened her mouth, she knew her emotions would be on display.

Joanne really set the scene for them with the candlelight dinner and the soft music playing in the background. The walls and the roof were made of glass, allowing them to see outside. The stars twinkled in the clear night sky, and the moon, which appeared to be resting on the top of a tree before continuing its journey, filled her with a peace she never thought possible. She looked at him and then looked away again.

"You appear to be looking everywhere but at me." His eyes were wide with amusement, and a smile played on his lips.

Her cheeks heated. "Am I? Sorry, it's just so beautiful out here."

"You got that right." He kept his gaze directly on her as he spoke.

She knew he didn't mean the stars or the moon like she did. The look in his eyes made her whole body wake up and take notice. She wiped her hands with her napkin before picking up her fork.

He took a bite of his food and ate silently for a moment but never once looked away from her. "I mean it, you know. You really are beautiful."

"Me? Yeah, right. I'm like a beached whale." She let out a short laugh.

They took a few more bites in silence before she finally decided to break it again. "Did you always want to help your grandfather run the family business?"

Alex gave a nonchalant shrug. "It's always been there, and I never really thought about doing anything else. My grandfather introduced me to the business as soon as I was old enough to work."

"What made you take over this office?"

"You didn't hear that we opened another office?"

She shook her head, her mouth full.

"We opened a new office in the States, and Brendan seemed to be the best person to move. He doesn't have family tying him down. He agreed to help establish the new office, and I took over this one."

"How come I've never seen you at the office before?" She'd been wondering about that for a while. They lived in neighboring cities, but they never met before, and Aidan never spoke about ever seeing anyone who looked like him. True, there were millions of people, so the odds of meeting were slim, but she worked for his family's company twice now, and yet their paths never crossed. She couldn't help but wonder if Aidan knew about him. He'd been so adamant about not wanting her to work. Could his excuse about her being attracted to her boss been a cover up just to get her out of the company?

"I've spent the majority of my time traveling, visiting different offices to oversee major projects. It was just a recent decision my grandfather and I made to take over for Brendan. The last time I was here was during summer of last year."

"Does your father work for the same company?"

For a second, he didn't speak. His eyes flickered to the candle in the center of the table and focused on the flame. "My father died before I was born." His voice was void of emotion, but his eyes carried a world of hurt.

"I'm sorry. I know how you feel."

"Do you?" His voice had such a despondent ring to it that her heart bled for him.

She reached across the table and placed her hand on his, which rested on the side of his plate, curled around a fork. "You aren't the only one to lose family, Alex."

Her words seemed to break him out of his mood and his features softened. "It's my turn to be sorry. I forgot that you lost your parents and your husband."

The last thing she wanted to talk about was her husband, but it was inevitable. She stood up and walked closer to the glass and rested her forehead against it. Moments later, his hands closed over her shoulders. She reveled in the moment and leaned back against him, drawing on his strength.

Tears spilled down her face and landed on the back of Alexander's hand. "I seem to have this effect on you. I can't say it's very ego boosting."

"I, well—it's just..." She just couldn't find the right words. "When I look at you, I can see him, and it brings all my memories back."

He removed his hands from her shoulders and wrapped his arms around her, letting his chin rest on the top of her head. "Your husband?"

"Yes."

"How long ago did he die?" he asked with a gentle and soothing voice.

"December." Her voice sounded hollow even in her own ears.

Alex had to force himself not to freeze up. If he had had a brother before, he certainly as hell didn't have one now. He turned her in his arms and placed a hand under her chin, making her look up at him. She resisted. He caught a glimpse of pain in her eyes before she buried her face in his chest.

He stroked her hair. "Do I really look that much like him that it hurts you to look at me?" he asked hoarsely.

She nodded her head.

"Do you miss him?"

Her shoulders rose as she took a deep breath. "Yes and no." She pulled away from him and wrapped her arms around herself before facing him. "I miss what we could have had. But...no. I don't miss him. I could never miss him." His chest constricted at the vehemence in her voice.

Her eyes widened, and her hands slapped over her mouth. "Gosh, I sound so horrible. What's wrong with me?" Without waiting for an answer, she turned and left him standing on the veranda alone.

"Absolutely nothing," he whispered to the empty doorway.

After last night, he thought she'd run the first chance she got. The girl has got more guts than anyone he'd ever met. What did Aidan put her through that made her hate him so much? His stomach cramped at the thought of Aidan hurting Laryssa, damaging her tender heart. Could he have hurt her as much as Valerie hurt him? He knew the time had come to discover the truth.

CHAPTER TWELVE

Laryssa entered her bedroom and found Joanne sitting on the bed, crying. In her hands she held the photograph that had landed under the bed weeks ago. Her heart started to pound at the look of dismay on the older woman's face.

"Joanne, are you okay?" she inquired softly.

She looked up at Laryssa, and her mouth moved, but nothing came out. She sat down and put her arm around Joanne's trembling shoulders.

"It's him, isn't it? It's really him." Joanne finally said, turning the photograph towards her.

"That's my late husband, Aidan."

"Aidan," she repeated as though testing the name. "They look so identical."

"Don't I know it!"

The older woman's face lost all color, and she stared at Laryssa as if her words just dawned on her. "Late, that means..."

Had Alex not informed her of what happened? Laryssa took a breath before speaking. "He died in an accident."

"What...what happened?" Joanne asked in a voice barely above a whisper, as a tear slid down her cheek.

"He'd been drinking and got behind the wheel. He wasn't able to react quickly enough to the corner. The roads were icy and..." Her voice broke, unable to continue.

Joanne didn't say a word for a moment, as if trying to process all the information. With an unsteady voice, she asked, "How'd you find Alex?"

"It's more like Alex found me. We met when he took over the company I worked for." She searched Joanne's face for answers but found none. "Is there something you're not telling me?"

Joanne ran her hands up and down her legs. "I knew one day this would happen. That's why I was so against their decision."

"Whose decision?" Laryssa rubbed Joanne's back, hoping to encourage her.

She pulled away from her and stood up on shaky legs. "I'm sorry. I can't. I made a promise."

"Joanne, please. These are Aidan's children. I deserve to know the truth," she pleaded.

Joanne reached out and touched her belly, her face ghostly pale. "I can't. Alex will hate me. He'll never forgive me for what I've done."

"Why would Alex hate you?" she pressed further. There was no longer any doubt in her mind. Joanne was hiding something. Hopefully, she'd finally get some answers to her questions. Provided her stomach, which had begun twisting in knots, cooperated long enough.

Joanne stood there, shaking her head. Her eyes frozen on the picture which Laryssa held in her possession.

"You know about Aidan, don't you?" Laryssa stared at her in shock.

They both froze in unison as footsteps resounded on the hardwood floor in the hallway. Alex appeared in the doorway. He looked from Laryssa to Joanne. His face softened with concern at the look on Joanne's face. "Are you okay?"

Joanne looked down at the photo Laryssa held in her hands and then back up at Alex. She opened her mouth as if to speak, but a sob came out instead. "Excuse me."

He walked over to Laryssa and snatched the paper out of her hand.

"Hey, that's mine." She tried to get it back, but he held it up out of reach.

"First, I want to see what has made Joanne so upset." He lowered the photo.

Waiting for his response, Laryssa chewed on her lip. She watched his jaw muscles twitch, and his forehead furrow.

"I don't recall this photo being taken." He turned it around and around in his hands as if maybe changing the angle might make photograph change.

"That's because the photo isn't of you. May I have it back, please?" She held out her hand, but he moved back away from her, shaking his head. The muscles in her neck seized up, and she wiped her sweaty palms on her slacks.

He paced the length of the bedroom, stopping every few seconds to stare at the photo. "It's not possible."

She watched him wage war with himself about whether to believe the picture. In this day and age, photographs could be altered and what looked like truth could easily be a lie. When he turned his ice-cold eyes on her, she knew he made his decision. Her heart lodged in her throat.

"You're good, but not good enough," he sneered. "It's a damn computer printout." He crumpled the paper and tossed it at her. "Did Valerie put you up to this?"

Laryssa stared at the scrunched-up picture on the floor at her feet. She fought back the tears that sought to form in her eyes. "You jerk! That was the only picture I had left of him." The one picture she allowed herself to keep to share with her children.

"Give up the act." He leaned down so his face was nose-to-nose with hers. "You, my dear little missy, are a plain and simple con artist, and a lousy one at that."

She shoved him away and massaged the back of her head where sharp spasms of pain radiated through her skull, right to the back of her eyelids. *Why now!* Alex screaming at her was bad enough. She didn't need a migraine on top of it all.

She squinted at him. "If you think I'm capable of something like that, then you don't know me at all."

"You're right." He threw his hands up in the air. "Anytime I try to find out anything you run away from me."

"Excuse me." She turned and staggered towards the bathroom but found herself being pulled back by a hand on her arm. "Get your hand off me."

"No!" He tightened his grip on her arm. "You are not running away from me again."

"I can do whatever I want." She stomped on his foot. When he didn't let go, she looked up at him.

"After the first couple stomps, I learned my lesson." With a smirk, he tapped on the toe of his boot. "Steel toed boots."

"Lucky me," she murmured. "Look, all I was going to do is grab some Tylenol before this headache gets worse, unless you feel like holding my hair while I puke in the toilet again?"

"If you go in, I go in. I'm not giving you a chance to lock the door." He steered her toward the bathroom and walked in with her.

A sharp pain throbbed behind her eye, making the side of her face feel numb. How could he not believe her? He had the proof right in front of him. What else could she say to make him believe her? She took the pain killers with a glass of water and turned to face him, massaging her temples to ease the incessant pain.

"If you don't believe me, then ask Joanne."

Alex moved to the side to let her out of the bathroom and watched as she settled on the edge of the bed. She had her eyes closed, and her fingers moved rhythmically against her temples. He glanced at the photo on the ground. Every pore in his body wanted to scream denial. In his mind's eye, he could still see the green eyes looking back at him.

He lifted his hand and ran it along his own chin. It was the exact same shape as the one in the picture. His fingers traced the bridge of his nose. Was his nose really crooked? He stepped back into the bathroom to peek in the mirror and breathed a sigh of relief to see his nose was straight as usual.

By the time he returned to the bedroom, she was lying on the bed with one arm draped over her eyes.

"Can you turn the overhead light off for me, please?" she asked in a weak, strained voice.

He walked over and flicked the light switch down. The room flooded with darkness. Knowing every inch of the room, he made his way deftly to her bed.

"Why did you lie to me, Laryssa?" When she remained silent, he continued, "Is it because of the stalker, or is there even a stalker?" He could hear her breath hitch, but still, she never said anything. "What is it? Your bills? Did you need to find a rich sucker to bail you out?"

He knew these descriptions didn't fit with the type of person she was. But thinking that more lies reigned in his life and resonated from his loved ones was too much to handle. The firm foundation he built his life on no longer seemed stable. He didn't want to believe it.

She flicked on the bedside lamp, which gave off just enough light for him to see her flushed cheeks. With a shaky hand, she pointed toward the door. "Get out. Just get out," she croaked.

"In case you've forgotten, this is my house." He crossed his arms and looked at her with raised eyebrows. "Where did you get the photo?"

"Fine. You wanna know where I got the photograph." She swung her legs off the bed and pushed herself up off the bed. "I got..." Her hand flew to her head, and he watched her body sway to the right.

He grabbed her arm and helped steady her. "What's wrong?" he asked.

"Let me go," she growled. "I'm fine."

They stood so close that he had to glance down to look at her. He found himself looking down the neckline of her dress. Her breasts were heaving up and down with each deep breath she took. God help him. She still had the power to arouse, despite her deceit. Taking a couple of deep breaths, he released her and stepped away.

"I printed that picture off my computer. He emailed it to me on one of his trips last year so I wouldn't forget him."

"How romantic," he said sarcastically. "You can't honestly expect me to believe that the picture is real." He released the top button of his shirt and slipped a finger in his collar, pulling it away from his neck.

She covered her forehead with her hand and squeezed her eyes closed. "Romantic? Sure, it was romantic, all right." Laryssa opened her eyes and looked at him, blinking rapidly. "You want to know about the email that went with it, hmm? You want to know the horror I went through with him." She walked towards Alex and poked him in the chest. "He sent me that damn picture and said if he ever found out that I've been with anyone else, this picture would be the last thing I'd ever see. Now, you tell me if that is romantic."

He cringed and rubbed his chest when she turned away from him. She walked to the closet and pulled out her suitcase. He watched as she moved to the dresser.

"Why would you bother to keep it?"

"What do you think this bump is?" She paused from her packing and pointed towards her stomach. "I kept it for them, so they'd know what he looked like."

"I can't believe it." He shook his head. His heart hammered in his chest, and an intense dread filled him.

"You know what? I don't care what you believe. I didn't come here to be yelled at."

"No, you just came here so you could get my money." He knew he'd delivered a low blow, but they just kept spilling out of his mouth. "And you running away proves there's no stalker."

Her hand froze on the shirt she just placed in the suitcase. "I never had any trouble with stalkers till you showed up. Maybe, *you're* my stalker."

The emphasis she placed on *you're* annoyed him. He opened his house to her, and she as good as accused him of being a stalker. "I'm no stalker, lady, but I have to wonder if *you* are."

Her face paled at his accusation, and she placed her hands on the edge of the bed. She breathed in deeply before speaking, "If you didn't believe me, then why did you kidnap me? Why bring me all the way here and, at the first real proof, attack me? You are no better than him." She slammed her suitcase closed and stormed to the door of the bedroom.

He watched her stop when she reached the door. Her suitcase dropped, and she hunched over with a moan, clutching her stomach. The thought that she was faking it jumped into his head, until he approached her and saw the look of sheer terror on her face. He wanted to smack his forehead.

Her pregnancy was high risk, and now he might have made it worse for her. No matter how upset she made him, the children weren't to blame. What if she was right? What if they were related? He didn't want to believe her, but a corner of his heart kept nagging at him. His chest tightened, and a chill ran through him.

"Are you okay?" He put his arm around her to help support her.

She struggled to push him away, but it didn't take long before she gave up and allowed him to help, and that alone worried him. He would give anything for her to attempt to step on his foot. That would, at least, let him know she was okay. Anything other than her standing there hunched over, moaning.

Instead, she spoke in a quiet voice, "What do you care?"

"I may be angry, but I'm not heartless. I'm calling an ambulance." He stuck his head out the door. "Joanne, get in here."

When Joanne reached the door, she glared at him. "What have you done to the poor girl?" She walked to the corner of the room and pulled a chair closer to Laryssa.

Alex helped her sit down. "Please, I already feel responsible. Stay with her while I call for an ambulance." He started to leave the room.

"Alex, just take her in your car. It will be quicker."

"Come on, Laryssa." He went to help her up, but she shied away from him and leaned towards Joanne.

"Joanne, I'm scared," she said, in a voice thick with worry.

"It's all right, my dear. You'll be fine." She gave Laryssa a gentle, reassuring squeeze on the arm. "Come now. Let's get you to the hospital."

Alex's hands gripped the steering wheel as he dodged traffic. Both women were seated in the back. He couldn't help but notice how Joanne avoided meeting his gaze. He wondered if maybe Laryssa was right, and Joanne really did know something. She'd reacted to him in a similar way when she saw the photo, like Laryssa did the day she met him in the office. With that thought, the evidence started to lean in a direction he didn't want to go.

He gave his head a shake and concentrated on the task at hand, getting Laryssa to the hospital safely. He pulled into the emergency parking and rushed inside to grab a wheelchair.

When he came back out, Joanne helped Laryssa out of the car and into the wheelchair. Once inside, the nurse directed them up to the maternity floor. His heart thumped wildly in his chest as they stood in the elevator. He glanced at the two women, wondering if they could hear it, too.

They waited outside while Laryssa was examined by the nurse. Alex sank into a nearby chair and leaned forward, placing his head into his hands. "What have I done, Joanne? What if she..."

"What's done is done. We can only pray and hope it all works out. We got her here pretty quickly." She gave his leg a pat.

"Somehow that doesn't make me feel any better." He sat up and leaned his head back against the wall. "I'm ashamed of some of the things I said to her."

"As you should be, she is your fiancée. Why would you take this out on her?"

"I don't know. Maybe because I've only known her a short time, and I don't want to believe that she's been more truthful to me than my own fucking family."

He waited for her to correct him on his language, like she always did, but she remained silent. Her hands repeatedly smoothed the wrinkles out of her skirt. When he stilled her hands, she looked at him with downcast eyes. "Joanne, I know there is something you aren't telling me."

"Let's concentrate on Laryssa, and go from there," she pleaded.

He thought about what Laryssa said before she attempted to leave the bedroom. No one would make things up about being abused. Would they? His gut told him she wasn't the type to lie, but his trust in woman waned years ago. Now, he could be facing a greater betrayal than anything he has ever gone through before. Where everyone he knew, except one person, might be involved in it. And that one person would probably never speak to him again. He fought against the thoughts that swirled around and around in his head. *Is this what insanity felt like?*

She affected him like no other. Even when he was mad at her, he still wanted help her. He loved her spunk and her tenacity. After everything she'd been through, she still had the guts to stand up to him even with having been abused by the guy who looked like him. *Wow, hold that thought*. He smacked the side of his head. Did he actually believe her story? The twinge in his heart gave him the answer. He couldn't deny it anymore.

He turned to Joanne. "There is something I need to know before I go in there. Do I have a brother?"

CHAPTER THIRTEEN

Alex's life as he knew it, hung in the balance as he waited for Joanne to answer. Just when he thought she'd speak, the nurse walked out of Laryssa's room.

"We believe it is just a false alarm. However, considering the pains are strong and occurring quite often, we are going to monitor her overnight and make sure it doesn't progress. We've also given her something to help her sleep. She needs to relax as much as possible so that she will carry the twins closer to term."

"Thank the Lord." Joanne clapped her hands together and hurried into Laryssa's room. Once again, she'd dodged the question. What did he need to do to get an answer out of her? Super glue her to a chair? She was usually a cheerful, talkative woman. But this was like trying to get into a bank safe with a small crowbar. Damn near impossible.

He walked into the room and found them huddled together. Joanne comforted Laryssa as a mother would comfort a daughter, evidence of the close bond between them. Something Joanne and Valerie never managed to do. Again, an ache rose in his chest. Everything was getting too close for comfort. Too much like a family, one that he would never have again. He had to get out of there, had to get out of the very hospital that claimed her.

"I'm going to wait for you in the car, Joanne." He walked up to Laryssa and bent to kiss her cheek, but she turned her head away. What was he thinking? As if she would let him kiss her after the way he acted. Unable to think of anything else to say, he gave a quick nod and left the room.

Laryssa leaned back in the bed and turned her head towards Joanne. "I'm sorry to have caused so much trouble."

Joanne put her hands on Laryssa's cheeks. "Listen to me, my dear. You have been no trouble at all. I've enjoyed having you around. It's Alex who needs to control himself."

"But I can't be the one he practices control on." She shook her head, and her stomach churned. Tears fell down her cheeks. She brushed them away, but they kept falling. "Take care of him for me, please, Joanne."

After all the troubles she went through, didn't she deserve to have at least one thing that went perfectly? Continuing to put herself and the twins in harm's way wouldn't allow her pregnancy to progress safely. She needed to keep control of her own life, think of the babies first and not her own heart. The same heart that wanted to beat twice as fast whenever he stepped in the room. She had to stop thinking about how her stomach fluttered with excitement whenever he was near and how her legs would go like liquid when his fingers created a magical trail down her bare skin.

"Are you hot, my dear? You're flushed?" Joanne placed a cool hand on her forehead.

"I'm sorry. I must have faded there for a minute." She let out a silent prayer of thanks that Joanne hadn't discovered the direction of her thoughts. "Thank you so much for all you've done for me."

"Why does this sound like goodbye?" Joanne let her hands come to rest on top of Laryssa's.

"I've got problems to work through myself. I can't handle his, too."

"He was just shocked, sweetie. After all, it's not every day you look into a picture and see another version of yourself." Joanne squeezed her hand. "Think of how surprised you'd be."

"It hasn't been easy on me either. For Pete's sake, I thought he was a ghost, or maybe I should say a poltergeist." She clutched the bed linen with both hands. "Sometimes, I'm not sure if I'm having a nightmare, or if this is really happening."

"But it did get better, and I know this will too. Please, just give him time to adjust."

Better? That was a matter of opinion. At times, she really enjoyed Alex's company, but today, after he exploded, it was just another piece added to the Aidan puzzle. One she'd been hoping to lose the pieces to.

"I know you love him, Joanne, and that you don't think he is capable of hurting me. But after the life I've led, I need to take care of me and them." She waved a hand over her belly.

Joanne lowered her eyes to the floor for a moment and clasped her hands on her lap. She looked up with a resounding sadness in her eyes. "I can't change your mind, can I?"

Laryssa shook her head, afraid that she might start to cry if she said anything else. She would miss the time they had spent together. She covered Joanne's hands, which still clung together on her lap. "Please say you'll come visit me when the babies are born?"

"I do wish I could convince you to stay. Alex needs you."

She snorted. "Alex doesn't need anyone. He most certainly doesn't want or need me. He made that perfectly clear earlier."

"He may not think so, but he does. There is one thing I've learned, sweetie. True love doesn't give up when the going gets tough. It grabs on and never let's go." Joanne glanced towards the door and pushed herself up off the bed. "I'd better go, Alex is waiting. Think about what I said."

She leaned over and gave Laryssa a quick kiss on the forehead, then limped out of the room. Remorse ran rampant through Laryssa. Joanne was a sweet old lady who didn't deserve to be lied to. They'd let her think they were in love. She didn't know why she didn't tell her the truth now that she was leaving. Sparing her feelings?

Sleeping in her own bed again would be pure sweet heave—

Laryssa's hands flew to her mouth and her insides tightened before she even finished the thought. She couldn't go home.

Alex rubbed his sweaty palms on his pants as he sat in the car. He looked at the hospital doors and dread ran through him. He sighed with relief when a familiar face walked out. Twice in six weeks now he'd been forced to visit this hospital. He'd managed to avoid it for nearly ten years, not counting the time he broke his leg on a job site, and they carted him here while he cursed like crazy.

Joanne climbed into the car and shut the door.

"About time. What took you so long?" He gunned the engine and sped out of the hospital parking lot, needing to get as far away as possible. Away from the death and pain that ate away at him. Hospitals were supposed to help people, make them well again. They did the opposite for him. The further he stayed away from them, the better.

Joanne remained quiet for the whole trip, until the gate opened. "You know she's planning on leaving, don't you?"

His eye narrowed, and his grip tightened on the steering wheel. "Maybe it's for the best."

"Oh, pish tosh. She's the best thing that has happened to you. Are you telling me you're just going let her walk away? She's your fiancée."

Alex looked at her through his peripheral vision. She was perched sideways in her seat, staring at him with her eyebrows knitted together, and her mouth pressed in a crooked line. He recalled her telling him ages ago that she'd lost partial use of her face muscles due to an accident she was in before he was born. Another way the hospitals had failed his family. She'd been left with a permanent numb spot on her right cheek. The same cheek as her droopy eyelid.

"Or were you guys really engaged?" she asked.

That he could answer truthfully. He didn't want to go any deeper into detail. They shouldn't have lied to Joanne. There had never been any reason to in the past, and he isn't sure why he started now. The guilt of doing so kept him awake at night. That, and visualizing Laryssa's naked body down the hall. Then it dawned on him, that even though he'd told Laryssa it was to get his family off his back, he'd forgotten to tell his family he was engaged, except for Joanne. She wasn't technically family, just a long-time friend and employee.

He should have been more truthful to Joanne about everything, but he didn't want her to tell his grandparents about the current situation. He was still trying to wrap his head around the fact that he might have had a brother. Why had they kept them apart? The thought squeezed his heart, and intense sharp pains shot through him. Almost no denying it now, he'd seen the proof.

The car pulled to a stop and Joanne opened the door to get out. He grabbed her arm before she left the confines of the car. "What do you know about the picture?" He heard her breath hitch. "Come on, I know you know something."

She shook her head and tears filled her eyes. "I can't."

"For God's sake, what is the big secret? If I have a brother, I have a brother. It's not like finding out the truth will release the bubonic plague."

"Please, don't ask me. I can't tell you what you want to know."

Her eyes pleaded with him to let her go, but he didn't want to relent. He'd never treated Joanne this way before, but he needed to know. "Why can't you tell me, Joanne? Did I have a brother?"

Her shoulders shook with quiet sobs, but she didn't say a word.

He lifted her chin to gauge the reaction in her eyes. "Look at me, Joanne."

She averted her eyes.

"Damn it, look at me."

She sniffled and wiped her cheeks with the back of her hands, then said, "Don't use that tone with me, mister." She wagged her finger at him, but her tone didn't carry the usual zest when reprimanding him. It was just a diversion tactic.

Keeping eye contact with her, he asked his question again. Before she lowered her eyes this time, he knew the truth. “Why didn't anyone tell me?” He let her go and banged his fists on the steering wheel. The horn blared.

Joanne took off out the door and towards the house as quickly has her limp would carry her. He watched her go and made no move to stop her. He'd gotten his answer. He hadn't meant to frighten her, and, for that, guilt would eat at him till he apologized.

“Damn it.”

Another person also needed his apology. One who was now in the hospital because of him. He looked down at the clock and knew that tonight was out of the question. He was even more certain now that she deserved his protection. If she left, where would she go? She certainly couldn't go back to her house, not with that loser stalker lurking about. The thought of her not being safely tucked away in his house was enough to make a ball form in his chest.

But a brother? He had a brother. A cold chill washed over him, and Laryssa's words came back to him. Her husband—his brother—had died in December. His only link to Aidan now was the children in her belly. He couldn't let her walk away. They were his responsibility.

Alex had to control his feelings for her and do what he could to help them. He couldn't give them the love they might need, but he could give them a safe place, and when the danger finally moved on, and he found the answers he was looking for, he'd let her go. He ignored the voice in his head that kept calling him a liar.

Alex couldn't let go of the thought about what *being* with her might be like. And using the passion they fought with for another, more fulfilling, purpose. He knew that her body would be ready for him. Her warm, wet heat would beg him to bury himself inside her. His groin jumped to life at the thought of her closing around him as he entered her. Knowing she hadn't lied to him added more fuel to the growing desire. If his brother abused her, it was up to him to make up for it. The thought that someone had been cruel to her ate him up inside. No, he refused to let her leave. The time had come to pull out the heavy arsenal.

After he convinced her to stay, and he hoped to God, he could, he would have two other people to visit. His grandparents.

"Melissa, can I stay with you?" Laryssa asked, cradling the phone in the crook of her shoulder while she pulled the lid off her breakfast tray. She'd just finished explaining the situation to her friend, and her mood lightened just hearing Melissa's voice.

"Sure, I'll come down to the hospital and pick you up after work. Can you wait that long? If not, I can send hubby down." Laryssa heard the beep of a horn, and her friend swore into the phone.

"Are you okay?"

"Yeah, I'm fine, just some idiot not watching where he's going," her friend said, letting a few more curse words fly off her tongue.

"I'd better let you get off the phone before you get into an accident. I'll see you later when you get here. Thanks again."

"No problemo. Remind me to kick Alex's butt for you later."

Laryssa laughed. She would enjoy staying with her, at least until they could figure out who the stalker was. For a few minutes before she called Melissa, she'd wondered if it was a good idea. If the stalker knew where she was staying, it may put them at risk. Thankfully, Jamie, Melissa's husband, was a police officer. He'd be able to take care of her. She'd have to tell them about the note. Something she wasn't too keen on doing, especially if the psycho found out.

She walked into the bathroom to freshen up. "Belch. Jungle mouth." She stuck out her tongue. After going through her morning ritual of getting ready, she stepped out of the bathroom. Her mouth dropped open.

Much to her surprise, Alex was stretched out on her bed, playing with the buttons on the television remote. "I think it needs new batteries." He tossed it on the bedside table.

She tied her robe closed. Her heart skipped a couple beats

beneath it. “What are you doing here?” she asked once she found her voice.

“I've come to take you home.” He ran his fingers through his hair, moving back a piece that had fallen over his forehead. His cocky, crooked grin made her heart pound. One of these days, he would cause a heart attack on her poor overworked heart.

She closed her eyes and took in a deep breath, resting her hand on the door frame for balance. “I'm not going back.” She opened her eyes and looked at him, annoyed at the unsteady waver in her voice.

His grin turned into a frown, and his eyes lost their sparkle. He held out his hands, palms up. “For what it's worth, I'm sorry.”

“I'm sorry, too.” She broke eye contact and wrapped her arms around herself.

“Please go.”

His shoes squeaked on the polished floor, and she knew he was coming towards her. He reached out to touch her, but she moved away. “No.”

“Please, don't do this, Laryssa. I already feel bad.” He reached for her again, but she slapped his hand away.

“You expect me to feel sorry for you? Let's see now. You yelled at me and insulted me. Why should I care that you feel bad? What planet are you from?” She shoved by him and walked towards the door to get help.

“Joanne, in a roundabout way, admitted that Aidan was my brother.”

His words stopped her feet and her heart. With her back to him, she asked, “Are you sure?”

“Yes. You already knew, though, didn't you?”

She turned back to face him and nodded her head as tears cascaded down her cheeks. “Well, sort of. I thought you might be, but until now I didn't know for sure.” She looked down at her growing belly; the outline of a butt protruded next to her belly button. “You hear that, guys? You have family.”

Not her, though. Her family was gone, and Alex didn't love her.

Not that it should matter. She didn't love him either. She'd be fine...as long as she kept telling herself that.

"I didn't want it to be true, and I took it out on you. I apologize."

"Those are just words, Alex. Words I don't accept lightly anymore."

"I don't blame you. He abused you. It makes me sick knowing we're related." His lips pursed and his fingers curled. "Please give me a chance to show you not all guys are the same, or at least make up for our family name."

How Laryssa wished she could believe him, but after their fight yesterday her belief wavered. "I can't risk it with your temper. I have my children to worry about."

His eyes widened at her accusation and mouth dropped open. "Do you really think I'm so cruel that I'd risk hurting them? They are my blood."

"How should I know? You're the one who screamed and yelled at me yesterday." The time had come to stand on her own two feet, to be the boss of her life. She'd been a wimp the first time around, not standing up to Aidan, and nearly lost her life by not getting out.

He raked a hand through his hair. "I've already apologized for that. How many times do I have to say sorry?"

"I accept your apology, but I'm still not going back." She shook her head and folded her arms.

"Why the hell not?" He started to pace back and forth in the hospital room.

She was glad the nurses were outside in case he went into a rage. "Your temper, that's why. I need to relax, and I can't when I'm with you."

He turned his back on her, and she could hear him mumbling but couldn't catch any of the words. His shoulders rose with each deep breath he took.

After a minute, he turned back around, his shoulders slumped and hands in his pockets. "How about if I propose a truce? Please, you're my only connection to my brother."

"A truce? How would we manage that? All we've done since we've met is fight."

The corner of his mouth curled up. "I can think of a few other fun things we've done."

Heat rose in her cheeks. "You mean the kisses you stole."

"No, which you allowed." He tilted his head and flashed a sexy smile that caused her legs to wobble.

She threw her hands up in the air and shook her head. "See, it's not going to work."

He walked towards her, stopping only an arm length away. He reached out with his hand and cupped her chin. "On the contrary, I think it could work very well."

She knew she should move, that she should back away, but her feet wouldn't listen. Even as he brought his lips a fraction from hers, his breath drying the moisture on hers, she still couldn't move. She opened her mouth to lick her lips. The minute she did, he closed the distance. He tried to draw her closer but moaned as her belly bumped into him.

He continued his attack on her lips and, try as she might, she couldn't push him away. Their tongues met in a frantic war she didn't wish to stop. The anger which existed inside her faded away, replaced by a need so strong it had her wrapping her arms around his neck, afraid he might disappear at any moment. His hands rested on her hips. Her robe clenched in his fists. Each stroke of his tongue sent shivers of delight straight down her spine.

"Ahem." Someone coughed loudly behind them.

CHAPTER FOURTEEN

"I figured now was as good a time as any," the nurse said, standing in the doorway with a bundle of red roses in her arms.

Alex watched Laryssa walk toward the nurse and run her fingers along the edge of a rose petal. Her cheeks still rosy, and her lips swollen from his kiss. If he could see her eyes, which were hidden by her dark eyelashes, he knew they'd reflect the same desire that ran like a waterfall through him. Try as he might, he could not deny how his body came alive when she was around. He'd never been so hormone driven in his life, never been so blunt when it came to the opposite sex.

She looked back at him. "These for me?"

The desire in her eyes packed a wallop on every cell in his body, causing him to pick up his jacket off the bed and flip it over his arm to hold it in front of him and hide his growing desire.

"Depends. Will you come back with me if I say 'yes'?"

"I don't know." She bit her bottom lip. A sight he'd grown accustomed to when she was unsure of things.

"Give the poor guy a break. If I were you, I'd jump him," the nurse said with a wink as she checked him over. "If you don't want him, I'd be happy to take him off your hands."

"Oh, shoo already." Laryssa pushed the nurse out the door and closed it. Alex couldn't help but grin at her snappy response. Obviously, she wasn't as immune to him as she wanted to be. He hoped he could use that in his favor. He wasn't sure why he wanted her around so badly. All he knew was he didn't want her to leave yet.

"Jealous, are you?" The look she gave him had him throwing his hands up in the air. "Sorry, sorry. Bad humor." If there was one thing he did well, it was putting his foot in his mouth. It would take him a lifetime to pull it back out.

"This is what I'm talking about. I won't be treated like dirt. I want respect and deserve respect. I won't live in a place where I don't have it, regardless of how..." She touched her lips with her forefinger. "...good you kiss."

He couldn't stop the smile that spread across his face at her words. She thought he was a good kisser, did she? Another point in his favor. This just kept getting better and better.

He walked up to her and took her hands in his. "I truly am sorry for the things I said to you. You didn't deserve it, plain and simple. Will you please give a big egghead like me another chance?" He removed one hand, reached into the pocket of his jacket and pulled out a small jewelry box. "I can't promise you that I'll be perfect, but I'll do my best."

"What's this?" Her eyes drifted to the box.

"Open it and find out." He placed it in her hand and rocked on his heels as he waited for her to open it.

She lifted the lid and gasped in surprise. "But this isn't the—"

He put his finger on her lips. "I admit the other ring didn't suit you. But, if you'd like, I could go and get it." Alex reached for the box, and she slapped his hand away. Elation soared inside him. She was softening.

"Don't you dare!" Laryssa wagged her finger at him before letting her gaze fall back on the ring. The solid gold ring had a medium sized diamond in the middle and one sparkling sapphire on either side. It was not as overwhelming as the other ring he'd made her try on but held a beauty all its own.

She looked up at Alex, and their eyes locked. The jolt that shot through her body when he looked at her was powerful enough to knock her off her feet, making her reach out to him to steady herself.

"The diamond is for you, and I had the sapphires added for your children. They are as much a part of this as we are."

Once again, tears blurred her vision. and her gaze dropped to the ground. "This is lovely, Alex. I don't know what to say."

He placed his hand under her chin and lifted her face to meet his. "You could put me out of my misery and say I'm forgiven."

She chuckled and sniffled at the same time making it turn into a snort, and she couldn't help but laugh. "How could I not, when you do such sweet things for me."

He let out a 'whoop' and pulled her close for a kiss before helping her pack the rest of her things.

Laryssa knew she should turn him down, but how could she refuse when he did something as kind and generous as this? Her one weakness was roses. The other was a man who was willing to accept her and her babies together. No matter what, she could not and would not live with a man who didn't.

Back in the safety of her own room at the mansion, she dialed Melissa's number. "Hey, girl, how's work going?"

"Being run ragged as usual. What's up?"

"I wanted to let you know that I decided to go back with Alex." Laryssa held her breath waiting for Melissa's response, certain that her friend would adamantly attempt to make her change her mind.

"Oh, Laryssa, are you sure?"

She explained everything that happened that morning.

Laryssa heard a clang of something drop and sharp indrawn breath. "Wow, so they really are brothers."

"Apparently so. I really don't know exactly where all this is going, but I needed to come back." She sat down on the bed, kicked off her shoes, and sprawled out across the bed.

"I wish you'd reconsider. You need to relax, and all you guys seem to do is fight."

"He's called a truce."

Although some truce that was. They argued half the time in the hospital room up until he pulled out his charm and turned into her dream man. Her defenses should have gone up at his manoeuvres, but they hadn't. Something about his behavior seemed genuine, like he was showing her the real Alex. The part of him he usually hid from the rest of the world.

"I don't like this idea, but I'm here to support you. If there are any issues, promise me you'll phone. That you'll leave right away and stay with us."

After promising her friend, they said their good-byes. Knowing she had Melissa to fall back on if this didn't work out lifted her spirits. She wasn't sure making the decision to come back was the right one, but Alex in the ride home seemed determined not to fight with her and for that she was grateful. Slowly, she drifted off to sleep.

She was startled awake by a gentle shaking of her shoulders and opened her eyes to find Joanne looking down at her with a smile. "Sorry to wake you, sweetie. I made you some lunch."

"Thanks, you're an angel." She breathed in the aroma of the chicken soup. "It smells delicious."

Joanne didn't speak for a moment and then said, "I'm glad you decided to come back. I'd have missed you terribly. Anyway, Jose Dimitre, the wedding planner I told you about, will be over this evening. Alex told me to go ahead and invite him."

"Do we have to see him today? I just got home."

"He's booked solid. He's only coming today because he owed me a favor. "

"Will Alex be sitting in with us?"

Joanne looked at her with puzzlement. "I'm afraid not, didn't he tell you?"

"Tell me what?" Laryssa pushed herself higher up in bed.

"That he was heading to England this afternoon to speak with his grandparents about...well...you know."

Typical, just typical. Just when he gets his way, he disappears again on her. She could understand why he wanted to go, but he should have at least told her his plans. "The inconsiderate pig," she mumbled.

"You didn't know?"

"Guess it must have slipped his mind, the bonehead." Laryssa slapped a hand over her mouth. "Sorry. I know this is a big time for him. I shouldn't be getting upset."

"That's right, missy. You should be relaxing, not working yourself into a tizzy. He shouldn't be gone more than a week."

She hoped that Alex would find the answers he was searching for, not only for himself, but her as well.

Alex sat on the plane, desperately trying to catch up on some last-minute work. He usually avoided visiting his family unless it was a business trip. They didn't understand what had happened between him and Valerie. His grandparents put the blame on him for their breakup and always rallied on her behalf. They were generally blunt with him. The last thing he expected was that they would hide something this big. Learning he had a brother was like having a rug pulled out from under him. The solid foundation he'd built his life on was slowly sinking in quicksand. He never doubted that his grandparents loved him, but that didn't explain what possessed them to do this. Determined beyond words, he would find out why, even if it killed him.

He looked to his right and found a blonde-haired woman who wore a white halter top and black shorts staring at him. He gave a quick polite smile and then turned back to his work. Moments later, she sat down in the seat next to him and sent a sparkling white smile his way. *Why, oh why, didn't I take the business jet today?* The last thing he wanted to do was engage in polite conversation with a woman who was practically drooling over him.

"Hey there, handsome. My name is Rachel." She stuck out her

manicured hand, nails painted with bright pink nail polish. When he made no move to grab it, she dropped it on her lap.

"Hi Rachel, I'm taken," he said, turning his attention back to his laptop.

Not being turned off by his blunt answer and, much to his annoyance, she continued, "Is this your first time in England? If it is, I'd love to show you around." She ran a finger down his arm in a bad attempt at flirtation. "Are you by yourself, handsome?"

He turned to face her. "Listen, lady—"

"Rachel."

"Whatever. Try those lines on someone else who's interested. You may be blond, but I'm sure you're not stupid." He placed his hands on his keyboard to begin typing again, but she leaned forward and shoved her breasts into his arm, looking at his computer.

"Business trip?" she asked.

"No," he gritted through his teeth. What would it take to get this woman to leave him alone without alerting the whole airplane?

"Personal?"

"Not your business." His tone came across rather harsh, but he was beyond caring at this point. She'd pushed her way into his personal space. Something he never enjoyed on public flights. He wanted to be alone.

"Boy, what flew up your butt to make you so grumpy." She flopped back in the seat and brushed her hair back from her face.

"Can you return to your seat, please? I have work to do."

"Oh, come on, relax. We have hours till we land, and I want someone to talk to. I'm lonely." She pouted, fluttering her eyelashes at him.

"I'm not interested in talking." He slammed his laptop closed, pinching his finger. He let out a curse and sucked on his injured finger. Too much was going through his mind to be cordial.

Shaking her head, she looked at him with wide eyes. "And you're taken?"

"As a matter of fact, I'm engaged," he blurted out. Who would have thought he'd say those words again? His thoughts strayed back to Laryssa. Trying to convince her to come back *home* had been a challenge.

Wow, back up.

Since when had he started referring to his home as her home? Maybe he did need therapy after all. When he made this agreement with Laryssa, he never intended to start caring for her, and now he found himself begging her not to leave. *Yep.* He definitely needed to have his head examined. Better yet, be locked up in a padded cell before he did something stupid.

Rachel kept talking for the whole trip, except for about ten minutes when she went to the bathroom and maybe another thirty minutes when she fell asleep. He'd tried to tune her out, but no such luck. And no matter how rude he was, she kept going. She'd put her hand on his arm or tap his shoulder when she wanted his response. He learned she was twenty-seven and single. *No surprise there.* She told him her whole damn life story.

When the flight ended, she held out a piece of paper. "In case you change your mind, here's my number."

"Thanks, but no thanks." He gathered up his belongings and walked down the aisle of the plane towards the door.

Maybe in another time and another place, he would have accepted her offer. She was the kind of girl who didn't hesitate to jump into an affair with no strings attached. He used to be interested in relationships like that. She was a gorgeous blonde, with penetrating blue eyes. Why hadn't he felt any stir of interest? *Not as pretty as Laryssa.* The thought had him standing up straight. Since when had he started comparing women to Laryssa? He shook his head. Even when he wasn't with her, she affected his life. His first impression of her being a siren was right on the money.

Within minutes he sat in a rental car on his way to his grandparents' house in Keswick. He'd lived there until he was nineteen. A year after he married Valerie, they moved to Vancouver into the house that had been in his family for generations. Now he wished he had realized the effect the move had on Valerie.

Moving her away from all her friends hadn't been the brightest move. Maybe if she hadn't been lonely, she wouldn't have betrayed him, and his daughter would still be alive. No, he wouldn't make excuses for her behavior. He could have cheated if he wanted to, but he promised on his wedding day to remain faithful till death.

"Damn it, Valerie." He thumped the seat cushion beside him. "How could you do that to me?"

Too bad time portals don't exist. He would take himself back in time and made sure he was home early enough to pick his daughter up from preschool. With remorse, he realized that was one of the things he never found time to do. The times with his little girl were few and far between, and time spent with Valerie even less.

He had been too young to realize the most important things in life and instead became an over-zealous workaholic. He worked his butt off for her, wanted to give his family everything. In the end, Valerie turned to his best friend for comfort. Correction, ex-best friend.

Every road he journeyed down seemed to be filled with lies and deceit. How much of his life was not what it appeared to be? He hadn't had an unhappy childhood, but he always felt like something was missing. Feelings of déjà vu would creep up on him at the strangest of times. Words and thoughts would pop into his head that weren't his own. Sometimes he'd get a strange sensation that someone was beside him, but when he'd turn to look, no one was ever there.

He never believed in the telepathic link between twins until today or was it empathy? With this recollection, he now recalled the exact day Aidan died. An overwhelming dizziness hit him, and fear rushed through him. The events of his life up till that point played like a movie in his mind. Moments later, the feelings and the connection had stopped.

He pulled the car up to the gate of his childhood home, and the security guard opened the gate to let him in. He drove up to the front of the two-story white house and put the car in park. The reality of all that was about to occur hit him. He laid his head back on the seat and squeezed his eyes closed, counting to ten to help calm his breathing. A technique he learned from one of the shrinks his family managed to drag him to. Once he felt that he was back in control, he opened his eyes and climbed out of the car.

His old, rusted metal swing set still sat off to the west about a hundred feet from the house. The same swing set he pushed his daughter on when they came for visits. He looked at the large bay window situated to the right of the front door. As a child, he would sit at that window for hours when storms passed through and watch the lightning flash across the sky. He never did figure out what was so fascinating about it. The surroundings looked familiar, but it didn't feel like home. The house no longer evoked positive emotions in him. He felt like a stranger.

Night had started to fall, casting strange shadows across the house. The home that once had been a safe haven to him suddenly seemed haunted. The main doors looked like a monster's mouth, teeth and all, threatening to swallow him whole. He began to wonder if coming here was such a good idea.

However, he'd never been one to shirk away from his fears. He'd come this far, literally, and he'd do what he came to do. His life might never be the same again, but at least he'd be able to hear from their own mouths. The truth they long since evaded telling him.

He forced himself to walk through the shadows and up the stairs to the front door. With one foot facing the stairs, ready to run, he reached out with a shaky hand and pressed the doorbell.

CHAPTER FIFTEEN

When he heard someone turning the lock on the door, Alex wiped his sweaty palms on his pants. *Stop being such a wuss*. He was the boss of a company for Pete's sake, not some child.

The door opened and the butler, wearing a tailored crisp black suit, greeted him. "This is a surprise, sir. We weren't expecting you."

"Hello, Robero. Are my grandparents here?" The butler moved, and Alex stepped into the foyer.

"Yes, I'll let them know you are here." He nodded and turned away.

"No need. I saw my grandson arrive." His grandmother, Ruth, gave him a hug and a quick kiss on the cheek, but he stood there, not returning the greeting. He just couldn't bring himself to hug her, knowing she had hidden the truth from him all these years. She sent him a puzzled look. He stared at her for a moment. She hadn't changed much over the years, except for having all gray hair, and a few new wrinkles next to her eyes.

She wore a three-piece suit, as usual. This one was the color of red wine, with a white blouse underneath. For being in her eighties, she looked surprisingly fit. No doubt a result of their chef's amazing ability for finding healthy and delicious recipes. However, she loved to cook, so she often kicked their chef out of the kitchen. Even though she married his rich grandfather, she never let it go to her head like some did. She enjoyed doing things for herself, even taking him outside to play when he was younger, rather than always making Joanne watch him. He gave his head a quick shake. He wasn't here to reminisce.

"So, to what do we owe this honor after all this time?"

"Is my grandfather here?" he asked, his voice calm and controlled while his insides continued to twist in a knot.

She slanted her head to the side and looked up at him, eyes narrowing a fraction. "He's in his study. What's wrong?"

Alex folded his arms and took a step back from his grandmother. The hurt inside him bubbled to the surface. "How long, Grandma? How long did you guys think you could keep this from me?"

She stilled at his words. Her features paled, and her eyes widened. "What?"

"You know exactly what I'm talking about." His fingernails dug into the palms of his hands as he tightened his fists. How could she ask him that? The knowledge hung like a dark shadow in her eyes.

"Am I interrupting something?" another voice called from the corridor beside him.

"Hello, Grandfather," he said with frost in his voice.

"Tell me, what has caused you to disrespect your grandmother? I thought we taught you better." Mitch, his grandfather, pulled his gray suit jacket down and straightened his blue colored tie as he approached them.

"You guys are ones to talk about respect. What was that favorite lecture you use to give me about how families shouldn't lie to each other?" His voice was low and laced with sarcasm. "That's what you told me as a boy, wasn't it?"

"Alexander Michael Richards, don't use that tone of voice with us." His grandmother wagged her finger at him.

"I'll use whatever tone I damn well please." Alex yanked at the tie around his neck and pulled it off.

"Not in my house, you won't," his grandfather ordered. "Your grandmother isn't well and doesn't need your attitude right now."

He studied her. She had bags under her eyes and, when she breathed, she sounded like she had swallowed a cat. Angry or not, he did love her and didn't wish any ill on them. "Are you okay?"

"I'm getting better, just getting over a bout of pneumonia." She waved her hand at the two of them. "No need to worry about me."

"It's late. Whatever Alex wants to talk to us about can wait till the morning. You need your rest." Mitch placed his arm around Ruth's shoulders and steered her toward the hallway.

"I don't want to wait. If she can't speak with me, you can." He grabbed his grandfather's arm.

His grandmother turned towards him and shook her head. "In all my years raising you, I've never seen you like this. What is wrong?"

"I..." Alex started to pace back and forth, his mind drawing blanks. He knew what he wanted to say, but for the life of him couldn't figure out how to say it. Now that he was here, and they were watching him with confusion, the words wouldn't come out of his mouth. He raked a hand through his hair. "Actually, sleep is sounding pretty good right about now."

Mitch helped Ruth up to their bedroom. The room which had been theirs for more than fifty-five years. They'd raised two generations here and would hopefully see another generation before long. If Alex got his butt in gear, that is.

Mitch couldn't have been prouder of the boy, but currently, he wanted to wring Alexander's neck for bringing this cause of worry upon his wife. She sat on the edge of the bed. Her face ashen, and her hands trembling in her lap.

Having just come home from the hospital earlier this week, she didn't need the stress. He sat down beside her on the bed and took her hands in his. She looked at him with panic-stricken eyes, and his heart bled.

"What have we done, Mitch?" she asked softly.

"Please do not worry, my darling. It may not be what we think." He lifted her hands and brushed them with his lips, but even as he spoke the words, he knew it was exactly what they thought. They hadn't seen Alex much since they tried to offer him therapy. He'd been quite insistent that he was fine, and he'd avoided them ever since, unless it involved the family business. For him to fly all this way, and be in this much of an uproar, it had to be something major.

"You and I both know it is." Ruth sighed.

"Do you think Joanne told him?"

"No, I don't believe she would. We were pretty strict on her when she worked for us. She was always a fearful wee thing. I doubt she'd say anything now. She's been with him for twelve years now, and we haven't heard anything till today."

"Maybe we should speak with her and see what this is about?"

Ruth nodded her head. The hurtful expression on her grandson's face ripped her heart apart. She'd give anything to go back in time to reverse the choice they had made. Surely, he'd never want anything to do with them again after this. They'd been afraid of losing him back then, and now they might just lose him anyway.

"Oh, Mitch, how could we have kept something this important from him?"

"It was for the best."

That was what they told themselves for years, but she didn't believe it any longer. Alex was their only remaining legacy of Scott, their son. They had to do what they did to keep him in their lives. Hopefully, he would understand once they explained.

"I want to believe that, but after seeing his face, I don't anymore." Her last word broke as she went into a coughing fit.

Mitch stood up and went into the bathroom. Moments later, he came out with her medicine. "Here, you better take this before we forget."

"Thanks, honey." She took the medicine from him and swallowed the pills.

He pulled her into his arms, and she leaned into him, resting her head on his shoulder. Oh, how she loved him. Even after all these years together, their love never waned. Not many couples last during the tough years. They would give up and go their separate ways. Their hardships had brought them closer to each other. She'd fallen in love with him when she was a teenager, even when he tried his hardest to discourage her interest. He thought he was too old for her.

He was her brother's ruggedly handsome best friend—her brother who had long since passed away. Mitch, in his mid-eighties, was even more handsome and refined now than when she married him. His balding head, with a patch of silvery gray hair, looked similar to Captain Picard of the Starship Enterprise. She had always been partial to balding men. His smoky gray eyes, though, were what initially captivated her. They seduced her before he had even touched her. He was so easy to read, even when he tried to deny his feelings for her way back in their younger days.

She hoped they had a couple more years left in them. Maybe, even reach their sixtieth anniversary. She also wanted to live long enough to see Alex happy. He deserved to have a family of his own. Someone he could truly love. Wasn't that every parent's dream? But as much as she didn't want to admit it, they weren't his parents. They were only his grandparents. He deserved an explanation. No more beating around the bush.

“Let's speak with Joanne.” Mitch picked up the phone next to the bed and handed it to her.

“Hello, Joanne. Do you have a moment to talk?” she asked when she heard the ‘hello’ on the other end.

“Hi, Ruth, did Alex arrive safely?”

“Yes, that's why we're calling. He came into the house all in a huff. Is there anything we should know?” Ruth asked. Mitch squeezed her hand in support.

She heard Joanne take a deep breath. “I had hoped the flight would calm him down before he reached you. He's found out about his brother.”

“How did he find out? You didn't tell him, did you?” Ruth couldn't keep the accusation out of her voice.

"I...well...not in so many words. It's kind of complicated," Joanne sighed.

"Joanne, you promised. How could you do that to—"

"For God's sake, Joanne never said a word. Talk to me if you want to find out," a third voice growled into the line, followed by the sound of the phone slamming down on its base.

"Oh dear," Joanne whispered.

Ruth stared at the receiver in shock. First, he comes to their house, yelling. Now he was eavesdropping. Did she even know who he was anymore? That scared her more than anything else. They had drifted so far apart since his family broke up. But she knew there was no one to blame but herself. They pushed him away by insisting he get help instead of just being there for him. She feared how he would react if they told him the whole truth. Her old grandson would understand the circumstances, or at least she had hoped he would, but this one, she just didn't know.

"I'm so worried," Ruth said.

"Alex is a good man, but he's full of pain right now. Anyone would react this way in his situation. We can't change the past or make up for the decisions we made, but hopefully we can help him come to terms with them," Joanne tried to reassure her.

She knew Joanne could rub it in her face, but she wasn't that type of person. Guilt stabbed Ruth in the heart at the way they'd treated her over the years. "I'm so sorry, Joanne. I know that doesn't make up for the choices we made, but I truly am sorry."

"I know you are, my dear. We all have our faults to bear, me included."

"Yes, but we should never have made you..." Ruth couldn't stop the cry that bubbled up from her chest. How could they have kept this from him? The magnitude of the secret made a knot the size of a brick form in her stomach.

"You gave me more than I hoped for, Ruth. My family pushed me away, I wasn't expecting anything more."

"You really are a sweetheart." Ruth's throat started to tickle as she tried to fight off another coughing fit. "I better—*cough*—go. Take

—*cough*—care." She hung up the phone and doubled over till the fit released her.

"Come on, honey. We should go to sleep. We have a big day tomorrow." Mitch helped her undo the buttons on her suit jacket. They changed into their sleep attire and climbed into bed. Ruth nestled close to her husband, and he wrapped his arm around her. "It'll be fine, you'll see."

She prayed Mitch was right.

"Is it true? That they were brothers?" Laryssa watched Joanne over the brim of her hot cocoa while sitting curled on the sofa.

Laryssa had sat on the edge of her seat during the meeting with the wedding planner, just itching to get Joanne alone to ask about Alex. Finally, the wedding planner was gone, and they sat in silence for a bit before she decided to pop the question.

Joanne stirred the tea bag around the cup and brought the spoon to her lips before picking up the cup and sitting back against the recliner. Only the grandfather clock ticking in the corner made any noise.

She couldn't blame Joanne for stalling, but the time had come for answers.

"Well?"

Tears filled Joanne's eyes. Laryssa got up and went to sit on the brown footstool next to her. She covered the older woman's hands with her own.

"Oh, my dear sweet child, we've done something terrible." Joanne's voice trembled and the look of despair on her face set alarm bells off in Laryssa's stomach.

"Do you want to talk about it?"

Joanne's whole body rocked, and Laryssa wondered if she was having a seizure, then a loud sob burst from her mouth.

"It can't be that bad." Laryssa put her arm around her and gave her a gentle squeeze.

"Alexander will hate us. He'll hate me."

"He won't hate you. You are the most wonderful, loving woman in the whole world. I doubt anything would make him change the way he feels about you."

Joanne lifted her hand and gave her a little pat on the cheek. "You really are a special girl. I always hoped Alex would find someone like you."

"Was Aidan really Alex's brother?" She asked.

"Yes."

There it was, in one simple word. She dropped a hand to her womb. Her children would never have to grow up alone like she did. They'd have a family they could call their own.

"How did they get separated, Joanne?"

"That, my dear, is a long and complicated story. Whatever I tell you here has to be kept in strictest confidence."

She nodded her head for Joanne to continue.

"My memory isn't what it used to be, but let's see what I can remember." Joanne took a deep breath. "There was a woman who had married a man that her father didn't approve of and got disinherited."

"How barbaric. Why would any family disinherit a child just because they were marrying someone they didn't like? It happens all the time. Sheesh, since when have any in-laws ever been happy?" She tried to lighten the mood by joking around, but Joanne was too caught up in the tale to notice.

"The two families were, I guess you could say, at war with each other, in a feud that had gone on for decades. She'd betrayed them by marrying into the other family, broke the family honor, or something like that. Even to this day I don't understand."

"That's so sad. I couldn't imagine ever doing that to my own children."

"Anyway, all seemed to go well for a while. They married, and then she got pregnant. They were ecstatic at the idea of becoming parents. When she went into labor, Scott drove her to the hospital. He was going through a green light..." Joanne's breath hitched, and she stopped talking for a moment.

"Take a couple of deep breaths." Laryssa rubbed the older woman's back. "There's no rush."

After a few moments, she began speaking again. "A car...a car ran the red light and smacked into the husband's side of the car."

"Oh my gosh." Laryssa's eyes widened, and she covered her mouth in horror.

Joanne continued, "He died on route to the hospital. The girl lived, along with the twins, but she was in a deep coma. Her head hit the window. The babies, thankfully, had no lasting injuries. Anyway, her family heard about it and came down, not to see her though, but to try and get custody of the little ones; God only knows why. Probably couldn't stand the idea of the husband's family taking care of them because they hated them so much." She shifted in the chair and stretched out her leg. "It's hard to sit long these days. Anyway, where was I?"

"Her family came down and tried to get custody."

"Yes, that's right. The courts tried to delay making a decision, but after a few weeks, it wasn't looking good. They had to decide something. They decided each family would get custody of one child. Due to the feud, the courts decided it would be best if they did not contact each other, and in the end, issued a no contact order. Because of that, they were not allowed to tell each child he had a brother."

"Did the mother survive, or did she die?"

"For a while, she remained in a coma, but miraculously she woke up. Not perfectly of course." Laryssa heard the wistfulness in Joanne's voice. "She was in bad shape. She was partially paralyzed, mostly her right side. She also experienced memory loss."

"Did she recover?"

"Yes. Well, mostly. It took two years before she was mobile enough to do anything. Her memory mostly returned, except for the accident. That day is still hazy and sometimes it's tricky trying to figure out whether something is a memory or a dream. A few other problems also lingered, but eventually she sought out her family and tried to get her child back. They still hated her for betraying them and managed to bribe their family doctor into declaring her unfit. She was no longer allowed to see her son. They threatened to institutionalize her if she didn't leave them alone."

"Could they do that?"

"They were rich. The rich can do anything they want and nearly everybody has a price. The girl didn't have any money to fight. The only thing she could do was hope and pray that her husband's family would allow her to visit her other son."

"Did they?" Laryssa got up off the stool and stretched. Her back ached from sitting too long.

"After what she went through with her own family, she didn't hold much hope. His family was reluctant when she arrived, as the child was all they had left of their son. They liked her, but with her having been declared unfit, and the restraining order from her family, they were worried about someone finding out." She stared down at the hardwood floor.

Tears fell down her cheeks, and her chin wobbled. Taking a deep breath, Joanne continued, "They'd established a home for the boy and didn't want to risk losing him. She begged them to let her work for them. She just wanted to be near him. After losing the son her family had, she didn't want to lose him, too, and would do anything to be with the boy. They told her to change her name and, once she did, she would be able to work for them as their housekeeper. The one stipulation was that she could not tell him who she was, or they'd fire her."

"The situation just seems so unreal. My mind can't absorb it. Why didn't she go to another doctor? Do something?"

"She was as poor as a stray kitten, and after the ordeal with her family, she just couldn't handle any more fighting. She accepted what they offered her and went to work for them. And even though it killed her inside not to tell him the truth, she kept her promise.

"It doesn't seem fair. Not after all she went through." Laryssa shook her head. "That is one of the hardest things to accept. Life isn't fair."

Joanne sat hunched in the chair, staring at the vase in the center of the coffee table. Her hands knotted together on her lap, knuckles white. She could tell Joanne was hiding something else.

Laryssa let the words sink in and slowly she tried to fit the puzzle together, but one piece was missing. One question kept coming to mind.

"How do you know so much?"

Joanne looked at her with tears glistening in her eyes. "Because, my dear, that sweet young woman was me."

CHAPTER SIXTEEN

"His name is Alexander Michael Richards," Matt told him.

The minute the stalker heard the name, his mouth soured, and his lips puckered. "Are you sure?"

"Yes. They were born in Keswick, the Lake District, England, to a woman named Joanne Richards."

"Gimme an address." He tapped his pen on the edge of the desk. Soon. It was only a matter of time and he'd see her again.

"*Yours, she'll be all yours again*," a voice gloated in his head.

This time no one will be able to take her from him. He'd be the last person she'd be with, or swear to God, he'd kill her. Matt didn't need to know that, of course. Good ole, reliable Matt never could turn his back on a mystery.

"Isn't it enough to know she's with a relative, safe and sound?" His ole buddy had a slightly suspicious tone to his voice, and it grated on his nerves.

"It's your job to track people down. I know you have the fucking address."

"I promised to find her and see if she was okay. She is. End of discussion. Good-bye. And please, don't call here for anymore favors." Matt hung up on him.

'He never really liked you,' a voice in the corner of his mind taunted him.

'He only used you.'

'Kill him, kill him, too.'

The voices screamed at him every minute of every day. Everyone looked at him like he was crazy, treated him like a weirdo. Said he'd never amount to anything.

Look at him, though, he learned how to build the most sophisticated spying software and sold it to agencies over the internet. No one knew the man behind the software. They came to his website, and he gave them what they wanted.

The time had come to take what he wanted. Nothing would be able to stop him. He wanted Laryssa, wild and naked. He wanted to take her as roughly as Aidan had. God, that man had her eating out of the palm of his hand, literally like a dog.

Now another man had his paws on her, but he'd get her back. He had a name and soon he'd have an address. She'd be his for the taking, or she'd be dead before his pants hit the floor.

Laryssa thumped her pillow and then dropped her head back against it for a second time. As hard as she tried, sleep just wouldn't come. With Alex gone, she thought for once she'd be able to get some sleep. But no, why would it be that easy?

Images of his half naked body had taken permanent residence in her mind. She visualized him in his bed, wearing only his boxers, with the sheets half kicked off. His hair disheveled from tossing and turning all night. Her hands itched to be able to reach out and smooth his sleep tousled hair.

No matter what she did, she couldn't shake the image. *I refuse to think about him. Think about... think about, uh...*What could she do that would help get her mind off how good he looked?

Laryssa eyed a book on her nightstand and picked it up. She groaned when she saw the title, *'Too Hot to Handle'*. Somehow, she didn't think that book would help put her to sleep. Already, the ache building inside her was ready to explode. If she read it tonight, she definitely wouldn't be reading Paige and Justin's story.

She dropped the book like a hot potato and continued to look around for something to distract her from her wayward thoughts. She picked up the remote and pushed the on button. The conspiracy thickened, even the television worked against her. Any channel she turned to presented her with a love scene. Her body tingled as she thought about Alex touching her.

"Darn, it's not fair. He's invading every part of my life, even when he's not here."

Turning off the television, she tossed the controller on the bedside table. She turned off the light and lay in bed, trying not to think about Alex's magic fingers trailing down her body.

"Shut up, Laryssa."

Sleep did find her. But, just like people always say, 'you dream about the last thing you think of before you fall asleep,' and that was what she did.

She wasn't pregnant in her dream, and he was walking towards her on a moonlit beach. They were in a cove, hidden from public view. The only sounds were the waves rolling against the shore and the beat of her heart. She wore a low cut, red dress, with a slit clean up to her hip.

Alex wore a white silk shirt that blew open in the wind, showing his very muscular chest and his washboard stomach, which looked as though the world's heaviest man could stand on it. His wet hair made him look as if he had just stepped out of the ocean.

Her gaze lowered until she met the top of his hip hugging jeans. His belt was loosened, and his top button undone. She could easily pull the zipper down and watch his pants fall to the ground. He came to a stop in front of her.

Were you supposed to feel sensations in dreams? Her body hummed with awareness. His eyes roamed down her body, creating a fire deep inside her. Hunger ravaged his features. By the time he reached out to her, she was a quivering mess, aching to be touched.

His fingers caressed her cheeks lightly and slowly moved their way downwards. His lips traced the heated trail his touch magically evoked, while his hands traveled teasingly over her breasts.

She let her head roll back as he devoured her neck. His fingers drifted lower to where she wanted to be desired to be touched. She arched, almost falling backwards. He pushed his way between her legs with his hand and ran his palm up her inner thigh, coming to rest against her mound. She was about to come already. She couldn't help herself.

Suddenly, the beach faded, and she found herself back on her bed, drenched in sweat, aching for release. The phone rang again, and she realized what had disturbed the best dream of her life.

"What?" she snapped.

"Well, hello to you too, sunshine." Alex chuckled.

The last person she wanted to talk to was him. The main object of the most sensual dream she'd ever experienced. "Did you have to phone?"

"Not happy to hear from me?"

"Not particularly." Her body still throbbed from his phantom touch, and the last thing she wanted to do was give him any indication of how much she wanted the real thing.

"I wanted to apologize for not letting you know about my plans. The trip was a sort of a spur of the moment thing."

"I can understand why you went. What I don't understand is why you have to call me tonight? I'm having a hard enough time sleeping already."

"You must be having the same problem as me." His voice deepened.

She fought back the raging desire that threatened to surface again. "And what might that be?"

"I'm here and you're there."

"And that's a problem, how?" She struggled to keep her voice cool. All the while her insides were like a forest on fire. Hearing his voice sent shivers of pleasure down her spine.

He chuckled. "Maybe it's a good thing I'm not with you tonight. I don't know if I could be a good boy or not."

His words caused heat to pool between her thighs. She crossed her legs under the covers and tightened her grip on the phone. "Gosh, will you shut up. I'm having a hard time already."

"You don't know the meaning of the word. I wish I could show you just how *hard* a time I'm having right now." His tone of voice gave his words a very literal meaning.

Another image of something hard popped into her head and she groaned. "I wish you..." She bit her tongue. Was she really going to say she wished he was there, too? She wasn't about to put her foot in her mouth. He would turn on the pressure, and with how she felt at this moment, she wouldn't be able to say no.

"Lara, you don't know what you do to me," he said, with a voice so tender and full of desire that another wall around her heart came crashing down.

"I think I can guess."

"I have an idea. Go to my office and turn on the computer."

"Alex, I'm upstairs in my bedroom. I'm not going all the way downstairs."

"Please, I want to see you."

She threw back the covers and swung her legs off the bed. She slipped on her slippers, and then waddled her way to the elevator to go downstairs. "I hope you realize I should be sleeping. I'm going to be a zombie tomorrow."

"I'll make this worth your while. Trust me."

"You really don't want to see me. I'm a mess," she tried to reason with him.

"Lara, Lara, Lara, there is nothing I want more right now."

She shivered in delight at the desire evident in his voice. On wobbly legs, she made her way to his office, unsure of what he had in mind. He made her feel like a real, desirable woman and for tonight, she'd do as requested.

"Once the computer has booted up, turn on the messenger app.

Let me know when you've got that far." The phone was silent, except for his heavy breathing.

"Okay, it's on."

"Click the webcam button."

She did as asked and saw a picture of herself pop up on the screen, horrified at the mess of her hair. She heard his intake of breath.

"My dear, sweet Lara, you are simply breathtaking."

Alex sat looking at the sexy goddess on his computer screen. Sadly, she was hours away from him. Her hair wild. Her face flushed. Was it from embarrassment or desire? He ached to know. He let his gaze drop to her bare shoulders. A thin strap of her nightgown lay nearly transparent on her shoulder. He gulped. He was in over his head.

His desire tripled as compared to what it was before the phone call. This woman haunted his mind day and night. Now, there she was, halfway across the world, and he couldn't touch her. Talk about modern day torture.

"Do you want to see me?" He watched her bite her nails as she contemplated his question. "I won't bite, honest."

A moment later, a box popped up on his screen asking permission for her to view. His whole body screamed out *yes*. His little siren was bolder than he thought.

Although, the moment the screen loaded on her side, she jolted out of her seat. He'd forgotten to mention one little detail.

"You're naked." She covered her eyes and peeked between her fingers.

"I can see you peeking. Come on, lower your hands." He watched curiosity get the better of her, and she lowered her hands.

"Why didn't you tell me?" Her gaze drifted downward, and her face flushed even more.

"Would you have viewed if I did?" He chuckled and leaned back in his seat.

"Alex," she moaned. "This is so mean."

More like torture, but she was so dang beautiful, and he'd rather have this than nothing. "Are you wearing anything underneath?"

Her breathing quickened at his question. "No." Her eyes widened as they came to rest on a certain part of him.

"Are you looking at what I think you are?" He watched her eyes jerk upwards to his face again, and she fumbled with the phone. "You're making me want to pack up and come home right now."

Her eyes were full of desire, and he wished he could jump through the computer.

Laryssa sighed. "This isn't going to help me sleep, you know."

"Did you dream about me?" He leaned closer to the screen to see her better and watched the blush rise in her cheeks a third time. "I take that as a yes. I want to hear about it."

"No way."

"Was it juicy? Were we, you know? Here, let me guess. Maybe, you had the same dream as me. We're in a secluded place, just you and me. I pull you close. Your breasts firm against my chest. You tilt your head up, and I brush my lips against yours. Slowly and agonizingly, I remove your clothes, one by one, and carry you to my bed." He watched her gaze fall on his aroused flesh again. "I rub myself against your swollen flesh as I lay over you. You are as gorgeous as you are right now. I trace your breasts with my tongue before closing my lips over your nipples."

"Okay, okay. Will you shut up." She squirmed in her seat.

"Your hands begin to explore and close over me." He mimicked on himself what her hands would do. He heard her whimper and grinned. She could try denying it, but she wanted him something fierce. Her hand traveled down her own body as well as she watched him.

He was getting to the point of no return just watching her. If he didn't be careful, it would be like opening a Pandora's Box. How much more erotic would it be to be able to remove her clothes in person and hold her, flesh against flesh? And be with her completely.

"If we were together now, I'd be doing exactly what I said. I'd pull that nightgown over your head and kiss every succulent inch of your body." He licked his lips.

Her hand went up to the strap on her shoulder.

"Do it, please. I want to see you."

Laryssa looked at her hand, which rested on her shoulder, and then back at Alex on the screen. She couldn't have been seriously contemplating removing it for him, was she? Alex would be turned off for life. "Alex, I have to go."

She turned off the webcam and struggled to her feet, her heart beating like a wild horse. For a second, she forgot about the phone in her hand, until his voice broke the silence. Warily, she brought it up to her ear.

"I know you're there, Laryssa."

"I have to go to bed. It's late." She crossed her fingers and hoped he'd let it go.

"Why'd you turn it off?"

"We can't do this."

"Why not? We're adults. We can do what we want."

He made it sound so easy, and for a second, she wished she could throw away her inhibitions and see where it could lead.

"No, we can't. At least I can't. I won't get myself lost like that. I'm not here to fulfill my fantasies."

What on earth had she been thinking? One second longer and she would have come on camera. Embarrassment colored her cheeks.

"You admit to having fantasies about us, do you?"

"Yes. No. Alex, just go to bed." She said, hanging up the phone. Her insides continued vibrating with need as she headed up to her room. His well-toned body was absolutely incredible and sexy. She pictured their bodies melded together as close as two human beings could get.

She walked to her dresser, dug behind her underwear, and pulled out her vibrator. With the tension built up inside her, she wouldn't be able to sleep until she sought relief.

~

Alex rolled over in bed as the rays of the morning sun shone in through the window. He groaned and threw the pillow over his head, trying to go back to sleep. He did not want to face the challenges that were sure to follow him the minute he got out of bed.

Last night had been the most enjoyment he'd had in a long time, and the most painful hard-on he'd ever experienced. He'd never done that sort of thing online before. If he could have flown back home last night to be with her, he would have. She looked gorgeous in her pink nightgown, swollen belly, and hair going in every which direction.

He'd wondered if she made herself orgasm after their call ended. He had been unable to go to sleep without first jumping in the shower and doing what he wished he could have been doing with her. Hopefully, they'd make love together soon. The anticipation might kill him otherwise.

He groaned and sat up. The sunlight pouring in through the window made his head pound. He looked over towards the wall and saw a picture of him riding his first bike, and his grandfather holding on to the back, grinning from ear to ear.

His grandfather, Mitch, always told him how proud he was of him. However, that word didn't even enter Alex's vocabulary when he thought of the people who raised him. The deceit they'd fed him over the years hurt. His own deceit didn't make him feel too guilty considering what they'd done. He couldn't wait to see their faces when he told them about his marriage. Well, once he could figure out how to start the conversation.

Alex rubbed his face with his hand and walked into the bathroom. "Who the heck am I?" he asked the reflection in the mirror. Was that the start of gray behind his ears? He leaned over the counter and closely inspected his dark brown hair. Hot damn. It was hard to believe someone else looked like him. He decided the time had come to suck up the apprehension and get it over with.

He found his grandparents in the afternoon tearoom. This had always been his favorite room in the house. It overlooked the lake and seeing the water brought back fond memories. The first thing he did every morning when he lived here was hightail it to the lake for a swim, only to have his grandmother come fish him out, telling him he had to have breakfast and do the chores first.

His grandmother's eyes were on him as he entered the room. He walked over to the window opposite of where they sat. Silence reigned in the room. He turned towards them, frantically searching for what to say and, in the end, he could only manage to speak one word. If he tried to say more, he knew he'd explode again.

"Why?"

CHAPTER SEVENTEEN

"How'd you find out?" his grandfather asked.

"Why does it matter how I found out? Are you going to go and get mad at them, like you did Joanne last night?" Alex crossed his arms and glared at them.

"There were complications, Alex. We did what we had to do at the time." Ruth's eyes pleaded with him to understand.

"What is so complicated about telling me I had a brother? I went through my whole life thinking I was an only child."

"Maybe we should have told you before, but we didn't know how. At least, you know about him now," Ruth said.

"Sure, I know about him, but what good does that do when he's dead?"

They froze in their seats, eyes glued on him.

"That's right, you heard me, D-E-A-D, dead."

"Mitch." His grandmother reached for her husband, who wrapped his arms around her.

He looked over her head at Alex. "What on earth are you talking about? Who told you that?"

"Oh, did I forget to mention that I am marrying his widow?" Guilt pricked at him. He should have delivered the news with more sympathy. They were still his grandparents, and they had just learned a grandchild of theirs had died, but he couldn't help it. He was angry and wanted to surprise them, just as he had been.

Ruth fanned her pale face. "Widow?"

"Yes. Your selfishness kept me from my brother." He clenched his fists.

"I'm sorry, Alex. I'm so sorry." Ruth's whole body trembled, and she swayed on the couch. Mitch smoothed her hair and whispered something in her ear.

His grandfather glared at him. "Alexander Michael Richards, the only one being selfish right now is you. Take a look at your grandmother. You will not continue to speak to us like this."

"This is not the way we planned on you finding out," she said, tears streaming down her face.

"Just how, then? Did you plan on me going through my whole life not knowing?" Alex took a deep breath, unsure of how long he could continue to carry on a semi-decent conversation before losing complete control.

"We took you in during the hardest time of our lives. Maybe we weren't going about it correctly, but we did what we had to do to keep you." Ruth pressed closer to Mitch.

"Did either of you think I might actually want to know about this? Damn it! Now I'll never have the chance." Alex turned towards the window, shoulders heaving. His stomach ached.

"If you'll calm down, I'll try to explain." Mitch said from his spot across the room.

He spun around to face them. "Calm down. Don't tell me to calm down. Did you hear what I said? He's dead, Grandpa. This Bullshit decision cost me my brother."

"We know you're upset, but I won't have you swearing at me. We taught you better than that."

Alex walked up to his grandfather and leaned down, one hand on the couch. "I'll speak any way I damn well please. I think I'm entitled to have my say. You lied to me my whole life. Don't think you can boss me around now."

"While you're in this house, you will show respect. I am still your grandfather."

"Really? For all I know I could be adopted, and you might not even be my real family at all. How can I believe anything you say?"

Ruth pushed up off the couch, her eyes blazing, and her lips pressed together. "How dare you! We took you in at the worst time of our life and this is how you repay us?"

"Ruth, sweetie, it's okay, let me handle this."

"No! I've had enough. I won't let him stand here and speak to us like this. Everything we did, we did out of love. If he can't understand that, then I want him out of my house."

"First, you are going to tell me why the hell you lied to me." Alex lost the remainder of his control. He deserved answers, and they were fighting him every step of the way. He felt like he was playing all around the mulberry bush. The monkey chased the weasel.

"That is it! Out! We lost your father on the day you were born." Her voice lifted an octave higher than usual. "We took you in out of the kindness of our heart, you ungrateful ignoramus."

Alex turned and stormed out of the room. He went up the stairs to grab his belongings with his grandfather hot on his heels. Mitch grabbed his arm and surprised him with the strength behind the old man's grip.

"If you cannot control your temper, you will not be welcome here."

"Don't worry. I have no plans on coming back." He threw his bag over his shoulder and stomped down the stairs. His grandfather followed him to the door.

He wanted answers, but tempers were raised and, if he didn't leave now, he might do or say something he'd regret later. "My brother is dead, got that? Dead! Nothing you guys can say or do will bring him back. I never knew him and will never know him thanks to you. I hope you're happy, and I hope this eats away at you for the rest of your damn life."

His grandfather raised his hand as if he was going to strike. Alex hurried outside and rushed to his car. Eager to put distance between them. If his grandfather's hand hit the mark, he was afraid he'd no longer be able to show any type of restraint.

He missed what happened next as he drove down the driveway. If he would have turned around or glanced in his rear-view mirror, he would have seen his grandfather collapse, and his grandmother kneeling down, shaking him.

Laryssa threw the book on the couch beside her and sighed. How is it that love always turns out so perfectly in romance novels? What she would give to have just one romance that turned out like that. Sure, all the characters had conflicts, but they always worked it out. The tall, handsome hero would ride to the rescue, sweeping the heroine up in his arms. She chuckled. Alex would need a forklift to lift her up these days.

The sharp sound of glass breaking broke her out of her reverie. She pushed herself up off the couch and went in the direction of the noise. Joanne stood there, in the kitchen, with the remains of a glass at her feet and the phone in her hand. Joanne turned to face her, placing the phone on the counter with a shaky hand. Her heart skipped a beat as she assessed the situation.

"One second, don't move." Laryssa walked to the pantry and pulled out the broom. She swept the glass out of harm's way and helped Joanne to the table.

"That was Alex's grandmother," Joanne said. "His grandfather collapsed. They are at the hospital now."

"Oh no!" She dropped into a chair next to Joanne. "What's wrong? Is he okay?"

"He's had a massive heart attack." Joanne took a deep shaky breath. "She said they aren't sure if he'll survive the next twenty-four hours. They can't find Alex either."

"Why not?"

"The meeting didn't go well. Alex took off. She says he just lost it."

"I don't think I could blame him."

Joanne bit her bottom lip and looked between Laryssa and the door. "Ruth is beside herself. I have to go to her, but I don't want to leave you alone."

"Go and stay with her. Don't worry about me. I can take care of myself." There were very few people in the world today like Joanne. One who was willing to go and be with someone in their time of need, regardless of how she'd been treated in the past. She was the perfect description of a modern-day saint. Laryssa couldn't help but love her as she would her own mother. She lucked out in the in-law department.

"Alex might get mad," she said hesitantly.

"If it makes you feel better, I'll either go stay with Melissa, or ask Melissa to come stay here." Laryssa gave Joanne's hand a re-assuring squeeze. "Ruth needs you more than I do at the moment."

"Sweetie, you are an angel. Please phone Melissa right away." Joanne pushed back the chair and leaned over to give her a kiss on the cheek. Once at the door, she paused and looked back at Laryssa. "I almost forgot. Let me get you the number of the hospital, just in case Alex calls or shows up."

Once her packing was done, Joanne left and caught the last flight that day to England. Laryssa half hoped that Alex wouldn't contact her. If he lost his temper with his grandparents, what lay in wait for the one who caused this avalanche? For her babies' sake, she knew she should call Melissa. If things got out of hand, she could act as a buffer. She decided to wait until the next day to phone. One evening alone couldn't hurt. She wanted to do some snooping and couldn't do that if other people were around.

Unanswered questions lingered in her brain. She wanted to find out who the old occupant of her room was. Alex never shared anything with her and refused to talk about it. There had to be something in this house that would tell her.

She made her way up to her own room, happy to not have Alex around to avoid. If she wanted, she could walk in the nude. “Ha, that would make even the ghosts flee.” Instead, she settled on her newly bought silver maternity lingerie.

She looked in the full-length mirror in the corner of her room and studied herself. Could she even remember what being skinny felt like? With her protruding belly, she'd lost her equilibrium and her mind.

Alex blew like a whirlwind into her life. Before she knew it, she was accepting a marriage in name only. She saw his inner man trying to break free of his chains. Chains he seemed to lose when he was with her. And she couldn't help but feel drawn to him.

Pity filled her. His family had lied to him and kept him from his brother. She didn't know what he would do when he found out that his mother had been living right under his nose, and he didn't know it. The revelation worried her.

Alex had so many people keeping secrets from him, and now she had one as well. What a great start to their marriage. The ordeal hung like a black cloud over them all. One bad thing after another kept hitting them, and she couldn't help but feel responsible.

Too bad she couldn't just blend into the shadows and disappear, forget about everything, but she couldn't do that. Her twins created the link between them, making it impossible to walk away. It was hard to believe she was here with Aidan's brother. A brother she didn't know existed. She ran a hand over her belly and watched her reflection in the mirror.

“I pray nothing like this happens to you two. I'll do my best never to let anything separate you. That's a promise.”

Alex wasn't sure how long he drove before finally pulling over. He looked at the scenery and realized he didn't have a clue as to where he was. He'd been so distracted that he hadn't watched which way he traveled. Did he go right or left when he left his grandparents place?

Looking down at his GPS, he finally discovered his location. The lake was coming up on his right. He drove further down the road and pulled into the beach parking lot. The water should hopefully help him relax and allow him to re-gain his footing. How much could one person take before they were finally lost in complete misery?

He got out and walked down along the water's edge. Picking up a flat rock, he tossed it across the water and watched it skip and sink. His life was sinking fast. How could he continue working for his grandfather, especially after he'd lost his temper like a child? For a brief second after he left, he'd thought about turning back, but doubted he would be welcome.

A nagging, guilty feeling persisted, but he had a right to be mad. They had kept him from his brother and tried to justify it by telling him there were circumstances. He could have laughed at the expression on their faces when he said he was marrying his brother's widow. Grabbing another flat rock, he chucked it over the water with all his might.

Time quickly passed by, and the sun was low over the water. His arm ached from skipping endless rocks. The work out helped ease some of the tension in his body. Wandering back to the car, he traveled to the hotel he'd stayed at the last time he was up this way.

He checked himself in to the Greystone's hotel and made his way up to his room. Pulling back the curtains, he looked out over the small town. Lights flickered on, one by one, illuminating the historic buildings along the street as darkness fell. Even though this was his hometown, the feeling of familiarity didn't hit him.

Everything that stared back at him seemed new, like he was looking at it through the eyes of a stranger. In a way he was. The last time he was here, he had no brother. He was the only child of a woman who deserted him, leaving him in the care of his father's family. Now he found out he had a brother who had lived out there somewhere. Did their mother raise him, or had she deserted him, too?

So many questions, and he couldn't even be patient enough to let them answer. Did he overreact today? Maybe, he did, but what did they expect? The rug, which had been the firm foundation of his life, was pulled out from under him, and he still felt like he was on his back trying to find out how he got there in the first place.

He'd come here searching for answers and, just like the idiot he always was, he'd let his temper get the best of him. He shook his head. He was thirty-four years old and couldn't control himself any better than a child. His grandparents had shown him nothing but love his whole life. Why had he thought his grandfather was going to hit him? He'd never struck him before, not even when he'd deserved it as a wayward teen. What on earth possessed him to think so? God, his life was a mess, and he just kept digging himself deeper.

All thanks to Laryssa. She'd brought the truth into his life. Had it not been for her, he might have remained ignorant his whole life. He wanted to be grateful that she helped him discover the truth but, rather than be happy, he was jealous. She'd lived with his brother for seven years and had the time to get to know him. Granted, from what she said, he wasn't a person he'd have really liked anyway, yet he still couldn't stop wishing things were different. His brother might have been a different person had they been raised together.

That was what irked him, not being able to go back and change the past. The future was in his hands, though. He could change the future. He'd start with Laryssa. Alex grinned to himself as he remembered her appearance on the webcam. How he'd wished desperately that he could have been there. She wouldn't have been able to turn him off as easily as she turned the webcam off. He wanted to toss the restrictions she imposed out the window and take her wherever she stood.

He continued to stare at the buildings surrounding the hotel, each having a beauty all its own. Resting up against the walls were bushes full of blue and pink flowers. They reminded him of Laryssa. Her inner beauty always left him breathless.

How could Aidan have abused a sweet little thing like her? He was not perfect himself, but to scare a woman so completely. He couldn't comprehend the logic behind it. When she looked at him with wounded eyes, he wanted to sweep her off her feet and kiss her senseless. He wanted to show her not all men acted that way.

They were caught in a game of tug-of-war. He didn't want to have feelings for her, and she didn't want feelings for him either, but here they were, attracted to each other like moths drawn to the light. He knew none of this was her fault. It was for that reason alone he found himself picking up the phone to contact her.

"Hello." Her voice was husky with sleep.

He mumbled under his breath at the sound of her voice and did a quick time conversion in his head. It was six in the morning in British Columbia. "I'm sorry, Laryssa. I didn't mean to phone you so early."

"Where the heck are you? We've been worried sick."

"Why, did you miss me?"

"This is no time for our word games, Alex. You need to phone your grandmother. Now!" she said, her voice no longer sleepy, but with sense of urgency laced in every word.

"I have nothing more to say to them."

"You better think of something, you big lug. Your grandfather is in the hospital."

He sat on the edge of the seat and tightened his grip on the phone. His grandfather, who always claimed to be the healthiest man on the planet, was in the hospital? The man certainly looked fine when he left, angry maybe, but fine none-the-less. "You have to be mistaken. It was my grandmother who was sick when I saw them."

"He had a massive heart attack right after you left."

"Sure, rub it in." He should have been more tactful when talking to them. They were not as young and spry as they use to be and couldn't handle stress very well anymore. This was exactly the reason why his grandfather allowed him to take over most of the basic operations of the company. "Stupid, stupid me."

"Alex, they don't believe he'll make it. You have to go back."

"I don't know if I can, Laryssa. I really blew it." He leaned his head back against the wall.

"I'm sorry all this is happening to you."

"I wish I could see you, hold you." The only ground that seemed solid beneath his feet was Laryssa. She was the only one who never lied to him.

"I really don't know what to say Alex, except—"

"Say that when I get back, you'll let me hold you," he interrupted.

"Let's not go there right now. You really need to call them," she persisted, much to his annoyance. "If you don't, you and I both know you won't be able to live with yourself."

Alex knew she was right. He just couldn't bear the thought of seeing his grandfather hooked up to the machines because of something he did. Lately, everyone seemed to be getting hurt because of him. "I can't seem to do anything right," he sighed.

"No one blames you, Alex. They know what they did was wrong. Where are you?"

"Why, you want to come visit me?"

"Stop it. You know I can't come," Laryssa said.

"I'm coming home then. I want to see you."

"What if he dies?"

"My brother died without seeing me," he gritted out through his teeth.

"I never figured you for the vengeful type, but that is beyond low. You went down there to find out what happened. Are you going to chicken out now?" She was baiting him, he knew it. She'd hit him where it hurts.

"I'm not a chicken."

"Then get off your lazy butt and march yourself down to the hospital."

"I know exactly where I want to march myself, and that is right back to you."

She made a low guttural sound. "Will you stop being an idiot and go to the darn hospital. I know it's hard, but you got to suck it up. You might not have another chance to see him. If I could go back in time and talk to Aidan again, I often wonder if I would have said or done something differently. Don't make the same mistake as me. I can't have a do-over. I can't change the things that were said or done."

"Lara, I'm at a loss here. I've always been so sure of my life. Now, it feels like everything I once knew is gone."

"I'm only going to say this once. Your grandmother phoned us. She wants you there. You need to be there. That's what family does in good times and in bad. I'd give anything to have a family like that. If you don't go, you are more like Aidan than I thought."

He heard a click and a second later the phone beeped in his ear.

CHAPTER EIGHTEEN

"Of all the nerve!" Laryssa grumbled. How could he even think about abandoning his family at a time like this? Much too awake to go back to sleep, Laryssa swung her legs over the edge of the bed and sat up.

"Gosh, you guys are going to kill me," she groaned, massaging her stomach.

Were all men born with an *idiot* gene? All the men she met had one. She thought that only applied to men who were young and inexperienced in life, but she'd just learned otherwise. "You two had better be girls."

After making her wish, she wondered if what she'd heard was true, that girls were harder to raise than boys. The doctor had asked her if she wanted to know what they were, but she'd said no. She had to admit, though, that the surprise of not knowing was killing her. It kind of reminded her of the feeling she got when she found wrapped Christmas presents in her foster parents' closet.

They weren't born yet, but she loved them dearly already. The only thing she wished was that Alex was the father instead of Aidan. *Wow, hold the phone.* Did she really think that? She could hardly believe that she had gotten so close to him already.

The last thing she would see before she went to bed was Alexander's face, and he was the first thing she'd picture when she woke up in the morning. At least, she thought it was Alex and not Aidan. Her body would get warm and fuzzy all over. Her pulse would do jumping jacks in her throat. Parts of her that she thought would never be aroused again throbbed with excitement. It reminded her of a cat in heat, except she was already pregnant.

She searched in her mind for the time she felt like that with Aidan. She could not recall one single time where her body hummed with the same sexual energy for him as it did when Alex was around. Talk about confusing. While her eyes saw Aidan, her heart sensed otherwise. For a moment, she felt like she'd just stepped into a house of mirrors and all of the mirrors reflected the face of the twins.

Eager to put her mind at rest from the images which plagued her, she went down to the kitchen to make breakfast.

After eating, Laryssa took the elevator to the top floor of the house and decided to explore the west wing. She walked all the way to the end of the hallway to the double doors and pushed them open. The large room was aglow with many colors. She looked up and noticed the ceiling was one large stained-glass dome that mimicked the solar system, and one incredible crystal chandelier hanging from the middle. It was beyond exquisite.

The artist had created it so that when the sun shone through the multi-colored window, it would light up the room with an array of colors, illuminating it with such brilliance that it left the observer breathless.

The walls were white like a projector screen. When the sun shone in through the picture it appeared on the wall, surrounding you. She felt like she could reach out and touch the moon. She had never seen anything like this before and was sure she never would again. She could envision holding a fairy tale ball in here, dancing around with her beloved prince. She gently and quietly closed the door, fearing that any loud noise would shatter the window on the other side.

Turning back around, she opened the next door which led to a huge library that held shelves upon shelves of books. One section of the library caught Laryssa's attention. On the lower shelf tucked away in the corner were children's books. Did they belong to a previous owner of her room? Laryssa grabbed a book called Children's Fairy Tales and opened the ripped and frayed hardcover. Inside the cover it read, "To Julia, love Daddy." The book appeared to be the most worn of the collection.

Laryssa looked at a picture on the wall to her right, which hung above an old rocking chair. There was a large Christmas tree adorned with ornaments and lights of every color. A young girl sat on a cherry-colored wooden rocking chair, dressed in a red frilly dress. Wrapping paper piled knee high surrounded her. The child had long, curly brown hair and eyes as big as walnuts that sparkled like the stars in the night sky. She held a white stuffed teddy bear close to her heart, smiling brightly for the camera.

If her children looked as cute as the girl in the picture, she'd be in heaven. Her stomach contorted as one of her babies stretched and tried to roll. Sometimes it felt like they were fighting. Laryssa remembered something she'd read. That babies in the womb could hear sounds.

She sat in the rocking chair with the book and opened to the story of Cinderella. The story seemed appropriate with the things going on in her life. Rocking in the chair gently, Laryssa started to read. She didn't realize how much time had passed until the grandfather clock struck noon.

Her belly grumbled. "Guess I better go feed us, eh? Or we might shrivel up like a pumpkin."

After she had lunch, Laryssa tried to spend more time wandering around, but found herself back in the library. In the opposite corner from the children's books, she found a big book about the Richards' family tree. Filled with curiosity, she took the book down, coughing as dust filled her lungs. She pulled up a chair to the nearby table and sat down to read.

The book went back to the early eighteen hundreds. No wonder the pages were so delicate. If she could trace her life back this far, what would she find? On the last page of the book, she found the name of Mitch and Ruth, with Scott mentioned as their only child.

Scott was the last entry on the page. Sadness filled her. She felt like filling in the names herself. How could they just stop writing about their history? It could never be finished if Joanne, Alex, and Aidan were left off the family tree.

Did Alex ever look at this, or did he even come into the library? She had never seen him come in here. He seemed to spend more time in his office. Laryssa closed the book and put it away. She would fill in the names herself one day, mark her words!

Ruth stood by her husband's bedside. "Mitch, sweetie, it's me. Can you hear me?"

The only response was a flutter of his eyelids. How could this have happened? There were no signs of heart problems during his last visit to the doctor. Nothing. What would she do without him? He was her pillar of strength. If he died, she'd die with him.

Life simply wouldn't be worth living without her other half. Losing Scott devastated her. She couldn't handle losing both Alex and Mitch on the same day. Mitch meant the world to her. He'd been her knight in shining armor. The one who whisked her up on his big, black steed and rode off into the moonlight.

She never regretted the choices she had made in her life, not even for a moment, and didn't want to have any regrets now, but she couldn't help it. If they hadn't kept this from Alex, they wouldn't have fought, and Mitch wouldn't be lying here, fighting for his life.

Thank God, Joanne came down to be by her side. Even after all they've done to her over the years, she still stood by them without a second thought. Scott couldn't have chosen anyone better or more honorable to be his wife. Life was cruel to have ripped those two apart, but she knew they were even crueler to have kept the truth from their grandson. She no longer had the strength to live a lie.

She was lost in thought when an alarm sounded. She turned toward the machine and saw a flat line.

“God, no. Someone help me.” She smacked the alarm button on the wall with the palm of her hand.

Alex heard the shriek from down the hall as he stepped out of the elevator. On the other side of the hall, he saw Joanne. He watched as the coffee she was carrying dropped to the ground at the sound of the voice over the loudspeaker.

“Code Blue. Code Blue. Room One-Eighteen.”

They met at the door of the room, as the nurse guided a frantic Ruth out. Joanne rushed over and helped her to a seat in the hall.

“I want to be with him.” Ruth tried to stand up. “I can't lose him now, I just can't.”

Alex shoved his hands in his pockets and watched Joanne attempt to comfort his grandmother. What was Joanne doing here? He shook his head. He'd find out later. He wanted to go to his grandmother and wrap her in his arms, but she probably wouldn't welcome it.

Laryssa's words played back to him as he watched them work on his grandfather through the ICU window. 'I can't have a do-over.' Now, here he was in the hospital again, and he may have just lost his grandfather. He wished he could have gotten here sooner.

“Grandma, I'm so sorry. This is all my fault.” He held his head low and shuffled his feet, not wanting to look at her. Afraid of what he might see in her eyes. Would they be filled with anger or maybe even contempt?

Her hand came to rest lightly on his arm. “Sweetie, you have nothing to be sorry about. We brought this on ourselves. If it's anyone's fault, it's ours. I was afraid you wouldn't come.” She grabbed a tissue and blew her nose.

He nearly didn't. “You can thank Laryssa.”

“Who?”

“My fiancée, the one I told you about this morning.”

Ruth looked at him with a blank look in her eyes, and her forehead furrowed.

“I'm sorry my brain is a little muddled at the moment.”

He sat down on the chair beside her and took her hands in his.

"I'm getting married, Grandma." He'd told them earlier, but in all the craziness, she must have forgot.

A small smile appeared on her face as more tears flowed down her cheeks. Her eyes were puffy and red from crying so hard. "Oh, sweetheart, that is great news."

He pulled her into his arms. Not the best time to spring news like this while her husband—his grandfather—sat on the verge of death. She wouldn't want to hear his blissful news if you could call it that. If Laryssa was there, she'd elbow him.

"I'm sorry again. I'm such an insensitive clod."

Ruth wiped her cheeks with a tissue. She couldn't help the ache arising in her heart at his words. Her grandson would be starting his life with someone, and that part of her life could very well be ending.

She looked up at the man Alex had become. She remembered all the times she'd nursed him back to health, held his hand during his first heartbreak. Well, tried to. Now that Alex was older, he didn't need her as much and that left a hollow pit in her stomach, or was it because there was one final secret left to tell him?

"It eases the burden of my heart, my dear. I've been hoping to see you settled down before I go."

Finally, he was putting the past behind him and settling down. Something she thought he would ever do again. He had met a woman he trusted enough to share his life with.

Her heart hurt because she knew they had lost his trust, but hopefully they could try to rebuild it. "Alex, I'm truly sorry for what we've done. Please forgive me. I can't bear to lose you, too."

He knelt in front of her, and gently took her face in his hands. "Grandmother, you haven't lost me. I'm right here."

Love swelled up in her heart and the flood gate of tears broke open. She wrapped her arms around him and cried. Joanne joined them. The three of them sat there, arms around each other. She couldn't have asked for more. She froze when the doctor appeared at the door.

To Ruth, everything happened in slow motion. The doctor could be about to give her the worst news she had ever had to face in her life. She wasn't sure if she had the strength to hear it. She had been with Mitch for so long and could barely remember the time when they were not together. Whatever the news, she knew that she was pretty lucky to have found someone to share most of her life with.

As a young woman that had been her one and only wish. If only someone could grant her one last wish, many more years to come with the man she loved. She leaned into Alexander's strong arms, and he wrapped his arms around her as they waited for the news.

“We got him back.” The doctor smiled. His eyes, however, remained serious. “We're not out of the woods yet, but we've stabilized him.”

Ruth let out a long breath and gave a silent prayer of thanks. She went straight to Mitch’s bedside and stared at the monitor that displayed the beat of his heart. She lay her head down on his chest, relishing the sound of his heart. When she lifted her head, she saw her grandson hovering in the doorway and beckoned him to come.

“I can't.” He had an innate fear of hospital rooms. After what he experienced, who could blame him?

“Your grandfather is strong. He'll make it.” She held her hand out to him.

Alex shoved his hands in his pockets and remained in the doorway. He wanted to be there, wanted to stand by her side, but he didn't feel as though he belonged in the room. Even though she held her hand out to him, seeing his grandfather on the hospital bed held him still. His chest grew tight as he listened to the machines in the room. He could still remember the noise of the machine when his daughter took her final breath.

Joanne walked up to him and led him away from the door. “What on earth are you doing? Why aren't you in the room?”

“What do you mean?”

“Your grandfather is in there, fighting for his life. Your grandmother could use your strength right now.”

“I want to go in there, but what strength do I have to offer?” He gripped the back of his neck as he watched Ruth through the open door. “Look at me. I don't even know who I am anymore.”

"Balderdash. Having a brother doesn't change who you are."

He released his neck and turned towards her. "What would you know? You've never had to live your whole life and find out it was a sham." He stopped dead when her eyes welled up with tears. "Are you ever going to tell me what brings that look into your eyes?"

Joanne lowered her head, blinking away the tears. How she longed to tell him. It had been going on so long that fear was the biggest factor that stood in the way. How would he react when she finally said, *'my dear boy, I'm your mom'*? Alex had been through so much over the years that her heart ached for him.

She wanted to take away his pain, as every mother wished to do for her children. When he was a child, she would wrap her arms around him when he fell, and felt at a loss when she couldn't say, *'don't cry, Momma's here'*. It was at times like this she felt the most helpless. She looked up into the eyes of her now grown son. Anguish was now the dominant emotion displayed in his eyes.

"Sweetie, there is so much I wish to say but..." She let her voice trail off.

"Does everyone here have secrets? Is this a 'let's see how much he can handle before he blows' day? Because I'll tell you right now, I can't take much more. What will I learn next? That you're my mom?" Alex looked away as he spoke.

She knew that if he had continued to look her way, he would have seen the truth written all over her face. She took a deep breath and wrapped her arms around him.

"Please do not ever forget that we love you very much. You having, or not having, a brother will never change that. We know you're angry, but look in that room, Alex." She pointed at the window. "You may not have another chance to re-unite with your brother, but your grandfather is still alive. If you don't go in there, and he dies, you'll regret it the rest of your life. Listen to them with an open mind and heart. Give them a chance to explain."

She sensed the struggle within him as he glanced in the window, then at the open door. She longed to shout out the truth to him, then and there. *I'm your mom, Alex.* The desire to share this with him was so strong that her stomach was tied up in knots. She rushed down the hallway, hoping she'd make it to the bathroom in time.

Alex watched her hurry away. Her words reminded him of Laryssa. How could they be so alike? They spoke the truth, and in his gut, he knew it. Gathering his strength, he stepped over the threshold. Fear gripped his heart. He couldn't tear his eyes off the machines, thinking at any moment the alarms would go off. The walls appeared to close around him. He squeezed his eyes shut and took several deep breaths.

For his grandmother's sake, he mustered up the strength to continue the journey to her side and wrapped his arms around her. He opened his mouth but found himself at a loss for words. She lay her hand on his arm as they stood vigilant over his grandfather's bed. Hospitals meant death to Alex. Nothing good had ever happened to him in one. The room was white, so very white. His grandfather's face was hollow and lifeless, almost like death itself. The machines were the only sound of life in the room, with the steady beeping indicating that all was well. But all was not well. It never would be.

His grandfather was no longer the one on the bed. He could see only his daughter's sweet loving face. Unable to handle much more, he released his grandmother and took a few steps back towards the door.

His heart raced like a stampede inside his chest, and his hands formed tight fists at his side. “Grandma, I have to go. I'm sorry.”

He rushed down the hall, past Joanne who was coming back. She gave him a strange look as he ran by.

CHAPTER NINETEEN

With sheets in a crumpled mess and pillows strewn across the floor of the room, Alex tossed and turned, sweat pouring off his brow.

"*No*!"

His eyes shot open, and he bolted upright, breathing heavily. Confusion flooded him. He closed his eyes tightly and reopened them, but he could still see her as clearly as ever. The torture of losing his daughter fresh in his mind.

The room had been white, like his grandfather's. The same white sheets. The same machines that monitored Mitch had monitored her.

He threw his legs over the edge of the bed and brought his head down into his shaky hands. "No. No. No. I can't remember. Don't let me remember." His heart hammered against his ribs. Her dark brown hair that had matched his swam before his eyes. He could see her bright blue eyes as though she stood there, staring at him.

The corner of his heart, where he kept her hidden, lit up like a two million candle watt spotlight. In a desperate attempt to stop the memories from surfacing, he walked to the bar fridge and pulled out a bottle of gin. He stared at the bottle. There was something he was supposed to remember, something Joanne told him, but his brain failed him. All he could see was his little angel. All he could hear was her sweet melodious voice.

"Daddy, Daddy," her voice would call out. "Play with me, Daddy. Swing me high like Grandpa does." She'd jump into his arms, and he'd swing her around and around. Her laughter was the sweetest thing he'd ever heard, and he enjoyed every single time she blessed him with it.

He'd never hear her voice again. Never see her sweet smile. He tossed the bottle cap on the floor and took a large swig of gin. His hands ached to take her in his arms and blow on her tummy, pretending to eat her. What he would give to hear her giggle and have her tell him that her tummy wasn't food. His heart hurt. He felt like it was in the paws of a grizzly bear, being torn to pieces. He held his hand to his chest, rubbing at the never-ending ache.

He watched the hotel room disappear in a cloudy haze, replaced by a bright white room. His grandfather, hooked up to machines, appeared on the bed before him. When he approached the bed, his grandfather vanished, and a much smaller figure lay in his place.

"God, no. Not this again." As hard as he tried, he couldn't prevent the nightmare from dragging him under.

"Please tell me she'll be okay." Alex looked up at the doctor from his seat in the waiting room, waiting for the prognosis. His heart skipped a beat when the doctor didn't speak right away. He tightened his fingers around the arms of the chair and braced himself for the news. *God, no. Don't let her be dead.*

"I'm afraid that she received internal injuries, mostly to her kidneys and her liver. And the force of the blow from the other vehicle broke the second vertebrae in her neck. We've had to place her on a respirator to help her breathe." The doctor took a deep breath before he continued, "We've stabilized her as much as possible, but the next twenty-four hours are going to be critical. We're doing what we can to see that she makes it through, Mr. Richards." The doctor tried to sound hopeful, but he recognized the look of consternation in the man's eyes.

"Can I see her now, please?"

The doctor nodded his head. "Try not to be alarmed by all the machines you see when you go in. They are to help us keep an eye on her." The doctor stopped at the door of the room, and Alex passed by him to walk in but came to an abrupt halt.

His only daughter lay there, hooked up to every machine a man could think of. One strand of her curly hair snuck out of a bandage that they'd wrapped around her head. Blood seeped through the material next to her right temple. She had a neck brace on, and more blood-soaked bandages were on her arms.

This was the first time he'd seen her so still. If the machines weren't beeping, showing signs of life, he'd have sworn she was dead already. His daughter was always on the move unless she was asleep. He approached the bed and looked down at her. There were cuts all over her face from the shards of glass. He could barely recognize her.

"Sweetheart, can you hear me?" He reached out and rested his hand on her cheek.

Her eyes fluttered open. "Daddy, is that you?" she asked with a quiet, raspy voice.

His gut clenched and his stomach churned at the sound. This was his baby. His only baby. She had to make it through. His chest constricted and tears gathered in his eyes. He turned his face away for a moment and wiped the tears before turning back to her. "I'm here. Daddy's here."

Her eyes clouded with frustration. "I can't move, Daddy."

More tears threatened to fall as the doctor's words replayed in his head. "I know, sweetie. You may not be able to move for a while." He just couldn't bring himself to tell her she may never move again. The lump in his throat grew with each passing moment.

"How come?"

He turned and lowered his head. Sharp pains radiated in his chest. He tried to massage the pain away, but it only grew in intensity. He had to be strong for her; he couldn't let her see how torn up he was inside. After a couple of deep breaths, he turned back to her.

"You've got a boo-boo that stops you from being able to move," he tried to explain.

"When will it go away?"

He couldn't prevent the tears from falling down his cheeks. "I'm not sure, sweetie."

Her eyes filled. "Don't cry, Daddy."

"I'm trying not to." He leaned down to kiss her forehead. Her usual scent had been replaced by the smell of antiseptic.

"I'll be fine, Daddy. You'll see. Please, don't..." She stopped talking, and her eyes rolled back into her head. The machine beside him started beeping. His heart pounded against his chest and the contents of his stomach rose in his throat.

"Julia? Julia?" he cried, tapping on her cheek. Shadows fell across the bed, and they pulled him away. He struggled with his captor. They couldn't take him away from her, not now. "No, let me go. I gotta stay with her. I promised to stay with her."

"Mr. Richards, please. You must give them room to work on her."

Twenty minutes past before the doctors and nurses finally emerged from her room. The downcast looks on their faces gave him an answer he didn't want to acknowledge.

"I'm sorry, Mr. Richards. We did all we could."

"You're wrong, you're wrong." He looked from one face to another. The nurses that surrounded the doctor had tears in their eyes. He grabbed the doctor's arm. "Please, do something. Don't let my daughter die." Tears streamed down his face and his legs became as weak as a newborn calf's.

"I'm sorry. Her injuries were too severe. Her body shutdown. We couldn't revive her."

Alex pushed by them and stumbled into the room on shaky legs. He sat down beside her on the bed and shook her gently. "Julia, please talk to me."

Silence answered back.

He framed her face and leaned his forehead against hers. "Please, baby. Please, don't leave me."

He threw back the sheets and picked her up, cuddling her in his arms. Great sobs ripped through his body as he rocked back and forth. He squeezed his eyes closed, lifted his head, and let out a loud cry. Anguish filled his soul.

When he re-opened his eyes and found himself back in the hotel room. The nightmare was bound to be with him for as long as he lived. He could remember her death like it was just yesterday. The pain as strong now as it had been on that day, ten years ago.

Subconsciously, he grabbed the china vase on the table next to him. It threatened to break under his intense grip. His body shook involuntarily, and his stomach churned. Anger bubbled up inside him and he threw the vase, smashing it against the far wall of the hotel room.

"It's not fair, God. Why did you have to take my baby away from me?" He raised his fists towards the heavens. He took a large mouthful of the gin that he'd nearly forgotten about, hoping it would ease his pain. He could not remember a time it had hit him this hard. His body slid down the wall, and he landed with a thud on the floor.

"Why couldn't it have been me, God? If you're out there, why couldn't it have been me?" he cried out. No amount of pleading helped. Nothing was going to change the past. The guilt that threatened to crush him grew stronger still. If only he'd have handled the situation differently, Valerie might not have been so quick to leave. If he had persisted, his daughter might still be alive. But, like the idiot he was, he had opened his fat mouth and uttered words that could not be taken back. Words that made her leave and take his daughter out on the icy winter roads.

Women. They were nothing but trouble. This was why he didn't want one. He took another sip of the alcohol, and the drink warmed his chest, releasing the death grip his daughter's memory had on him. Hospitals always brought it back. If only he hadn't phoned Laryssa, he would never have known his grandfather was at the hospital and would never have felt obligated to go. She was the perfect example of trouble. She was the one who set him on this roller coaster ride.

Her. Everything always led back to her. He couldn't get through one conversation with himself without her seeping into his brain, making him wish for things he no longer thought he needed or wanted. How did she keep wiggling her way into his thoughts? She must have cast a spell on him. Yes, she was an enchantress who cursed him with the spell of love.

He'd fight her, though. He had no intention of letting her pull him into her evil clutches. Control would be his. They'd have their fun. He'd make love to her like she'd never been loved before, and then he'd tell her to leave before she left with someone else. For now, he'd simply call her.

Laryssa finished her breakfast and stood at the last door she hadn't manage to explore the previous day. "I wonder where this goes."

The door creaked as she opened it and revealed steep stairs leading high above her. She ran her hand along the wall, hoping to find a light switch, and felt something crawl over her hand. She pulled it back and found it covered with cobwebs.

"Spiders."

She shivered at the thought. They were the one animal that frightened her ever since the one jumped out at her from the garbage when she was a child. This called for a flashlight. After rummaging in the kitchen, she returned to the door.

She found the light switch and made her way up the stairs carefully, unsure whether the creaking stairs could support her weight. Once at the top, she looked around the room, which looked much like an attic. An old Victorian Armoire stood in the corner, half covered in cloth, and a Victorian vanity desk sat next to it. If it wasn't for the dust an inch thick, she'd have thought she had gone back in time.

Stashed in the opposite corner she saw a purple and pink toy chest, which appeared out of place among the other more ancient furniture. She ran her hand along the top of the chest, disturbing the dust. She lifted the lid and saw a child's stuffed white teddy bear, which was missing an eye. Didn't she see one like it in the picture in the library? Laryssa had a feeling these toys belonged to the same girl. She closed the lid and turned her attention to the box next to the chest.

She sifted through the children's clothes in the box and her hand connected with something hard. Pushing the clothes aside, she noticed a yellow and white striped photo album. Unable to let sleeping ghosts lie, she picked up the album and took a seat on the dusty rocking chair next to the attic window.

Her babies shoved relentlessly against her stretched skin. She ran her hand over her belly and started to rock back and forth. The dust made her sneeze, but curiosity plagued her as she opened the book. The first picture was a wedding photo of a groom and bride dancing. The woman had long blond hair and was wearing a white satin wedding dress. Her eyes sparkled, and there was a huge smile on her face as she stared up at the man she was dancing with, leaving no doubt that she was thoroughly captivated by the man holding her.

Even though she couldn't get a good glimpse of the man's face, she knew it was Alex. The way he stood, his broad shoulders, and dark brown hair stood out prominently in the picture. He wore a tuxedo with a long tail, covering his very firm and sexy bottom.

She turned to the next page and saw the same petite woman, heavy with child, wearing a bikini. She was smiling wildly at the one taking the picture, cradling her bare womb. The woman could have been a cover model. Laryssa felt ugly in comparison. Stretch marks covered her stomach and breasts. She doubted that would be very appealing to a man.

On the following pages were pictures of a little baby, born out of love. And one in particular caught her attention. She saw Alex and a little girl in the middle of an open field. The girl's brown hair glittered in the sunlight. He held her high in the air, her hair flying as though he was spinning her around. A proud father and husband.

"What happened to you, Alex?" She flipped to the next page of the album and noticed another wedding picture, except this time the head of one of the party members was missing.

The final page held a miniature picture of the one she'd seen in the library. Carefully, she pulled it from the plastic cover and flipped it over. On the back it said, 'Julia, 4 years old, Christmas 1998'. It looks like she found the ghosts that plagued him, part of the past he kept hidden from her. She wondered if they would ever be close enough to share their stories. She stood up from the chair, put the book back in the box, and wiped the dust off her dress.

Hungry yet again, she made her way back down to the kitchen and pulled a can of soup out of the pantry. She doubted she'd ever get use to cooking in a restaurant style kitchen.

Once the soup was cooking, she sat at the table and let her mind drift to the present. Had Alex taken her advice and visited his grandfather? She hoped to heck he had. He sounded pretty distraught the last time they talked, and she hoped the rift growing between him and his family would heal soon. She never wanted this to happen.

Would he phone and let her know how the visit went? Considering he'd phoned every day so far, it wouldn't surprise her if he did. She hoped the next phone call would be on a happier note, but things never happened the way she expected. He could be as passionate as wildfire or as angry as thunder clouds on a stormy night. Sometimes all at once, and it left her bewildered and excited. The powerful combination always left her wanting more.

Her cheeks warmed as she recalled how sexy Alex looked during their previous encounter on the webcam and what she just about did. It was times like that she was glad she was pregnant. They couldn't act on the intense emotion flying between them. The distance between them should have helped, but it didn't. Her body hummed with desire as though he were in the room with her.

His fully aroused manhood had been caught on the webcam, and he'd caught her looking at it. Talk about embarrassing. As hard as she tried, she couldn't look away. It was like a beacon guiding a plane in for a landing. What would it like to guide him home, to have his eyes on her as he slid into her?

This wasn't doing her any good. Her underwear was wet and uncomfortable, and her breasts tingled. She shook her head and tried to erase the pressing images of him. She turned the stove off and reached for the ladle when the phone rang.

"Hello?" she answered.

"Larysssa." He phoned like she thought he would, but his voice sounded slurred as he said her name.

"I've been worried about you. Is everything okay?" She took her soup and sat down at the table, aware of his heavy breathing.

"I gots a bottle of gin, an empty hotel room, a hard on like you woodin' believe. My gran'pa in the hostibal. What could pobisly be wrong?"

"How much have you had to drink?"

"Nos nearly enuff."

Concern didn't even begin to explain how she felt. "Alex, drinking doesn't solve anything," she tried to reason.

"Listen to you, miss high and miggy, mity, mighty. Gets off youz high hoose. I didn't ask for any of this so shudup."

She made a mental note to never let him drink too much. He was not a fun drunk. "You're upset and I understand, but don't take it out on me."

"And whyz not, yourz the reazon I'm in this mez. If it wazn' for you, none of dis woodin have happened."

"So, sue me for living. It's not my fault you stuck your nose into my business." She took a deep breath. No use arguing with a drunk.

"My bro is my bisiniss. The sooner youz relis that, the better. Youz babies are my bisiniss, too."

She couldn't do it. She couldn't keep talking to him. His voice reminded her too much of Aidan's the night of the accident. He'd come home drunk as a skunk and threw his weight around.

"I'm going now, Alex. Get some sleep and phone me when you're sober."

Alex, Aidan, Aidan, Alex. The names bounced around in her head like a ping pong ball. Repulsion ate away at her stomach until she had to rush down the hall to the bathroom. She hadn't expected the phone call to turn out quite like that. Alex had reached his breaking point and was searching for some way to handle it. Why did she always get the brunt of someone's frustration? People enjoyed using her as a scapegoat.

It was as though someone had stuck a sign on her back that said, 'take your best shot'. She wouldn't be a scapegoat again, and she had every intention of telling him the minute he got home. After living with a man who got plastered every week, she had no intention of letting him do the same. If he did, she'd walk out the door before he could even so much as blink. He probably wouldn't even remember talking to her after being drunk out of his mind. But if they planned on living together for any length of time, then he needed to know how strongly she felt on the subject.

The twins pushed against her stomach in what appeared to be agreement. They deserved the best, and she planned to give it to them. She didn't want to take them from the family she just learned about and hoped they could work something out.

Most of all, she hoped Alex's grandfather would live to meet them.

Alex groaned and grabbed his head, unable to ease the pressure that squeezed his brain. The last thing he remembered was picking up the bottle of gin from the fridge and the rest was history.

He staggered to the bathroom and grabbed the Advil. His stomach chose that moment to cramp, and he doubled over, trying to breathe, as a wave of nausea washed over him.

"Bright move, ex-lax." He looked up into the mirror. His face was pale and his eyes bloodshot. He looked like the grim reaper had stuck him with his scythe. Drinking himself into oblivion sounded like a good idea at the time, but he regretted it now. The last time he drank himself nearly to death had been when his life fell apart, until Joanne knocked some resemblance of sense into him and made him get help. He'd been sober for nine years until last night.

Satisfied that his stomach was calming down, he walked into the kitchen to make some coffee. Within the hour, he'd pulled himself together and drove back to the hospital. As much as he didn't want to go, he knew he needed to.

He found Joanne and Ruth asleep on the couch next to his grandfather's bed. He shook them awake gently and told them to go to cafeteria and eat something. His grandmother refused.

“Grandma, how do you expect to be here for him if you wind up in the hospital yourself from malnutrition and dehydration?” He encouraged, and she finally agreed. Joanne led his grandmother out of the room, and they went down to the cafeteria.

Alex sat down in the other chair next to the bed. “I don't understand what's going on. I wish you'd wake up so I could straighten my life out. I'm at my wits end here.” He rested an arm on the railing of Mitch's bed. “I'm sorry for the way I acted. No doubt, if you were awake, you'd make sure my butt met the bottom of your boot, as you always threatened to do when I got out of hand.”

He watched his grandfather for any signs of life, beyond the wavy lines on the heart monitor, but found none. “I drank more than I had in a long time, last night. I know I promised Joanne I'd never do it again, but this is more than I can handle. First, I lose my wife and daughter because I'm an idiot and couldn't see it coming. Then I find out I lost a brother I didn't even know I had. Now you're in here because of me.

“Damn it, Grandfather, wake up.” He pounded on the metal guardrail. “I couldn't handle it if I lost you, too, because of my bloody temper. I'm a lousy grandson.”

The machine next to him that shared the steady rhythm of his grandfather's heart started to beep wildly. A pale, wrinkled hand reached out from under the sheets and grabbed his arm.

CHAPTER TWENTY

"Never say that again," his grandfather said with a stern and raspy voice.

Alex jumped out of his chair and rushed to the door. "He's awake," he yelled towards the nurse's desk. He ran down the hallway to the cafeteria, almost knocking over the volunteer delivering the patients' lunches.

He burst through the doors and searched the room for Joanne and his grandmother. "Joanne, Grandma, come quickly. He's awake." He held the door open for them, and they all rushed back to the room.

The on-call doctor was already there, checking him over. "It's great to see you awake, Mitch. You gave us quite the scare there."

His grandfather groaned and struggled to sit up. Ruth pushed him back down. "Just lay back and rest, my dear." She rested her hands against his cheeks and bent down to give him a kiss. "I thought I'd lost you."

Mitch lifted his arm and wrapped it around his wife. "Can't get rid of me that easily, my little dove. I'm not going without a fight."

Alex watched the exchange and wished he could have experienced what they had, an undying love that nothing could match.

His grandfather turned his head and looked at him. "Come here, boy." Sadness and regret past across his face.

"I never meant—" Alex started to say, but his grandfather held up a hand to silence him.

"If anyone is to blame, it's us. We knew we'd have to face this one day, and we did it rather badly."

Ruth placed her hand on Mitch's shoulder. "Sweetheart, let's not get into this today. You just woke up."

Alex knew she was concerned Mitch might collapse again and understood her fear. He decided to do the first grown-up thing since he'd learned of this. "Grandma is right. Another day or two won't hurt. After all, it has been over three decades already, right?" He tried to keep his words light but couldn't prevent a slight hardness from sneaking its way into his voice.

Joanne tugged on his arm, and he followed her from the room. "Why don't you go back to Laryssa? It may be a while before he regains his strength."

"I came here to learn the truth."

"And you will. Why don't you just invite them to the wedding, and let them meet Laryssa. We can all sit together and discuss this."

He clenched and unclenched his fists, struggling with the desire to know the truth. "I need to know."

"Yes, you do. I agree. But not at the expense of your grandfather's health."

"Then you tell me."

"I..." Joanne stared into the room and pulled the door closed.

"I know you know."

Joanne sighed. "The only man more stubborn than you was your father, who got his stubbornness from the man behind this door."

"Please. My rope broke, and I drank for the first time in years. I can't keep doing this."

She slapped his shoulder. "Alexander Michael Richards, you told me you wouldn't do that again."

He lifted his hands in surrender. "I had no plans to, but seeing him in there and my...my daughter..." He stopped speaking and ran a hand through his hair.

"I think it would be good to go home to Laryssa. Give yourself a break. Your grandfather is on the mend, and by time he's ready to come over, you'll both have had a bit of breathing room. Invite them to the wedding," she reminded him again.

"I don't know if I can wait that long."

They had planned the wedding in July, and it was only the beginning of June now. Snippets of what he'd done last night shot through his mind.

"Oh, God, Laryssa." He slid his hands down his face.

"What did you do now, mister?" Joanne looked at him, her hands on her hips.

"I phoned her last night." He cringed at the thought of what he may have said to her. He remembered parts of the conversation, but not all.

"You phoned her while you were drunk. What am I going to do with you? If you hurt that poor girl, you'll have to answer to me." She wagged her finger at him.

He went back into his grandfather's room with a new purpose. His concern was that Laryssa might not be there when he got back. Damage control would be the first priority upon his return. "I have to head back home, but I would like to invite you to our wedding. We're getting married next month on the ninth."

"You weren't serious about marrying his widow, were you?"

The complexity of the situation rose to the surface, and his desire to know the truth pushed forward again. He bit it back. "Will you come or not?"

Ruth and Mitch exchanged a glance. His grandfather held out his frail hand and Alex shook it. "If I am well enough, we'd love to come."

"I'd love to stay longer, but I don't like to leave her alone for too long."

"I told her to call Melissa, but knowing her, she probably didn't." Joanne turned towards his grandparents. "She's a stubborn one. He's got his hands full."

He wanted to stay and question them about what happened, but Joanne was right. Distance is what they all needed right now, and time to find out the best way to approach this. "I'll go for now, but we will talk." He gave them a nod and left the room.

~

"I never expected to be doing this again." Laryssa stared at the mirror next to the dressing room of Angel's Bridal Gown Shop. The shop was run by a woman about her age. She was skinny and tall, with short hair, dyed white and silver.

"I've never seen a more radiant bride." Joanne sat perched on a chair.

"Just a few more adjustments and your dress should be ready for pick-up tomorrow." Angel stuck a few more pins in the hem the dress.

"Thanks, you've been great. I was not expecting it to turn out this good, especially as I look like a barge."

"It's my job to make you look good. Your man is going to love it. You look absolutely beautiful." Angel stood up and took a step back to survey the dress.

Her man? It was true that Alex had been a little kinder since he returned from England a month ago, but she wasn't holding out her hopes that he considered himself 'her man'. She wasn't even sure she wanted to view him as such herself. When he arrived back home, he immediately apologized for his behavior. He even promised to never get drunk again. She'd heard it all before.

How many times had she forgiven Aidan for the very same? This was why she made the promise never to be gullible again, and here she was marrying a man who might not be any different. Her heart thumped against her chest as if in disagreement. The most disconcerting fact was that she liked him, even with all his faults. When they weren't arguing, he was the sweetest guy she'd ever met.

He told her to spare no expenses for the wedding and to pick whatever dress she wanted to. She settled on a short, pink silk maternity wedding gown. Being summertime, she wanted something she'd be comfortable in. The gown had a dipping neckline, which initially made her nervous. She'd been worried about bending over and having her breasts pop out. Her breasts had swollen to almost two times their original size due to the pregnancy. The dress came down to her knees and was covered with a rose design made of fine lace.

Joanne and the clerk both insisted this was the dress she should settle on and, after a few twirls in the mirror, she'd been as hooked as them. She'd felt glamorous for the first time in her life.

Most of her clothes were bland. More suited for a wallflower, made to blend in with her surroundings. If Aidan couldn't see her, he couldn't hurt her. No longer would she hide away. She was her own woman now. The queen of her own life. No one would rule over her. If Alex didn't like the dress, tough!

If she was honest with herself, that wasn't entirely true. A small part of her hoped he'd like it. The same part of her that hoped she was doing the right thing by marrying him, and that for once something would go her way.

"Do you think I'm doing the right thing, Joanne?" She looked over towards Joanne who had a confused look on her face. She clarified, "Marrying Alex, I mean."

"No one can decide that but you. I will tell you this though, you've been good for him. I know, at times, it may not seem like it, but you have."

She spun one final time in front of the mirror to inspect the dress and then went back into the dressing room to change. She hung the dress up on the hanger and ran her hand along her belly. The twins were having another wrestling match. "Easy, little ones. I'll have none of that now," she said. Her back ached from all the activity.

"Are you almost ready, Laryssa dear? Mitch and Ruth should be arriving shortly," Joanne called through the door.

Butterflies filled her stomach at the thought of meeting Alex's grandparents. In mere hours, she'd meet her children's great-grandparents. Today seemed more like a dream than reality. After Aidan's death, she thought it would only be her and the babies. Never in her wildest dreams did she imagine an extended family. She wasn't sure of the welcome she'd receive after how they had treated Joanne in the past, but she kept her fingers crossed. Laryssa sat in the back of the limo, chewing on her nails.

"If you keep biting your nails, we'll never manage to salvage them for the wedding," Joanne said, taking her hand.

"Do you think they'll like me?" she found herself asking. What did it matter whether they did or not? It wasn't like she'd be here long term. She knew Alex didn't think that way, either. Once they met her, she was sure they'd view her as a gold digger—only interested in their money. "Forget I asked."

"They really are wonderful people. I'm sure they'll love you." Joanne gave her a re-assuring pat on the knee. "Just like I do."

As they pulled up to the house, Alex came out to meet them. "They just phoned me from the airport, they should be here shortly." He offered her a helping hand out of the vehicle. "Are their rooms ready, Joanne?"

"Quit worrying, my dear boy." Joanne stepped aside to let Laryssa out.

Once she climbed out, Alex put his hand on Laryssa's lower back and guided her into the house. Her dress clung to her body under the heat of his hand. "How'd everything go?" he asked once they were inside.

"Great, I found—"

Joanne tugged her aside and whispered, "Shush. Leave him guessing. Anticipation is half the fun."

She looked back at Alex, and a tidal wave of sadness washed over her. What fun? There would be no magical wedding night. No coming together of man and wife in every sense of the word. Was she robbing him of the chance to find his soulmate? They had chemistry, there was no denying that, but what hope could there be if love wasn't involved?

She allowed Alex to lead her inside, and they sat down on the tan-colored sofa in the sitting room. He leaned down and helped her remove her shoes, placing them on the shoe rack inside the closet.

"Why couldn't we have just gotten married quickly? Why all the fuss?" Laryssa struggled to reach her foot to massage away the pain. "My back is aching. My feet are sore. I can't take much more of this."

"Only one more week, and all this will be behind us." He pulled up a stool and sat down in front of her. He gently lifted her foot onto his lap and began kneading the tender sole.

She leaned her head back against the cushion and moaned softly. "You don't have to do that you know, but gosh it feels good."

He smiled. "I know, but I want to."

His fingers sent mini shocks ricocheting up her leg. For a moment she thought about pulling her foot away, but she loved feel of his hands on her skin. She took a deep breath and her nose tickled with the scent of his fresh citrus cologne.

"I feel so helpless at times. I can barely get out of bed and put my own clothes on these days."

His hands paused, and his eyes roamed down her body. "Now, there's an image I wouldn't mind seeing." His voice lowered an octave, and a deep chuckle rumbled in his throat.

"That's such a typical guy answer." She shook her head and laughed. "But trust me, it's not a pretty sight."

"Why don't you let me be the judge of that?"

She lowered her head to look at him and wished she hadn't. His darkened lustful gaze threatened to release the love and pleasure she kept locked away in her heart. She'd placed them in a double locked chest and thrown away the key long ago. That was the only way she survived when she lived with Aidan. When he was home, it was all about him. There was no giving. No affection. If he wanted sex, she gave it. Her pleasure long forgotten.

With a simple touch and gorgeous eyes like oceans of the Caribbean, Alex awoke every nerve in her body and every desire that she'd long since suppressed. Never did she think a massage could arouse her, but as his fingers massaged the instep of her foot, heat spread through her and pooled like a tornado in her belly.

"Where did you learn to do that?"

"When Valerie was preg..." A shadow passed over his eyes, and he dropped her foot abruptly.

He started to stand up, but she placed a hand on his cheek. "Alex, please, don't run."

He covered her hand with his and leaned his face into it, before turning his face to brush his lips over her palm. When their eyes met, her chest constricted. The lust in his gaze was replaced by despair. A sorrow so deep that not even a submarine could reach its depth.

"What happened?" she asked.

He shook his head and stood up, turning away from her. When he turned back, the pain in his eyes disappeared, replaced by an emotionless mask.

"Please, don't close yourself up again," she begged. "Talk to me."

"Just like you talk to me, eh?"

"No, you don't. You are not going to turn this one back on me." She struggled to get up from the low couch, and he held out his hand. She pushed it away and continued her attempt to get up.

"Don't be stubborn." He grabbed her wrists and pulled her up. She stumbled over the stool and bumped into him. He tightened his grip and held her while she regained her balance.

"Geez, this is so not fun," she grumbled.

"You've certainly—"

"If you're going to say grown, I'll bop ya one," she threatened, hoping to put a sparkle back into his eyes.

His eyes drifted down to where her belly rested against his hip and then back up to her face. "Okay, I won't." He winked at her.

She slapped his shoulder.

He took hold of both of her wrists. "Hey, I didn't say anything. I object to that type of abuse."

They stood there a moment. She wanted to learn all about him and have him reveal all the deep dark secrets that hid behind those ocean-colored eyes. She wanted him to trust her for a change, just as she trusted him. Well, sort of trusted him. There were still things she kept hidden from him.

She didn't have a second chance to ask what was bothering him. All thought fled from her mind when his hands ran down her arms, coming to rest on her waist. Being pregnant and the size of a hippo didn't dull the sexual desire building inside her. Knowing they couldn't take it anywhere, she started to pull away.

"Where are you trying to go?" He tightened his grip on her.

"Away from this fire," she whispered. No point in trying to mask what he no doubt already guessed.

"Sometimes, the only way to deal with this particular fire is to give it what it wants," he murmured as he lowered his lips to hers.

Alex hadn't planned on kissing her, but as she looked up at him with her big brown eyes and flushed cheeks, he couldn't resist another taste, despite the pain inside him. Her lips were soft and tasted of strawberries, his favorite fruit. She turned slightly, which moved her belly out of the way slightly, and wrapped her arms around his neck. Her fingers played with the hair on the nape of his neck.

Unable to resist the urge, he ran his fingers over her breasts. She shivered beneath his touch, which increased the ache building in his gut, his jeans growing more uncomfortable by the minute. His erection pressed hard against the zipper. He wanted to pull her flush against him, but her belly prevented that close contact he desperately craved. He grabbed her hand and guided it to him. He expected her to resist but she didn't. She gasped when she came in contact with the bulge behind his jeans.

"That's what you do to me," he groaned as her hand pressed against him.

She pulled her hand back and looked around. Her face went a deep crimson. "Alex, what if Joanne walked in."

She had a point. The things he wanted to do to her were best done in private. He took her by the hand and started to lead her toward his office. "Come with me."

Her heart pounded beneath his thumb, but she still resisted. "We can't. You know we can't."

"We may not be able to make love, but we can still have fun, can't we?"

Laryssa went as still as a statue.

CHAPTER TWENTY-ONE

Laryssa gaped at him. *Love?* Since when did he call having sex with her making love? Not that they'd done it, yet, but still. The phrasing, and the tone behind it, opened up old hopes and dreams. She couldn't let herself go down that road, especially as he might have just gotten caught up in the moment. As it was, she had started to care for him. If she let herself believe it was deeper and it wasn't...

She shook her head. She wouldn't let herself think about it. No matter how much her heart wished it so. In Alex's face, there was a promise of pleasure, and her body ached to take him up on his offer, but she'd only hurt herself in the process, literally and emotionally.

"Your family will be here soon, Alex. We can't."

"Joanne will show them in." He pulled her close and nuzzled her neck, nipping at her earlobe.

Her insides melted, and she rolled her head back. "Gosh, you know how to make this difficult, don't you?"

"It's already hard for me. It's only fair," he murmured. His voice muffled by her hair.

A picture of him gloriously naked, and very much aroused, popped into her head. Wet heat seeped onto her panties. She shifted uncomfortably. "I don't think you know how to play fair."

His hands slid up her sides and brushed the edge of her breasts. She let out a small moan, which was drowned out by the doorbell. Alex leaned his head on her shoulder and mumbled incoherent words under his breath.

"We should probably get that," she said.

"I'd much rather do this." He framed her face with his palms and went to lower his head to hers again. She turned her head sideways, and his lips met her cheek.

"It will be your grandparents. We can't ignore it."

"Joanne will get it." His face radiated apprehension, and his body stiffened. The muscles in his jaw tightened, creating little crevasses along his jawbone.

She swallowed hard. Now she understood the persistence behind his actions. He didn't really want her. He wanted to forget what was about to happen and having her within arm's reach was one way to do it. However, as much as she wanted to be mad at him, she couldn't be. If she found herself in the same situation, she'd reach out for someone, too. Her life had been upheaved, but not nearly as much as Alex's.

"I'll go in there with you if you want," she offered.

Alex stared over her head and down the hall, listening as Joanne greeted his grandparents. He heard the low baritone voice of his grandfather, and the alto voice of his grandmother. The five weeks of waiting were finally over. He'd thought by this time he'd have more of an idea of how to speak with them. He was no closer to an answer than when he stood by his grandfather's bed in the hospital. Even with Laryssa by his side, he needed something to ease the nerves that threatened to choke his airway. He grabbed her hand and followed the trail of voices.

Joanne had led his grandparents to the living room. He glanced at his grandfather and noticed that he looked much better, although still slightly pale and more fragile in appearance. He had taken a seat in Alex's favorite recliner and was looking at a western-type novel. He remembered his grandpa doing this many times when he was younger. After all the hype of the day died down, he'd lie back and enjoy a good book. His grandmother was sitting with Joanne, sipping a cup of tea as she relayed the events of the last few weeks.

The room went quiet when they walked in. He immediately went to the bar on the opposite side of the room. "You guys want anything?"

Everyone shook their heads. He poured a stiff glass of whisky and drank a mouthful, letting it burn in the back of his throat before swallowing.

"You shouldn't either," Ruth said quietly.

His eyes narrowed and he lifted his head to look at her. "What I do in my house is my business."

He may have promised Joanne not to get drunk, but that didn't mean he couldn't indulge in the occasional drink, especially if it helped him relax. With the tension building inside him, he needed something that would take the edge off and help make the conversation go easier.

"And the choices we made were our business, Alex," his grandfather piped up.

"We did what we thought was right at the time. You were too young to understand."

"What about now, huh? What about the last fifteen years? I couldn't have been too young then."

"We admit we waited too long. Is that what you want to hear?" Ruth looked down at the cup she held in her lap. The tea swished dangerously close to the edge as her hands shook. "We didn't expect this to happen."

"Life never turns out the way we expect." He slammed his shot glass on the counter and walked towards the window. He turned back to face them, half sitting on the windowsill.

"We were going to tell you. We just didn't know how. You weren't the easiest boy as a teenager. We thought if we told you, you'd run off," Ruth tried to explain.

"Son, you were—are important to us, and we'd do it a second time if we had to." His grandfather spoke with a certainty in his voice. "Sit, and we'll explain."

"I'm comfortable where I am."

"After we lost your father in the accident, your mother's parents fought to get custody of both of you. We lost Scott, and we weren't about to lose contact with all that we had left of him. We tried to get custody of you both, but it didn't work out that way. The judge, knowing he'd have a long and drawn-out court battle on his hands if he didn't decide something quickly, chose to separate you boys. We got you and your mother's parents got your brother. The only stipulation was that we couldn't tell you about Aidan. If we didn't agree to all the conditions, they were going to put you boys into foster care."

Alex shook his head in bewilderment. "You expect me to believe that? No judge would refuse a child the right to his grandparents."

Joanne spoke up for the first time since the start of the conversation, "Let them finish, my dear boy."

Mitch explained the family feud that had existed for generations. How a member of the other family had been killed while working for them. He'd injured himself and fallen in a ditch. No one discovered him in time. They'd tried to bridge the gap, but the other family refused to forgive them.

"Their son shot my father because of it. Once the police learned who the shooter was, he spent time in jail. After that, they hated us even more. They thought we should have been punished, not them. When their daughter and Scott, our son, got married, the newlyweds hoped a peace would come between the two families." Mitch stopped and squeezed his wife's hand.

Ruth grabbed a tissue off the coffee table and blew her nose. "It didn't work out that way. Her family disowned her."

"I don't understand. If they didn't want her, why would they want us?"

"Revenge, plain and simple. They wanted custody of you both to get back at us and her. Their lawyer must have realized the judge wouldn't go for it and put in the suggestion of splitting you boys up. We had no choice but to agree. We weren't about to lose both of you if it went to a full-blown custody trial," Mitch said, adjusting his position in the recliner.

"The judge saw we couldn't get along and decided that we shouldn't contact each other, or they'd take you boys away as a result, considering the past history. Once your mother's family got a hold of Aidan, they disappeared and we never heard from them again," his grandmother said, her eyes watching him with hope and wariness.

Alex hopped off the windowsill and turned his back on them for a few moments, looking out into the yard. In light of the new information, he had a better understanding of what happened. Nothing could lessen the pain of never knowing his brother or having a chance to be part of his life, but it helped. As he looked out the window, he could imagine the two of them wrestling in the grass as they reached for a football. Something he'd seen his friends' families do.

Sadness threatened to overtake him as he realized his whole family was gone, except for his grandparents. Only a moment later a light bulb went off in his head. They knew his mother and her family, yet they said only Scott had died. If that was the case, how did his mother fit into the story after the accident? The equation didn't balance out. The thought that she might be dead too went through his head. Why else would the judge have been faced with custody issues?

He spun on his heels and faced them. His grandmother sunk back into the couch, and all hope fled from her features. "My mother. What happened to her?"

Mitch and Ruth exchanged glances before looking back toward him. The room was so silent that he could hear his heart pounding.

"We wanted to tell you, but by the time you were an adult we were afraid and were never quite sure how to bring it up." Ruth's voice trembled as she spoke.

"You guys always avoided talking about her. Did she die?"

Joanne sat beside Ruth and took her hand. "It's time for him to know."

Mitch sat back in the recliner with a resigned sigh. "Your mother didn't die, and she didn't desert you. After the accident, she was in a coma for a while. She was too sick to care for you. It's how we ended up with custody."

"She's alive, and you never told me?"

Joanne, Mitch, and Ruth exchanged glances again and it aggravated him. Obviously, they all knew the secret.

"There were..."

"Circumstances. I know. Okay, let's hear this one." He took a deep breath and plopped himself on the couch, settling in for another tale of the bizarre. It couldn't be any stranger than the last.

"When she was finally up and about, she went home, but her family didn't welcome her. They got a doctor to declare her an unfit mother. She had no choice but to leave," Mitch said.

"How could they refuse a mother the right to see her own child?" Alex gawked in amazement. Crooked doctors? Was there anything this story didn't have?

"It's amazing what money can do," he heard Joanne mumble and glanced over at her. She and Ruth had a death grip on each other's hands.

"Not long after that, she came to us, scared and alone," Ruth told him.

He clenched his fists. "Let me guess, you guys turned her away, too?"

"At first, we thought about it because we were scared to lose you. But Ruth and I realized that if it had happened to us, and we weren't allowed to see Scott, it would have killed us. So, we offered her a job. We knew we were risking a lot due to her being declared unfit and the restraining order. If anyone found out, we could have lost you. That's when we told her to change her name and then come back."

"If she was working for you, why didn't she tell me who she was?"

"We asked her not to. I realize now that was the wrong choice, but we did what we had to do to protect you. We couldn't let you accidentally tell someone she was working for us. You were too young to understand at that point. Her family is very influential, even more than us. If they'd caught wind of it, we might have lost you."

Alex rubbed his aching head and Laryssa stood behind him,

resting her hands on his shoulders for support. He only had one question left. "Where is she now?"

He watched Joanne lean over and whisper something to Ruth, who responded with a nod of her head. Joanne stood up and took hold of his hand. "Come with me, dear boy. Let's give them a break for a few moments."

Joanne walked with Alex outside and into the garden. Her heart beating a mile-a-minute.

He stuffed his hands in his pockets as they entered the gazebo. "I can't believe all this is happening."

Joanne looked up at him. He towered over her by at least a foot and a half. He certainly had become a handsome man. She still remembered the day when he asked her to be his housekeeper after he moved into his own house. She ached to tell him that she was his mother, but she'd resigned herself a long time ago that this was all she'd be. Losing her strength, Joanne collapsed onto the gazebo bench.

Alex came up and knelt in front of her and took hold of her hands. A lump formed in her throat as she looked into his eyes. She trembled under his gentle touch.

"Oh, my dear boy. I wished all these years that you would grow up to be a kind, compassionate man, and I got my wish." She sniffled.

He pulled out a hanky from his pocket and gave it to her. "I'm not kind," he said.

"Yes, you are. You try to act otherwise, but you have always been a man with a caring heart. No matter what you go through, you always will be. That is why Laryssa is still here. She sees that herself."

"You didn't bring me out here to speak about Laryssa, did you?"

She shook her head. His eyes watched her with curiosity as she blew her nose into the handkerchief. She'd spent years praying for this day. The time when she could finally tell him the truth and not have to worry about anyone taking him away from her. One question remained. How would he take the news? Would he accept her? Fear curled in her stomach. She wanted to tell him, but she couldn't seem to make her mouth move.

She remembered back to when he was a boy. She'd kissed his boo-boos all better and comforted him after he had had a bad dream. She'd nursed his injuries after a school yard brawl. Never being able to hear him call her 'Mom' broke her heart, particularly one night when she held him in his arms after a bad dream and he'd said, '*I wish you were my mom*'.

Now here they were, years later. She stared up at the man he'd grown into. There was a hardness to him that only bad life experiences could bring. Hopefully, Laryssa could crack his shell and break the facade he hid behind.

Eager to get it out of the way, yet frightened all the same, she took a deep breath. "Your mother still works for your family."

He stood up and began to pace the length of the gazebo. Anger evident in his stiff stride. His fists clenched tightly at his side. "Who, Joanne? Tell me who she is."

Her heart thumped erratically, and a knot formed in her chest. She took hold of his hand and held on for dear life. Opening her mouth, she spoke the one word that had always rested on the tip of her tongue. One she was never allowed to speak, till now.

"Son."

No other word needed to be said. She knew the moment realization dawned on him. His eyes met hers. Mouth open wide.

"You."

CHAPTER TWENTY-TWO

The stalker drove up and parked his black Cadillac across from the mansion and read the address. Excitement coursed through him. Three months of searching and he'd finally found her. If Matt hadn't been such a dick, he'd have found her sooner. No matter. He was here now.

The grounds looked like Fort Knox. The large perimeter wall stood over ten feet tall, with what looked like an alarm running across the top of it. No doubt he'd have guards patrolling the grounds with a place this large. He might not be able to get in physically, but he'd get to her somehow. Nothing would stop him.

He spotted the mailbox off to the side and a brilliant idea popped in his head; and as if on cue, he saw the red and white mail truck coming down the road.

"*You're a genius.*"

Just before the truck reached the mailbox, he pulled into the driveway and stopped at the gate. He saw a short, blonde-haired lady step out of the truck, and he opened his door to meet her at the box.

"Hey there, how's your day going?" he asked. "I'm Alex Richards." He held out his hand, hoping that she didn't really know the real Alex.

"Hi, Mr. Richards. I'm Kayla."

"I don't think I've seen you along here before?" He took a shot in the dark.

"Are you stupid, why'd you ask that?"

"Take her out. Take her out now." His eyes twitched, and his heart thumped wildly in his chest.

"You okay, sir?" she asked, resting a hand on his arm.

He shrugged and shook his head to silence the voices. "Yes, I'm fine. Sorry, ice pick headache."

"I know what those are like. Here you go." She handed him the mail. "And you're right. This is my first day along this route. But that's enough about me. I won't keep you out in the sun any longer than you have to be. Have a great day."

He watched as she walked back to the truck. Her hips swayed slightly as she moved, beckoning him to follow her.

'Go get her. Take her.'

'Quick before she gets away.'

"Shut up. She's not Laryssa," he growled at the voices, although he did have to admit that it sounded tempting. But for now, he had what he came for and that was enough.

This was much more fun than taking candy from a baby, and hopefully more rewarding. He hurried back to his car and waited for the truck to drive off, then took off in the opposite direction. Making a right on the next street, he pulled off the road and looked through the wad of mail he'd stolen. Junk, junk, and more junk. His hands stopped on a smaller, card-sized envelope that said return to sender and tore it open.

Inside was the address, date, and time of the wedding. That was all he needed to know.

"You've been in my life all this time, and you didn't even care to tell me?" Alex's voice rumbled, shaking the gazebo.

Joanne shivered at the tone of his voice as all her fears came forward. "I was afraid."

"Afraid, damn it? Afraid? How scary could it be to say, hi, I'm your mom?" He pinched the bridge of his nose in frustration.

She would normally have given him a scolding for speaking to her like that, but this time she would let him vent. There was no point in adding fuel to the already full-blown forest fire.

"I wanted to tell you for so long, but I was afraid to lose you. I'd already lost Aidan and your father. I would have died had they refused to let me see you." She looked at him, hoping to see understanding in his face, but was unable to read his features. "When you got old enough to move out and asked me to come, I couldn't refuse. I should have told you then, but I started to fear that if I told you, you would have fired me."

Alex stared at the woman sitting on the bench. How could he not have seen it? He'd always felt a strange closeness with Joanne, but this was not what he expected. It was a cruel twist of fate that kept her bound from telling him the truth. He looked into her eyes and noticed they were the same shade of green as his.

She gave him a shaky smile. "You look a lot like Scott, you know. You have his smile."

"Grandma use to show me pictures of him. I always found it funny that none of them included my mother...you." Now, here he was, standing only a few feet away from her. She looked like a whole different person today. She was usually cheerful, but this woman had her hands folded in her lap, wrinkles prominent around her downcast eyes. The worry made her look years older than she was, complimented by the strands of gray hair that glistened in the sun.

He'd dreamed of her being his mother when he was a child until the hope of having a mother of his own faded into a dim corner of his mind. He wanted to be angry, but sympathy bombarded him instead. The fact that she didn't feel she could trust him with the truth was the only thing that perturbed him, but he did understand her terror and probably would have done the same in her shoes.

She didn't abandon him like he thought she did. How many times had she comforted him when he cried out for the mother he didn't think he had. He finally recognized the look she'd always had in her eyes when looking at him. He'd always felt it too. The love a mother would have for her own child.

She continued to fold and unfold her hands in her lap, her anxiety obviously increasing due to his silence. "I'm sorry, Alex. Please, don't hate me."

He could only stare at her for a moment before his laughter rang out through the garden and through the open kitchen doors. He sat down on the bench and pulled her into his arms. "How could I possibly hate you? I think I've always known on a subconscious level that you were my mom. In my dreams as a little boy, you were the one helping me when I needed it. Not Grandma or Grandpa. When I hurt myself, you were the one who came running, not them."

She rested her head against his chest. "Oh sweetie, it's such a burden off my chest. Ever since you found out about Aidan, I've been so afraid. Laryssa said you wouldn't hate me, but when I saw how angry you were, I—"

His happiness faded, and his hands dropped to his side. "Laryssa knew?"

"Please, don't be mad at her, I told her not to tell."

"This affects me the most. Why am I the last one to know?" He stood up and grasped the railing of the gazebo. Laryssa knew and didn't tell him. He may not have been the easiest to talk to lately, but he deserved to have at least one person he could trust. Trust?

Since when had he begun to trust Laryssa? That scared him more than anything else. He didn't want to trust another woman. With anger coursing through his veins, he stormed back toward the house, with a stunned Joanne following close behind.

Laryssa watched Ruth pace back and forth across the room. Occasionally, she would pause at the hallway where Alex and Joanne disappeared, no doubt wishing she could be a fly on the wall. There wasn't much they could do but wait. The newly revealed mother and son deserved their privacy.

Guilt ate away at her for the umpteenth time. If it wasn't for her, they wouldn't be going through this. "I'm sorry that all this is happening."

Ruth came over and sat next to her on the couch and put her arm around her. "It's not your fault, sweetie. The truth needed to be told, we were just never sure how to go about it." She looked down at Laryssa's belly. "Do they really belong to Aidan?"

Laryssa's eyes widened. "How'd you know?"

"Alex, actually. He told us quite bluntly that he was marrying his brother's widow." Ruth must have seen her cringe because she continued quickly, "Not quite the way we wanted to hear he was getting married again, but we're happy none-the-less. We thought he'd never settle down. Not after what happened."

His grandfather grunted in agreement. "That kid is as stubborn as a mule."

Laryssa desperately wanted to pry more information out of them but ran out of time when she heard the sound of boots stomping down the hallway. She didn't even have time to take a deep breath before she was confronted with a red-face Alex, eyes blazing.

"You knew about all of this?"

She was at a loss for words, never having expected it to turn out quite like this. She had no part in this event, and yet the anger on his face was directed at her. "I—"

"I thought I could trust you. God knows why, but I did."

"You can trust me," she said softly.

He took her by the shoulders. "Really? Can I? You knew and didn't tell me. I don't like people keeping secrets."

"So, it's all right for you to keep secrets, but no one else?" She shook his hands off her shoulders and took a step back from the ferocity in his gaze. Every time she looked at him, she could see the secrets hiding in his eyes. They guarded him from any future hope of happiness.

"Alex, why don't we all sit down and talk?" His grandmother's voice broke through the tension crackling in the air.

Seemingly at a loss for words, he stood there letting his gaze pass over them, coming to rest once again on Laryssa. "Forget it! I'm going for a walk." He walked out the door, not bothering to close it.

Laryssa stood at the door and watched him cross the field. Within moments, a gentle hand came to rest on her shoulder. His grandmother had taken up the space beside her, watching her grandson.

Laryssa sighed. "Oh, Mrs. Richards, he has so much pain and won't even share it with me."

"Please, call me Ruth or Grandma. We're family, after all." The old woman gave her hand a squeeze.

The bond between Alex's grandmother and herself formed as they stood at the door of Alex's house. They watched him disappear into the forest. She couldn't deny the warmth that spread inside her at knowing she finally had people who cared about her.

"I hope we haven't caused too much stress for you today. You don't look like you need it." Ruth led her inside and shut the door. "I'll talk to him when he gets back. He shouldn't be upset at you."

"No, no. That's okay. I'm sure we'll work it out." Laryssa fought against the lump forming in her throat. She'd never thought she'd be part of a family again, nor did she expect to be accepted so readily. They didn't question why she was marrying him, didn't accuse her of marrying him for their money. Nothing. They just took her in as one of their own.

Could she finally have a family of her own, too, not just a family for her children? She didn't want to think on that for now, not when Alex was as angry as he was. Who knew what she could expect once he returned. She hoped he would understand. He might be her fiancé, but it hadn't been her place to tell.

Ruth led her down the hall and into the kitchen where Joanne was bustling about, making tea for everyone.

"If he gets mad at you again, I'll be sure to whip his butt into shape." Joanne sat at the table next to her.

She mustered up a small smile and stared down at the tea in her cup. "He has every right to be mad at me. If we wouldn't have met, he wouldn't be going through this."

"He'll thank you one day, you'll see." Joanne sent her a knowing smile.

She wasn't so sure about that but crossed her fingers anyway.

"Why, God?" Alex shoved hard at the branches in front of him and made his way through the grove of trees and bushes. The family he'd known and loved his whole life had kept the biggest secret from him. Not only was his mother alive, but damn it, she lived right under his own roof, and he didn't even know it. That was worse than finding out he had a brother. He always had a close relationship with Joanne without knowing why. He'd never gotten close with any of the other help, but she wormed her way under his defenses, like Laryssa managed to do.

When had he started to trust Laryssa? His words back at the house shocked him. He needed to get out of there and go somewhere where he could think. He pushed his way into the clearing and heard water trickling downstream. A clear, shallow river ran through his yard from one end to the other. This was his favorite place. He paused next to the river and took a deep breath. Leaning down, he picked up a flat rock and skipped it across the water.

He'd promised himself he would never trust another woman. Never get close enough to care about what they did, so why did her actions bother him? He could hardly fault Laryssa for showing loyalty to Joanne. He'd have lost his respect for her had she done otherwise.

What he didn't like was the fact that this entire situation gave him a deeper glimpse into her character. She was kind and trustworthy. A woman any man would be lucky to have. As much as he didn't want to accept it, common sense had him acknowledging that it wasn't her business to tell.

He didn't want to have this revelation, not now. Not when their wedding was only a few days away. The thought of caring about another woman made him pick up another rock. He chucked it as far as he could. Off in the distance, a bird chirped angrily. He couldn't let himself care for her; not when he was already so dangerously close to falling in love with her. True love was out there for some, but not for him.

After being burned once, he had no intention of trying again. That's one of the reasons he chose Laryssa, because there was no way she would fall in love with him.

She did deserve an apology though, but what could he say that didn't sound stupid. “I wasn't mad because I couldn't trust you. I was mad because I knew I could and didn't want to.”

That sounded lame, even to him. Trusting someone was supposed to be a good thing. Valerie forever messed him up on that one. An image of his daughter flashed in front of him, and the tightness in his chest soon followed. His brown-haired, blue-eyed wonder. He fell to his knees and closed his fist around a rock.

God, would the pain ever go away? He let the tears fall freely. His arms ached to hold his little girl again. How could she have been taken away from him so young? She should have been allowed to grow up and to have kids of her own.

“Son,” his grandfather's voice broke into his thoughts.

Alex flinched. He released the rock and brushed his eyes with the back of his hand before standing up.

“Sorry, I didn't see you coming,” he said, his voice thick with emotion.

“I just wanted to come and make sure you were okay.”

He looked around to see if anyone else would emerge from the forest.

“Don't worry, I'm alone. I left the women back in the kitchen.”

Alex let out a breath. “No! I'm not okay.” He walked away a few steps before turning back to his grandfather, arms open wide. “Will I ever be able to handle losing my daughter?” Annoyed having been caught in a moment of weakness, he turned away as tears threatened to fall again.

"I know how you feel, son. It killed us when we lost Scott. But as much as we wanted to live in the past, we can't. We had to move on. We had you to care for." His grandfather walked up next to him and placed an arm around his shoulder. "The pain never truly goes away. We still miss him to this day, but we did learn that life doesn't stop, and you have to find a way to keep going. You helped us do that."

"Me?"

"You gave us a reason to go on, and a reason to remember. Initially we wanted to forget, but as we watched you grow, you reminded us so much of Scott. Your laughter. Your demeanor. When I played with you, you helped me remember the good times I had with him. You know your mischievous look? It was just like his." His grandfather took a step away and leaned down to pick up a rock, holding it tightly in his hand. "Grab a hold of her memories, son. Don't let yourself forget them. If Julie was watching you now, what would she say about the hole you've put yourself in? You work till you're about to drop, and you've closed nearly everyone out of your life."

"I didn't put myself in a hole. I was thrown in by Valerie." He clenched his fists as he spoke her name. Even now that name could squeeze the air from his body.

"No one can keep you down, but you, boy. You were always stubborn. If you keep letting this drag you down, you will miss a lot of good things in your life, and a lot of good memories to come." His grandfather took a deep breath, as if contemplating whether he should keep going. "You may not want to hear this, but I'm going to tell you anyway. Marriage is a two-way street. You both have to contribute to it. If you don't, it won't last."

"But I—"

His grandfather held up a hand to silence Alex, and then threw the rock he was holding into the creek. "I know we made our share of mistakes in raising you, and in the way we acted when you and Valerie broke up. We don't condone what she did, but she was not the only one to have made mistakes. You spent so much time working and away from home. You left Valerie with a small child and the running of your house when she was barely an adult herself. Your relationship suffered because she didn't feel special to you. She didn't want the money. She wanted you. If a relationship doesn't get the loving care and attention it needs, it won't work."

Alex folded his arms and glared at him. "Are you saying it's my fault?"

"I'm saying you both were young when you got together. Neither one of you had a chance to live your lives. Neither of you knew what to expect or what was needed to keep your relationship alive. You've avoided her all this time because you blamed her for what happened. We never forced you to see her, but I think it's time to talk to her. You need closure. You're older now. and I think if you talk to her, you will be able to understand things better."

"We said all we needed to say back then," he gritted through a clenched jaw.

"If that is the case, then let it go. You are letting this eat you up, making you forget the special memories with your daughter. It's not letting you move on with your life. There are good women out there. Your grandmother is one of them. If you aren't careful, you'll lose the one good woman in yours. I may have only just met Laryssa, but I like her. She cares for you. I can see it."

His grandfather gave him a manly smack on the back and then left him staring out over the river. The sound of the water soothed his aching soul. The words that were spoken rang true in his head. She really was a wonderful person. Could she really care about him? *Nah*. She only cared because of what he could give her. He had to keep telling himself that before he let himself get in any deeper.

He had no intention of giving her the power to hurt him when she finally did decide to leave. He didn't want to hurt her either, although, he'd done a bang-up job already. He could be in the Guinness Book of World Records for being the man who said sorry the most.

He pushed and shoved his way through the bushes and went back to the house. Hopefully, Laryssa would accept his apology, or else he'd have to face the wrath of Joanne again.

CHAPTER TWENTY-THREE

Alex found the women gathered in the kitchen, working together to cook supper. Laryssa barely glanced at him when he walked in, and he couldn't blame her.

With a shaky hand, she picked up a carrot and started to peel it.

"Could I speak with you?" Alex asked.

"Now is not a good time." She pointed to the unpeeled carrots on the counter.

"We still have lots to do before supper."

"It's all right, my dear. You go with him. We'll be fine here." Ruth gave her a light kiss on the cheek. "We'll call you when it's ready."

She looked at Joanne with pleading eyes, no doubt hoping for an escape route. Before Joanne could say anything, he took Laryssa by the hand and coaxed her gently out of the room. He continued down the hallway towards his study and closed the door.

She wrapped her arms around herself and looked at him with guarded eyes. "If you plan on accusing me of something else, then tell me now. I'm not in the mood for another battle today."

He motioned towards the chair and watched Laryssa stretch her back as she glanced at the door. He wondered if she might attempt to make a run for it. She allowed him to guide her to the love-seat, and they sat down. He breathed a sigh of relief.

"Your grandparents really are wonderful people," she said, breaking the silence that hung over them.

"Yes, they are." Again, they collapsed into silence. He got up and walked to the little fridge, pulling out a bottle of water for his parched throat. "I'm sorry," he blurted out. There he said it. *That wasn't so bad.*

She tilted her head and looked at him with raised eyebrows. "You're sorry? Those are just words, Alex. Ones I've heard many times before. I bet you don't even know what you're sorry for," she said cynically.

He stared at her a moment and leaned back against his desk. *God, she's beautiful.* Even though she was pregnant with another man's baby that didn't lessen the beauty he saw in her. Pain shot through him. She made him wish for more, but he couldn't stand the thought of having another child and she was carrying two. She deserved a real relationship, and he felt like a jerk for offering her less, but he didn't have more to give. Sometimes, especially in moments like this, he wished he did. That thought rattled him and made him forget what he'd come into the office for.

"Well, do you?" Her voice broke through his thoughts.

He gave his head a shake. What were they talking about again? "I, uh..."

"Right, didn't think so." She got up from her seat and walked towards the door. No sooner had she got up, he moved to block her.

"Please, don't go." Taking her by the hands, he led her back to the sofa and sat down with her on his lap. She attempted to get up, but he held her there.

"Alex, I'm going to squish you. Let me go."

"Relax, I'm fine," he said. Her body relaxed against his, and he lightened his grip. Reaching up, he wrapped a strand of her long hair around his finger. "I'm sorry I snapped at you earlier. I was overwhelmed, and you didn't deserve the way I treated you."

"I know this hasn't been easy for you. It's not a picnic for me either, trust me."

Trust me, she says. That was the last thing in the world he wanted to do, but she had this uncanny knack of drawing it out of people. "I'm an insensitive clod sometimes and really bad with words." He buried his face in her hair, breathing in her tantalizing scent. "Please forgive me. You really are wonderful, and my family loves you."

Laryssa wasn't sure how to respond. She ached to ask him whether he loved her, but she knew he wouldn't welcome the question. He fought his feelings with an iron will. The only thing he didn't fight was his desire for her. She wrapped her arms around his neck and kissed him, letting her actions show that she forgave him this time.

His hand tightened on her arm, and his free hand cupped the back of her neck, pulling her closer. She dug her fingers into his hair and held on for the ride. He traced her lips with the warm tip of his tongue. Desire raced through her. The fresh smell of the forest clinging to his clothes sent a shiver all the way down to her toes. Did this turn women on in the cave man days when their men use to return from hunt? If so, the myth that the men had to use clubs was probably a lie. The women would have gone willingly, instead of having to be knocked out. They'd be intoxicated and seduced by their man much more easily. Of course, there would always be the man who'd do it anyway.

Laryssa pulled back slightly and a whole different tremor went through her body. She took a deep breath and pulled a small leaf out of Alex's hair. He continued to send trails of kisses down her neck. Could this man, who made her body come alive, be capable of the same evils? Had she ever responded to Aidan's ministrations the same way she did when Alex touched her? Had her toes curled when Aidan gently caressed her cheek, or when their legs accidentally brushed together when sitting at the table?

She'd asked these questions over and over in her mind and never found an answer, till now. Nobody in her past had ever made her feel this way, and she was darn certain no one else ever would. She sighed when he removed his soft, moist lips from her neck, then groaned at the emotions that were making themselves known inside her.

Crap.

She couldn't be in love. She didn't want to be. Suddenly, the phrase ‘love catches you unawares' flashed brightly in her mind. She'd been watching for it, guarding her heart closely, yet, somehow, the seed had been planted and was beginning to take root.

He lifted his hand and rested his palm against her cheek. “What is it about you, Laryssa Mitchell?” he asked. “How is it you set my whole body on fire?”

Fire? She muffled a chuckle. Her body felt like a blazing inferno. She desperately needed to cool down. “I...uh...need to go check on supper.”

“Are you afraid to be alone with me?” His lips brushed the side of her neck where her pulse raced like a horse.

“Considering my present state, yes.”

His gaze dropped to her belly. She realized he took her comment the wrong way, but that was okay with her. He didn't need to know she had a bad case of 'should I, shouldn't I love him'. If he took her now, she'd surely fall deeply in love with him, if that hadn't happened already. The feelings were still too fresh, too raw, not to mention confusing. Aidan kept popping up into the picture, and it was hard to be sure that she wasn't just falling in love with the man he could have been and not Alex himself.

Their relationship was bound to be a complete disaster. Alex didn't want love any more than she did. Her old lifelong fantasy was to meet a tall, dark, and handsome man who would love her more than anything she could ever imagine. Now she had met two and neither loved her, not to mention they were identical. No, a long life together wasn't possible. They both had way too many issues to deal with to make any type of a life together, regardless of the growing emotions inside her. She wouldn't even be here now if it wasn't for Alex and his family being related to the children inside her.

His hands caressed her breasts through her shirt, and his lips continued their pursuit on the tender shallows of her neck.

“What were we arguing about again?” she asked breathlessly.

“About how beautiful you are.”

Oh, yes, dangerously close to falling in love. She needed to get out of there and stop him from touching her. "I'm going to go check on supper now." Standing up, she walked over to the door and let out sigh of relief when he didn't follow her. This wasn't something they were ready for.

In fact, she wasn't sure she'd ever be ready for it. The only other man in her life that she'd ever felt anything for had turned into a monster. In a strange turn of fate, the man, who now stirred even stronger feelings in her, had her abuser's face.

How could one combat that?

Fifty minutes left and counting. Not long from now she would be walking down the aisle again. Her hands shook, and her knees banged together, which caused unending grief for the hair stylist, Desirae.

She placed her hands on Laryssa's shoulders to stop her from bobbing up and down. "S'il vous plait, Mademoiselle, hold still. We be done in a moment," she said with a thick French accent.

No matter how hard she tried, her knees kept knocking, and her stomach flipped for what felt like the thousandth time, and not because of the babies in her womb either. Desirae wrapped a wisp of her hair around the curling iron then let the strand fall against her cheek.

"Voila, magnifique." She clapped her hands with delight.

Melissa, Ruth, Joanne, and the hairstylists working on them all turned to look at her. She bit her lip as she waited for their appraisal.

"Wow, girl! You look awesome." Melissa, her maid of honor, glanced at herself in the mirror. "Much better than me. My hair is like a useless mop. Jamie won't let me cut it."

Laryssa looked in the mirror. "Hard to believe that's me." Her hair was swept up into a classic French twist mixed with baby's breath and two curly strands framed her face.

"Oh, my word! You look lovely," Ruth gasped.

Joanne sat there and stared at her, with tears streaming down her face. Laryssa got up and walked over to her. She picked up a box of tissue and held it out to her. "What's wrong?"

Joanne blew her nose and sniffled again. "I can't believe you asked me to do this. I-I never expected to—" A loud sob ate the rest of her words.

She wrapped her arms around the older woman. "We're both starting a new life with Alex. You deserve it more than anyone." She wasn't under the illusion of a happily ever after, but Joanne would be his mother forever and deserved to be recognized. "This might not be conventional, but I read in a magazine of others having their mothers walk them down when there was no one else. You are the grandmother of my babies and my future mother-in-law. Not to mention, over these past few months, you've been like a mother to me. There is no one else I'd rather have walk me down the aisle."

Behind them someone snorted, and she turned to see Ruth crying. "I never thought this day would come." Ruth dabbed at her eyes with a tissue. "He's been so wrapped up in the past, never letting himself have a chance at happiness."

Laryssa gave Ruth a hug and then turned to stare at the dress on the bed. Getting into the dress would prove tricky as she couldn't even bend down and touch her toes anymore. She stretched to the side attempting to dislodge one of the twins who'd taken resident under her ribs. They'd been far more active lately. She could have sworn they'd taken up kickboxing.

"Need help?" Ruth asked.

"Yes, please," she said and held the dress out to her.

Thankfully, once the whole truth had come out, the family seemed much closer than they'd been previously. Alex had been even more attentive and outgoing towards her over the last few days. She couldn't tell whether that had been because his family was around, and he felt the need for charades, or because he really had feelings for her. Not that they'd really spent any quality time alone together. Most of his time had been focused on Joanne. After their last meeting in his study, he had avoided being alone with her. She couldn't help but wish that he had made a way for them to have some alone time.

But she didn't want to dwell on any bad thoughts or feelings today. For all intents and purposes, it was her wedding day. Today, she would allow herself to dream, to forget that it was all a sham created to deceive the people she'd come to love. Laryssa was determined to make sure this was a day Alex would not forget.

She put her arms inside the dress and stood there as Ruth carefully zipped it up.

"Are my lovely ladies ready?" Mitch's voice called from the other side of the door.

"One second," Laryssa called back. She walked to the mirror. Desirae put the tiara with a veil attached on her head and secured it in place.

Mitch stepped into the room and placed a hand dramatically over his heart. "I must have died and gone to heaven. I've never seen so many beautiful women."

"Can I steal him, Ruth? My Jamie is nowhere near as flattering." Melissa grinned.

"Sorry, girls! I'm a one-woman man." He pulled Ruth close and made sloppy kissing noises.

"Mitch, you are going to ruin my make-up." Ruth scolded but wrapped her arms around him anyway.

"I think I'm going to have to bring Jamie around these two. He could learn a lesson or two," Melissa commented.

Laryssa wanted to cry as she watched them. Love radiated from the two of them. They appeared to be trapped inside a bubble where only the two of them existed. Would she ever have a chance at a love like that? She stopped believing in love after her experience with Aidan, but after watching Mitch and Ruth, who had been married for over fifty years, she couldn't deny that true love existed. Life was cruel. How could it throw two men in her path that didn't love her?

Alex just wanted her as a means to get what he wanted. Freedom from being hounded by his family. He wouldn't allow himself to love her even if he wanted to. He had too many of his own demons. Ghosts that sucked him into a world all his own. Hers weren't completely gone either. Each time she looked at him she couldn't help but wonder when he'd start to take his frustrations out on her physically.

Little by little though, she saw through the cracks and saw a man who wouldn't physically abuse her. His cold façade would disappear, and she would see him for who he was, and it entranced her. The other day she saw him walking through the garden with Joanne, his arm around her shoulders. He was capable of love, even if he didn't believe in it himself.

"Well, ladies." Mitch's voice broke her out of her deep thoughts. "It is time to go."

Melissa took her by the arm and led her down the hallway. Laryssa gave her best smile and allowed herself to be led to the waiting limousine. She ducked into the limo, sending up a prayer of thanks for having chosen a knee-high dress and not a full length one. How anyone could climb into a car with a full-length dress she didn't know.

"Is Alex already there?" she asked.

"Yep, he's been there for a few hours now, overseeing the last-minute preparations." Ruth took a seat across from her.

Laryssa turned and looked out of the window as they went through the gate and on to the road. Even with the slight cool breeze, the weather was blistering hot. Beads of sweat gathered across her forehead and threatened to ruin her make-up. She picked up the phone and asked the driver to turn on the air conditioner. There was a buzz of excitement in the limo, but she couldn't gather the strength to muster the same. Her legs bounced up and down and her hands refused to relax. She tried to calm her nerves, but they gathered in a tight ball in the pit of her stomach, making it churn. She hoped it would ease in the time it took to reach the church.

They'd been at the church the previous day for rehearsals. She could barely make her feet move as she did the practice walk down the aisle. Today, there would be people watching and that doubled her anxiety. She had wanted a quiet wedding, but Alex wouldn't hear of it. He said his family wouldn't believe him if he did things any other way. She would have been fine with eloping. The thought of standing in front of everyone, under false pretenses no less, didn't make her feel like a good person inside. Sure, she'd begun to have feelings for him, but his were a completely mystery. She knew he wanted to make love to her, but he remained emotionally distant.

After a while, she could see the church in the distance. The large cross on the roof stood taller than the buildings around it. As they got closer, she could tell the building had been repainted recently. The stained-glass windows looked as good as new. She knew it was one of the older buildings in the area, yet it blended right in with its surroundings.

The limo pulled up to the front of the church, and they got out. Laryssa stood there and looked around. Various colorful summer plants decorated the walkway that led up to the doors. The light breeze brought a flowery aroma her way. She took a moment to breathe it in. Shades of white, pink, and red clouded her vision.

She smoothed out her dress, which had crumpled slightly from sitting in the limo, trying to delay the walk up to the doors that held her uncertain future. Joanne rested her hand gently on her arm. "Come on, sweetie. We'd better get inside."

They started walking forward when the scent of a plant filled the air around her. She looked around, and her eyes homed in on a plant with crimson flowers that stood out from all the others. It might have been because of the placing. The plant was surrounded by pure white roses. Anyone would have spotted it immediately, but only one word came to Laryssa's mind as she stared at it.

Love.

It was the color of love. The childhood dream of every young girl. She had dreamed she would walk down the aisle in a beautiful white wedding dress, hanging onto her father's arm as he escorted her to her one true love. Tears formed in the corner of her eyes. No father would be here to give her away. No man to truly call her own. Not even the man who would be her husband.

I can't do this! Her stomach lurched, and she looked around quickly for a place of refuge. She spotted a willow tree with branches that hung low and bolted for them as quickly as she could, holding her belly.

CHAPTER TWENTY-FOUR

Laryssa shoved the branches aside and came to rest against the hard base of the tree. How, for the second time, could she marry a man who didn't love her? Why in her right mind would she settle for anything less?

Outside the tree, she heard Melissa speak, "Why don't you guys go inside and tell everyone we're here. I'll go talk to the bride with cold feet."

She looked up as her friend joined her in the hidden alcove. "Oh, Mel, I don't know if I can do this," she gasped breathlessly.

"You've got a bad case of wedding jitters. It's perfectly natural." Melissa pulled her into a hug.

"It's more than the typical wedding jitters. I'm scared."

"Scared of what?"

"That he'll turn on me. That he'll..." She was about to say that he'll never love her but bit her tongue before she did. Even though Melissa was her friend, she never really shared much information about their arrangement. Her friend, being as outspoken as she was, might have risked her job and given Alex an earful.

"Alex adores you. Anyone can see that. He might be arrogant, pigheaded, and stupid at times, but I can't see him being abusive."

Her friend nailed him to the letter and Laryssa couldn't help but smile a little.

"I'm not sure if I can take that risk."

"Life's full of risks. Some good some bad, but if you don't give it a shot, then you'll never know what could have been. When Jamie and I first got together, I was scared out of my tree. I'd finally managed to leave a bad relationship. I didn't want to risk my heart again. I wanted to lock it in a box and toss it in a river, but he fished it out. Now I couldn't imagine my life without him."

Laryssa pushed herself away from the tree and wrapped her arms around Melissa. "You really are a great friend, you know that?"

"I know. Tell you what, if Alex needs a good ass kickin', you call me, okay? I'm more than happy to come over and whip his butt, 'cause no one messes with my friend." Melissa pretended to kick at an invisible foe.

"I'll take you up on that offer if I need it."

"And another thing, girl. If you ever need a place to get away, you can always stay with us."

"What would I do without you guys?" She wiped her tears away. "How's my makeup?"

Melissa reached up and rubbed under her eye gently. "Mascara ran a little, but it's fine now." She took Laryssa by the shoulders. "Look. If you go in there, look him in the eye and decide you don't wanna do this, I will get you out of there with minimum fuss. Okay?"

"Promise?"

Melissa lifted her eyebrows. "Would I ever lie?"

"Knock, knock." Mitch pushed the branches aside and joined them in the little alcove. "It's time for us to walk the lovely bride down the aisle. The crowd is getting restless, and Alex is getting antsy that his bride might have taken flight. You ready to go, my dear?"

"Ready as I'll ever be." She placed her arm in his, and they worked their way back out of the mess of branches.

"You definitely picked a good hiding place," Mitch said laughing.

"I was always good at hide and seek." Laryssa shrugged her shoulders.

As they reached the lobby of the church, trepidation hit her again. Mitch must have noticed because he stroked her hand gently and whispered, "Take a deep breath. You'll be fine."

Down the aisle, Alex pulled at the tie choking his neck and tapped his foot endlessly on the ground. Nerves stretched the muscles taunt in his neck and created a dull ache in his upper back. Was she thinking about backing out? When Mitch told him, she needed a few minutes outside, his stomach dropped. If she spent too much time thinking, he knew she'd back out. He didn't trust that Melissa would convince her to continue to go through with the marriage.

The thought of her running away had his heart racing. He took a step toward the door, but Ron put a hand on his shoulder. "Don't tell me you're worried?" His friend chuckled. "Just give her a moment."

"Melissa doesn't like me. Who knows what she's saying out there."

He took another step off the platform when the wedding march started. He stood frozen in place as the doors opened. Melissa's young children walked down the aisle first, followed by their mom, who gave him the evil eye. Nothing at all prepared him for what he saw after they reached their destination.

The two most important women in his life appeared at the door, regally standing there. Everyone got up out of their seats and turned to get a better look. Murmurs broke out through the crowd as they saw something different to the usual orthodox choice. The bride was on the arm of the groom's mother! The decision had been made yesterday at the rehearsal. She'd insisted on Joanne walking her down. Mitch had offered, but she'd declined. They'd all finally settled on Joanne walking her halfway and Alex meeting them in the middle, which is what he'd do if he could get his feet moving.

She wore a pink dress with a low neckline, highlighting her breasts. His fingers itched to touch her. Below her breasts a ribbon wrapped around her, tied in a bow in the back. The dress flowed freely over her cute round belly and stopped at her knees. There, he caught a glimpse of shapely legs as she made her way towards him.

He managed to find his feet and started walking down the aisle.

Behind the pink veil she wore, he could see a shy smile on her face and pain in her eyes. The desire to protect her from all problems and troubles filled him. The need to touch her had him walking towards her at breakneck speed. They told him to walk slowly at the rehearsal but screw it. All he wanted was to be next to her.

The crowd let out a few chuckles. Others murmured about the groom being impatient. He stopped two feet in front of her and kissed the hands of his mom.

"Thanks, Mom."

His words sent more whispers through the crowd. Even though he knew almost everyone here, no one had yet heard that Joanne was his mother. She placed Laryssa's hands in his and took a step back to allow them to walk the rest of the way together. When they reached the altar, he lifted her veil and placed it behind her head.

He leaned in close and whispered. "If we were alone, I'd have my wicked way with you right here, right now."

He watched her face flush and pupils dilate with interest. Her cute pink tongue darted over her lips. His body reacted instantly. He wanted to ravish her all the more. He kissed the palm of each hand before wrapping them in his own. Her hands trembled, or at least he thought it was her hands, it could have been his own.

"Who gives this woman away?" the Minister asked.

"We do," Joanne, Ruth, and Mitch piped up.

"We are gathered here today to join Laryssa Mitchell and Alexander Richards in holy matrimony."

He continued to speak, but Laryssa could no longer hear him. Alex kept circling her palm with his thumb and looking at her as if he wanted to gobble her up. Well, two could play that game, and so the silent sensual war began. She looked into his eyes and smiled coyly, then let her gaze drift slowly and deliberately down his body and back up again. *Gosh, he's handsome in that tux.* She groaned when she couldn't catch a glimpse of a certain part of him. His pants and suit jacket hid him from her view.

Giving her head a shake, she let her eyes come to rest on his parted lips, which looked all too inviting, before meeting with his gaze again. The fire that danced in his eyes made her pulse hop against her throat. He lifted his hand to caress her cheek, and she leaned into his touch.

The Minister's hand passed in front of their faces, and he cleared his throat.

"Alex, this is the part where you're supposed to say I do."

Everyone laughed. Alex's ears and cheeks turned a bright red, and Laryssa could only imagine what her own face looked like.

"Don't worry. You guys can ravish each other later." The minister winked at them.

Alex leaned in and whispered, "I'll get you for that later."

"You started it," she said cheekily with a grin.

A few minutes later, the minister finished by saying, "You may kiss the bride."

Ever so gently, Alex took her face in his hands and took possession of her waiting lips. Hot passion sizzled between them. She lifted her hands and held on to his arms for support. Tears formed in her eyes. He could be so gentle when he wanted to be, and he was all hers.

After a few moments, they turned to face the cheering and clapping crowd. "I present to you, Mr. and Mrs. Alexander Richards," the Minister announced.

The elation quickly disappeared when an eerie feeling washed over her and the hair on her arms stood on end. She surveyed the room and saw a man slipping out of the back row. He wore a dark trench coat and a hat with the brim down low over his face. She hadn't seen him when she first entered the room. He must have come in after her.

A strange feeling of familiarity washed over her. He was the man from the funeral. She hadn't told any of the people who were there where she was, or what she was doing. The fact that her past had caught up to her made her chest tighten. She squeezed her eyes closed. When she opened them, the only evidence he'd been there was the door closing behind him. Why couldn't the past stay in the past?

But no such luck of that happening as a memory hit her. He was back. *The watcher*. The one Aidan commanded to keep tabs on her at all times. How did he find out where she was today of all days? Was it too much to hope that everything would end when her husband died? What was the watcher's name again? Donald, Dominick, Darren? The letter 'D' bounced around in her head.

Alex's hand squeezed her arm. "What's wrong, sweetheart?"

"I... uhh..." She looked at the empty doorway and then back up at him. "Yes, I'm fine."

The look in his eyes told her he didn't believe her but wasn't about to argue. He tucked her arm through his, and they made their way back down the aisle. They walked through the doors, and she came to an abrupt halt. In front of them, across the street, a black Cadillac pulled away from the curb and raced down the street.

"Shit. Shit. Shit." She generally avoided swearing or using slang words. Her foster parents had hated it when she swore and would rinse her mouth out with soap. She could still taste the soap whenever she misspoke, but she couldn't prevent them from slipping out this time.

Was he the man who sent the threats? Damn it, what was his name, D...D...something? How could she have forgotten about him? The man slobbered all over her whenever Aidan left the room. It had to be him. She shivered.

"Okay, now I know something is wrong." Alex turned Laryssa to face him, his hands resting on her arms. "What is it?"

She turned her head and watched the car disappear into the distance. A tremor raced through her, and her knees buckled. Alex tightened his grip to prevent her from falling.

Laryssa's fingernails dug into his arm. "He was here."

"Who was?" Alex asked.

She shook her head in frustration, wondering if she'd lost her mind. "I'm not sure. I think the person who wrote the note."

"Are you sure?"

She wasn't sure of anything, but she was sure of the fact she didn't invite that man to the wedding. How did he get by the attendants? Everyone needed to bring their invitation.

"Let's get you safely in the limo, and then we'll call the police." Alex wrapped his arm protectively around her waist and guided her through the crowd of rice throwers and helped her into the waiting car.

"What are they going to do? Track down all the people who own black cars?" she said as she sat down.

When he joined her, he had a white-knuckle grip on his cellphone. "Fine, but I'm adding another security detail to the house and you..." He gripped her arm tightly. "You're not to go anywhere without security, do you understand?"

All she could do was nod her head. The rest of the wedding party climbed into the limo, and they began their journey back to the house. She shifted in her seat, trying to get comfy. Pain radiated throughout her lower back, wrapping like a snake around her. Her stomach tightened as hard as a rock.

"I wish these guys would be born already. They are little invaders." She sat up and shoved one hand behind her back, trying to relieve the pain. "I think one is sitting on my sciatic nerve."

"Are you sure it's just the nerve?" Melissa looked at her with concern.

"Feels like it or maybe not." Laryssa wasn't really sure. Sciatica pain usually shot down her leg. This one hurt all over.

She asked them to stop the limo numerous times. She needed to stretch. "I'm sorry, guys. It's really hard sitting at the moment."

"We better have the doctor look at you when we get back," Joanne suggested.

"I'm fine. Well, I will be once these little monsters move. Let's just get the reception over with, and then I can lie down."

"The doctor will look at you," Alex said, leaving no room for question.

They had made so many trips to the hospital because of her pain. She didn't want to inconvenience them again today. There was always a certain amount of pain. The doctors informed her she was having intense Braxton hicks. They explained that it was the body's way of preparing for labor.

"The doctor earlier this week said everything was fine. I was having pains then, too." She was looking forward to the time when she'd be without pain and discomfort again.

"How about we compromise, I'll give you thirty minutes. If the pain continues, you see the doctor," Alex said with a frown.

"Agreed." Laryssa laid her head back against the seat and took a moment to rest. When they pulled up to the gate, she sat up and noticed a familiar glint through the back window. The black car pulled up beside them as they waited for the gate to open. She'd rolled the window down earlier to get some fresh air and wished she hadn't. The man behind the wheel pointed to his eyes, and then back at her before pulling away.

Her past had come back to haunt her. Surely, life couldn't be this cruel? This man had no business in her life. Not before. And definitely not now. "No, no, no."

Alex looked at her questioningly.

"I, uhh..." She watched the car disappear down the road, as another spasm of pain clutched her belly. Nerves, it was probably just nerves. She took a deep breath and then said, "I thought I saw something."

He swore, and everyone looked at him. "Sorry." He sat up straight in his seat, his mouth pressed in a firm line, and his eyebrows knitted together. He picked up the phone and asked the driver to wait.

She watched him get out and whisper something to the guards waiting at the gate, before climbing back inside. "I asked them to only let in people on the guest list and to not let any black cars inside, even if they have an invite." He gave her hand a squeeze.

Alex helped his new wife out of the car. Her face as pale as the white flowers which had lined the church walkway. The only time he'd seen her so frightened was when she'd discovered the note. He couldn't stand the scared look on her face and would do anything to bring her smile back.

When he said his vows, he made a promise to always be there to protect her. That was the only reason he hadn't given the note to the police. He never anticipated that the man would be able to find her so quickly before they could find out who he was.

For the first time in a long time, he was glad he'd gone through the trouble of installing a security system and choosing an onsite security team, looking carefully into their backgrounds. As a child, he had always dodged the security detail his grandparents set up for him. He didn't care for it, hated being watched and loved sneaking off without them. As an adult, he understood the need for it. The police, as good as they were at public service, couldn't be everywhere at once.

He and his friend had been in a major scuffle with a group of teenagers who thought they were treading on their turf and their girls. His friend barely survived and lay on the ground, unconscious, before the police even arrived. He'd learned his lesson and stopped sneaking around.

Alex looked at Laryssa. The fear he saw in her eyes as they darted back towards the gate clawed at him. She shouldn't have to be afraid. It wasn't fair. He wanted her to feel safe with him, not have to live life constantly looking over her shoulder. And now that she knew she had been found, what would stop her from leaving just to keep him safe?

She didn't think the note posed any threat to her, only him. But what if she was wrong, and the man was just waiting to get her alone? The only way to do that was to try and get him out of the picture, hence the note Alex surmised. The man would kill him without question to get to her. He couldn't stomach the thought of anything bad happening to her.

After the wedding photographs were taken, they all migrated to the ballroom, which had been decorated by the wedding planner. Circular tables were covered with white cloths, with gold-colored lace skirting the floor. All were strategically placed along the wall to leave the dance floor open for the couple's first dance together. The head table was in a spot all its own, with a gold-colored tablecloth and a white laced skirt. Each table had a pretty bouquet of pink, blue, and white flowers surrounded by baby's breath. A lit candle resting in the middle. Slowly but surely the rest of the guests arrived and were seated.

Laryssa scanned the crowd for the imposter. Even though she couldn't see him that didn't mean he wasn't watching. She learned that a long time ago. He didn't have an invitation. She hoped he wouldn't circumvent the guard and get in somehow. She forced herself to take a deep breath. This was supposed to be a happy day, her wedding day. She wasn't going to let some psycho mess it up for her.

She tried to listen to the speeches given by the Best Man and the Maid of Honor, but the pain in her back increased throughout dinner. She managed to catch a comment or two here and there. Ron mentioned that he had never seen anyone who captivated his partner's attention from the get-go. Not even with all the blind dates he convinced him to go on. Of course, Alex always threatened to strangle him after each one.

She struggled to smile at Melissa's joke about how she literally swooned when she first met Alex, but her mind and body wouldn't let her enjoy the moment. Thankfully, no one seemed to notice, other than her new husband, who kept sending her inquisitive glances every few minutes.

Alex stood up with an eagerness she could only wish for. "Thank you all for joining us to celebrate this very special occasion. If you had asked me a few months ago if I planned on getting married again, I probably would have run in the opposite direction. I'd sworn off women, thought they were nothing but trouble. No offense to the women in my life, especially my mother who's been there for me my whole life, even though I just learned who she really was. It's been a time of surprises, most of them good." He leaned over and gave Joanne a kiss on the cheek. "I love you."

He stood back up and stared at Laryssa with a goofy lovesick smile on his face. "Anyway, I really didn't have any plans on doing this again, and no one was going to change my mind, or so I thought. One day, I bumped into this exquisite creature in the elevator at work, and for the first time in ten years I felt alive. Her smile, her laughter, the gentleness in her voice blew me away. It wasn't long before I knew I wanted to spend my life with her. Thank you for saying yes, Lara." He lifted her hands to his lips, and everyone cheered.

Her heart skipped a beat when his warm lips brushed her skin. He should have been an actor. He would have had an Emmy by now. If she didn't know the truth behind their marriage, she'd have believed him herself. "Thank you for asking." She took a deep breath as another spasm attacked her back.

He frowned as he studied her face. In the background, she heard the clinking of a glass.

"It's time for the lovebirds' first dance," the wedding planner said.

Alex took her by the hand and led her on to the dance floor. Her belly prevented them from getting too close, but he placed his hands on her hips, and she placed her arms around his neck. He leaned down and whispered in her ear. "I can't wait for these little ones to be born so I can hold you properly."

She hadn't counted on another pain hitting her again and groaned. "You might get your wish." She felt a strange pop in her stomach, followed by warm fluid running down her legs, gathering in a puddle on the floor.

CHAPTER TWENTY-FIVE

Laryssa froze in Alex's arms. "I think my water broke." Her legs trembled as fear passed through her. It was too soon. Her babies were only thirty-three weeks. Her obstetrician, who was attending the wedding, rushed over.

He looked at the floor and then appeared to do a quick assessment of her. "Joanne, can you go get her hospital bag. Alex, go pull your car around to the front doors. We're going to want to get her to the hospital as soon as we can," Doctor Martin ordered.

"Thanks everyone for coming. I'm afraid the reception has to be cut short. Please accept our apologies. If everyone would file out to their cars, it would be appreciated."

Alex led her to the closest chair, and then high-tailed it out of the room to get his car out of the garage. Within ten minutes, they were on their way.

"Will you stop going over the bumps so fast," she groaned, tightening her grip on the armrest.

"Sorry," he mumbled and eased off the accelerator.

Doctor Martin met them at the emergency room doors with a wheelchair. They rushed up to the maternity wing, and Alex went to the desk to finish registering her.

After a few minutes of examination, the doctor looked up at them. "I'm afraid there is nothing we can do to stop the contractions this time. You are five centimeters dilated already. The good news is we don't have to do a caesarean by the looks of things. Baby A has his head down already. He's fairly low, which is why you've been feeling pressure."

"Feels like I have to take a gigantic poop." She gripped the edge of the bed as another contraction hit. After experiencing stronger contractions in the car, she'd finally figured out when one was about to hit. Her stomach would start to tighten, followed by an agonizing pain. If anyone told her it would have hurt this much, she would have threatened Aidan with a sledgehammer before she'd let him touch her.

She'd heard people say that women forget the pain once they hold their newborn baby for the first time, but there was no way she would forget how much this hurt. No way. No how. Not even her broken arm hurt this bad.

Another blinding pain attacked, wrapping right around her abdomen. She clenched her fists and squeezed her eyes closed, shaking her head back and forth. "I can't do this."

"Laryssa, look at me." She'd nearly forgotten about Alex and opened her eyes to look at him. He brushed the hair away from her face. "I know it hurts, but you can do it. When your next contraction hits, I want you to take some deep breaths with me, okay?"

All she could do was nod her head. Joanne, who stood on the opposite side of the bed, wiped the sweat beading on Laryssa's forehead. The doctor entered the room with an anesthesiologist. "Would you like something for the pain?"

She glared at the doctor. "What do you think?"

"Me thinks the lady would like something." The anesthesiologist winked at her and administered the epidural.

The wonderful pain medication kicked in and took the edge off, allowing her to breathe again. "It's not gone, but it's not quite as sharp anymore."

~

"You've progressed quickly, nine centimeters dilated. Nearly there now." Dr. Martin checked the machines. "The babies are doing well, too."

"I swear I'm never doing this again," she gritted between her teeth. Alex could feel her stomach tighten underneath his hand.

The doctor leaned toward Alex and chuckled. "They all say that but guess who's usually back the following year."

The ball in Alexander's chest grew and threatened to cut off the air to his lungs. He couldn't bear to see his wife in pain and did his best to comfort her. Feeling helpless, all he could do was allow her to have a death grip on his hands. His bones probably wouldn't thank him later.

Today had been beyond eventful. First, he stood at the end of the aisle again. Now, he stood in a birthing room surrounded by doctors, watching his wife give birth to his brother's babies, who, by all rights, could genetically pass as his own. Would they look like her? He didn't think he could bear it if she had a girl who looked exactly like his daughter. Maybe she'll have a boy, having a son might not be so hard. That might be easier to adjust to.

His wish went right out the door when her first child slipped out into the world, followed by her sister. They weighed in at four pounds one ounce and four pounds three ounces. Alex walked over and took a quick peek. Ann Nicole Richards and Ashley Marie Richards. His heart fell into his stomach. They looked identical to his daughter when she was born. He shook his head and backed up, bumping into Laryssa's bed.

"We're just going to transfer Laryssa into her private room now. Fathers are welcome to stay over. I could get a roll-away cot if you'd like," the nurse offered.

He breathed a sigh of relief when Laryssa said, "Alex probably would like to go home. He's had a long day. The babies aren't bunking with me so there really is no need for him to stay overnight."

"Are you sure you're okay?" he asked.

"I'll be fine. I know what you're thinking, Alex. I can see it in your eyes. Go home, and take some time to breathe. I'm not going anywhere for a while." She patted the hand he had resting on the bed beside her.

~

"They are growing like weeds." Melissa gasped as she looked at the babies inside the incubator.

"Amazing, eh? I'm still afraid to hold them. They feel so breakable." Laryssa slipped her hand inside, and a little hand closed around her finger, melting her heart into a puddle on the floor. She'd fallen completely in love with them. It was beyond imaginable.

"Any idea when you can spring them from their mini jails?"

"Well, they are four weeks old now and doing well, from what the doctor says. But he wants them to stay at least another week. Ashley had a little bit of trouble breathing at the start but seems to have caught up to her sister."

"Makes me want to have a little baby again." Melissa sighed. "Kara is four years old now."

"Going to try for another?"

"As much as I'd love to have another little one, the two I got are holy terrors already. I couldn't handle anymore." Melissa walked over to the other incubator and pushed her hand through the opening, brushing the baby's cheek. "How's Alex doing with this new father thing?"

She'd hoped that this would break down the last barrier between them, but it only created a new one. The twins bore an uncanny resemblance to his daughter. It was like destiny was playing another cruel trick on them. Everything that happened seemed to push them away from each other instead of closer together. Was this a sign that they weren't meant to be together?

Laryssa shrugged. "Your guess is as good as mine. I've hardly seen him since they were born."

"You're kidding me." Melissa's mouth dropped open. "How could he not come and check up on them? He's related to them."

"He's popped in maybe once a week, only long enough to say hello to me. I don't think he can bear to look at them. They look so much like his little girl."

"Don't make excuses for him, girl. He married you. They are his kids now, too."

What else was she supposed to do? If she didn't make excuses for his actions, she'd lose what little hope she had left. She could have been discharged weeks earlier, but thankfully Alex pulled some strings that allowed her to remain at the hospital with the babies. From what it sounded like, he wanted to be alone, and that was fine with her.

"I'd better go and let you feed them. They look hungry." Melissa pointed at the squirming infants. "Don't forget, I'm always here for you." After a quick hug, she hurried out the door.

The nurse picked up Ann from the incubator and motioned with her head to the chair. "Don't worry, they won't break. Every half an ounce, sit her up like this and burp her. If you don't, little air bubbles will get caught in her tummy, and she'll spit up." The nurse handed Ann to her, and then stepped back. "Do you have help at home, or are you by yourself?"

She wasn't surprised that a nurse finally asked that. For all intents and purposes, she was single. That's how it felt anyway. *Gosh, darn him.* She wouldn't be alone if he'd just get his butt to the hospital. He was such a wimp. They did agree on a no strings attached marriage, so he probably thought he didn't need to help her out. But if that was true, then why on earth had he stayed with her in the delivery room? Since she'd had Joanne there, his presence was unnecessary. Although, she couldn't deny that she had wanted him there.

"I have help, thankfully."

Laryssa looked down at the child sucking on the bottle and smiled. Her heart swelled with pride at having given birth to such an angel. Nothing prepared her for the depth of love that filled her heart for them. They were the only good thing that came out of her loveless marriage. She knew Alex would love them, too, if only he would just spend some time with the three of them and hold the little bundles of joy.

Ann's small fingers wrapped around her own. "Oh, my little angel, I pray that your uncle will come to his senses someday."

Alex stared at the phone in his hand. Laryssa dropped the bombshell. They were coming home today, and she wanted him to pick them up from the hospital, or she would walk out on him. The one thing he knew about Laryssa was to take her at her word. With all the times she'd made her displeasure known by stepping on his foot, he knew better than to question her.

He felt bad that he hadn't gone to the hospital more often and knew it had hurt her, but each time he tried to go, his stomach rolled over at the idea. He was a jerk, and he knew it. There was no getting out of it this time, Joanne and Laryssa would both wring his neck if he tried. Not that his neck wasn't already tucked away neatly in a noose.

Two times he'd nearly turned the car around to drive back home, but the thought of Laryssa leaving him made his gut clench. He didn't want to lose her. That he knew for a fact, although he wasn't sure how to keep her, either. His experience in relationships didn't tend to lean toward the positive. Would she forgive him when she saw what he had made for the little ones? For the last few weeks, he'd worked on a surprise for her. Hopefully, that would make up for his less than admirable qualities.

He pulled to a stop at the hospital doors and parked in the patient pick-up area. He took the elevator up to the paediatrics wing and walked up to the nurse at the desk. "Is Laryssa Mitch...I mean Richards ready to go?"

"Yes." She gave him the evil eye and pointed towards an open door.

He gave the nurse one last look before joining Laryssa in the room. “What was that about? I have a distinct feeling that nurse hates me.”

“Ya think? The whole floor knows I've been looking after these two by myself.” She folded her arms and glared at him. “They think you're a deadbeat.”

He held his hands up. “Okay, I guess I deserve that cheap shot. You know how I hate hospitals.”

“And you think I don't? I had bad times in them, too, you know. Everyone has.” She knelt next to a carrier and finished strapping Ann into it, and then did the same with Ashley, dropping a kiss on her nose.

The scene nearly undid Alex as he recalled doing the same with his beloved Julia on the day they brought her home. It was like a punch to the stomach. He rested his hand on the chair next to him to steady himself as he swayed. Laryssa looked at him with concern. “Are you okay?”

“No, I'm not okay. You dragged me out here, knowing I hate hospitals.”

“I don't think it's the hospital. You're remembering her, aren't you?” She rested a hand on his arm. “I've seen her picture in the library at home.”

“Forget about it. Just get them ready so we can get out of here.” He backed away from her. The last thing he wanted to do was hurt her, but he didn't want to talk and didn't want her sympathy. He just wanted to get the twins and get the hell out of there.

Hurt clouded her eyes as she bent down to finish getting the girls ready by tucking their blankets around them. “You'll have to sweep aside your fear of kids and help me out here.”

“I can carry your bags.” He gestured towards the ones on the bed.

She let out a long breath. “You'll carry one of the twins and a bag. I'll do the same.”

He stared at the carriers.

“Contrary to popular belief, they aren't going to leap up and bite you,” she joked.

"I know, I know." He leaned down and grabbed the twin closest to him and walked to the door. "Let's do this."

He hurried to the elevator down the hall and pushed the button, wiping the sweat off his brow. The infant at his side squeaked, and he looked down. She'd pulled the blanket over her face. Knowing he had no choice, he reached down and lowered the blanket. Her face scrunched up, and she let out a wail. The air squeezed from his lungs.

Laryssa caught up to him and rested a hand on his arm, kissing his cheek. "I do appreciate this. I know how much you hate hospitals." She leaned down and popped a pacifier in the infant's mouth. The crying miraculously stopped.

"You can pay me back later."

She looked at him with raised eyebrows and shoved by him to step in the elevator. "I don't have anything to pay you back for. If anything, you owe me."

He stepped in and the doors closed behind him. "I definitely don't mind owing you." He ran his fingers down her arm. She stiffened and pulled away.

She walked to the other side of the elevator and turned back to face him. "I hate that you do that. Anytime something gets uncomfortable for you, instead of talking about it, you attempt to seduce me. I think I deserve more than that now, don't you?"

"You're right. You do." Alex turned away from her and faced the elevator doors. He knew he owed her an explanation. He just couldn't bring himself to tell her about what happened. Laryssa had her hands full with the twins and didn't need him burdening her with his sob stories.

The elevator grounded to a halt on the main floor and the doors slid open. He exited the elevator first, making her rush out after him.

Laryssa couldn't keep up with him and found herself short of breath. "You know you might slow down a little, I'm not quite as strong as you."

He slowed down and allowed her to fall into step with him. *Wow, he's changed.* The old Alex would have been all over her in the elevator, not taking no for an answer. What was going on inside that head of his? Had he finally decided he'd had enough of her and that she wasn't worth the pursuit? Why on earth did she care? She wanted to keep her distance from the start and now she could, although she couldn't help but wonder if she'd done something to make him upset.

They rode home in silence, but she snuck side glances at his hard profile as he stared out over the road. Something was going on. She could sense it. The question was, would the end result be good or bad?

Joanne was waiting at the door when they arrived at the house. She gave Laryssa a big hug when she stepped out of the car. "I'm so happy you're home. The nanny is unpacking in her room upstairs. I'd just let it be us, but I'm afraid I'm not quite as agile anymore. My arm gives out once in a while."

"You guys hired a nanny?" She wasn't sure what she thought of someone she didn't know helping with her babies.

"Don't worry. She is a dear friend of mine and very good with kids." Joanne walked to the back of the car and pulled out a bag.

They piled into the elevator and went up to the second floor. "I guess I'll have them in the bedroom with me for now since we never had the chance to prepare the nursery." Laryssa stepped out of the elevator and into the hallway.

Joanne and Alex exchanged a secretive look. She looked at the two of them. "Okay, what's going on?"

"I'll leave you guys alone." Joanne placed the bags she carried just outside a closed door and limped away from them.

"I realize that I've been a mess the last few weeks, and I wasn't sure how to make it up to you, so I've worked on something that I hope you'll like." He lifted a hand to caress her cheek, then moved behind her and covered her eyes.

"Hey, I can't see."

"It's a surprise."

She heard the click of a door opening, and he carefully guided her forward.

They stopped when they reached what she assumed was the middle of the room. He stood close behind her, his breath hot on her neck. She ached to lean into him and feel his lips on her skin again. When he pulled away, she moaned at the loss of contact.

"Don't worry. I'm not going anywhere." He chuckled.

"Oh, shut up," she said, laughing. "Can I look yet?" Warmth spread across her cheeks and a sliver of light appeared through her closed eyelids. He must have opened the curtains.

"Okay, look."

CHAPTER TWENTY-SIX

Laryssa opened her eyes, and her jaw dropped at the sight before her. Around and around, she spun. Her feet sunk into a plush pink carpet that rested in the center of the room. Every piece of baby equipment imaginable filled the room. Two cribs at opposite ends of the room caught her attention.

She walked to the crib next to the adjoining bathroom that led to her room. A name plaque with Ashley's name on it hung above it on the wall. She ran her hand along the edge of the white pine crib. It was lined with pink Disney princess sheets and a comforter that matched the freshly painted rose pink walls of the nursery. A matching mobile hung over the crib.

She wound up the mobile and let the Brahms' lullaby play throughout the room as she continued to explore. The crib on the other side was identical, except for the name plaque that had Ann's name on it. Next to the crib stood the most gorgeous dresser she'd ever seen. It looked like it was from the Victorian era. The base and the handles were gold in color. The rest was pure white. She opened the drawers to find it stocked with clothes.

"I wasn't sure what sizes to get so I got newborn up to six months."

She was shocked to say the least. Not too far away from the dresser stood a matching changing table already stocked with all the necessities. Anything that a baby might need.

Alex took her hand. "Here, come try out the rocking chair." He pulled her to the chair next to the window. "I didn't want to get a hard-wooden rocking chair. I figured you'd want to be comfy."

She let herself sink into the rich blue upholstered rocking chair. "It's perfect." She rested her head back against the seat. After a moment, she lifted her head to survey the room again. Tucked away in the corner rested a box that caught her attention.

She got up, walked over to it, and knelt down. It was the toy chest she had seen up in the attic. All the dust had been cleared away. Small chips of paint were missing along the edges, showing it had been used before. With her finger she traced a painting of Mickey Mouse on the side of the box and looked up at Alex.

"This belonged to my daughter, Julia. She was a huge fan of Disney." His voice was husky and full of pain. He cleared his throat before he continued, "I wanted your daughters to have it."

"I don't know what to say." She held her hand out, and he helped her up. "This is absolutely wonderful. I can't believe you did this for us."

"There's more." He led her over to the changing table and opened a drawer. "I thought you might like a baby monitor so you could keep an eye on them at all times." Inside the drawer lay a baby monitor, equipped with a camera and everything.

She turned away and walked towards the window, her heart near the breaking point. He didn't have to do all this. They hadn't planned on forever. Yet here he was spending who knows how much to create a nursery for her children. "Why? Why would you do all this for us?"

"I knew you were hurting because I didn't come up to the hospital. I was kind of hoping this would make up for it."

"I'm not someone you can buy, Alex. I already told you that. I don't need you to buy us all this stuff."

"Maybe not, but I needed to. This was my way to contribute."

"Why should you care about contributing?"

He was silent for a moment and, when he finally spoke, his voice was low, barely above a whisper, "Because I didn't contribute much the first time around."

With that he turned and walked to the door. "I'll leave you guys to get settled."

What did he mean by that? Did he feel he was somehow responsible for his daughter's death? Could that be why he hadn't been able to come to terms with the tragedy? If anyone knew how it felt to be responsible, it was her. Maybe they would be able to find healing in each other.

"Excuse me." A plump woman with short black and gray speckled hair appeared at the door. "I'm Sarah, the nanny."

Laryssa shook her hand. "It's nice to meet you. I'm hoping to do most of this myself, but I'm happy for the extra hands in case it gets too crazy. I'm guessing you've had a lot of experience around young children?"

"Born and raised seven of my own, but none quite as tiny as these two precious angels. They must have frightened you terribly."

"Ashley gave us a little scare, but all in all, they were pretty healthy from the start. Speaking of Ashley, maybe you can change her diaper while I warm up their bottles?"

"It would be my pleasure." Sarah scratched her head and looked from one twin to the other. "Which one is Ashley?"

Laryssa laughed. "On their ankle you'll find a bracelet with their name on it. I don't usually use it anymore, but occasionally I have to check to make sure."

"I can just imagine the fun we're going to have when they're older." Sarah knelt down and checked the ankle bracelet.

"I can just imagine. When I was younger, I knew a set of twins. They were always pulling jokes on people." She walked over to the diaper bags and pulled out two bottles. "I haven't seen them in over twelve years." Ann let out a squeak, and they both looked down at her.

"You'd better go get their milk ready. I'll cover here for you." Sarah leaned down and placed the soother back in Ann's mouth, and then reached for Ashley. “Well, aren't you just a little treasure.”

Laryssa's heart skipped a beat as Sarah picked Ashley up. New mother jitters, but this woman knew how to handle children. There was no reason for her to be nervous.

“Are you okay?”

“I'll be fine, sweetheart. Don't fret.”

She rushed to the first floor and flew into the kitchen, colliding with Alex, who was just around the corner in front of the fridge.

“Wow, where's the fire?” He grabbed her shoulders and steadied her. The bottles fell out of her grasp and rolled to a stop next to the counter.

“You startled me.” She took a deep breath and tried to calm her racing heart, unsure of whether it was from the near collision or his close proximity.

“I'd say sorry, but I rather like the position we ended up in.” He pulled her into a full embrace. Their first embrace since the children were born. No stomach to get in the way.

She rested her forehead against his chest for a moment. For weeks she'd been run ragged, taking care of the twins. This was her first moment of peace if she could call it that. She sighed softly when he ran his fingers through her hair and tilted her face up to look at him.

When their eyes met, her mind clouded, and she no longer remembered what she came down for. “I came into the kitchen for something. I can't remember what.”

“Could it be this?” He tightened his hold and pulled her close to him, lowering his mouth to hers. The ground opened beneath her, and she wrapped her arms around his neck to keep from falling. There was nothing she could do to stop the free-fall and held on for the ride. She was certain she didn't come here to kiss him, but she'd missed his touch and couldn't pull away.

Alex let his hands drop to her hips and pulled her against his arousal with a guttural growl. Liquid heat gathered low in her belly. She stood on her tiptoes and pressed against him. How could one man make her feel this way? She wanted to rip his clothes off in the middle of the kitchen, without giving a darn who walked in on them. He backed her up and lifted her onto the counter, tossing the salt and pepper shakers aside. He came to rest in the conjunction between her thighs.

His hands snuck under her sweater, caressing her bare skin. *Gosh darn it, what was I supposed to remember?* His lips worked their way down her slender neck. She angled her head to give him better access.

"You taste and smell so good." His deep and husky voice sent shivers through her body.

His fingers traced the outline of her bra, then ran his thumbs over the tips of her breasts. Her nipples hardened instantly, and she sucked in a breath.

"I've missed touching you like this." He bunched up her sweater and unclasped her bra, making her spill into his waiting hands. He flicked his thumbs over her beaded nipples. Lowering his head, he flicked his tongue over her sensitized tips. Her breasts tingled and she arched against him.

"Hmm...sweet. I can see why babies love to suckle," he groaned. When he pulled back, she saw drops of milk on his lips, and she slapped a hand over her leaking breast.

"Babies, oh my gosh." She shoved him away, re-adjusted her bra, and then hopped off the counter. "I forgot. I can't believe I forgot."

"Forgot? Forgot what."

"I came down here to warm up the bottles for the babies, you dolt, and you distracted me." Her words were raspy, her chest heaving. She tried to regain control of her breathing. She straightened out the rest of her clothes and looked around for the bottles.

"And here I thought you came searching for me," he said with a playful pout.

"In your dreams."

"Real life is much more fun." He grabbed her arm to pull her close again.

"You know, as much as I'd love to stay here and have verbal foreplay with you, I have..." The look in his eyes and the sensual smile that played on his lips made Laryssa wish she had used a different selection of words as her voice trailed off. She spotted the bottles and leaned down to pick them up.

Alex ran his fingers over her backend. "You have a very sexy butt, you know that."

"I have a fat butt."

His arm reached out for her again, and she ducked underneath, making a beeline for the stove.

"I object. You've got one mighty fine ass." He gave it a slap when she hurried by.

She walked to the sink and rinsed off the nipples, and then pulled out a pot. She filled it with water to warm up the bottles and placed it on the stove. Alex came up behind her and placed his palms on the edge of the stove, trapping her in between.

"Do you mind?" she asked.

"I don't mind at all. Please continue what you're doing." He leaned over and brushed his lips against her neck, sucking gently.

She tilted her head his way, closing off access. "This isn't helping. I can't think when you're touching me."

"That could be a good thing." He switched to the other side and took a deep breath. "I've missed you. You smell so good."

"I mean it, Alex." She elbowed him in the gut and heard him grunt. That should show him. When she looked back at him, she saw a grin on his face as he rubbed his belly.

"You're a spoil sport," Alex said playfully.

"No, I'm not. Sarah is upstairs and probably has her hands full with the two of them, and I've taken too long already. Would you mind checking on them while I finish warming up the bottles?"

The sexual tension in the air changed to one of discomfort, and she turned to look at Alex. He was frozen in place and his features as pale as the white shirt he wore. "I, uh...well, how about you go up, and I'll finish warming the bottles up."

She hesitated.

"Don't worry. I know how to prepare bottles."

She wished he would tell her what happened that made him so afraid to be with the babies, but she knew better than to try. He bit her head off any time she asked. If there was one thing she learned, it was that he didn't like people intruding on his private thoughts, especially ones that held him captive in a prison of pain, crying out for peace and freedom but finding none.

She looked down the hallway and back towards him again. "If you're sure?"

"I'm sure. Now, take that adorable, delectable tooshie of yours upstairs before I ravish you again." His voice was a little shaky, but she knew he spoke the truth.

For a second, she thought of testing his words, and a shiver of desire ran through her. If she stayed, she knew what would happen, and it wasn't something they were ready for. Not when he was only doing it to forget his pain. She saw his hands shake as he lifted the nipples out of the water.

"Whatever is bothering you, I'm here to listen if you want to talk."

"Just go. I'm fine," he said.

"Fine." She spun and left the room as quickly as she entered.

Alex warmed up the milk and put the nipples back on the bottles. He walked over to the sink and smacked his hands on the edge of it. Why couldn't the hurt go away? Pain hit him each time he thought about going near the twins, and it wasn't fair on any of them.

Even the bottles reminded him of Julia, of the few times he managed to sit and feed her. He thought of Laryssa's offer to listen and realized he should probably tell her. She would most likely understand why he couldn't be around the babies.

The thought of taking a trip down memory lane made his heart feel like a thousand needles were poking into it. Not even the simple solution of telling himself they were his nieces helped. How could his brother, who abused Laryssa, wind up with two adorable babies while he lost his? It didn't seem fair. What did he do to be punished to this degree?

He picked up the bottle and checked it on his wrist. The temperature was perfect. He grabbed the other bottle and headed upstairs to the nursery. As he reached the door, he heard a cry. Unable to cross the barrier of the door, he knocked on it.

Laryssa came out with a red-faced baby squirming in her arms, rooting for her nipple hidden behind the sweater. "You couldn't have been a little quicker," she snapped.

"Sorry," he mumbled, unable to take his eyes off the infant as her face scrunched up and another wail burst from her lungs.

Moments later, Laryssa's hand passed in front of his face. "Aren't you forgetting something?" She gestured towards the bottles.

One fumbled in his grip, he caught it before it fell to the ground. "Sorry."

After he handed over the bottles, she turned to walk back into the room. "Lara, wait."

She gave him a glance over her shoulder. "What?"

"I know I've been making a mess of things. I don't suppose you'd let me make it up to you by taking you out to dinner tomorrow. You know, to celebrate their homecoming."

She looked down at the baby wiggling in her arms, and then back to him again. "I don't know. I really shouldn't leave them yet. This is a new place for them. They might get scared if I'm not here."

"How about I give you a week to get settled in, and we'll go from there?" He reached out and pushed a lock of hair out of her eyes, letting his knuckles skim her cheek. "Then we can try dinner. Please, let me make up for my stubbornness."

"Alex, you already made this nursery. You don't need to torture yourself by spending time with me. I know you don't want to be around *us*."

He cringed at the emphasis she placed on the word 'us'. It wasn't her that he had a problem with. Time with her was something he definitely wanted. It was this baby thing he wasn't sure he could do again. Their blue eyes, brown hair, tiny fingers, and button noses created an ache the size of Mount Everest inside his heart. Their first cries and red faces reminded him all too much of what he'd lost. She deserved better, and he knew that, but he wanted to give her what he could. And right now, he wanted to give her his time.

"I know I haven't spent much time with you lately. I want to fix that. Give me a chance to explain."

Her eyes widened and filled with disbelief. "In the kitchen you shooed me away for even suggesting that I lend an ear."

"I know, I know. This isn't easy for me."

She studied him for a moment before speaking, "Give me a week. We'll go from there."

He turned and walked down the hall. Before he realized it, he was on the third floor in the library. He walked to the corner of the room, fell back into the recliner, and looked up at the picture of his daughter on the wall.

"Julia, my love, Daddy misses you so much." Tears filled his eyes. "Everyone expects me to let you go. How can I do that? You're my baby. Why did you have to leave?"

Leaning down, he picked up Julia's favorite book of fairy tales and ran his hand over the frayed cover. There was no changing what had happened. He couldn't change how careless and stupid he'd been in the past. His doctors told him that it was because of the guilt he felt that he couldn't let go and move on with his life. Guilt over decisions he'd made to spend so much time away. He had only a few precious memories of her, and they were wrapped so tightly around his heart that there didn't seem to be room for anything or anyone else. He'd tried to forget that he was the cause. He worked himself to death even worse than before so he wouldn't remember, but it kept coming back.

How could his ex-wife move on so easily with her life? Wasn't she hurting over the loss? How could she have gotten remarried so quickly? He knew what was going on in her life because she'd kept contact with a few of his friends. Didn't she still care about their daughter? He couldn't even look at the twins without being filled with agony.

Alex laid his head back and squeezed the bridge of his nose. If it wasn't for this insufferable attraction to Laryssa, he'd still be locked away in his safe haven, tucked away from this pain. But no, she had to be in the forefront of his mind every day, drawing it out of him. This need for her just didn't want to go away.

He kept telling himself it was because of her connection to his brother, but that didn't explain the intense burning desire to have her naked in his bed. Denying it wouldn't work anymore. He'd been around her too long. Her scent acted like a drug, traveling through his veins. He had to have her, had to make himself part of her. He'd give her a week like he promised, but after that it would be a no holds barred seduction.

CHAPTER TWENTY-SEVEN

Laryssa plunked the baby monitor on the kitchen table and sat down, exhausted. “Can I put them back inside, please?”

Joanne laughed. “I'm sorry, dear. Once they come out, there's no going back in.”

“But...but...maybe someone could make an invention that teleports them back inside.” She tried to make a serious face but burst out laughing instead.

“I think if that were possible, someone would have invented it a long time ago.” Joanne pulled up a chair and sat beside her.

“You had to go and burst my little bubble, didn't you?” She stuck her tongue out and grinned. “Even with Sarah here, it's still hard.”

“Don't worry, it does get easier,” Joanne said as she reached out and squeezed her hand.

“Gosh, I certainly hope so. If it keeps going like this, I don't think I'll live to my thirtieth birthday.” She dropped her head to the table.

“You know what you need.” Joanne smoothed Laryssa's hair. “A night out.”

Laryssa lifted her head, her face scrunched. “Don't tell me you've been talking with Alex?”

"Guilty as charged. Have you thought about his dinner proposal? He said he asked you last week."

"I don't really want to leave the babies yet. I did just bring them home." She stared at the baby monitor on the table and turned on the screen, only to find the babies fast asleep. "I don't even have a sitter, and Sarah...well, I couldn't really leave her alone with both of them."

She should change her name to procrastination. Sarah didn't even need her help. The thought of being alone with Alex frightened her. Her brain stopped working whenever he was around, which was more than a little scary. She knew exactly what would happen if they went anywhere by themselves.

"Why don't we set up dinner on the veranda again, like we did the last time. Just the two of you?"

"I'm not sure I'm ready yet." She bit her lip, and her heart doubled its pace.

"Don't be frightened, my dear. You'll be fine." Joanne put her arm around her.

Having dinner at the house was an even scarier prospect than going out to a public restaurant. He'd have no chance of getting her alone with everyone else around, but here...

She shuddered.

Her pregnancy used to act as their chaperone, but now she had no physical barrier to stop her from going all the way. No doctor's orders. No medical reason to refuse him. She knew she'd have no strength to fight him off on her own.

"Alex is an intimidating man, Joanne."

"Indeed, he can be. Humor me, though, let him take you out. If you don't like it, I won't ask again." The older woman gave her a huge, exaggerated pout, and the same puppy dog eyes that Alex was famous for.

Laryssa laughed. "There is no saying no to you either, is there, Joanne? Like mother, like son."

"Nope. Now scoot. Go find Alex." Joanne picked up a dish towel that was resting on the table and whipped it in her direction.

She looked up at Joanne with wide eyes, hands on the edge of the table. "You mean tonight?"

"Yes, the babies will be fine. If we have any trouble, we'll call you."

Reluctantly, she agreed and pushed herself back from the table. She made her way down the hall. What would she say to Alex when she found him? The thought of spending an evening alone with him made a shiver sneak down her spine. She took a look at the elevator and decided to check on the little ones. Alex could wait.

Standing in front of the elevator, she leaned over and pushed the up button. She went to step into the elevator when hands grabbed her from behind, scooping her up off the ground. She shrieked.

"Ouch, you're hard on the ears," a familiar husky voice chuckled.

She placed a hand over her racing heart, smacking him on the shoulder with the other. "You jerk. I thought you were the stalker." It shocked her how she'd nearly forgotten about it until he'd grabbed her. The knowledge must still have been in the back of her mind, even though they hadn't received any threats since she'd been home.

"Didn't mean to scare you. I wanted to head you off at the pass before you disappeared on me."

"Put me down, Alex." She pushed against his chest.

"All in good time." He strolled to the door, flung it open, and proceeded to walk through it.

She grabbed the frame of the door and jerked him to a halt. "I'm not going anywhere. I have to change." Most of her clothes were in the wash, covered with spit up. The only thing she had to put on this morning was an old gray sweat suit that had seen better days.

"You'll be fine. I have a change of clothes in the limo for you." He started to walk forward.

She didn't release her hold on the door frame. She held on to it as if it were her lifeline. Joanne had dropped the bomb on her about going out with him but failed to mention he had plans to hijack her.

"I'm not changing in front of you."

He glanced down at her body and then back up to meet her eyes. A devilish grin played on his face. "I'm more than willing to help you change." He adjusted her in his arms and tried to pull her hands away from the door frame.

"Please, Alex. Just let me go to my room and get ready. You can even wait outside the door to make sure I don't make a bolt for it, okay?"

"I could wait inside."

The thought of letting him inside her room was a temptation she could do without. The heat from his hand seeped through her heavy sweatshirt, making her skin tingle. If his hand moved one inch higher, he'd be touching her breasts. They perked to attention. Thankfully, she'd chosen a heavy shirt, or he'd have seen exactly how attracted she was to him. And being this close to him, he definitely wouldn't miss it.

"No, thank you. I'm willing to go out." *Liar.* "Just let me get ready on my own, please."

"Aw, please." He jutted his bottom lip out in an exaggerated pout and looked at her with pleading eyes.

"That look isn't going to work on me. I already said I'd have dinner. What more do you want?" Okay, maybe that question didn't need to be asked. She swallowed hard as he eased her down the length of his body until her feet touched the ground. Her highly sensitized body parts brushed against his. She didn't need to look in his eyes to know he felt the attraction too, not with the blatant evidence of his arousal pressed firmly against her belly.

"Heaven help me," she whispered.

"My words exactly." Alexander let out a deep breath and released her, taking a step back. "You have exactly one hour to get ready, then we head out."

"Where are we going?"

"That's for me to know, and you to find out. Dress nice, though." He made her jump when his thumb brushed her bottom lip. "A wee bit jumpy, are you?"

She didn't grace him with an answer. Instead, she rushed up to her room, shut the door, and leaned against it. "Oh boy." They were in for one interesting night. If she read him correctly, there was only one way this night would end. Her nipples rubbed painfully against the rough cotton of her shirt in agreement with her.

One hour to get ready didn't leave her a lot of time. If she wasn't ready in that hour, she knew Alex would not think twice about barging into her room. She walked over to the closet, grabbed a towel, and then headed into the bathroom. The door that led into the twins' room was open. She couldn't resist taking a peek inside. Leaning down, she gave the sleeping babies a kiss on the cheek. They were sleeping side by side in Ann's crib. They were less fussy when they had each other to keep them company.

"Sleep tight, my sweethearts. Wish mommy luck."

Alex stared at his watch, three minutes to go. Joanne had worked her magic on Laryssa and convinced her to go, but he knew she still wasn't sure if she wanted to go out with him. Apprehension coursed through him when only one minute remained. If she was going to go, she'd be down here by now.

Mildly annoyed, he watched the last second tick by. There was no way he was going to be duped out of an evening with her. He'd made plans and was going to follow through with them, even if he had to dress her himself.

He started to climb the stairs when a noise at the top caught his attention. He lifted his head and saw her. She wore a long, hip hugging red velvet dress with a plunging neckline. Her long brown hair was pulled back and a few wisps of curls framed her face. From where he stood, he couldn't tell if she had make-up on. She never usually wore any, but he didn't mind. Her beauty didn't need make-up.

As she started to descend the stairs, he gulped. The dress had a slit that nearly reached her hip. His heart threatened to jump out of his chest. There was a shy smile playing on her face as she neared him. He held out his hand and she took it.

"You look beautiful tonight." He lifted her hand to his lips before resting it in the crook of his arm.

"You don't look half bad yourself," she said, short of breath. He hoped it was because of him and not because of rushing around trying to get ready to go. Tonight could definitely have its advantages, especially if she wasn't as immune as she tried to be.

When she scooted over in the limo her dress rode up, revealing a long, slender, mouth-watering leg. He wanted to reach over and run his hand down it, then back up again.

Ducking inside, he sat down beside her. "I really do love that dress."

She re-adjusted the dress and covered her leg up again, running her hands down them to smooth the material. "Does it really look okay?"

He could hear the hope in her voice. "My dear, you look absolutely delicious. Good enough to eat." He gave a playful growl and attacked her neck with light kisses, nipping on her lower ear.

"That tickles, Alex." She giggled and eased away from him. He simply moved closer and continued his rain of kisses. "You're relentless, you know that." She sighed with pleasure as she opened her neck to him.

Need spiralled through him. It would be heck to make it through dinner. All he wanted was to have her back home and in his bed, but he knew they needed to take this time to talk. If he so much as suggested they turn the car back around and go upstairs, he was certain she'd run off in the other direction. Her body was sending out all the right signals. However, she was still running scared. If he admitted to himself, the intensity of the desire he felt for her was a little overwhelming even to him.

"It doesn't sound like you're complaining." He blew softly against her ear and relished in the tremor that traveled through her body.

"How can I complain when it feels so good?" Her face turned to look at him. They met in a kiss that held promises of other hidden pleasures to come. Tonight was all about her and making her happy.

She'd pushed herself so hard to keep up with the twins, and guilt hit him endlessly for not helping her out.

The limo slowed to a stop. Alex pulled back and looked out the window. “I believe we're here.”

The driver got out and walked around to open the car door.

“Thanks, Jason. I'll contact you when we are ready to leave.” Alex helped Laryssa out of the limo. Her dress revealed her tantalizing leg again. He groaned in displeasure when it disappeared beneath the fabric again. “You know, Lara. That dress is definitely more arousing than the one I picked out.”

Her face flushed bright red, and her eyes dropped to the ground. “I... uh...wasn’t—”

“Don't be embarrassed. You are stunning.” He held out his arm to her. “Shall we?”

“Are you sure we'll be able to get in? The place looks awfully busy.”

The place had people milling about the door and a crowd that leaned against the window, waiting to be seated. “I made a reservation a week ago,” he said.

“What if I didn't accept?”

“I'd be having one lonely dinner. After you, my dear.” He held the door open, guiding her in with one hand on her lower back.

The restaurant was fancier than Laryssa expected. The lights were turned low and soft music from the live entertainment filled the room. Alex signaled a waiter who guided them around the edge of the restaurant.

The white linen covered tables were placed on the left side of the room, while there was a dance floor on the right, next to the stage, for the customers to dance the night away. The overhead strobe lights created unique designs on the polished wooden dance floor. She could see herself in Alexander's arms as their bodies flowed in unison to the beat of the music.

“Here you are.” The waiter motioned to a table tucked away in the corner, secluded from the others. “This is the best table in our whole establishment, as you requested, sir. I'm Paul, and I'll be your waiter for the night. Please excuse me. I'll be back in a moment."

Alex pulled the chair out for her and waited until she sat down, before taking a seat across from her.

Paul returned with a bottle of Dom Perignon, popped the cork, and placed it on the table. "Chilled on ice, sir, as you requested." He leaned over and lit the two candles in the middle of the table. "I'll be back to take your orders in a moment."

Alex picked up the bottle and poured them each a glass. She thought about refusing it. She needed a clear head tonight if she wanted to keep her wits about her but found herself reaching out to take the glass from him. "I'm not sure I want to drink this."

"Why not?" he asked.

"I do have to take care of the twins when I get back." Flimsy excuse, but it was the best one she had.

"Don't worry. I don't plan on getting you too loaded. I want you conscious for the other things I have in mind." He placed the bottle back on ice and flashed a sexy smile her way.

Her hand shook, sloshing the wine dangerously close to the edge of the glass. She placed the glass on the table and fanned her face. He couldn't possibly mean what it sounded like. "What other things?"

"I'm afraid that kind of talk will have to wait till later. You wouldn't want Paul to overhear what I have to say," he said, laughing. His laugh had a husky tone that wasn't there before.

"I don't think I wanna know." Laryssa held the menu higher than necessary to block her face from Alex, certain she'd gone bright red. The last thing she needed was sexual innuendos in a public place. Her hormones were already wacko.

When the waiter returned, Alex ordered a ten-ounce sirloin steak, and she ordered a chicken teriyaki bowl. Sadly, when the waiter left, he took her shield with him. When she looked up at Alex, laughter danced in his eyes.

"That reminds me of when you hid from me in the hospital." He sat back in his seat and watched her.

"I was not hiding from you." Unnerved by his gaze, she turned her attention to the people on the dance floor.

"You covered your head with a blanket." Alex leaned across the table and cupped her chin, turning her face back towards him gently. "If I didn't know better, I'd say you were avoiding looking at me."

He was right. She couldn't think when she looked at him. Her only thought was how handsome he looked in his black suit jacket. His hair was slicked back, and one strand hung over the right side of his brow. A sexy grin played on his face. His face looked as smooth as a baby's bum.

Oh gosh.

She just compared his face to a baby's bum. Her hands flew to her mouth as she suppressed laughter. It definitely proved she was a mommy now. That never would have happened had she not been changing endless diapers over the last few weeks.

When she braved herself to look at him, he was sitting there scratching his head, looking taken back by her sudden laughter.

"I'm sorry, I—" she tried to explain, but another giggle escaped.

"Okay, I'm fairly certain I don't have anything stuck between my teeth. We haven't eaten yet." He ran a finger over his teeth, confusion evident in his voice.

"No, you look fine. Really." She took a deep breath to regain control of herself. He looked more than fine. All the women seated at the tables when they walked in had their eyes glued on him, looking like they wanted to eat him for dinner.

"Good. You had me scared there for a second." He placed a hand over his heart in exaggeration.

"You scared? Never!"

Alex looked over toward the dance floor, then back at her. "Shall we have a go? Considering our meal will take a while?"

The stalker tipped his hat low as he watched them step onto the dance floor. From his position at the bar, he could see them clearly and still remain semi hidden from their view. Not that they'd have noticed him anyway with how damned absorbed they were in each other. He itched to reach out and touch her. He hadn't seen her up close in months, and it was killing him.

If only he could get her alone. He just wanted thirty damn minutes with the whore to punish her for marrying the other guy. She belonged to him and only him. He'd love to run into Alex in a dark alley and kill him for taking what should have been his.

'Beat him with a baseball bat,' a voice in his head piped up.

'Make her watch, that'll teach her,' another agreed.

He downed his shot of vodka and groaned as Alex's hand played with the slit in Laryssa's dress. His body hardened as the parted material exposed the bare skin of her thigh. *God, she's a sexy whore.* He looked around to see if there were any available ladies who might help cure him of his hard-on. There was a lady in the corner who appeared to be watching him rather intently. He spared Laryssa one last glance and made his way over to the scantily dressed lady.

"Care to help a guy with a hard problem?"

"Follow me." The woman took his hand, led him out of the restaurant, and around the back.

It was only a matter of time before Laryssa's luck ran out. He'd catch her alone. He just had to be patient and watch for it. Each day he got one step closer. One day she'd mess up and he'd be there waiting for her.

CHAPTER TWENTY-EIGHT

"Stop that." Laryssa smacked his hand as it slipped underneath her dress.

"Spoil sport," Alex said teasingly, letting his hand slide back to the slit as they slow danced. "It's been driving me crazy ever since I saw you coming down the stairs."

"Alex." She pulled his hand back up to her waist. "I'd rather not give everyone a show, thank you very much."

Her heart fluttered as fast as a hummingbird's wings. She was sure he could feel it pounding against his chest. The last time they danced together was at their wedding and her stomach got in the way. Now, they fitted together perfectly. Her hands were linked behind his neck, and his were all over the place. They would slide up her sides and skim her breasts before traveling back down to her waist again. Her breasts tightened, and she ached to brush up against his bare skin.

She never wanted something so badly in her life. His attempt to touch her in public was strangely erotic. It was not something she generally did with other people around. When his hand sneaked back to the slit a third time, albeit discreetly, she didn't stop him. Far too turned on to care. Tonight, she'd let herself have fun for a change. Drop all inhibitions and go where the wind took them.

They moved sensually to the music. Her fingers rhythmically danced in his hair at the nape of his neck, her head resting against his chest. His leg brushed her awakened mound whenever they turned, permanently finding a place there as they danced.

"You're an incredible dancer." She pulled back slightly and looked up at him.

He leaned down and whispered. "I'm also incredibly turned on." His eyes spoke of a desire she'd never experienced before. His eyes were so dark and dangerous she could barely see the ocean green color anymore. She shuddered at intensity behind them. He was looking at her like she was the last woman on earth and no one else mattered. She felt an odd sense of power when he crushed her hips against his arousal.

"I think I might have to stay here all night to avoid embarrassment." He ran his hand along her thigh.

She laughed. For the last few weeks, she didn't feel very beautiful. In fact, she still felt as large as a house. Carrying the twins had done a toll on her body. Seeing Alex this turned on made her feel sexy. She may not be a beanpole anymore, but he didn't seem to mind, so why should she?

His leg brushed up against her mound again, and her panties grew damp. "You think you'll be embarrassed? If you keep rubbing me there, my dress will end up with a wet spot."

"Gah! Don't tell me that," he groaned, leaning his forehead against hers. "I'm about ready to burst here."

All of a sudden, it was like a dam broke open inside her. Emotions she never felt before rushed through her. For the first time in her life, she felt like a real woman. A woman who could bring a man to his knees with a simple look or touch. With her new-found sense of power, she ground her hips against his.

"I'm warning you, if you play with fire you're bound to get burned." He ran his hands up her ribs, gently brushing the sides of her breasts. Thankfully, she was wearing a strapless bra, or everyone would see how her nipples jumped to attention.

She raised her eyebrows at him. “Question is, who will get burned more?” She took advantage of her new-found bravery and pulled his lips down to hers. All movement stopped, and his arms tightened around her.

His mouth was warm and light on hers. She ran her tongue along his bottom lip and sighed with delight when he opened for her. She couldn't deny how right it felt to be in his arms. They fitted together perfectly, even though he was inches taller than her.

His pulse on his neck pounded against her palm. He pulled back and looked down at her. “You really do want to play dirty, don't you?” He spun her in a circle and dipped her backwards before pulling her close to him again. His hands dipped down and cupped her rear, his eyes widening in surprise. “God, don't tell me you're not wearing anything under that dress?”

“That's for me to know and you to find out.” She winked at him. “Oh look, the waiter brought our food. Why don't you go back to the table? I have to go to the ladies’ room for a moment.”

She'd never been so physically aroused in public before and wondered what it would feel like to be with him in the most intimate way. She'd nearly had an orgasm on the dance floor with the way his hand and leg kept finding ways to touch her. She turned to walk away, and let her hand brush the front of his pants.

He grabbed her arm and dropped a hard kiss against her lips. “You really are trying to kill me here, aren't you?” he asked with a deep, husky voice.

He released her, and she rushed towards the ladies’ room, holding her breath until she stood in the washroom. She'd never acted this way and certainly never got so hot and bothered in a public place before. Must be the fantasy of it all, but she loved the way Alex was looking at her. His eyes spoke of a passion yet to be released. One didn’t even realize existed outside of romance novels. She had an overwhelming urge to take his hand and pull him into the bathroom with her.

She looked into the mirror and covered her face with embarrassment. Her face was flushed, and her lips swollen from his kiss. She leaned closer to the mirror. Is that what pure desire looked like? The eyes looking back at her didn't even seem like her own, and the conjunction between her thighs throbbed. Why didn't she think to bring a second pair of underwear and stuff it in her purse? Her body had no plans on behaving. She'd have to sit through dinner in discomfort, hoping there was no wet spot on the back of her dress when they left.

She tilted her head, lifting her fingers to her lips in newfound discovery. Tears threatened to fall. Only now did she begin to realize the scope of the feelings she had for him. It may not be love but felt pretty darn close to it. How would she know if it was love? The feeling was too weird and too strange to connect it with any word yet. One thing she did know was that she wanted him, and she wanted him bad.

Earlier, once she'd gotten over the distress of going out with him, she'd thought about how hard she'd been on him over the last few months. Most of their fights were due to her over-reacting. All he had been trying to do was help her out, and she'd acted like some frigid ice queen. She'd hoped tonight would mark a new beginning for them.

Looking down, she surveyed the dress she had on. The choice was a spur of the moment decision and really there was only one reason why she chose it. She wanted to knock him off his feet. And that she did.

Alex took off his suit jacket and held it in front of him. Again. Something he'd been doing a lot lately. God, she excited him in the way no other woman has. The last time he had to hold a jacket in front of him was when he was a teenager, and the girl he'd had a crush on sat down across from him.

He desperately wanted to follow Laryssa into the bathroom, but the last thing he wanted to do was get them kicked out of the restaurant for indecent behavior. He took his seat back at the table, glad to be able to hide his blatant erection under the tablecloth. He shifted himself, attempting to relieve some of the pressure.

Not wanting to be rude and start eating before her, he waited for Laryssa to return to the table. Finally, his body started to relax, and the pressure eased behind his dress pants. However, his body was acutely aware of when she re-appeared and started walking back towards their table. He could feel her presence. His arousal returned with a vengeance, threatening to break his zipper.

Turning, he saw her through the crowd, and their eyes locked. She gave a feminine toss of her head to clear the hair back from her face and sent him a playful smile, which excited him further. When she reached their table, she ran her fingers along the back of his neck as she moved around him to take her seat.

"Are you trying to torture me tonight?" From the moment she'd walked down the stairs at their home, it had been pure lust. He wanted to drag her right back up the stairs and tear the red dress apart to find the birthday gift underneath.

"Haven't you heard? Anticipation is half the fun?" She cocked her head sideways and sent a sensual smile his way.

There it was. She'd tossed the gauntlet on the floor, and he was more than willing to pick it up. "Sweetheart, I've been anticipating for months. If this continues, it will be over before we even start."

"You could have followed me into the bathroom," she teased.

He slid his hand across the tabled and danced his fingers across the back of her hand. "I was sorely tempted, my little siren, but I didn't figure you'd want to get caught and charged with indecent exposure."

"Somehow, I don't think Joanne would approve," she grinned.

"Nope, she'd probably bop me on the shoulder with the nearest spatula."

"How are things going between you?" Laryssa picked up her fork and dug into the food.

"Pretty good. It's still hard to believe she's my mother. I'm slowly getting used to it, though." He took a bite of his own food before speaking again. "I never did thank you."

She stopped eating and looked up at him. "For what?"

"For everything, I guess. Without you, I would never have learned that I had a brother, and that my mother was right under my nose."

"I wish it could have been on a happier note," she said softly.

"We've never really talked about ourselves much, have we?" He was surprised by his need to know all about her. "Mind if I ask how you met him?"

"Much the same way as we met, actually. We literally bumped into each other. My friend, Clarisse, was on the look out for hot guys." She smiled at him or most likely at the memory itself. "I was shy and always avoided guys. When she pointed out a couple of hot guys, I took off in the other direction and ran smack into him."

"It seems to be a habit, eh," Alex chuckled.

She laughed in return. "Yep. She always used to say my shoulder was a guy magnet."

"You can use your shoulder on me anytime. Did he sweep you off your feet?"

Her face turned somber, and her eyes took on a haunted look. "I always got tongue tied when it came to cute guys..." she started to say.

"It doesn't look like you have that trouble anymore. You've put me in my place plenty of times." He had hoped the joke would make her crack a smile, but only the corner of her lips turned up at his lame attempt. Guilt filled him. The last thing he wanted to do was make her get lost in memories she'd rather forget.

"Comes from experience. Anyway, he tricked me into having lunch alone with him, and I fell hard. At least, I thought I fell hard at the time." Her eyes narrowed, and her voice held a certain edge to it.

"You say that as if it were a bad thing?"

"If I had known how it would have turned out, I would have stood my ground and not gone along with anything he offered." She placed her fork down on her plate and stared at it. "Suddenly, I'm not hungry anymore."

Alex leaned across the table and placed his finger under her chin to make her look back up at him. "Tell you what, let's not discuss this tonight. Let's focus on enjoying ourselves."

"You don't mind?" she asked, her voice uncertain.

"All I care about is making you happy." He half stood and leaned across the table, placing a kiss on her cheek. He didn't want her to share anything she wasn't happy or comfortable with sharing, especially as he hadn't shared his past with her either.

"Why don't we finish eating, and then go for a walk on the beach?" He picked up his glass and took a sip of wine.

Her face lit up. "That sounds wonderful. I've always loved the water."

They made small talk for the remainder of their meal, and then headed outside towards the beach. He took a deep, cleansing breath. The saltwater smell filled his senses as the wind blew in his direction. The night air was warm and the sky clear. The stars twinkled high above them, and the sounds of the water slapping the shore made him feel at peace. It was the perfect night for seduction, although he had to wonder who was seducing whom.

They walked hand in hand along the beach, until Laryssa stopped him. "One second." She held onto him with one hand and leaned down to remove her high heels.

"It's hard to walk on the sand with these things."

"I never did figure out how a woman could walk in those." He took her hand again, and they continued their walk up the beach.

"With great difficulty, but it's worth it. Guys won't generally mess with a woman in heels." She waved the high heels at him.

"You don't have to tell me twice. I've already found out what your feet can do without heels." He pretended to hobble on his foot, almost knocking them both down.

"If you make me get this dress dirty, I'll use these heels on you," she threatened, laughter dancing in her eyes. She gave him a quick slap on the shoulder.

Feigning pain, he clutched his shoulder. "You wound me. You know what this means, don't you?" He looked from her to the water.

"You wouldn't dare." She backed away from him, eyes widening.

"Wouldn't I?"

"Don't forget I have these." She pointed to her high heels.

"Somehow, they don't look quite as menacing as they did a minute ago," Alex said smugly while walking like a predator towards her.

She screeched and started to run, throwing her head back wildly with laughter.

Her dress swirled open in the breeze and showed off a tiny red thong. Alex groaned. In less than a minute, he had her up in his arms, with his cell-phone open, calling Jason to come and collect them.

"All right, my little minx. You're all mine now." He continued to carry her back up to the road as they waited for the limo.

"Aw, but I was having so much fun." She faked a pout.

"I always did love that pout of yours." He nipped at her bottom lip. "Did I ever tell you how arousing it is?"

She didn't know how he could find her, of all people, attractive, but she wouldn't dwell on that. Tonight, she'd let passion take over and stop thinking for a change. She used her fingers to explore, running them through his hair and down his chest. He shivered beneath her touch. The feminine flame that normally lay dormant inside her roared to life. She knew instantly that one night wouldn't be enough to put out the embers of lust burning inside the two of them. If anything, it would ignite it all the more, turning their desire into a full-fledged uncontrollable fire.

Without waiting for Jason to open the door for them, he opened it himself and all but tossed her in the limo and dived in after her. "Drive us home."

Jason gave a knowing grin. "With pleasure, sir."

CHAPTER TWENTY-NINE

Laryssa had known for a while that this night was coming. She could no longer deny it, not when she could see the hunger evident in his face. Alex sat there, feasting on her with his eyes, while she was sprawled on the seat of the limo where he'd tossed her. She'd never thought about having sex inside a moving car before, but it sounded rather appealing right about now.

Alex moved forward and dropped onto his knees in front of her. "God, you're a temptress." His fingers traced the outline of her thong. "And not to mention absolutely gorgeous."

"I look like a whale." She knew she hadn't lost all the weight from having the twins, especially the flab on her belly, which had her feeling a little uneasy. Would he notice?

"Woman, you look good enough to eat. Besides, I don't like my women frail anyway." He looked at her hungrily and scooped her up in his arms as he took a seat, turning her so that she straddled him on his lap. She lifted her dress to fit more comfortably. He hadn't even really touched her yet, but her nipples strained against her dress and her thong barely contained her excitement.

She ground against the bulge in his dress pants and reveled in the hardness of it. Letting her hand wander down his chest, she stopped just above the waistband of his pants and heard his sharp intake of breath. She dropped her hand even further and cupped his hardened flesh through his clothes, squeezing gently.

"Woman, you're killing me," he groaned.

She flashed him a womanly smile and ran her hands back up his chest to link them around his neck. He took her face in his hands and brought her lips down to his. The heat from his lips seared through every vein in her body. Her heart pounded frantically inside her. She immediately opened to him and thrust her tongue out to meet his. She wiggled closer to deepen the kiss, glorying in his swollen state by rubbing herself against him.

He groaned, "Patience, my dear. I want you home before I..." She ignored his words and moved again. He griped her hips to hold her still. "If you continue to do that, I'll make a mess in my pants. I'm only human, you know."

"Let's get you out of your pants then." She reached for his zipper.

He whipped her around, facing her away from him. "Not so quick, missy. As much as I want you, I don't want our first time to be in a limo." His voice was hoarse with desire. She tried to turn around, but he wouldn't let her.

"Okay, you win," she said with a pout.

"Not the pout. God, not the pout," Alex moaned. One hand dropped from her waist, but the other still held her securely. His free hand slowly slid up her side and teased the corner of her breast. He kneaded her taunt nipple between his thumb and finger.

She sighed and rested her head back against his shoulder, instinctively arching her back to give him better access. Anytime he touched her, she didn't expect to feel such pleasure. Never did she imagine a man touching her in this way could feel so good.

His other hand moved away from her waist, only to give attention to her other breast. "Can't let this one feel left out," he commented huskily.

The ache between her thighs tripled, and she didn't want to wait any more. "Alex, please." She grabbed his hand and lowered it to the one place that desperately wanted the attention.

He chuckled, dropping a kiss where her neck joined her shoulder. “All in good time, mi’lady. We're home.” He nodded towards the window. She saw the gate being opened. “Thought you might want to gain your composure before Jason opens the door.”

He was right. She was an absolute sexual mess. Her legs were like jelly, and her whole body ached for release.

“You may have to carry me. I don't think I can walk,” she murmured against his neck.

Somehow, they made it up to his bedroom. She couldn't quite remember how, her mind far too caught up in how his hands were roving over her body. He shut the door and slid the lock into place before turning back to look at her.

“I finally got you where I want you.” He walked over to her, his eyes not once looking away. Her whole body tingled with anticipation.

“In the middle of your bedroom?” she asked with a cheeky grin.

“One place I want you.” Alex pulled her into his arms and greedily took her mouth, all the while searching for a non-existing zipper.

“Over my head,” she said breathlessly, her breathing still erratic from their foreplay in the limo.

He knelt down and slowly raised her dress up, inch by agonizing inch, letting his hand run over the newly discovered skin. Her dress finally reached her waist, and he stopped for a moment.

“I sat in the restaurant all night wondering what you had on underneath.” He ran his finger along the fabric of the thong. “Then I saw this, and it drove me crazy.” His face snuggled against her, and he breathed in deep. “You smell so good.”

Her thong grew increasingly wet at the intimate position of his face. He ran his finger over her dampened thong.

“Just a bit excited, eh?”

That was enough. She whipped her dress up over her head and leaned down to attack his shirt. Her breasts heaved beneath her strapless bra with each ragged breath. “You did say I only had to wait till we got home.” She brought out her famous pout.

All her life she'd read about passion that could rock the moon, book after book. Hiding herself away in a dream world she didn't realize truly existed and read about kisses that could curl your toes and make you forget everything, including your common sense. She thought it only existed in books, in fairy tales, but as Alex stood there, shrugging out of his shirt, she realized it could be real. That is, unless she was asleep and dreaming again. She reached out and pinched his arm. He definitely felt real.

"Okay, now you'll pay." He scooped her up and dropped her on the bed. She laughed as she bounced twice. Towering over her, he made short work of her bra and thong before removing the rest of his clothes. In awe, she stared at his massive erection. She reached out to touch him and swallowed hard.

He grabbed her wrist. "Don't," he warned, "unless you want it to be all over now."

"You're no fun," she grumbled and flopped back against the pillows.

He joined her on the bed, propping himself up on his elbow. "I still can't believe I finally have you here."

"It feels like a dream." She reached up and caressed his cheek.

His hand closed over her breast, and his head leaned down to take her nipple in his mouth. She felt the tingling sensation of the let-down of her milk. He looked up at her, and a dribble of milk rested on his lips.

"Please, Alex, take me now," she pleaded.

He moved up over her but didn't take her as his. Instead, he traced his fingers down her chest and circled around her belly button. Self-conscious of the disaster the pregnancy made of her belly, she tried to move his hand.

"No, don't. Your belly is beautiful." He bathed her with kisses as he slowly moved down her body. She gasped with surprise when she realized his next destination.

"So wet." His fingers brushed her engorged flesh, and she bucked against his hand. He parted her and slowly entered her with one finger and then two, using his thumb to rub the overly sensitized bud between her legs.

The ache grew stronger and stronger until she was ready to explode. "Alex, please." She almost died when he removed his fingers, but his mouth soon replaced his thumb and closed over her clit. Around and around, he flicked his tongue. She had no hope in heck of holding back.

"Come for me, Lara." He suckled and licked, pressing into her with his fingers.

She gripped the sheets tightly." Alex!" she cried out. Her back arched, and her butt lifted off the bed. The most intense orgasm rocked her entire body. Tremor after tremor ran through her. Her eyes squeezed closed at the intensity, and she shook her head from side to side. Tears pushed against her eyelids, trying to escape.

She'd just had her first real orgasm that she didn't overtly cause herself. The realization hit deep inside her heart. She didn't realize he had moved up until she felt his hardened flesh press against her opening.

"Look at me, Lara. I want you to look at me when we join together."

She opened her eyes and looked up into his face. His eyes darkened with the need to fill her.

"Make love to me," she whispered huskily.

Alex looked at the gorgeous woman beneath him, amazed that this night had finally come. For months they'd played a sensual game of cat and mouse, but his patience had paid off. Never did he realize she would be so responsive to him. He was almost ready to come even before he had a chance to slip inside her. Something about her stood out from the rest of the women he'd dated over the years. No matter how hard he tried to keep himself distant from her, he couldn't. She called out to him in a way no one else ever had.

He filled her with one thrust, and then slowly pulled out, teasing her, before driving back into her again. Her body molded itself around him.

She lifted her hips to drive him in deeper. "Harder, please."

"If I go any harder, I won't be able to control myself," he gritted through his teeth.

"Who said I wanted you to control yourself?" She grinned slyly and wrapped her legs around him, burying him deeper inside.

She matched him thrust for thrust. He could no longer tell where he ended, and she began. He'd never experienced this level of ecstasy in his life, and it was all due to the woman beneath him. Harder and harder he plunged into her depths, her groaning and moaning nearly doing him in.

She bucked against him with her hips and cried his name, over and over, as she reached her second peak. The excitement of watching her orgasm and feeling her flesh close around him was just too much.

"I can't hold on anymore. I'm coming, Lara," he cried out as he emptied his seed into her, thrusting harder and harder until all energy left him, and he collapsed. Neither spoke for a few minutes as they tried to re-gain control of their breathing.

"Wow." She let out a long breath.

"You can say that again," his voice muffled by the pillows and her hair. He lifted his head to look at the woman who quite possibly gave him the largest orgasm he'd ever experienced. He knew from the moment he met her something monumental was going to take place, but he had never expected this. This topped anything he'd ever experienced with Valerie.

Unwanted thoughts filled his mind. He pulled out of her and climbed up off the bed, paced a few feet away before he turned back around, running a hand through his hair.

"Are you okay?" She'd pulled the sheets up to her chin and eyed him warily.

He looked down at his erection and then back to her. "Please tell me you're on birth control." He could hear the desperation in his voice but couldn't prevent it. How could he have been so stupid as to forget a condom?

There it was. The mother of all questions, and he had to fire it at her right after they made love. Laryssa clutched her stomach where a bowling ball took up residence.

“I knew this was a bad idea.” She shoved the covers back and got up out of bed, walking over to where her clothes had been strewn on the floor.

“Answer me, damn it.” He grabbed her arm. It was Aidan's face all over again. Why did she even try to think he was different? She was a different person now though, and she'd stand up to him.

“No, I'm not.”

“Didn't the doctor give you any?”

“What was the point? I wasn't having sex. I didn't need any.” She pulled her arm away.

“What do you call what we just did?” he growled, pointing toward the rumpled sheets.

“A mistake. One which will never happen again,” she spat back at him and pulled the dress over her head. She leaned down and grabbed her bra and underwear, then walked to the door. Out in the hall, she raced down the hallway towards her bedroom.

It didn't take long before he stormed into her room. She tried to get into the bathroom before he got close enough to stop her, but she didn't manage to move quickly enough. He shoved the door open and stomped inside, shutting the door behind him. She'd never been claustrophobic, but the walls started to close in around her.

He smacked his hands on the counter, his eyes held the look of a scared little boy. “You knew we'd eventually have sex. Why didn't you ask for some?”

“Why didn't you wear a condom?” She tried to pass by him, but he wouldn't move. “It's as much your fault as it is mine.”

“Maybe it's not your fertile time.”

She could hear the hope in his voice, and her heart dropped. This was a man who couldn't and wouldn't accept children in his life, as much as she wanted him to. It was something he didn't seem capable of.

“What if it is, Alex? What then?”

"I don't want any more kids, I can't." His voice rumbled in the confines of the bathroom.

"I knew this marriage wasn't a real one, but I thought you'd love my kids because they are a part of you. A part of your brother. I can see I was wrong." Gathering what strength she had left, she shoved by him and pulled the suitcase out of the closet. Why had she thought they could get along and become a family of sorts? This was all one great big mistake. That was all too clear.

He'd stepped out of the bathroom and now leaned against the door frame, but she refused to look at him.

"What are you doing?" he demanded.

She didn't answer him and continued to pack. If she opened her mouth, she'd start crying like the fool she was.

"I asked you a question." He walked over and tossed the suitcase away from her.

She collapsed to the floor and buried her face in her hands, shoulders shaking uncontrollably. Was there no end to her being taken for a fool? When would she learn that she was doomed to grow old by herself? That no-one would ever love her. There was no decent man in the world that would claim her as his own. Not in the way a husband should anyway.

"Oh, hell. Don't cry. I hate it when women cry." He gave her an awkward pat on the shoulder.

She pulled away from his touch and scooted across the floor. "Just leave, please."

"Ten years ago, I was married." He took a seat on the edge of the bed. She looked up at him, wiping the tears from her eyes, curious to see what he was going to say. "My wife's name was Valerie. We had a beautiful baby girl named Julia."

"I saw her photograph in the library."

"That was taken at Christmas." He looked down at the floor before continuing, "I spent a lot of time away from home. I thought I was doing the best thing for my family by bringing in as much money as I could. One day I returned home from work and found my wife leaving me for another man. She bundled up my little girl and said she was leaving." Tears formed in his eyes. His voice laced with pain. "I begged them not to go. The roads were icy, but she insisted on leaving with him then and there."

The torment in his eyes was almost too much for her to bear. She placed her hand on his knee, despite the frustration she was feeling.

"They hit black ice and began to spin. A truck came around the corner and plowed right into my daughter's side of the car. She didn't stand a chance." Despair overtook him. He buried his face in his hands.

"Oh Alex, I'm so sorry." Losing a child had to be one of the most devastating experiences a parent could ever go through. After nearly losing her twins while pregnant, she could almost understand.

"It's all my fault. If I'd been home more, it never would have happened. If I'd insisted that they left her behind, then..."

"You can't play the 'what if' game, Alex. It will destroy you," Laryssa interrupted.

"You sound like Joanne," he mumbled.

"A smart lady," she smiled.

"I care about you, Lara. I don't want to see you go." He lifted his eyes to her, his body trembling.

"I can't fight your ghosts, Alex. As long as the ghosts are there, we can never be a family. I need a man who can be part of my children's lives, too, not just mine."

"We're attracted to each other. Why do you want to mess that up?" His fingers closed over the sheets on the bed, gripping them tightly.

"You think you are the only one with problems? Aidan made me miserable. He was a control freak who cared only about himself. I discovered one day that I was pregnant and had hoped he would be thrilled, despite the fact he didn't want children." She got up and walked over to the window. "I was wrong. He accused me of forgetting to take my birth control pills."

Alex winced at her words.

"Yes, just like you did," she said. "He accused me of getting pregnant on purpose. He even went as far as to say I cheated on him because a few weeks earlier he was away on business." Pain arose in her chest, and she placed her hand between her breasts attempting to ease the ache. She couldn't prevent the tears from starting to fall again. "He slapped me, and his last words were, I hope...the baby... dies," she said the last few words between sobs."

"Dear God." Alex reeled back in shock. He got up and started to walk towards her. She held up her hands.

"That's not the end of it," she said scornfully. "After he slapped me around a few more times, I yelled 'I hate you,' and he stormed out of the house. Two hours later, I got a call from the cops saying that he'd been drinking and had been driving too fast. He went around a corner and lost control, tumbling headfirst off a cliff."

"No wonder you responded to me the way you did." Alex gaped in dismay.

She gave a hard, short laugh. "You may not have hit me, but you reacted nearly the same way he did."

"I'm terribly sorry for the way he treated you, and for what I did here tonight. Now that you've heard what I've been through, I hope you'll give us a chance."

If it wasn't for the desperation in his voice, she'd have said 'no' immediately, but she didn't want to add to his pain. "I don't know why you're so desperate to keep me here. I'll give us one last chance, Alex. That's all I can do."

She didn't hold out much hope for their situation. Unless he could find a way to overcome his ghosts, they didn't stand a chance.

CHAPTER THIRTY

Three weeks later, Laryssa stood at the door. Joanne's arms were wrapped around her, begging her not to go.

"Joanne, as much as I love you, I can't stay with him. My children need a father who they can rely on. Someone who will love them as much as I do."

She'd tried to be patient, hoping he'd come to his senses, but the talk they had that night made no difference at all. He still didn't help take care of the children and barely said anything to her. She feared he would always be stuck in the past. She just couldn't live with him anymore. Couldn't stand by and watch him destroy his own life.

The older woman stepped back and looked down lovingly at the twins, who were surrounded by travel bags. "I really thought he'd seen the light when he married you, and that he had finally pulled out of the past."

"He will. I'm just not the woman to do it. I realize that now."

Joanne pulled a tissue out of her waistband and blew her nose. "I'm really going to miss you. Promise me you'll stay in touch."

"I will. You'll have to come and visit me when I'm all settled." Laryssa patted her pockets to make sure she had her house keys and felt the envelope that contained the note she'd written to Alex. "Can you give this to him for me?"

"Will do, and I'll give him a whipping for you, too." Joanne took the envelope and crushed her with another hug.

After they piled everything into the cab, she turned back to Joanne. "Please take care of him for me."

"I wish you wouldn't go. He really does care for you and them. He just doesn't know how to get past his pain."

"Well, when he's ready he'll know where to find me." She squeezed the older woman's hands, and then climbed into the cab next to the twins. "I'll give you a call soon."

She closed the door and gave Melissa's address to the driver. The cab pulled away from the house that had been her home for nearly a year. Alex wouldn't be happy, but what did he expect. A marriage couldn't thrive on avoidance.

They'd reached a stalemate, barely saying a sentence or two in passing. She guessed he must have been afraid that if he opened his mouth, he'd hear her say she was leaving. Tears rolled down her cheeks. She did go into this marriage knowing it wouldn't last. The year he'd offered her wasn't quite up yet, but her heart couldn't take the emotional roller coaster ride anymore. Just when she thought she could love the big egghead or that he might possibly love her, he had to go and ruin her dream.

Their night together would be forever burned into her mind. He'd shown her how fiery and passionate lovemaking could be. He took her to a place where her body hummed with a desire she never knew existed. She had felt as though she were on a magic carpet ride. Sadly, the night didn't end up exactly how she thought it would.

Her last night with Aidan didn't either. Now she'd done the next worst thing and fallen into his brother's arms. Once they made love, he tore her heart apart. What was she thinking by agreeing to marry him? Was she somehow looking for justification for Aidan's actions? Yes, that's what it was. Justification that he might somehow make up for how his brother acted. With him she couldn't walk away. This time she could with her head held high. Be proud of who she was. No man would ever knock her down again, verbally or physically.

The pregnancy test she'd taken a few hours earlier strengthened her resolve to take back her life. For the last week she'd known something different was going on inside her, and the test confirmed it. Her stomach didn't quite feel like her own, and her already sensitive breasts were more painful.

There was no way Alex would accept this miracle. He would not even accept the two she'd already had. The time had come to say good-bye. She couldn't stay with a man who couldn't even look his nieces in the eye. Watching him ignore the child they'd made together would hurt too much.

Someday, when he was ready, she'd tell him about his son or daughter, but right now she couldn't bear the thought of seeing him react to the news the same way Aidan had. She didn't have the strength to go through it twice.

She looked down at the twins on either side of her. "Well, little bugs, it's just you and me for now." She brushed her finger over their tiny hands. They instinctively wrapped their little fingers around hers.

The cab pulled up to her friend's house. "I'll just be a moment. I need you to take me to my house next."

"Hurry, lady. Clock is ticking."

"Thanks." She rushed up to the door and gave it a quick knock. Melissa opened the door and pulled her into a protective hug.

"Let me guess, Alex is being an asshole again?"

"Sort of, I'll fill you in later. Taxi is waiting." She gestured to the driveway.

"Mind if I ask a favour?"

"Sure, anything."

"It's a lot to ask, but can I take you up on your offer to stay with you? Only for a few days till I find somewhere else."

"Not a problem." Melissa leaned down and tickled the twin's bellies. They gave her toothless grins and cooed at her. "They are just so precious. We'd love to have you guys."

"I'm afraid I have one other favor to ask. I have to go back to the house and gather some things. Can you watch them for me?"

"Your timing couldn't have been better. I have today off." Melissa grinned.

"My kids are going to have a field day."

"You sure it won't be too much?" Laryssa looked down at her babies. The only time she'd been away from them was the night Alex took her out and look how that turned out. The pain of what happened still remained in her heart. It was as though someone took a butcher's knife and plunged it into her chest, twisting it left and right. How could he not want these precious bundles? They were so sweet and loving. What on earth was going on inside that head of his?

"No, we'll be fine." Melissa grabbed the carriers and took the twins into the house before coming back for the diaper bags.

"There are four bottles and lots of diapers. Everything they need should be in the bag. I'll try not to be too long." She planted a kiss on each of their heads and rushed out to the taxi.

Within thirty minutes, they were parked outside her Surrey home. She paid the fare, rushed up the path, and unlocked the door, stepping inside. The place had a stuffy smell, and an eerie feeling wormed its way into her mind. All she wanted to do was grab a few things and get the heck out of the house before the person who left the note came knocking.

Alex leaned back in his chair. His last client of the day had left the office, closing the door behind him. They'd just closed a deal on one of his larger projects, and he should feel elated, but for some reason the emotion wasn't there. A persistent feeling of dread had lodged itself in the pit of his stomach ever since his last chat with Laryssa. Every time he saw her, words failed him. The look of sadness on her face killed him any time their paths crossed.

Being an insensitive clod, he'd wrecked the most special night of his life. All because he couldn't let go of the past. There was nothing he could say or do to take back what he had said. When she told him what his brother had said, he knew he made the biggest mistake and ruined whatever relationship they had started to forge. To make things easier on her, he immersed himself in his work, hoping she'd be willing to stay if he gave her space.

Hopefully, he could convince her to go out to dinner tonight and celebrate the latest deal. Alex walked out of his office and grabbed his jacket off the coat rack.

"Jenny, I'm going home. Can you lock up for me, please?"

"Yes, sir, not a problem. I'm just going to finish up the last bit of my work before I go." Her fingers continued to clack endlessly at the keyboard as she spoke, moving at a speed he could only dream of.

"Thanks."

On his way home, he stopped at a florist shop and ordered a dozen red roses.

"Must be for a very special lady," the clerk inquired.

"That she is." He paid for his purchase and continued to drive home.

The minute he stepped out of his car, he knew something was wrong. Joanne was waiting for him on the porch, tapping her foot impatiently. He should get rid of the porch. It seemed to cause nothing but trouble.

"I've tried calling you. Where have you been?" A frown marred his mother's face.

"What is it? What's wrong?" He eyed the envelope in her hand with apprehension. His heart fell to his feet. "She's gone, isn't she?" It wasn't so much a question but a matter-of-fact statement.

"Yes, a couple hours ago."

"Is...is that for me." He pointed to the dreaded white envelope. Joanne held it out to him, and he took a step backwards as if it was a rattlesnake.

"I have half a mind to whip you, you know that," his mother threatened. "We warned you."

"I know." He sighed deeply and took the envelope from her, before moving into the house.

Once in his study, he shut the door and sat down at his desk. Reaching across, he reached for the letter opener and ripped open the sealed envelope. He pulled out the letter and unfolded it. He ran a hand over a tear stain which smudged a few words in the middle of the page.

Dear Alex,

I'm writing you this note to say thank you for the generosity and kindness you've shown me over the past few months. You opened your home when you didn't have to and gave me your name to protect me, which is beyond any man's call of duty.

But, as hard as this is, it is time for me to let go. At first, I thought that what we agreed on would be enough, but I realize now I was wrong. When you took me in your arms and made love to me, you opened up a whole new world to me and made me feel things I never felt before. It was then I realized love does exist, and that I deserve it as much as anyone else.

After settling for less in my first marriage, I won't do that now. I don't know why I thought I could, especially now that my children are here. They deserve more. They deserve a father who loves them, who will be there for them when they need him.

When you held me, I thought for a fleeting moment that maybe, just maybe, we had found something special. Then, you tore out my heart the minute you climbed out of bed. I tried to stay once you told me about your daughter, but I can't go on with you ignoring us. Time away doesn't make the heart grow fonder, Alex. Whoever said that was an idiot.

You have so much to offer a woman and would make a great father if you'd open up your heart and soul. When you are capable of doing that, you'll know where to find us. Please, don't just show up asking me to come back, not without accepting my children as well, and any child that may come in the future. Pretty words and fancy gifts won't bring me back. Not this time.

I can't fight your ghosts anymore. Mine are bad enough. Hopefully, one day you will be able to find the woman who is able to unleash the love you keep locked in your soul. I'll always regret that I couldn't have been that woman. I wish you the best of luck in all that you do.

Your lonely wife, Laryssa

He didn't want to believe it, but her words stared up at him from off the paper. They had something special. He could feel it. She said that in the note herself. How could she have left him?

His grandfather's face appeared before him, and the words he spoke echoed in Alex's ears. Mitch had drilled into him the fact that he'd never contributed much to his marriage, never made Valerie feel special and loved. That he spent all his time away working, rather than attempting to contribute to his marriage in the most important way. He slumped in his seat and let the note fall to the floor. His heart squeezed tight, and tears threatened to gather together and fall.

Was his grandfather right all along? Had his actions played a part in his breakup with Valerie, like it did now? He was so hell-bent on the idea that it was all Valerie's fault, not once giving her a chance to explain. All the words he'd shouted at her made him cringe. God, he was a prick. Even though they'd fallen out of love, she never deserved the things he'd said. Once the accident happened, he was so out of shape that he needed someone to blame, not once thinking that he'd played a part in what happened. His daughter's death had been no more his ex-wife's fault than it was his.

If only he'd paid attention to the changes in Valerie and realized when she starting to withdraw from him, then it never would have gone as far as it did. His grandparents were right, and now he'd done the same to Laryssa because he ignored his grandfather's advice. He'd warned Alex that he'd lose the one good woman in his life if he wasn't careful.

Now, he sat there in an empty house. The only sounds he could hear were that of the old house settling. As a child, he had been certain ghosts were coming to take him away. The sounds which use to fill him with fear now filled his heart with loneliness, weighing it down like he'd swallowed a lead weight. His shoulders sagged under the pressure.

Noise from the twins could almost always be heard around the house. That morning, while getting ready for work, he heard them stirring in their cribs. At times, he would lie awake at night and listen to Laryssa sing them to sleep. The desire to join her and be a part of their family created an ache in his chest that nothing could take away. Their gurgles and cries wormed their way into his soul and settled into the corner of his heart. He would miss hearing them. Startled, he leaned forward in his chair and shook his head.

When had he started caring about them? There was no denying what he felt, and the thought of it scared him. If he revealed his feelings and something were to happen, he wasn't sure he'd be able to handle it a second time. Laryssa was right. Ghosts still haunted him, and the ghosts weren't going to go away until he settled his past. There was only one thing to do.

Leaning down, he pulled open a desk drawer and pulled out his address book. He flipped through the pages and stopped at the letter 'V'. He picked up the phone and dialed the number in front of him.

"Hello." The voice was that of a young child.

He rechecked the number to make sure he dialed correctly. "Is Valerie there?"

"Yep."

He waited a moment, but the child continued to breathe into the phone instead of calling her. "Can I please speak with her?"

He heard the child put the phone down. "Mommy, it's for you," the young child yelled.

Mommy? Did he have the wrong number? His question was answered the minute her voice came on the phone. "Hello?"

He froze. Memories assaulted his mind, and he was unable to speak.

"Hello?" she said again.

"Valerie," he said hoarsely, unable to muster any other words at this point. He hadn't heard her voice in ten years.

More silence reigned before she finally spoke, shock evident in her voice. "My God, Alex? Is that you?"

"I know I shouldn't be calling, but I was hoping we could get together and talk." He crossed his fingers. She had no reason to see him, especially after their last parting.

"I don't know," she said slowly.

He could hear the reluctance in her tone and couldn't blame her one stinking bit. "Please, I really need your help."

"Okay, did I just enter the twilight zone? Since when does Alexander Richards beg?"

"I seem to be doing a lot of it lately." He raked his hand through his hair before running it down his face. "Please meet with me."

"One second, I'll be right back." There were muffled voices in the background, and then she came back on the phone. "When do you want to get together?"

"As soon as possible."

An hour later, Alex sat on a bench near Valerie's house. When he saw her, he sat in awe. She was no longer the young, unsure girl he'd married. She was a new woman and sophistication emanated from her. She'd even changed her waist long blonde hair style that she told him she'd never cut. Now she had short bangs and hair which curled just under her chin. Her eyes shone with happiness, and yet, weary at the same time. The weariness, no doubt, was because of him. Not that he could blame her, as he had been a complete louse when they'd been together last.

When she agreed to meet him, he wondered what he'd feel for

her when he saw her. Would any of the old feelings that existed still be there? The ones he'd pushed away after their incident.

The answer came rather quickly when she embraced him in an awkward hug. She no longer stirred him. The only thing he felt was sadness at all they had been through. The connection he'd shared with Laryssa did not exist with Valerie, and looking back now, he realized it never did. He hoped they could part on better terms this time.

"You look good, Valerie."

"So do you," she said as she sat down on the bench. "I must admit, I'm surprised to hear from you."

"I'm surprised you actually agreed to meet with me. How have you been?" He leaned back against the bench, trying to look relaxed, although his mind was far from calm. If he couldn't figure out how to let go of the past, he'd never stand a chance with Laryssa.

"Good, good. You?" She sat with her hands folded in her lap, eyes staring straight ahead.

"To be honest, I've been better. I'm curious, who was that who answered the phone?"

Valerie brushed her hair behind her ear and looked at him. "That was my son, Zach. He's six now."

"Does Zach belong to Jeremy?"

She looked away and kicked at the dirt on the ground. "Alex, contrary to what you believed happened, I never cheated on you. Jeremy was there for me, a shoulder to cry on." She sighed with sadness. "When you caught us in the foyer, he was comforting me because I'd been crying. My aunt had just died, and you weren't there. I couldn't take being alone anymore, and he agreed to drive me to my family's place. After we had the accident, I never saw him again."

His stomach dropped and lodged like a football in his gut. When he'd found them in each other's arms, he'd assumed the worst. They'd tried to tell him, he realized, but he'd been too busy screaming at them to give them a chance. "I'm sorry."

"We were young, Alex. We threw ourselves into an adult relationship. Something we weren't ready for."

"Still, you didn't deserve the way I acted. The things I said." He remembered the extent of his language and bile rose in his throat.

She stood up from the bench and wrapped her arms around herself. "What's this about? Certainly you didn't just come up here to clear your conscience." Pain filled her eyes, and guilt assailed him for having put it there.

He pushed himself up from the bench and paced a few steps before turning back to her. "How'd you do it, Valerie? How did you move on with your life?" He pointed to the ring on her finger. "You're married and have a child."

Valerie stared intently at him for a moment as if searching for something. Her face broke into a smile and recognition twinkled in her eyes. "You've met someone. That's great, Alex."

He shoved his hands in his pockets and mumbled, "Not so great. She just left me."

Pity flashed in her eyes. "Look, why don't you come back to my house. Michael, my husband, is there watching Zach. We can all sit down and talk."

"You sure Michael won't mind?"

"No, he won't. You'd probably get along with him. You guys can talk while I get supper cooking."

Her voice was so full of love as she spoke of her husband, and it made Alex feel hopeful. If she was able to be happy, maybe he could find happiness again too.

Back at the house, she introduced him to Michael and then rushed into the kitchen. The two of them stood there looking at each other, as though they were sizing each other up.

"You know, if I had met you years ago, I would have taken your head clean off." Michael stood there, looking very much like a man who could have fulfilled his threat, one whose height and weight matched his own.

CHAPTER THIRTY-ONE

Alex widened his stance, hands flexing at his side, unsure of what to expect.

Michael tilted his head back and let out a roar of laughter. "Don't worry. I'm not going to pummel you. If you two hadn't broken up, I never would have met the love of my life." He turned and flopped down on a blue futon.

Alex let out a sigh of relief and relaxed, glad that the man appeared to be good-natured. "I hope I'm not imposing."

"It's fine. Tell me, what brings you out this way? A woman?" Michael asked with certainty.

"How'd you guess?"

"There are only two things that can put that look on a man's face. One is their favorite hockey team losing in the Stanley cup finals, and a woman." He gave Alex a wink. "Do you want a beer?"

Knowing the man didn't hold a grudge against him, he joined him on the futon. "Hell yeah."

Michael leaned over the back of the couch and pulled two beers out of a mini-fridge. "Never have to get up and miss a game."

Alex laughed and pressed the tab to open the can.

"It sounds like it is going good in here. No heads being torn off I see." Valerie walked in, wiping her hands on a towel. Alex moved over so she could sit next to her husband.

"Tell us about her." Michael put his arm around Valerie and pulled her right next to him.

A pang of jealousy hit Alex deep. Not for the usual reason, but because theirs was the relationship he wanted to have with Laryssa. Free from all ghosts and demons that haunted him for so long. He shared how he met Laryssa and the events that transpired since then. "Now, because of the idiot I am, I've lost her."

The pitter patter of little feet shuffled down the hallway, and a child's head peeked around the corner. "Mommy, who's that?"

"I thought I told you to stay in the kitchen and color?" she scolded lightly, pulling her son into her arms. "Alex, this is Zach. Zach, this is an old friend of Mommy's."

"Hello, Zach." He smiled. The boy moved behind his mother. "How about a big manly handshake?"

The boy peeked around Valerie and stared at Alex's hand, then looked up at his mother who nodded at him. "We've been teaching him to be wary of strangers. It's all right, sweetie, you can shake his hand."

Zach held out his hand and let him shake it, but still clung to Valerie with his other.

"It's a pleasure to meet you, Zach."

Valerie stood up and swept Zach up in her arms, awarding him with a tummy tickle.

"She's incredible with him." Michael gazed lovingly at his wife as she disappeared down the hall.

He leaned back against the couch and rubbed his forehead. Seeing her with Zach brought back a lot of memories of how great she had been with Julia. She was happy again, and she deserved as much. Within a few minutes, she returned to the living room and took her place on the couch.

"How did you do it? How did you let go?" he asked.

"It wasn't easy. For the longest time I did the same thing as you. I was too afraid to love. Too afraid to care for anyone in case it happened again. If it wasn't for Michael, I'd still be stuck down that dark corridor alone." She squeezed her husband's hand. "Funny as it sounds, he was my therapist."

Alex gaped at the man who could pass as a football player. "I wouldn't have pegged you for a therapist."

"She didn't believe it at first either. She thought I'd stuffed the real therapist into a closet." He laughed as Valerie bopped him on the shoulder.

"Anyway, I went through a real rough time." Valerie took her husband's hand, and then continued, "I even thought about ending my life just to be with Julia. A friend of my family went to Michael for therapy once and gave my parents his card. I didn't want to go but agreed to do it for my parents' sake. When they were out of sight, I made sure Michael knew I didn't want to be there. He was patient with me, and I found myself drawn to him in a way I couldn't explain. Before I even knew what hit me, I poured my heart out to him and told him everything. Things I never told anyone else, and he understood me."

For a moment they sat there, lost in each other's eyes. The love the two shared shone as bright as the hot sun on a summer's day. "After months of weekly therapy sessions, I started to have feelings for him, and by the way he looked at me and how he would find ways to reach out and touch me, I knew he felt the same. I told him how I felt, and he told me it wasn't uncommon for a patient to become attached to their therapist. I got mad and ran off, disappeared."

"She scared the daylights out of me when she took off, and I couldn't help but go after her." Michael grinned sheepishly.

"I didn't want to love again. Gosh knows I tried hard not to. It scared me to think that another person I love could easily die at any time. I also thought that if I loved someone else, I'd start to forget about Julia, and then she'd really be dead. The guilt of her dying, instead of me, ate me up inside. I knew if I did anything that might make me forget her, I wouldn't have been able to stand it. Michael showed me that she would always be right here."

She reached out and touched Alex's chest, which constricted

upon her touch. "No matter what, she would always be in my heart. If I started thinking otherwise, he'd pull out the photo album, and we'd look at her pictures. Julia was a part of me. A part of us, and she always will be. I learned that by holding back, I wasn't cherishing her memories. I wasn't doing her life justice. Anyway, Michael led me through the storm, stuck by me through the hard times, and showed me how to love again." She leaned into her husband's arms, and he kissed her head.

"Aren't you ever afraid?"

"Yes," she answered honestly. "Every time Michael is late, or every time Zach gets sick. However, as much as I am afraid, I wouldn't change a thing. She'd want us to be happy, Alex, I know it. One thing my experiences have taught me is that you have to treasure every second, and if by some chance tragedy does come your way, you have to remember the good times. If you forget those, they are truly dead."

Valerie got up from the couch and walked to the bookshelf. She ran her hand over the top shelf and pulled out a photo album. "Julia meant the world to me. It still hurts, but I've realized that I'd rather have loved and lost than not to have loved at all. Cliché or not, I understand it now. The pain may never be completely gone, but don't lock your love away because you have so much to give. You won't forget her, I promise."

Alex shoulders slumped when Valerie sat down beside him. He knew she was right. "You know the final memory I have of her is in the hospital just after the accident."

Michael looked between the two of them and seemed to understand that a private moment was about to take place. "I'll let you two have a moment together." He leaned over and gave his wife a kiss before wandering out of the room.

"I'll always envy you," Valerie said with a quiet voice, her hand resting on the cover of the photo album.

"Envy me, why?"

"Because you got to spend the most important final minutes with our daughter. You got to say good-bye." She looked up at him with tear-filled eyes.

"It was the worst day of my life. She was so tiny," he said. His voice strained with emotion as a lump took resident in his throat.

"I'm so sorry," she whispered.

Alex pulled her close, and they wept in each other's arms for the first time. They mourned together over the loss of Julia. He rested his chin on top of her head. "I'm sorry, too, even though I know that the things I said don't deserve to be forgiven."

"I forgave you a long time ago. It is how I was able to find love again."

"You're happy?"

"Yes. Don't get me wrong. I'll always cherish what you and I had, and the angel we created." Valerie paused for a moment. "But what I feel for Michael, well, I never knew I could love another person this much."

That should have made him jealous, but instead Laryssa's face shone before him, like an angel with a halo. He couldn't help but smile. "Last year, I didn't even want to give love a try. And Laryssa, well, she blew my feet right out from under me before I even knew what was going on."

"Why don't you go to her?"

Alex took a deep breath. "Would you talk to me if I said those things to you?"

"I'm talking to you now, aren't I?"

"Okay, point taken." He laughed and sighed at the same time.

"Have you ever told her how you feel?"

"No." He hung his head in shame.

"Then go to her. Tell her how you feel. If I'm correct all she wants is someone to accept her and her babies. Give love a chance. If you don't, you'll become a grumpy old fart like my grandfather." She framed Alex's face with her hands and looked at him tenderly. "Live, Alex. Fight for what you want. You deserve it."

He gave her a kiss on the cheek and strolled out of the house. His steps took on a new determination as he walked out of her house. He would do whatever he took to win her back.

"There. That should do it." Laryssa piled the last of the boxes next to the door and collapsed in exhaustion on the couch. The room darkened slightly as the sun passed behind a cloud. Evening had fallen, and it would be dark soon. Staying any longer would not be a good idea. During the day a lot of people walked up and down the streets and cars traveled down endlessly, but at night everything came to a standstill.

She'd been jumpy, to say the least. Every noise had made her want to run for cover. Whether it was because she expected Alex to show up in a rage, or whether her mystery note-writer would make his appearance, she didn't know. Alex would have gotten the note from Joanne by now and likely wasn't too impressed with her right now. He'd be less happy after he received the divorce papers, once she'd had time to visit a lawyer.

Her stomach cramped at the thought. She didn't want to divorce him. The thought of living without him left a void larger than life in her heart. She was a survivor. She'd get through it. If the last few months taught her anything, it was that she was the only one who could shape her destiny. No one else.

As much as she'd love to have a life with him, he must willingly want one with her, and after the way he acted when they made love, there was no chance of that happening. She tried to fortify her heart by telling herself that his reaction was no different than Aidan's. If she kept telling herself they were alike, then, maybe, she'd survive.

"Darn you, Alex." Tears formed in her eyes. She reached for a box of tissue on the coffee table and blew her nose, then she stood up and walked to the door. There was still a bit more to do around here before she could contemplate selling it, but her mind had been made up. She couldn't live here anymore, not with the memories.

She leaned down, picked up the closest box, and then headed to the door. Balancing the box on her hip, as she so often did with the twins, she turned the lock and went to open it. The door slammed open, knocking her off balance. The box dropped out of her hands as she reached for something to steady her. Her foot caught the edge of the welcome mat and she fell to the ground, banging her head on the stack of boxes.

Dazed, she looked up at the figure that loomed in the doorway. There was an unmistakable familiarity about him. She searched her memories and gasped when one came to the forefront of her mind. This was the man who Aidan ordered watch over her; the one who constantly hounded her whenever he was away. He was the man who couldn't take his eyes off her.

"Hello, Laryssa. Long time, no see," he jeered. "I've been waiting a long time for this moment."

"Aidan's dead. Why can't you leave me alone?" she cried, crab crawling backwards to put a bit of distance between them.

"Do you really think I watched you only as a favor to him?" He grabbed her by the upper arm and hauled her up against him. His pungent odor filled her lungs, and her stomach churned. "You really are one sexy woman."

His fingers closed around a fistful of hair and yanked her head back. He leaned forward and tried to crush his mouth to hers. She turned her head to the left and right. He tightened his grip on her hair and held her head in place.

"Let me go, Damon," she cried, but her words were eaten when his mouth closed over hers. The contents in her stomach rose into her throat. He reeked of stale beer. Her heart pounded, and body trembled. She bit down hard on his lip.

"You little whore." He pulled back and backhanded her across the cheek. She lost her balance and fell back against the couch. He advanced on her, pulling a gun out of the back of his jeans.

"God, no. You've got to be kidding me." She climbed up over the couch and crouched behind it while he stood there, grinning.

"God, yes. You're going to give me what I want, sweetie. I'm going to take it from you one way or another anyway." He advanced around the couch. She backed away from him.

"Why, why me?"

"You were supposed to be mine, damn it. Back in college, you were supposed to be mine."

"We went on one date." She'd dubbed it the date from hell. The man was a slimy pig who did whatever he could to get his paws on her. He'd taken her to a sleazy drive-in and expected her to *suck his dick*, as he so eloquently put it.

"A date I've never forgotten. Do you know what it felt like when you started going out with my best friend and forgot I even existed. Well, now he's dead, and you were supposed to be mine, yet you went and got married again." He made a clucking sound. "Bad, bad idea. But no matter, I've got you now."

"Alex will be coming for me, you know."

He threw his head back and laughed. "You left him, sweetie. You think I don't know that? You dropped your kids off at that woman's house."

Her eyes widened, and her stomach twisted. *Oh God, what if he's hurt them?*

"Don't worry. I haven't touched your precious cargo. They could be worth a lot to us. We're going to go and pick them up shortly, but first I want what I came for."

She swallowed hard. He grabbed the top of her shirt and ripped it down the front, revealing her blue silk bra. Backing away from him, she pulled her shirt together again and wrapped her arms around herself to hold it closed. "Don't do this."

He grabbed the front of her shirt and pulled her towards him. "Don't tell me what I can and cannot do, bitch," he snapped, placing the gun under her chin. "I got the upper hand this time." He shook his head then spoke in a voice she could barely hear, "No, I'm not going to kill her yet."

Her heart skipped a beat as the cold metal touched her skin. *It can't end like this. It just can't.* She cried out silently, praying for an escape route. Her knees buckled when the doorbell rang. He held her up by the hair and moved towards the door, looking out the peep hole.

"Well, well, well. What do you know! Alex has come for his

prodigal wife." He tightened his grip and made her look up at him. She tried to cry out, but his hand clamped over her mouth. "No, no. Not allowed to do that. You wouldn't want me to blow his brains out would you, dearie?"

She shook her head madly.

"Good, because I would do it you know. We're gonna play this cool, you and me. You're going to act like my lover and what better way to show for it than this."

He leaned over again and sucked on her neck, leaving a bright red mark. She squirmed to get away, but his grip was iron clad. When he seemed to be satisfied that he'd left a good enough mark, he pulled back and held the gun on her. "You're going to open the door and send him on his way."

She looked from him to the door. There was no way they could outrun a bullet. If she didn't put on a good enough show, he would kill them both. He wasn't stable, not with how he kept talking to unheard voices. The man needed help, needed to be in a mental hospital, but she wasn't going to be the one who pointed that out to him, not when his finger hovered over the trigger.

Alex knocked on the door again, and Damon waved the gun towards the door. "Open it."

Her hand shook so hard she could hardly grasp the handle. She prayed her voice would be steady enough to sound convincing, yet she hoped that he would be able to read her thoughts. She opened the door. Sweat beaded on her neck and trickled down her back. Damon hid behind the door and held the gun at her side.

She swallowed hard and peeked around the corner. "H-hi." Her hand tightened on the door handle, and her knees knocked together.

Her shirt slid down her shoulder, and his gaze followed it before narrowing slightly. "I was hoping we could talk."

She turned her head and looked at the armed madman who shook his head. There had to be some way to get a message to him that something wasn't right, but she didn't dare do something obvious.

"I, uh...don't think so. I said everything I needed to in the note."

She blinked her eyes rapidly, not daring any other action. She had no clue about Morse code, but she had to try something, anything.

Alex tilted his head to the side and stared at her. “Is everything okay?” Before she could answer Damon appeared behind her and slung his arm over her shoulders.

“Everything is fine, isn't it, sweetie.” The man slurred, dipping his head and running his lips along her neck, drawing attention to the hideous hickey that pulsated with each beat of her heart.

She shivered and pleaded to Alex with her eyes. Hurt flashed across his face, but it was quickly masked as he took a stumbling step backwards. His fingers flexed at his side, and she wanted to tell him it wasn’t what he thought, but, with the cold barrel of the gun pressed to her side, she didn't dare. The thought of putting him through another betrayal killed her inside. Even if it wasn't real, he obviously believed the act.

His eyes focused on something behind her for a moment before turning his attention back to her. His jaw tense and lips pressed in a firm line. His fists clenched against his side. “I came here hoping we could work things out, but, seeing this, I don't care anymore. You can have her. Just give me back my ring.” He held out a hand and wiggled his fingers at her.

When she placed her ring in his hand, he turned and walked down the path, never turning back once. Her hope of making this out in one piece faded. Damon yanked her back from the door and shut it, locking it behind them.

“So how does it feel to watch your one and only love walking away?” He ran the barrel of the gun down her cheek and dragged her to the window to watch Alex climb into his car.

CHAPTER THIRTY-TWO

"You won't get away with this." Laryssa pulled up the sleeve of her shirt and glared at him.

"I already did. No one else knows I'm here, but him." Damon gestured towards Alex's car as it backed out of the driveway.

"What do you want from me?" she asked. Her sweat dampened shirt clung to her breasts, drawing his attention.

"I want what has always been mine." His gaze traveled down her body, and he licked his lips hungrily. "Years I've tortured myself watching you undress and having sex with Aidan."

A gasp tore from her throat, and her body chilled as though she'd jumped into a lake in the dead of winter.

"Ah yes, you didn't know, did you? Aidan bugged the whole house. The bathroom, your bedroom, you name it. I used to jack off while I watched you in the shower."

The contents of her stomach rose higher still, and she slapped a hand over her mouth. "You make me sick."

"I used to watch you guys and wish it was me on top of you. I'm finally going to get my wish, and there is nothing in hell you can do about it. All I wanted was a quick fuck in college, but no, you had to act all high and mighty. It could have been good, you know. You and me."

"I wouldn't have let you touch me with a ten-foot pole." She mustered her courage and spat in his face.

In an instant, he had his arm around her neck and the cold barrel of the gun pressed firmly against her temple. "I wouldn't do that again if I were you," he warned. "I'd hate to put a bullet into that pretty little head of yours."

He'd do it. She knew he would. His hand was far too steady to indicate otherwise. The familiarity with which he held the gun made her realize he'd probably used one before. She gasped for air and pulled at his arm. "Please, don't. My babies need me."

"We're going to have some fun first, and then we'll pick up the little shitheads. We're going to be a family."

She nearly sighed in relief when it was clear he didn't want to kill her, although she knew he wouldn't hesitate to if she struggled. Maybe she could bide her time, make him think she accepted the idea. "Okay, okay." She lifted her hands in the air. His grip loosened a little, and she felt the barrel pull away from her head.

Tears pricked the back of her eyes. Life couldn't be so cruel as to throw her into the path of another lunatic. *Please, Alex. Don't leave me here.*

Damon slid his gun wielding hand down her side and pulled her shirt free from the waist band of her skirt. His fingers touched her bare skin and slowly wormed their way up her shirt, pulling it off her body.

He groaned as his hand closed over her breasts. His touch sent a disgusted shiver through her body. Goose bumps covered her skin, and her nipples tightened in response to the chill. "I knew you'd like that," he said, sounding pleased with himself.

Could this be her escape, acting turned on by him to the point that he would let his guard down? She may not be an actress, but judging by his behavior, it wouldn't be too hard.

She nearly gagged in repulsion when he unclasped her bra and ran his fingers over her bare breast. "Oh, that feels good." She forced the words out of her mouth. "Wouldn't you feel more comfortable if we went upstairs?" Her voice came out shaky, and she hoped he'd buy her pathetic attempt.

He threw her over his shoulder and lugged her up the stairs like a sack of potatoes. "I knew you were a wicked slut of a woman." He slapped her butt, and he kicked the bedroom door open.

This man was going to get it, and he was going to get it good, she'd make sure of it. Damon tossed her on the bed and tore off the rest of her clothes, making her wish she'd worn jeans instead.

Stay calm, she told herself, bide your time. Laryssa sat up and pulled his shirt over his head. Her hands shook, and her heart raced so hard that her ear drums felt like they were about to burst. "My, aren't you a handsome devil," she ground out between her teeth.

He lay down on the bed beside her, the gun still in his hand. "I like a woman to ride me, so get up there," he ordered.

"I love a man who knows what he wants," she purred. Straddling him, she tried to think of a plan. To her left on the nightstand was a glass vase. She averted her gaze, not wanting to let him in on the plan. "I bet I know something else you'd like." She put a hand between her legs and pressed it against the bulge in his jeans.

"Take them off," he demanded.

She undid his jeans and pulled them off. Her stomach churned.

"Touch me." He grabbed her hand and placed it on top of his erection. She bit back a gag reflex and did as he ordered. After a few moments, his groans filled the room, and his eyes closed. Very carefully, she kept the rhythm going and reached for the vase with her free hand.

His eyes flew open, and he grabbed her hands. "I knew you'd try something like that." He flipped her over onto her back and trapped her hands above her head.

When he thought she was secure, he placed the gun on the table beside them. "Nothing is going to stop me from taking what I want, my sweet Laryssa. I've waited a long time for this."

He kept one hand on her wrists and the other trailed down her body, stopping at the conjunction between her thighs. She crossed her legs to prevent him access, and he laughed, drawing her into her own private horror movie.

"You think that's going to stop me." He shoved his leg between hers. At that moment, Laryssa saw her opportunity.

She swung her free leg up and knocked him off balance. He freed her wrists while he tried to steady himself. She reached up and gouged his eyes as she'd been taught in her self-defence class. He tumbled to the side and smacked his head on the nightstand as he fell off the bed.

Without waiting another second, she jumped off the bed and fought with the lock on the bedroom door. Damon groaned on the floor behind her. She flung the door open and bolted down the hall, taking the steps two at a time.

"You bitch," his voice roared from the second floor.

She stumbled to the front door and fumbled with the lock. "Damn it. Fingers, work. Please," she cried. The thump of his feet on the stairs told her she only had seconds to get out the door. Just before he reached the bottom of the stairs, she managed to get the lock open and rushed outside, naked. Rocks tore into her feet as she tore down the little path towards the driveway. She heard something which sounded like a siren, but then it stopped.

She lifted her head and saw Alex, her knight in shining armor, step out from behind a vehicle next door. She propelled herself in his direction, waving her arms in warning. "Alex, get out of here. Run."

"Watch out," Alex yelled, as he ran towards her. They reached each other as a shot rang out in the evening air. Alex tackled her, twisting in mid-air so that when they landed on the ground, she was beneath him. She laid flat on her stomach with her hands covering her head. Another shot rang out, and he jerked against her back. She wanted to turn and look at him, make sure he was okay, but his weight prevented her from doing so.

"Drop it. Drop it now," another voice shouted. She looked out from beneath Alex's arm and saw the boys in blue. The cavalry had arrived. Damon had no choice but to lower his weapon to the ground.

"Down on the ground, now," the cop barked.

When they finally subdued him, a cop approached them. "Hey, are you hurt?"

"I'm fine," Laryssa said. Fear ricocheted through her when she was the only one who said anything.

The cop knelt beside them and carefully rolled Alex off of her. "We've got a man down. Get the paramedics down here, pronto," the cop yelled to his partner.

Another cop came over and draped a blanket over her shoulders, then purposely blocked her view of Alex. "You okay, miss?"

"I'm fine." She tried to look around the cop to see if he was okay, but the cop moved again blocking her view. "Please, I need to see if he's okay."

She managed to get a look at Alex and saw the one cop pressing his hand against his shoulder. "No. No. No!" she screamed and shook her head wildly from side to side.

He wasn't moving and blood poured from his wound, seeping between the cop's fingers. Her vision blurred, and she leaned over on all fours. What little energy she had left seeped from her body and the world swayed around her. The last thing she remembered was her face meeting the cool grass as her world went black.

"Alex!" Laryssa screamed.

"It's all right, sweetie. You're okay now."

She heard the soothing, familiar voice and struggled to open her eyes. The only thing she could see was a shirt covered in blood. Was it her blood or his? A dream. It had to be a dream. Any minute now she'd wake up and be in her own bed.

Giving her head a shake, she tried to open her eyes, but all she could hear were Damon's feet stomping down the stairs as he chased after her. Her heart pounded and the sheets were damp from her sweat.

"Alex, get down. He's got a gun," she cried out.

She felt pressure on her shoulders. "Laryssa, listen to me, sweetie," said the familiar voice sternly. "You are fine. You are in the hospital. He can't hurt you anymore."

"The hospital?" She squeezed her eyes closed and then opened them again. Her vision was blurred, but she could make out the white walls of the room and Joanne sitting on a chair beside her bed.

Her mother-in-law brushed Laryssa's hair back from her face. "That's a good girl. How do you feel?"

"Like I've been run over by a truck." Blood rushed from her face as Alex's bloodstained body filled her mind. If he was fine, wouldn't Joanne be sitting with him? "Is Alex—oh god! He's dead, isn't he?"

"He's fine, Sweetheart. A little worse for wear, but he'll recover." Joanne took her in her arms.

"It's my fault, it's all my fault. If I hadn't left, then he wouldn't have...and Damon wouldn't have..." Tears flowed down her cheeks.

Joanne made a soft soothing sound. "You couldn't have known, sweetie."

"Oh, Joanne. If he had died, I wouldn't have been able live with myself." She struggled to get out of bed. "I want to see him."

"But he didn't die, my dear. He's alive. The doctors have him in surgery currently, so we can't see him yet."

Her eyes widened, and a mangled gasp tore from her throat.

"He'll be okay. They are repairing some of the damage the bullet caused, aside from that he's just fine. Alex is as tough as they come." Joanne patted her cheek.

The doctor came in and smiled. "I see you're up and awake now. How are you feeling?"

"Alex, how is he?" Her fingers grabbed a fist full of the hospital sheets as she stared at him, waiting for an answer.

"He'll be fine. The bullet didn't hit any vital organs. I'll let you know when he is out of surgery."

The reality of it all hit Laryssa, and her hand flew to her mouth. "My gosh, he saved my life."

"That he did, young lady, although I don't recommend him dodging too many bullets. It's not good for his health." The doctor winked at her, then left the room.

Why was he still at the house? Had he called the cops? She had so many questions that needed answers. Aidan wouldn't have even contemplated stepping in front of a bullet for her. The final ghost that connected the two faded away. They were nothing alike. She could put her life in Alex's hands, and he'd take care of her. He proved that today. Just as her twins were as different as night and day, so were Aidan and Alex. Was there a chance that he actually loved her?

"Okay, don't get ahead of yourself, Laryssa. Alex could have just been too angry to drive and decided to take a walk," she mumbled under her breath.

While they waited to see him, she gave her statement to the police. "I really never thought I'd hear from Damon again after my husband died."

"Often people become obsessed with their targets. It looks like he was just biding his time. You don't have to worry though. He'll be going away for a long time," the cop assured her.

"If you hadn't got there so quickly, we both would have been toast. Thank you so much." She gave each officer a hug.

"All in a day's work, Mrs. Richards." The cop tipped his hat. "I think that just about does it. We may want to talk to Alexander when he's up to it, but I think we have all we need."

Her doctor walked in a few hours later. "Alex is out of surgery, and I can take you to him if you'd like. He's groggy, though. Don't be surprised if he falls asleep on you."

"I don't care, as long as I'm with him." She followed the doctor down the hall and into the elevator. They went into a surgery recovery area, and the doctor pulled back a curtain, revealing a pale Alex lying on his back, covered with a white hospital sheet.

Unable to contain herself, she burst into tears and ran up to him, burying her face in his chest. She was careful to avoid the injured shoulder that was covered with bandages.

"Oh, sweetie. I'm okay, really." He wrapped his good arm around her. The force of her sobs rocked her whole body.

"I thought I had lost you." She pulled back slightly and took a moment to look into his glazed, ocean green eyes.

"Not going to get rid of me that easily." He rewarded her with a weak smile before it turned into a yawn. "I'm so sleepy." His eyelids blinked rapidly as he tried to keep his eyes focused on her.

"Don't fight it, sweetheart." She leaned forward and kissed his forehead. "You need your sleep."

"Don't leave me again, please," he pleaded, struggling to watch her.

She knew he was trying to make sure she'd stay before his eyes closed. His voice was so soft and tender that it stole its way into the depths of her heart. She knew at that moment, that no matter what happened between them in the future, he'd remain in her heart until the day she died.

"I'll be here, I promise you that."

After a few hours in the recovery room, they moved him up to a private room where she collapsed on the brown recliner in the corner. She groaned and turned over in the chair, aware of the ache in her neck.

"Hello there, beautiful," Alex said from his bed.

Her eyes shot open, and there he sat with the sun shining off him like a bronze God. "Have you been awake long?" She got up and walked over to him.

"Long enough."

"Why didn't you wake me up?"

"You looked so peaceful. I couldn't bear to disturb you." Alex took her hand and pulled her down next to him on the bed.

"How are you feeling?" Her fingers brushed gently over his injured shoulder.

"Not too bad, considering. The nurses gave me some more pain meds." He pointed towards an empty cup on the table beside him.

"I was afraid I'd lost you." She curled up next to him, and he pulled her into his arms. "Why'd you do it, Alex? Why did you risk your life for me?"

"Because I love you." The words flowed so easily from his lips. If he hadn't been looking directly in her eyes when he spoke, she probably wouldn't have believed him. The love that she craved her whole life shone brightly in their ocean green depths. The love she'd read about in books, but never thought possible, radiated from him.

"Oh, Alex, I love you, too." Tears slid down her cheeks at his admission.

"Can you ever forgive this old fool?" He lifted his good hand and rested it on her cheek, brushing the tears away with his thumb. She couldn't speak, and he must have thought the worst, because he continued quickly, "I've been such an idiot. I didn't realize it till I came home, and you, *Ashley,* and *Ann* weren't there."

He emphasized their names, and her heart swelled with delight. This was the first time he'd ever said their names. He was a changed man. The look that usually haunted his face when they spoke of the twins was gone.

"When I saw his gun in the mirror, my heart dropped," he said. "A life without you flashed before my eyes. Walking away from that door was the hardest thing I'd ever done. I knew how scared you were."

"More than I'd ever been in my life." She shuddered thinking about it.

"When you came running out and he pointed that gun at you, I realized that I'd rather die than face a life without you. You stole my heart even before I realized that it was out there for the taking. You hold it in the palm of your hand. Please say you'll take me back," He shifted to face her then grimaced when he tried to move his arm.

"What about when the ghosts come knocking again, Alex?" As much as she loved him, she didn't want to spend a lifetime fighting his past. How would he react if she told him about the baby they'd created? "I can't fight against ghosts."

"I took my grandfather's advice and went to see Valerie." He pushed the button on the bed and raised it to a sitting position.

Shock rippled through her. He never went to see Valerie, never wanted to. The fact he had gone spoke volumes to her. "Boy, you've definitely had a busy night, fighting ghosts and a bullet."

"Only for you, Lara, no one else. I'd give my life for you. I promise that my ghosts are long gone and buried," he said huskily as tears swam in his eyes. He cupped her chin and studied her face. "And you? What about your ghosts."

He no longer resembled Aidan. They may have been identical in looks but nothing else. His features were soft while Aidan's were hard. No, they were nothing alike. The last ghost connecting the two of them fell away, and a love stronger than anything she'd ever known stood in its place. She knew she'd never love anyone else the way she loved Alex. She held his face between her hands and brushed her lips against his.

He pulled back slightly with a hopeful look on his face. "So, you'll take this old fool back?" he asked, sounding only slightly unsure.

She pulled back and looked at him with a sly smile. "On one condition."

"God, you know how to make a man suffer." He groaned and laid his head back against the pillow.

She laughed and placed a hand on her stomach. "How do you feel about more children?"

Alex lifted his head and looked at her. His eyes widened, and a grin spread across his face as he stared at her hand on her belly. He reached out and covered her hand with his. "Does this mean?"

She nodded her head. His shout of joy bounced off the hospital walls, and the nurses rushed in to see what the commotion was.

"I'm having a baby. I mean, she's having a baby."

The staff cheered and offered their congratulations, then slowly filed out of the room, leaving them alone. He turned back to her. "You've made me the happiest man in the world." He leaned his forehead against hers and whispered, "I've never met anyone like you, Laryssa Richards. I love you so much. And I promise I'll be there for you till death do us part."

"And I you, my dear sweet husband."

He pulled back and smacked his forehead with his good hand. "Can you go into my jeans and check the pocket. There is something there that belongs to you. Can you bring it to me, please?"

In his pocket lay the ring that she had given him earlier. She pulled it out and placed it in his hand.

"Months ago, we married under false pretenses. I don't want it to be like that anymore. Will you be my wife in every way that counts? To love this old fool and have my babies, the whole nine yards?"

She brushed away the tears that gathered in her eyes as she looked down at her beloved husband, still disheveled from the injury that saved her life. "I will."

He placed the ring on her finger and kissed her hand. True love did exist, and it had finally found them. For the first time in her life, she knew that everything would be okay.

EPILOGUE

"It's your turn," Laryssa groaned and covered her head with the pillow. The cries from their latest addition to the family came through the baby monitor next to the bed.

"I got up last time." His own voice muffled by his pillow.

The crying stopped, and they both looked at each other before they bolted out of bed, heading in the direction of their son's room. Inside, Joanne sat with the baby in her arms in the rocking chair.

"Took you two long enough." She gazed down at the young child with a twinkle in her eye. "I thought this little man would pop a blood vessel."

"We're sorry, Joanne. Here, let me take him, and you can go back to bed." Laryssa held out her arms.

"Bed? Why would I go back to bed? It's ten in the morning."

Alex and Laryssa both turned towards the window and saw the light of the sun peeking around the corners of the curtains.

"Sarah has already taken the other two downstairs for breakfast. You two were dead to the world."

"We're sorry. Justin kept us up all night."

"Don't apologize, I love helping you with him. Oh, your grandparents are flying in next week to visit the new wee one. They said for me to tell you that it was about time you added another addition to the family."

As they were filing down the hall towards the elevator, Laryssa thought about what Alex's grandparents said and a light bulb went off in her head. "Hey, I'll meet you guys downstairs. I have to go get something."

She found what she was looking for in the library and hurried to catch back up to everyone who had piled in the kitchen. She dropped the heavy book onto the kitchen table.

"I found this in the library a few months back. It's the family tree. I thought it was about time we finished filling it out."

They filled it out, name by name, ending with the birth of their newest addition, Justin Ray Richards.

Joanne placed a hand against her heart. "I never thought I'd see this day."

"I'm glad you're here to share it with us, Joanne," Laryssa said.

The telephone rang and Alex picked it up. "Yes?" He paused before continuing to speak, "Escort him to the door, please."

"Who was that?" Laryssa asked.

"A man claiming to be your uncle is at the gates."

She sat back in her chair. Her uncle? She didn't think she had any family left. No one came to claim her when her parents died or during the twenty years since.

"I'll go let them in." Joanne stood up and limped down the hallway.

"Are you okay?" Alex asked softly.

"I'm not sure." Her hands had gone numb, and her legs didn't want to work.

He helped her stand up and allowed her to lean on him as they walked towards the door. They found Joanne and a very well-dressed, handsome, older gentleman staring at each other, neither speaking. Joanne's cheeks were flushed with color, and a shy smile played on her face.

Alex and Laryssa looked at each other and a secret passed between them. It looked like the love bug was about to hit again. This time to a woman who deserved it more than anyone. She could only hope that the man standing before them was worthy of it.

"Hi, I'm Nathan Mitchell. Your father's brother."

To be continued in "Her Ghosts Reborn."

HER GHOSTS REBORN

HLF – BOOK TWO

by

Patricia Elliott

CHAPTER ONE

"It has to be here somewhere," Ebony growled anxiously as she dumped out another drawer from the luxury designer desk in the living room.

If Seth Peters didn't know any better, he'd say a burglar had torn through his home and not his young mistress racing around in front of him. She was normally poised and in control.

Not today though. She was in hunt mode, and as a result, there were only a few things left in the house that hadn't been turned upside down. The newspapers in the basket had been picked apart, couch cushions tossed into the corner, and now the contents of three drawers were strewn across his floor, and she was marching her way towards the planters.

"You could at least help," she snapped. "You have as much to lose as I do."

He glanced at his watch. "I would, but I have to get to the hospital. They said tonight could be the night."

"Maybe you can get the old bag to tell us where it is before she croaks."

"Why are you so sure there's another will? I was there with her when the last one was made."

"Exactly," Ebony said sharply as she picked up a ceramic planter, dumping the entire contents, dirt and all, onto his pristine beige carpet. He cringed.

Seth took a breath and looked over at the maid huddling in the corner, her eyes downcast and her hands clasped tightly in front of her. "Clean this up when she's done. I don't want to see a speck of dirt in this place when I return."

"Yes, sir," she said timidly, still not looking at him.

The young maid, who was only in Canada because of him so she could support her family overseas, was a sharp contrast to the woman who was tearing up the living room. One obeyed. The other couldn't be tamed. And he didn't mind. Ebony had brought excitement into his dull life. She took guff from no one, including him.

"Damn it! Where the hell is it?" Ebony stopped in the center of the room, hands on her hips, casting him a look filled with impatience. "You must know whether she had a favorite hiding spot."

"She didn't hide things from me," he said.

Ebony laughed that haughty laugh of hers. "You don't know much about women, do you? We all hide things."

Judith, his wife, didn't have the guts to go against him, not even when the shit hit the fan after Joanne, their daughter, had her accident. He still couldn't believe his own flesh and blood had betrayed him by marrying his enemy's son. That made him pause for a moment. Maybe Ebony was right. If his daughter betrayed him, was it possible that his wife could do the same?

Seth shook his head. During their entire marriage, Judith never questioned his decisions, wouldn't even open her mouth to offer her thoughts. Not even when he specifically asked her. She would just say, 'whatever you think, dear.' God, she was boring. But he had to admit that a pussy-whipped woman allowed him to have more freedom to do as he pleased, so there were pros and cons to their odd family dynamic.

"I still think this is the only one," he said, sticking to his guns as he held up the envelope containing his wife's Last Will and Testament.

She picked up another plant and dumped it out, examining the pot. "No, it's not. There's another one. I can feel it in my bones."

"What makes you think so?"

Ebony stopped her path of destruction and looked at him, her eyes blazing with anger. "I can see it in her eyes every time we go to visit her. Now stop questioning my intuition, or I'll leave and never come back."

"Okay, okay," he said, holding his hands out. "I just don't think we have anything to worry about. Everything she has belongs to me anyway. I paid for it. So, I don't want you to worry your pretty little head. It isn't healthy for you or our unborn son.

She waved her hand in dismissal. "I'll be fine, but we're running out of time. We need to find it and get her to rewrite it before she dies. I have the solicitor on standby."

Seth sighed. Ebony wasn't going to let this rest until she found it, or until she destroyed his whole house in the process.

"Women are crafty, especially a scorned one," Ebony warned him.

"I gave her everything she ever needed. Why would she be scorned?"

"Uh, how many women have you cheated on her with?"

"We had an open relationship," he argued.

"Open according to whom?"

He opened his mouth to answer, but then realized he had nothing to refute her with. It wasn't something he and his wife had ever discussed. They just stopped having sex years ago because she was never interested. And after being refused so many times over, it seemed like the only logical decision. What else was he supposed to do to get his needs met? Once he made that decision, he never bothered to hide it. Not like some other weak ass men he knew.

"She never had an issue with it," he said, chuckling. "And she wasn't going to leave even if she did."

"Maybe not, but women plan for the worst, so don't put it past her. And she has a soft spot for her kid. Now go on, get out of here," she said, shoving him in the direction of the door. "See if you can get her to tell you anything. And don't come back until you know."

"If it were me, I wouldn't worry about it until there was something to worry about," he said, shrugging his shoulders.

"Good thing I'm not you."

He laughed as he put on his shoes, then he pulled her close to kiss her forehead. "I'll let you know if I find out anything, but she wasn't very lucid the last time we were there."

"Careful, you'll ruin my makeup, and I have a shoot later."

"Break a leg," he said before heading out the door. Things were about to get interesting. Very interesting indeed.

"Hi, Laryssa, I'm Nathan Mitchell," the stranger said. "Your father's brother."

Joanne Richards found herself captivated by his bright chocolate-colored eyes, encircled with a ring of black around his irises. She barely heard what he had to say because his eyes were locked on hers, too, and she had been struck dumb.

"That's impossible," came a voice from behind her, breaking the temporary spell. "I don't have any family left."

Joanne stepped back and placed her arm around a shaking Laryssa. They never spoke much about Laryssa's past. The only things she knew about Laryssa were that her parents had died in a boating accident, and she'd spent the remainder of her childhood in and out of foster care. She had also been the wife of her late son, Aidan and was currently the wife of her other son Alex, Aidan's twin. Life couldn't get more bizarre than that.

"Why don't you come in, and we can continue the discussion in the living room," Alex suggested, as he held his hand out to him. "Hi, I'm Alex, Laryssa's husband."

Nathan gripped his hand in a firm, steady handshake. "That sounds great, thank you."

"I'll go put on some coffee," Joanne said, eager to put some distance between the newcomer and herself to ease the flutter in her stomach. She was too old to get butterflies over a guy. Besides, who would want a woman with a limp anyway?

"Sarah, can you handle the kids?" Alex asked their nanny.

"No problem, sir," she replied.

Joanne watched as Alex guided Laryssa with a hand on the small of her back to the living room with Nathan in tow. She couldn't help but notice the man's wide shoulders and his smooth gait. One she wished she still had. His crisp dress shirt and tailored black dress pants spoke of a man who cared about his appearance. Either that or someone who wanted to put on a good show.

That's not the feeling she got from his gaze, though, but it was easier thinking that way than letting her heart run away on her. Her heart had been broken once, and half of it was still buried in the grave with her husband, Scott. The trouble that ensued from that ordeal was enough to last a lifetime. Taking a deep breath, she reached for the coffee in the cupboard and dumped some into a new paper filter.

"Are you okay?" Sarah asked as she picked up a fussy Justin from the playpen, propping a bottle in his mouth as she moved to sit at the table with Laryssa's young seventeen-month-old twins.

Joanne could hardly believe her son had three kids to raise now. She'd begun to question whether he'd ever settle down again. "Sorry, I just had a very weird feeling about Nathan."

Leaning over, Sarah whispered, "Would that weird feeling have anything to do with how great his ass looked in those pants?"

Joanne's face burned, and she knew it was as red as a tomato. "Really now! We're two almost gray-haired grannies. We shouldn't be looking at a man's butt. That time has passed." Yet, a vision of his hot ass flashed in her mind.

"Speak for yourself, I'm a blonde."

"Salon dyed doesn't count."

"Oh shush. We're not dead yet, and as long as we're alive, we can enjoy a sexy man's ass," the woman said, winking at her. Letting Joanne know that she took no offense to her words.

Joanne waved her off. She was still getting used to being a mom and a grandma after hiding it for so long. Adding a man to that would take away from the time she had with her family. Eighteen months have passed since the news got out that she was Alexander's mom. Hearing him call her mom made her heart leap every time. They were finally a real family now.

Joanne smiled at that thought. He'd forgiven her for keeping it a secret and welcomed her new role in his life. Mind you, he did try to prevent her from working for him as a result, telling her that he'd happily hire a housekeeper, but she liked doing stuff around the house. It kept her busy, and it was what she was most familiar with.

However, her body had begun to plan a revolt whenever she did anything strenuous like lugging a vacuum up and down the stairs in their monstrous house. They had an elevator, but some areas were only accessible via a staircase. And being sixty-one years old, she had to accept she had limits, especially with a body like hers that still felt the effects of her horrific car accident.

"Say it! Say you thought his butt was hot."

Joanne's eyes widened, and she felt the heat return to her cheeks as she tried to cover the ears of at least one twin. "I most certainly will not say that. We have innocent ears in the room."

The nanny rolled her eyes. "Girl, it's time for you to live for a change."

"Changing diapers is enough change for me."

Sarah shook her head and lifted Justin to her shoulder to burp him. "Go on. Go be with your son and Laryssa. I'm sure Nathan could use a cup of coffee. I've got the kids covered." Just then, Ashley dumped her cereal bowl on Ann's head, and the young girl burst out crying. "Okay, maybe not."

Joanne walked over to the kitchen sink to get a dishcloth, and then wandered over to Ann to clean her up. "I definitely prefer toddlers over grown men."

"You need to get a life, Jo!" Sarah sighed, settling Justin back into her arms to finish the bottle."

She couldn't think of a life better than the one she was living right now. She didn't want for anything. Her son hadn't kicked her out of the house when he found out her secret. And her late-husband's parents, Ruth and Mitch, didn't give her any trouble—at least not really.

They were a pretty close family now, and they treated her like a daughter-in-law again. And even though Scott—her husband and their son—had been dead a long time, they told her she would always be family. Her eyes watered as she stood there in the kitchen. She quickly wiped the tears away with the sleeve of her blouse.

Sarah looked at her, her brow crinkling with worry. “Did I overstep my bounds?”

"No, dear. It's fine," Joanne replied, waving off her concern as she gave the highchair one final swipe with the cloth. "I think this little one is going to need a bath."

"She'll survive until the visit is over." Sarah said, nodding towards the coffee pot. "Coffee's ready.”

The last thing Joanne wanted to do was impose on a private conversation. *Okay,* she groaned to herself. That was a lie. She wanted to know what was going on, but she didn't want him to look at her again with that steady, unnerving gaze.

One would think by her age, she'd have this man thing down pat, but she'd been out of the game for so long she wouldn't even know what to do with one...like a dog chasing a car.

Taking a deep breath, she picked up the tray and carefully walked with it into the living room, concentrating hard, trying not to spill the coffee with her limp. She wished they would have been able to fix her leg when she was younger because now it was getting harder to move these days.

Joanne glanced around the room. Alex was sitting beside Laryssa in the middle of the couch. Nathan was by himself on the love seat, leaving the other cushion open beside him. The only other available seat was the recliner, but it was covered with clothes that she hadn't gotten around to folding yet.

Nathan patted the cushion beside him. "Please, sit. You look exhausted."

"I really shouldn't. Sarah needs help with the kids."

"Please stay, Mom," Alex said, gesturing towards the love-seat and consequently towards Nathan. The tenderness of his tone, and the use of a word she never thought she'd ever hear come out of his mouth, made her throat clog. She didn't think she'd ever get used to it.

"My dad never mentioned that he had a brother," Laryssa commented.

"You were probably too young to remember," he replied, his voice gentle and serene. "You were only four when it all happened."

"Why didn't you ever come for me?"

"In all honesty, it all happened so fast, and I wasn't in a position to adopt you at the time. My life had gone off the rails with the loss of my brother, and by the time I managed to get it together, you were gone, and no one would tell me anything. If I wouldn't have seen the article of your wedding in the paper, I wouldn't have found you.

Joanne was glad she'd encouraged the newspaper article after the danger of Laryssa's stalker had passed. She had a feeling Laryssa had family out there. The girl deserved a full family after all she'd been through. It took a bit to convince Alex to go for it, but she was glad he eventually did.

Nathan seemed genuine. But as soon as those words fluttered through her mind, he turned and looked at her. His eyes locked with hers, and it was like the room disappeared. If she wouldn't have been sitting, she'd likely have swooned. Heat rose to her cheeks again, and she fanned herself with her hand.

"Is it hot in here?" she asked the others, certain that someone had turned the thermostat up. Not even her worst hot flash was hotter than this.

Her son and daughter-in-law shared a knowing glance, and Joanne watched Alex squeeze Laryssa's hand, and it made her blush all the more. She knew the type of stuff fluttering through their newlywed minds.

They'd been married just over a year and were still very much in love. It had eased the ache in Joanne's heart that she bore for Alex ever since the loss of his daughter. He deserved his happily ever after more than anyone.

"So does anyone want to introduce me to this wonderful lady?" he asked them, sending a brilliant smile her way.

"Nathan, this is my mom, Joanne," Alex said.

"It's nice to meet the one who raised such a marvelous man for my niece."

She opened her mouth to correct him, but Alex spoke up instead. "I wouldn't be who I am without her or Laryssa."

"I firmly believe behind every good man is a good woman," Nathan replied, letting his knuckles brush Joanne's shoulder.

Goosebumps appeared on her arms as a warm shiver rustled through her body, making her leg stiffen painfully. She'd missed her morning dose of medication which helped with the pain.

"I couldn't agree more," Alex said. "Would you like a coffee or a beer?"

Joanne made a 'tsk' sound. "It's too early to be drinking, and he might have to drive somewhere." She leaned forward and poured everyone a cup of coffee. After losing her husband to a drunk driver, she wasn't about to let anyone in this house drive after drinking.

"Where are you staying?" Alex asked him.

"I actually just got into town, so I haven't had a chance to scope out any areas."

"Hey, why don't you—" Alex started to say, but Laryssa interrupted him.

"Wait here a moment. I have to talk to my husband."

Her son was probably going to suggest that he stay with them. He had a habit of bringing stray puppies home. That was what he had done with Laryssa when they first met. He felt like he had to help everyone in need, and while Joanne was normally okay with that, *her needs* were currently going in a different direction. To avoid temptation and to give herself a moment to breathe, she got up to follow her son, but the man took her hand.

"Won't you keep me company?"

The warmth of his skin against hers made her pause, and she

recalled the first rules of hospitality, which was to make the guest feel welcome. Biting back a groan, Joanne sat down, folding her hands on her light purple slacks. "Do you live near Vancouver?" she asked him.

"In all honesty, I only have a motorhome. I sold my place a long time ago to travel."

There was a hitch in his voice that was barely perceptible, but it was there. "Don't you need a physical address?"

"I have a spot for my motorhome in Alberta, but I travel more often than not. Would you like to see it? It's parked out front."

Joanne swallowed hard. "Maybe when they get back, we can all go take a peek."

"You're a cautious one, aren't you?" Nathan said, grinning.

"Well," she said, shrugging her shoulders. "You don't get to be our age by being stupid."

The smile disappeared from his face, and his hands closed into tight fists as he looked away, his eyes taking on a despondent look.

Joanne looked towards the hallway where Alex and Laryssa disappeared, hoping they'd be back soon. She had a feeling there was a lot more to be discussed.

ABOUT THE AUTHOR

Patricia Elliott lives in beautiful British Columbia with three of her children and her amazing, incredible partner. Now that her kids are all adults, she has decided to actively pursue her passion for the written word.

When she was a youngster, she spent the majority of her time writing fan-fiction and poetry to avoid the harsh reality of bullying. Writing allowed her to escape into another world, even if temporarily; a world in which she could be anyone or anything, even a mermaid.

Dreams really can come true. If you believe it, you can achieve it!

For more titles, please visit Patricia Elliott's website:

https://patriciaelliottromance.com